Curio

THE COMPLETE SERIES

CARA McKENNA

Third Edition

Curio originally published 2010

Coercion, Craving, Reversal, Confession, Exposure originally published 2011

Edited by Kelli Collins

Cover design by Cara McKenna

ISBN 978-0-9977834-6-9

For the ugly ducklings and the nervous wrecks.
Pick your fruit from the highest, most improbable branches and leave
the bruised, mealy cast-offs to those not willing to risk a fall.

CURIO

THURSDAY

The First Visit

Didier Pedra is the name of a male prostitute who lives at sixteen Rue des Toits Rouges, in Paris.

It's a relatively quiet street amid the greater bustle of the Latin Quarter, his flat on the top floor of a long tenement, two blocks from the river. I'd never expected to find myself standing on the stoop of a prostitute's building in the rain, on what should have been an unremarkable Thursday evening in March.

Then again, I'd never expected to be five weeks from my thirtieth birthday with my hymen still intact.

As I stood on Didier Pedra's front step—precisely six minutes early for my appointment and unwilling to go in, lest I appear too eager—I knew only a few things about him. I knew he was in his early to mid-thirties, that he'd always lived in Paris and that he had a reputation for being supremely good in bed.

As if I had any basis for comparison.

I knew also, beyond the shadow of a doubt, that he was gorgeous. I use that word without gushing, without girlishness. I say *gorgeous* as though I'm speaking of the most luscious and decadent cake you ever laid eyes on, one you can taste from ten feet away. So beautiful that not only do your salivary glands tingle, your eyes water. So beautiful that cutting a slice and consuming it would feel wrong, because you are beneath such a specimen.

As an aside, you might wonder what sort of woman would visit a male prostitute. I can only speak about the one I know, which is of course myself.

I'm not what I might have pictured.

I'm younger than I'd have guessed, not quite thirty as I said, and I suspect I'm better-looking but less well-off. I'm not beautiful, but I'm an inch or two taller than average, perhaps a bit underweight, though in this city of chain smokers my measurements seem standard. I have curly hair, neither short nor long, neither blonde nor brown, neither sloppy nor tidy. I pin the sides back with a barrette behind each ear. For some reason I dressed this evening more for a job interview than a first date, likely because Didier intimidated me tremendously. My flats collected rain on the walk from the Metro and the cuffs of my slacks were wet and shapeless by the time I reached number sixteen, Rue des Toits Rouges. The Street of Red Roofs.

I was scared and thrilled, shaky from excitement and nerves and anticipation.

There was no doubting Didier's aforementioned gorgeousness. I work at a museum in Paris—no, not the Louvre but still very nice— and two of my best friends work in the gallery next door. Paulette is from near Provence and Ania is Polish, and they are both insatiable perverts. I say that affectionately. When customers wander out of earshot, Paulette and Ania are never more than a breath from discussing some man or other or the exploits of a mutual friend.

Ania first told me about Didier Pedra when the gallery displayed a half-dozen daguerreotypes. You may have seen some—photographic images burned onto shiny silver plates, like dark mirrors. It's a delicate, temperamental, antiquated medium. The artist behind the exhibit was a local woman and her model was Didier.

He is without a doubt the most stunning man I've ever seen, both burned onto metal plates and in person, burned forever onto my retinas. He's so beautiful I actually felt an ache in my chest when I viewed those images.

Noting my fixation, Ania had declared herself the model's greatest fan and disappeared into the storeroom, emerging with a large binder filled with prints. Didier has sat for many photographers and other artists since he was in his late teens. Ania had plopped the portfolio down on a table and proceeded to flip through the images. I'd immediately wondered how I might possibly steal the binder and sleep with it beneath my pillow, though of course I never would. But if given the chance, I might borrow it on a long-term basis without permission.

Definitely without permission, because there's some defect in my personality that prevents me from admitting my attraction to handsome men. I've always been that way.

I was an extremely homely kid, growing up in northern New Hampshire. I wasn't quite the ugly duckling who blossomed into a beautiful swan… I merely developed into an okay-looking duck. But back then I was inarguably gawky, and because I knew it would be laughable for me to profess my love for the cutest, most popular boys at my school, I chose to act as though I couldn't care less about them. That I was above such nonsense.

In truth they intimidated me, because they had the power to disappoint and humiliate me, and confirm everything I feared about my own awkwardness.

I carried this facsimile of haughty superiority with me through college and beyond, and though I shrug off accusations that I might have a crush on this man or that and pass my attitude off as contempt, secretly of course I'm simply terrified to hear it made official that they're out of my league.

Beautiful men terrify me because, deep down, they're the only kind I want.

I could probably do well, dating guys as passable-looking as myself. I even suspect they're nicer people, yet I have what feels like an affliction—an affinity for beauty. A fetish, perhaps, to further belabor that overused term. It's what led me to museum work, to art appreciation, to entire weeks of my life lost window-shopping for mouthwatering furniture and trinkets that could bankrupt me with a single swipe of my bank card. I have expensive taste, my father always said. Though surely he'd meant my refusal to settle for less than the fancy brand of macaroni and cheese, with its seductive silver packet of gooey Velveeta. Not home furnishings or Parisian prostitutes.

But that's enough about me for now.

When it finally struck six fifty-nine, I gave myself permission to enter Didier's building. I shook my umbrella off on the stoop and studied the tenant list. I pressed the brass button beside 5C PEDRA, D. and waited, my breath held.

I should mention that Didier and I had only corresponded in postcards, because a) I hadn't had his number at first; and b) once he gave it to me, I was too chickenshit to use it. The voice I'd speculated and fantasized about didn't greet me, though the door buzzed as it unlocked and I let myself in.

It was probably once a dazzling building, now thoroughly worn around the edges. In addition to attractive men, I fear elevators, especially the ancient kind here in number sixteen, with the accordion-style door, so I found the slightly less claustrophobic stairwell and dripped my way up four flights.

Flat 5C is at the very end of a long, dim, narrow corridor with a ceiling at least a foot shorter than the lower levels'. As I took my final breath, knuckles poised to knock, the door swung in.

Didier was taller than I'd anticipated. He was more of everything than I'd anticipated. Which is saying a lot, because I'd purposefully conflated him in my mind, so grand he could only fail to measure up and hence give me permission to do as I always do and declare myself above the bothersome magnetism of lust.

But Didier did not disappoint. My mouth went dry and I must have looked stoned, standing there with the blank expression I rely on when desperately trying to appear unaffected.

"Good evening," he said. "You're Carolyn?"

I managed to say, "I am." My name is, in fact, Caroly, a misspelling on my grandmother's prospective baby name list that my mother found exceedingly fetching. No sympathy for her daughter, doomed to be addressed as Carol or Carolyn for the rest of her days. And because of how "Caroline" is pronounced in France—*Caroleen*—nobody here ever gets my name right when I introduce myself. But that's fair, considering how badly I mangle their entire language every time I open my mouth.

"I'm Didier." He shook my hand and I marveled at the gesture, how he could manage to make it feel so casual yet confident. "Come in." His English is strong, though his accent heavy. Ania had told me he could speak several languages, and that his father was from Spain.

He closed the door behind me as I stepped into his garret.

It was the single most sensual space I'd ever been in. There was nothing extravagant about it, yet sex seemed to drip from every square inch. His furniture was all dark wood, a mix of mahogany and walnut. More estate sale than antique broker, but it worked. It matched the stained beams of the sloped ceiling and set off the walls, painted the deep red of a dying rose, two weeks past Valentine's Day. The lighting was perfectly inadequate, allowing the eye to take in only a handful of immediate details at one time. Very soothing, like blinders. The living room was long and narrow, and through the few windows not shrouded by gauzy curtains you could see an enviable skyline view to the east. It smelled nice, as well, something I couldn't place, the oddest mix of clean and musty.

I'm babbling about Didier's décor because I was afraid to look at him at first, and those were the minutiae I lost myself in. But eventually I turned to face him.

"You have a lovely flat."

"Thank you. Would you like a drink?"

"Sure." I'd never needed a drink so badly in my life.

"Have a seat." He waved toward the settee and armchair in the corner before heading for another room. "And you prefer English?"

"If you don't mind. Thank you." I set my umbrella and purse by the door and crossed the room to sit on the chair. Pigeons paced on the ledge outside the window, their little bird motors idling, purring and cooing their contentment. I envied their ease.

Didier's voice carried from the far room. "I see you did not escape the storm."

"No, sadly."

He reappeared with two glasses of red wine, handing me one as he took a seat on the couch.

I have avoided describing Didier, I know. That's because I worry I'll never be able to paint him properly, to do him justice. But here goes.

I'll start with his voice. It's deep and gentle, warm and relaxed. I'm terrible at guessing heights, but he's tall, over six feet. His image in those photos and sketches from the gallery binder are elegant, which he is in real life as well.

I can't find the right word for his build. Though he's quite trim, he has a large frame—wide shoulders, broad hands—making him seem heavy and strong. In person, his muscular body was of course hidden, and it was maddening to know what he looked like nearly naked and to then have to suffer his sweater and slacks. He had on socks but no shoes, which for some reason I found reassuring.

We sipped our wine and I have no idea what we talked about. The rain, how this spring was stacking up to previous years, perhaps. I took in only what I was looking at.

I know you must want to know about his face, one worthy of so many artists' awe and my clumsy prose. It's a stern face, as you'd expect of a male model. A strong jaw, though not square. Cheekbones that bend light, of course. Expressive eyebrows, black in the dim room. His hair is a shade lighter than his brows, and not as unruly as mine—a wavy sort of curly, long enough to clutch but not to wrap around one's fingers. His eyes are deep brown with heavy lids that give him a slightly sinister, slightly sleepy expression. His nose is strong, not quite *big*, with the faintest hook to it. Like so many Parisian men, he has an air of caustic wisdom about him. Unlike many Parisian men, he does not have an aroma of cigarettes to accent the attitude.

Didier is the type of man who, even if you can't stand seafood, makes you crave oysters. There is something raw and primal yet utterly refined about him that leaves you hungry for such a thing. He pairs with liver and black caviar and hundred-dollar champagne, this extraordinary delicacy of a man. A rare animal, worthy of hunting to extinction lest anyone else lay claim to the beauty of him.

"So tell me what exactly brings you here," he said.

Ah, a question I had no answer for. "I saw pictures of you at a gallery, and heard that you... You know."

He nodded.

"You've modeled a lot," I said.

"I did. Not so often anymore." The only imperfect thing about him was his teeth—white but a bit crooked, which I didn't mind at all. Mine are just the same.

"Have you lived here long?" I asked, aiming my gaze all around his flat.

"Ages. Nearly ten years." He had a way of leaning forward, bracing his elbows on his knees and locking his eyes on mine even as he sipped his wine. Though it sounds unnerving, it makes you feel you're the most fascinating woman on earth.

Normally I shy from a stare as intense as his, strong as a floodlight, but all I felt then was blank.

"And you?" he asked. "How long have you been in Paris?"

"Two years, next month."

"School?"

I shook my head. "Work. At a museum. Assistant curator."

He made an impressed face. "And so what brings you to me?"

My delusions of charisma faded. "Um... Do you have a confidentiality thing with your clients?"

A smile that melted my muscles. "We never met," he said simply.

"Right. Well. This is embarrassing..."

He let me trail off, no prompting, merely sipping his drink while I gathered my thoughts.

"I'm not very experienced with men."

Didier nodded, as though he were fluent in evasive English. "You're looking to change that?"

"Maybe. To be honest, I don't know what I'm looking for."

He leaned back against the couch cushions and crossed his legs. "Not to put too fine a point on it, but it is a flat rate." I pictured the check in my purse, ready to be dropped in his mailbox upon my departure. "You get me for the evening, and what we do is entirely your choice. Nothing is off-limits with me." He gestured with his free hand, presenting his body as a package.

"Right."

"But that goes the other way as well. It's your time, and if all you want to do is talk and drink, then that's what we do."

I wondered how often that *was* what women wanted from him—a date with no pressure, no fear of rejection. That's what I wanted, after all. I've even heard that plenty of men who patronize female prostitutes want simply that, companionship.

"That would be good, to start."

He nodded, stern face striking and sage. "Do you mind my asking, how inexperienced are you? Or what would you like to learn from me?"

"I've kissed men, but that's really all."

Let me pause here and explain how it felt to admit that. I'm sure plenty of girls lie about how many guys they've messed around with when they're younger, not wanting to seem too easy. Well, there's another stigma that comes later, as you edge closer to true adulthood, especially if you run with a liberal, artsy crowd. I always pray my friends assume I'm a real freak behind closed doors, just stingy with the details. I think you can get away with being a virgin until you're, say, twenty-three or so, and still pass it off as choosiness or cautiousness or plain old willfulness. But twenty-nine? By then people start to wonder what's *wrong* with you. Including yourself.

Didier was the first person I'd actually admitted the extent of my inexperience to, ever. I even lead my gynecologist on. When she asks, "Are you sexually active?" I always reply, "Not at the moment." If the truth has always been embarrassingly apparent, she's been kind enough not to tell me so.

And it was in *that* moment in Didier's living room that I realized, maybe not tonight, but some day not too far off, I could leave this place with that weight lifted from me. I could walk down his street and be like everyone else. I could have a *lover*. This is Paris, after all.

Having a lover is like having a pancreas. I was suddenly very ready to quit being a medical anomaly.

All Didier said to my pronouncement was, "That is very interesting." He paused and squinted as though he were taking a drag off a psychic cigarette. I worried he was about to tell me he had a policy against deflowering his clients, but instead he went on. "It's very flattering that you've come to me."

"Oh. Good."

"Yes. I would be very honored to corrupt you in whatever ways you like."

I laughed at that, relaxing further. The wine suddenly tasted extraordinary, and it dawned then that I was turned-on. I'd worried that wouldn't happen and I'd officially get stamped DEFECTIVE and sent back to the factory.

I cleared my throat. "I have no idea what ways I'm looking to be corrupted. I'm usually pretty nervous around men."

"That's very normal, for the first date."

Ooh, *date*. I liked that. I'd happily pretend I'd scored a date with this perfect man.

"There's no rush, by the way," he said. "I rarely get to bed before five a.m., so if you want to just sit here and drink and talk all night, you're not wasting my time or keeping me up in the least."

"Okay, great." And necessary. I'm a slow thaw.

"Here." Didier stood and crossed the room to switch on a radio. I love listening to French talk radio. Even after two years, I struggle to follow the pace of the language but I adore the sound of it. He kept the volume low, and I felt he'd read my mind, meeting some need I hadn't even realized I had. He filled the silence without making it feel like a pointed seduction or an awkward distraction, and my brain quieted.

The etiquette is odd, when you visit a prostitute. On the one hand, Didier was mine to do with what I wanted. That was my privilege.

But even if I wanted to treat him like a piece of meat, I suspected I wasn't capable of it. He might be a slice of cake, reserved specially for me, but it felt very strange to actually consider enjoying him. Which of us was I worried about demeaning?

He fetched the wine bottle from the kitchen and set it on the table before us, taking his seat. "So tell me. You're an attractive woman. You seem successful and clever."

"Thanks."

"May I ask what it is about men that's made you cautious? Do you not like being touched, or you simply haven't met the right one? Is it a religious decision?"

"No, definitely not religious. And I don't think I mind being touched, really… It's hard to explain." I folded my legs beneath my butt and addressed his hands. "I guess I don't want to settle for a man who isn't really, truly attractive to me. But I'm afraid to try to date those guys, because I'm afraid I'll find out I'm not enough for them. It's always been easier and less scary to just not take the chance."

"You won't be rejected here."

I nodded. "That's the appeal. Well, and you." I met his stare. "I'm sure you've heard a million times that you're handsome. You, um… I think you may be the most attractive man I've ever seen."

His smile was warm and humble, and it gathered the skin beneath his eyes into adorable little rolls. "That's very kind. I hope it pleases you that I'm yours to enjoy."

"It does. It scares me, too."

"Of course."

I drained my glass and Didier refilled it. His mix of matter-of-factness and perfect calm was disarming. I'd feared he'd be cocky or sleazy or aggressively flirtatious. I mean, countless women pay to sleep with him. How could that not give a man a gigantic ego? I'd also feared he'd be a sweet-talking, God's-gift Don Juan and I'd feel as though I were being coerced. But I didn't. If this was a seduction, it was very covert and exactly my speed.

We chatted some more about the city and when the sky grew dark, Didier lit at least a dozen candles, a mound of them all melted together on an old metal card table behind the couch. Beeswax—that was the pleasant, musty smell I'd noted.

Didier by candlelight was obscenely stunning. At long last, my mind was wandering. I studied the tendons in his neck in the warm glow and recalled the images of his bare chest that I'd seen. He must've been used to such scrutiny, as he merely sipped his drink and watched me watching him.

I feel so predictable saying it, but add wine and candles and a Parisian skyline at dusk and this prude is suddenly a hussy.

"I don't suppose you could, um…" My voice dropped to a mumble. "Take your sweater off?"

Didier nodded and stood, stripping away his top and undershirt in one motion.

As he sat, I gave myself permission to be curious, not bashful. I decided to treat him as what he was to me—living art. His bare skin looked warm in the flickering light, and I understood with true clarity what artists mean by "muse". He's magic. A man who poses merely by sitting, a hundred thousand angles waiting to be discovered. I wished I were more artistic so I could capture him, every last shadow and contour.

"You're beautiful," I finally said.

"Thank you."

"It's okay if I only want to look at you tonight?"

"I'm yours for whatever you wish to do. Or not do."

When you're as inexperienced as I was, there's a ton to learn from a man before you even touch or kiss him. I considered what I wanted. To see him naked, but not too soon. To watch him bathe. To watch him masturbate, above just about everything else. That's always turned me on, and I'm sure it's because I nearly never fantasize about actually being with a man. Even in my own imagination, I fear rejection. My mental porn is almost exclusively comprised of one-man shows, with an occasional faceless woman stepping in as choreography demands.

"Could you take your pants off?" I asked him.

"Of course."

Before I knew it, he'd stripped to his underwear. And it was the sexiest underwear I'd ever seen on a man. Nothing fancy, just briefs, but they were made of silk or some other fine, explicit, clingy fabric. His thighs looked strong, his shorts full. He was an Armani campaign, lounging on his old couch in this moody, elegant apartment, candles flickering.

Note to self: find out if clients are allowed to take photographs.

"Is it weird," I asked, "having people stare at you?"

"No, not really. I modeled for so long, I'm used to it now."

"And you don't model anymore?"

He shook his head. "Very rarely. My priorities have shifted."

"Oh. Well, I guess it's just weird for me, then, doing the staring."

"You're here with permission to do far more than stare," he reminded me with a smile. "Believe me, I'm not bothered."

"Would you feel weird if I asked to watch you, later? You know, like watch you…" I couldn't find the right verb, all of them sounding too clinical or too juvenile.

"Touch myself?"

Oh, that'll do.

I nodded.

"No, that would not bother me at all."

I sipped my wine and considered something. Male prostitutes can't fake it the way female ones can. What if the time came for Didier to take me and he wasn't *up* for it, as it were?

"Something is worrying you," he said.

I smiled dopily, owning my nerves. "Sort of. I was just thinking about how… About what happens when you're not attracted to your clients."

"Whether or not I can perform?"

I nodded again.

"Well, I have a few unwritten policies. The first is that no one in this flat does anything they aren't comfortable with. If I don't think a woman is absolutely, perfectly ready for me to do what she's asked, I won't do it."

"And what about if *you* aren't into it?"

Another smile, but this time he lowered his gaze to the glass in his hands. "If I've managed to make a woman really, truly ready to have me, I'm into it. It's very seductive to me, a woman who can make demands of my body."

"Oh. That's a good answer."

He met my eyes again. "The truth always is."

"Have you always known… When did you first realize you're, you know. Good-looking?"

He made a thoughtful face, just another intriguing flavor of handsome seasoning his features. "I suppose when I was about fourteen, I started to realize, or people started to tell me."

"Did you always want to model?"

"No, it was very accidental. Photographers kept asking, and I kept being broke. It seemed a natural solution."

"What about…" I gave a little nod to mean this room, the two of us and what had brought me here.

"That was accidental as well. It never struck me as such a great divide, the step between modeling and selling my physical body. And I never had a drug problem or anything so desperate, if you were curious."

"That hadn't actually crossed my mind."

"I've never been modest, and I've never felt that sex is something so precious it needs to be reserved for some mysterious 'one'. That's a very American way of thinking, isn't it? This modern obsession with monogamy. Exclusivity."

"Probably. Did you want to be something else when you were younger?"

He smiled. "I certainly never went around saying, 'when I'm grown, I want to be a whore'."

I blushed, unsure if he was offended by my question.

"I wanted to make women happy. That was all I knew."

"That's an interesting thing for a boy to realize."

"You would have had to have known my mother to understand. She was a very cold woman. To me, at least. I'm sure a psychiatrist would have plenty to say about that. But I suspect that's some part of why I'm here, doing what it is I do."

"Do you enjoy it?"

Didier nodded. "Very much."

"A friend of mine said your father's Spanish."

He shook his head. "Portuguese."

"Oh, sorry. Does he live in France now?"

"No, he never lived here. I used to visit him in the summers, when I was a child, but not for years and years now. My parents never married. Though I don't think my mother ever stopped loving him."

It was interesting to me, how freely Didier spoke of such things. Then again, surely no part of him was off-limits, not his anatomy or his past, his views on sex and love. I was reminded then how differently Europeans—and in particular the French—view love compared to Americans. When I first moved here I found it bleak, borderline nihilistic, but I can understand now how our version must seem to them—delusional and sloppy and grasping.

As I sat staring at Didier's near-naked body, I ached to learn how to be blasé about the whole affair, how to be *French* about it. I ached to be a woman who, when viciously dumped or informed her boyfriend was cheating, could merely curse and spit at the ground and shake her delicate fist, then move on.

Though if I were really so unaffected, I'd surely have gotten laid long ago. So no, I'm no more fluent in France's romantic pragmatism than I am its language. Though perhaps in time, with practice.

"I'd like to watch you," I said quietly.

Didier offered me a subtle, genuine smile. "I would like for you to watch. Where? Right here?"

"Where do you usually…"

"On my bed."

His bed. Shiver. "Is that okay?"

"That's perfectly okay. Come." He stood and lifted the table from behind the couch, carrying it, lit candles and all, to the far end of the flat. I followed, fear and curiosity tightening my belly, eyes torn between his ass and shoulders and the black threshold of his room.

His bedroom was dark, even more so than the rest of the apartment, its lone window obscured by a curtain. He set the candles by the wall so they illuminated the head of his bed. It was a fascinating piece of furniture, and I bet it had been in this flat for decades, too cumbersome to bother removing. Dark wood, with a canopy—curling, carved posts draped with the same red, chiffony fabric as the curtain. Sensual without being feminine, antique without stodginess. His bedspread was black and I hoped one day to be able to report on the color of his sheets. Beside the bed was a small side table displaying a half-dozen bottles with glass stoppers, massage oil or lube or both, I could only assume.

He waited patiently while I took in the room, as I imagined him fucking on that bed to the noise and flash of a thunderstorm, rain hammering the window. Note—I did not say I imagined him fucking *me* on that bed. I really need to get better at participating in my own fantasies.

"It's a lovely room," I told him.

"Thank you."

"It's very…relaxing. I was worried before I got here that there was no chance I'd be able to relax."

He pulled a chair from the corner to the center of the room for me and took a seat on the bed. "You have a lot of worries about all this."

"I have a lot of worries about most things," I admitted. "Though hardly anything's ever as bad as I let myself expect."

"And me? I'm not as bad as you feared?"

I grinned down at my hands. "No, not at all. You're very disarming."

"I'm glad."

Seeing him nearly naked on his bed had me coursing with heat all over again. This was where he lay when he touched himself for real, without an audience.

"Are you ready?" he asked.

"I think so. I've never watched a man before. In person."

"Does it intimidate you, to feel like a voyeur?"

"Kind of."

"That's fine. Here is what we do." He stood and got the setup going. A dark wicker changing screen from the corner of the room was arranged between the bed and the chair, all of the light on the bed's side. I took a seat and could see him quite clearly through the gaps in the weave, sitting on the edge of the mattress. He could surely see only candlelit lattice.

"This is better?" he asked.

"Yes, this is perfect."

He grabbed a silk scarf from a side table and handed it to me. "This is all at your pace. When and if you're ready for me to finish, just drape that over the screen."

Didier is a genius.

As he sat once more, his expression changed as though he'd convinced himself I wasn't there. His eyes half closed and he cast them downward, looking meditative. He ran a slow hand across his throat, down his chest, circling his living sculpture of an abdomen before finally cupping himself. My pulse rocketed, arousal so potent I held in a gasp.

His hand slid up and down, up and down, over his hidden cock, glacially slow and volcanically hot.

He looked up and addressed the screen. "Is it all right if I make noises?"

"Yes, that's fine."

He braced his other arm behind him on the bed and leaned back. His right hand rubbed lower, fondling his balls, stroking deep between his thighs.

"I'd like to see," I murmured.

I knew he heard me, but he didn't take the order right away. I might have been in charge, but Didier's not entirely obedient, I was discovering. He slid his hand inside the front of his shorts with a low, shallow moan. It was the most exquisite torture, watching the flex of his arm and the shape of his stroking hand, but being denied the view.

"Does it feel good?" I barely realized it was me talking. I felt disembodied.

"Feels wonderful. You want to see?" As if he didn't know the answer.

"Yes."

Still, he made me wait.

Let me be clear. I was nearly thirty and a virgin, but in my head, I'm not a prude. Between me and my hand—and occasionally my vibrator, when I'm lazy—I'm no stranger to arousal or orgasm. I knew what it was like to be worked up beyond belief, and right then, watching Didier, I could honestly say I'd *never* been that wound up before. My entire body was tight and fevery and impatient to the brink of madness.

At long last, when I thought I'd go crazy from the lust, he let me see. Easing the waistband over the tip of his cock, he drew his shorts down, revealing each thick inch with slow precision.

And all at once, I was in the same room with a naked man. An aroused, naked man, and the best-looking one I'd ever seen.

It was almost unfair, that he got this body and this face and voice, all these gifts, and that his dick should also exceed expectations. Not so huge that it intimidated me, though.

It was then that I knew I'd made the right decision, coming to him, and waiting for all these years to have these experiences with a man so extraordinary. I might be ruining myself, setting the bar this high.

Fuck it.

I watched not only his hand and cock, but the tensing of his stomach as he breathed, and the shift of his hips. For a minute he concentrated his strokes just below the head until a clear bead appeared at his tip, then more. With a soft moan, he crested his palm over his crown and slicked it down his shaft, skin glinting in the warm light.

"I'm so ready," he said. There was no pressure in the statement. No request. The thought that my presence was linked to this man's arousal felt like a miracle. And the idea that I could have him, if I wanted…

"Come closer," I said.

He stood from the bed and stepped forward a pace, keeping just far enough away that our eyes couldn't meet above the screen. He dropped his shorts and kicked them aside. As he pleasured his cock, his other hand caressed his belly and chest, all the places I longed to touch myself.

"I'd like to watch you bathe sometime," I told him. Warm, soapy water dripping down his abdomen, between his legs…

"You can have anything you want."

What I wanted right then surprised me. I wanted to be close to him.

"Go back to the bed, please."

He did as I asked and I watched him for another minute or two. A strong, hard, pantingly horny man is a marvelous creature, everything the gender ought to be…yet so frequently isn't, in this day and age. This was how Didier looked when he was by himself. Who did he think of, when he did this?

His groans grew harsher, driving the bad thought away and drawing my attention back where it should be.

I stood and skirted the shade, intending simply to move it aside. But my fear was gone so I let my body lead me, and it led me to sit right next to him on the edge of the bed and watch from close up. His lids looked leaden as he turned his face to me. I could have kissed him, I'm sure. I even leaned in, but when we made contact it was forehead to forehead. Yet it felt more personal than any kiss I'd ever experienced, more explicit by miles. His skin was hot and damp, breath sweet from the wine and scratchy with arousal. The moment was nothing like I'd feared. It was nervous but somehow natural. Sweet. I nestled against his shoulder and watched his hand, wondering what his cock must feel like…surely as hot as the cheek pressed to mine. But I wasn't ready for the tease to end and real exploration to begin.

The smell of his sex was something I hadn't anticipated. Heady and dark as rum, dark as his eyes and brows and the tidily trimmed hair between his legs.

He pulled away an inch to whisper, "What do you want from me?"

"Keep going. Until you absolutely have to…"

He nodded, and even in the candlelight I could see how pink his lips and ears and cheeks were. His cock was flushed as well, his shaft dark against his stroking hand. It was a revelation to know his excitement was so real, when I'd imagined his experience must have turned him into a cold machine, going through the motions.

I thought, *I could kiss this man, so easily.*

Just as easily, I could discover all the things I'd denied myself. I could find out what a hard cock felt like against my palm, what it tasted like, how it felt to have a man in my mouth. What it was like to have Didier above me, sliding inside me. What it felt like, the first time. If you were really turned on, it wasn't supposed to hurt very much. No problem there. What would it be like, to feel his cock rushing in and out? And how would I feel to him? Did it actually feel different with a virgin?

"Have you ever done this… Has a woman come to you, I mean, who's a virgin?"

He nodded, lost in his own pleasure or the struggle to keep from losing it.

"Does it feel different?"

"Every woman feels different."

"Oh." Another good answer.

"I know if you decided you wanted me," he said, "you would feel extraordinary."

Fuck, that melted me. If I decided *I* wanted *him*. As if his wanting me were beyond speculation. Maybe it was even true. Maybe I was one of his prettier and younger clients. Maybe he'd even have smiled at me, had we met in line at a café and not under these strange circumstances.

I tried to imagine what other women might come here to do… To have a beautiful man kneel between their legs, take them roughly on this stately old bed, or ride his hard cock until they got their fill. He'd said nothing was off-limits. I imagined him tied down, or doing the tying. Getting spanked or doling out that punishment. He was whatever that evening's client wanted, and right now, he was exactly mine, intuitively guiding my experience. I wondered what else he'd know I wanted, before I knew it myself.

"I'm imagining you," he whispered.

My heart stopped, tangled in what he'd said. "What are you thinking about?"

"Imagining what you might have me do to you. Maybe undress you here on this bed. Taste your mouth and neck, and your breasts. Your sex."

"I don't know what I want yet."

"I can't wait to help you find out."

Oh, but he could wait, surely. I bet no one could delay gratification like Didier Pedra.

"Do you like being watched?" I asked.

"I like pleasing a woman, so yes. I like the way you watch me." His eyes were nearly closed, voice strained. "You still want this?"

"Yes." So badly I prayed it would never end. "Would you stand? In front of me?"

Didier got to his feet and it felt precisely how I'd hoped with his body looming, just the slightest streak of intimidation warming me. I glanced at the little bottles beside his bed.

"Do you ever use any of those?" I asked, pointing.

"I do. Would you like that now?"

"Please."

He reached for the largest bottle and lifted the sphere from its top, drawing out a glass wand and dripping a measure of clear liquid onto his palm. I recognized the smell—mineral oil.

"Slowly," I said, surprised again by this new ability to make demands.

He obeyed, running his cupped hand along the underside of his shaft with perfect control. Next he smoothed the oil along the base, drawing his fist halfway up, then back down. With each stroke he came closer to the head, until his entire length shone in the dancing light.

"Does it feel good?"

"Yes, wonderful." His hips joined the motion of his hand, thrusting his cock into his grip. Arousal obliterated a dam inside me, flooding me with heat and urgency.

I rose to stand at his side and study him from every angle. He seemed to understand what I wanted from this show, intensifying the movements. With his free hand he reached up and clasped the canopy rail, leaning forward to emphasize everything that had me so mesmerized. He held his fist still, fucking it with his cock and letting loose a deep groan. The sound sucked the breath from my lungs. I circled to the back, imagining this vision—the undulations of these strong hips and ass and shoulders—was how he'd look, taking me.

With a shallow, fearful inhalation, I reached out and touched him, trailing my fingertips down his spine. He moaned from the contact and I pulled away, but only for a moment. When I touched him again, I let myself linger. His skin was hot, as though he'd been standing in front of a fire, and damp with the finest sheen of perspiration. I traced the crests of his jutting shoulder blades, then down his back to his hip. Beneath my palm I felt the strength in his muscles and I marveled simply to be touching a man this way. To be touching a man this flawless. It was a glorious crime, like breaching security to run my fingertips across *Starry Night* and memorize its luscious brushstrokes.

As I rounded him, I dragged my palm across his lower back. I admired the flex of his arm, with my eyes as well as my touch. How extraordinary, that this was actually happening to me, that I was allowed to enjoy the most beautiful man I'd ever seen and he couldn't break my heart.

I went back to the bed, kneeling on the mattress in front of him. As he fucked his fist, I mustered the nerve to touch his face. His gaze, half-mast though it was, felt too intense.

"Close your eyes."

He did.

I memorized his cheekbones and the rasp of his stubble, the shapes of his ears and nose. I held his jaw, awed by how real he was. How he could look this astonishing yet still be flesh and blood. I rose enough to graze my closed lips against his lower one, not quite a kiss.

"I'm close," he whispered. The words brushed our lips together, the most potent and personal caress I believe I'd ever felt.

"I don't want it to end yet."

He nodded.

"Can you stop now, or are you too close?"

"I can stop." And he did. He straightened, chest and belly rising and falling with each harsh breath.

"Could I watch you bathe?"

"Of course."

"When you're ready, I mean."

"Thank you." He ran his hands through his hair and gulped a few inhalations, until his composure returned.

"That was… That was exactly what I wanted," I told him.

"Good."

I felt myself blushing but continued anyway. "Does it make any difference, that it's me here with you when you were doing that?"

"Of course." He met my gaze and as intense as it was, I welcomed it. "Everything I did was for you. Every thought that ran through my mind was of you. And it thrills me to be the only man you've watched, that way."

The blush raged to a full-blown fire. "Oh."

"Whatever you desire tonight, I want to be the one who gives it to you."

I felt too many things, at that moment—lust and awe, and a romantic thrill quickly eclipsed as my traitorous brain reminded me we were only together because I was paying him. But the illusion felt too good for the ugly thoughts to win. That was the magic of Didier—he let you believe this romance was real. Because for the hours you'd reserved with him, it was.

"You want to watch me bathe now?"

I nodded.

"Come."

I followed him to an adjacent, tiny bathroom, lit by the clear bulbs framing the cabinet mirror. This is a garret, I'll remind you, so don't imagine he has an actual tub, merely a shower cubicle. But it's an elegant little nook, tiled in teal and turquoise and indigo, with antique copper fixtures. I took a seat on the wooden lid of his toilet and marveled at how close his naked body was. He got the water running, leaving the glass door wide open.

For whatever reason, this seemed more intimate than sitting beside him on his bed. There was his shampoo bottle, a brand I'd seen in the drugstore a hundred times. On the sink, the razor he shaved with—however infrequently—his toothbrush, his comb. All of these things felt more explicit than his bare cock, perhaps because they negated the illusion. He was an actual man, and I'd been invited into this, his actual home.

"How hot do you want the water?" he asked me.

I balked, worried he thought I wanted to join him.

"Choose for me," he elaborated.

"Oh." It felt like an odd request, but when I rose and put my hand under the flow, it made perfect sense. Did I want him to be warm and comfortable? Cold and tense? Scalded to within a gasp of fainting? I opted for the temperature I like myself, hot but not too hot. I took my seat.

"Thank you," he said, and stepped inside.

I don't know what it is about a man in the shower… His eyes shut and his dark hair turned black as the water cascaded over his face and shoulders, down his chest and stomach and legs, slipping from his oiled cock. My pulse sped as he took a bar of soap from a tray, turning it around and around. He taunted me until the lather was thick and dripping from his hands. His eyes opened, holding me hostage.

He slicked a palm across his throat, his shoulder, down his arm. As he stroked his chest, the suds slid along the crests of his abdomen and between his legs. He broke eye contact to turn, letting me watch as he soaped his hair and his elegant back. He slicked lather between his ass cheeks with a slow, explicit sensuality. The caress unleashed strange, taboo possibilities in my head, ones that had never held much interest before that precise moment.

He turned to face me again, leaning back against the tile with his feet braced at shoulder-width. For what felt like ages he soaped his chest and neck and stomach, before he finally slid his hands lower. Those dangerous eyes closed as he cupped his balls, fondling and lingering, the filthiest act of ablution I've ever seen.

After a few more slippery turns of the bar in his hands, he lathered his cock.

"Good," I murmured.

He didn't touch himself as he had on the bed. This was for me, first and foremost, not merely a voyeuristic glimpse at private acts. He gave himself long, lazy strokes, as if he knew exactly what I wanted—to savor every wet, glistening inch of his bare body.

"Tell me what you think I want," I said. "Not just tonight. But eventually."

Eyes still closed, he paused before he spoke. "I think you want me to take you."

"How?"

I could have sworn his fist gripped tighter, his strokes no longer a show meant only for me, but pleasure for himself. "Slow," he said. "Slow at first."

"Where?"

"In my bed. You want me on top."

My throat and pussy tightened.

"You want to be taken, your first time," he went on. "You need to be passive before you can feel ready to take for yourself. When you trust my body, then you'll explore."

"Explore how?"

"Find out what it feels like, to have a man in your mouth."

"That usually comes first, doesn't it? Before the actual sex?"

He smiled. "That *is* actual sex. And yes, it does often come first, but I don't think it should."

"No?"

"No. I think that act is more explicit than mere fucking."

I shivered, wondering if maybe I shared this view.

"To trust someone when you can barely see their eyes," he murmured. "To give up your own comfort and control and take pleasure in their commands, their experience. And for the one who receives, the vulnerability of being seen so close up, smelled and tasted."

"I never thought about it like that. It always seemed like…like the thing you do between fooling around and going all the way."

"It can be, if you like. But it isn't to me." His brown eyes finally opened. "When sexual pleasure loses its mutuality, that's when the fear and the trust emerge. That's real intimacy. To me."

I was being offered lessons on real intimacy from a man who fucked for money, yet I was inclined to subscribe. Then again, with that deep voice and nasty-sexy accent, Didier could tell me how to strip wallpaper or press flowers and I'd still be riding on the brink of orgasm.

"I like that," I told him. "Your views about it all."

"This is just what I've learned from the women I've been with. When you leave here, I'll have learned something from you as well, I'm sure."

I found that hard to believe. I was the least sexually experienced person I knew. But the way he said it had me *wanting* to believe it, which was enough.

"You'll teach me what it's like to get a private woman to open up, perhaps."

"I hope so. I'd like to learn that, myself."

"What else would you like to learn?"

"Well, how to be with a man, I guess."

He gave me a strange, crooked smile. "You want me to teach you how to be a good lover?"

"Maybe. Well, no. Not really. I just want to know all the things I should by now. What it's like to touch a man, what everything feels like."

"I can only teach you what it will be like between you and I."

You and I. I could've sighed aloud at that concept, the two of us encapsulated as a couple. "Then that's what I'd like to learn. At my own pace."

"At your pace," he agreed.

Didier's own pace had me hypnotized—the slippery, gliding pulls that had his cock looking so hot and thick. How would I want it to be, when I touched him for the first time? Who would be above whom, or how could it be made equitable? I thought perhaps I'd like to touch him as we kissed…or did I want both our pairs of eyes on my hand, his cock? I was already trapped in the worries of what would come, wasting the magic of the present.

"Are you enjoying this?" he asked me.

"I am. But I'm making myself anxious, thinking about whatever's going to happen next."

"Did you think when you first arrived that we'd come this far?"

"No, I didn't."

"What happens will happen, exactly the way it's meant to."

As I nodded, I truly believed him.

"All you need to do is be honest with yourself and with me about what you want. You've done that perfectly so far."

"Thanks."

"What are you wanting?" he asked. "Right now?"

"I think I want to touch you. But not here. Maybe on your couch."

He released his cock and set the soap aside. As he rinsed his magnificent body, he said, "Then we will go to the couch and find out if that is meant to be."

I preceded him to the living room, turning on a dim reading lamp and refilling our glasses while Didier dressed. He joined me on the couch in his pants, his shirt unbuttoned, to my great delight. He accepted his glass and took a deep drink, staring at me over the rim.

"So," I said.

"So. You are pleased with how this is going?"

"Very. You've made me way more comfortable than I'd imagined was possible."

"Good."

I leaned a bit closer, addressing his chest. "You're very intuitive. What else do you think I want, tonight?"

"I think you want to control when I come. You want to feel some control, but also feel safe. Passive."

"I think you're right."

"You've seen that before, I'm sure. A man pleasuring himself? Coming?"

"Yeah."

"Do you enjoy watching? Videos? Or looking at pictures?"

I shook my head. "I've been curious enough to check them out, but I don't really enjoy it for more than a minute or two. I'm never attracted to the men, and I don't want to see the other women, in case I start comparing myself to them."

"I think you're possessive, maybe?"

"I think I'm too fussy. And I think I've spent too much time in my own head, imagining things I'll never be able to have, and no one in real life could ever live up to my ideas."

"You can have those things with me."

"I hope so. But once I leave…I'll never really be able to have you, a man like you. But I want to experience it anyhow. Like a wonderful feast I'll never be served again."

Didier's face turned thoughtful and he sat up, drawing a knee to his chest and wrapping his arms around it, obscuring my view. "What do you mean, a man like me? Why can't you have whatever you want?"

"I'm not pretty enough," I mumbled. "And even if I could land a man as perfect-looking as I want, I don't think I could ever relax, I'd be so worried he'd leave me."

"Do you think maybe that's not what you're afraid of at all?"

I *did* think that, sometimes, but I just shrugged.

"Maybe," Didier said, "you're more afraid of being left by a man you see as your equal. So you tell yourself you'll only ever be satisfied with one you think is better than you are, and you give yourself permission to not bother."

"But I don't want to settle. I don't want to spend my life pretending the man I'm with turns me on if he really doesn't."

"What turns you on, aside from the perfect face and body?"

I blinked. "I'm not sure. Charisma, maybe."

"Wit? Kindness? Talent?"

"I guess."

"You like the way I look, yes?"

I nodded. "Very much."

"Say we fell in love, got married."

35

"Okay." I shifted on my cushion, unnerved by the impossibility of such a notion.

"All of this," he said, circling his face, "will become mundane. What if you do not like anything beyond what's on the outside?"

"You make me sound like a man, after a trophy wife."

"And if we are together forty years, for maybe ten of those I might still be the object you crave. What then?"

"Are you trying to make me feel bad?"

He smiled. "No. I'm trying to understand why you've constructed these rules for yourself. Why you seem to want permission to opt out of love."

"It's scary."

"Of course it is. That's what makes it so exciting."

"Maybe."

"On your end," he said, pointing at me, "you fear the rejection of a man you deem too attractive to ever want you. On my end, I might fear that what I have on the inside will only disappoint you, once my looks are gone. Put out on the pavement like a once-loved chair, after the cushions are stained and worn."

I frowned, a potent pang of sadness twisting my insides. "I don't think about men that way. Really."

"I'm not suggesting I understand you," he said in a kind tone. "But I'd like to. That's why I'm asking all these questions. You're a very exceptional client. You interest me very much."

I blushed at that. "You must think I'm some kind of reverse-chauvinist or something."

"I don't. I think you're just scared. I want to know what you're scared of."

"Of being left, I guess. Of not being good enough."

"Did that happen to you, when you were young?"

I laughed, partly uncomfortable, partly amused. "You *are* a prostitute, right? Not a shrink?"

"If I'm prying too much, tell me so."

"No, I don't mind. And I wasn't ever really left as a kid. Both my parents were around until I was in high school, and when my mother moved out it was actually a relief. But I was a really awkward kid. I know, all children are at some point, but I was like, properly homely. I didn't really get it together until I was out of high school."

"And your classmates were cruel to you?"

"Yeah, but not just because I was weird-looking. I was mean, too. Bossy and rude when I thought I was smarter than other kids." Why was I telling all this to the sexiest man I'd ever met, sitting open-shirted and wet-haired mere feet from me? And why precisely did it feel so good?

"You were a bully?" he asked.

"No, not quite. I didn't go after anyone, wanting to hurt their feelings. I was just clueless and reactionary. I didn't know how to hold back whatever I was feeling. I couldn't separate emotions from reality, my dad used to say. Everything hit me on this intense, visceral level, and if I was angry or insulted, I couldn't step back and calm myself down before I reacted."

"I could see how that would be alienating."

"My mother was the same way, sometimes. But she's severely bipolar. I'm not, but I learned how to interact with people from her. It wasn't until she left and I went to college that I really realized how not-normal it was, living that way. I'd grown up seeing that my dad always caved in the face of her mood swings, until the day he filed for divorce. So my kid brain thought, hey, that's how you get your way."

"Usually it is the parents who teach the child that tantrums are not the way to get what you want."

I nodded. I felt odd, woozy from having told this stranger so much. Much more than I'd ever shared with anyone since moving to France.

"It's nice," Didier said, "getting to hear about you."

I laughed. "Really? I must sound like such a mess."

"Everyone is a mess. If you and I are meant to make love, I wouldn't want to do that without trying to understand you first."

"I thought this would be way different."

"That I'd be some object?" he asked.

"Kind of. Just that it'd be all about appearances. I mean, I figured the women who come to see you are looking for the fantasy, the illusion. Like a place where they don't have to worry about sharing anything personal."

"I suppose some whores offer that."

It gave me pause, hearing him use that word. An ugly, blunt word, though his heavy accent made it less a cinderblock than a strong shot of liquor.

"For me," he went on, "I think the experience is better for everyone when there is a connection. And you cannot connect to someone if you know nothing about them aside from their body. A woman could have a scar across her throat, and I cannot help it—I want to know, was that from an assault? A surgery? A cycling accident? I'm curious. Every woman goes beyond a body and a collection of kinks, even a personality. Each woman is like a landscape to me, and I want to know the history, not just the placement of the rocks and trees."

"That's rather poetic."

Didier grinned, a smile that made my middle melt.

"Would you like to kiss?" he asked.

My stomach gave a flip. I hadn't expected him to initiate anything, but he must've sensed that I needed coaxing if I was to get anywhere. "I'd like to try that."

He lowered his leg and turned onto his hip, draping one arm along the back of the couch. I scooted closer and did the same, pulse speeding.

"Do you like to kiss, or be kissed?" he asked.

"Somewhere in the middle."

"I will kiss you first. As I would if we were coming to the end of a very good first date."

"That sounds nice."

Annoying worries clustered in my brain—I would hate the way he kissed and my attraction would die, tossed into the mass grave alongside so many others.

"Close your eyes," he said, pushing aside all the buzzing thoughts.

I did. I held my breath as his palm cupped my jaw. He spoke and his words warmed my lips. "I want this very much."

"So do I."

His mouth brushed mine, and suddenly, this *was* a date. This was my fantasy, one I rarely let myself indulge, a scenario that actually included me. I'd had a date with the best-looking man I'd ever seen, and he wanted me as much as I wanted him. And it occurred to me then...I'd kissed perhaps a dozen guys in my life. But I'd never before this moment kissed a *man*.

And I'd never before felt like a woman, doing this. Always a girl.

Another graze of his lips, the faintest drag of skin. Tight, urgent heat spread from my mouth down my neck, through my chest and belly to pool between my thighs. Eyes still closed, I found his throat with my palm. The skin I'd watched him bathe felt as clean as it smelled from his olive oil soap. He took my lower lip between his, then the top. I slid my hand back to feel his damp hair, the heat of his neck. He cocked his head, the kiss still closed-mouth but promising more, soon.

I let myself imagine the acts he'd mentioned doing with others, and though they'd thrilled me before, now I couldn't picture such things. In this moment he was my cautious first date, my maybe-a-boyfriend. He was no other woman's, and he'd never kissed any girl and made her feel this way before. His body was far from innocent, but I fantasized that his heart was as untouched and virginal as mine.

As with everything else about Didier, he did not kiss as I'd expected. There was no showing off, though I'm sure his skills are untouchable. I realized in those moments that he might be the most intuitive human being I'd ever met. Part psychiatrist, part psychic, part prostitute.

I pulled away millimeters to whisper, "Kiss me deeper."

"You want to go further?"

"I think so."

"Do you want to watch me as we kiss?"

My pussy ached at such a thought. "Yeah, I'd like that."

Didier kissed me again, more insistent than before. Fire shot through me as his tongue penetrated, our mouths locking, his chin scratching mine. For only a moment did I freeze up from his forwardness. I gave in to the fear, to his maleness and his lead.

His palm left my neck and I could sense it as he opened his pants. I broke away to watch. He slid his hand under his shorts, the flex of his forearm taunting me for a minute or more. I could see his erection growing, framed in his open fly.

"You are always welcome to touch," he whispered.

"I know. But not yet. Not tonight."

He nodded. A deep shiver ran through me as he eased his waistband down to expose his cock.

"You're big," I mumbled.

"I suppose I am."

"I hoped you might be."

That earned me a mischievous smirk. "Then I'm glad I've pleased you." The arm draped behind my shoulders shifted and he held my head gently as he began to masturbate. Putting his lips to my temple, he kissed me there, then down to my ear. His warm mouth took my earlobe, breath so close and ragged I shut my eyes, overwhelmed.

His whispered words tore through me. "You're going to make me come."

I opened my eyes and cast my gaze at his pumping hand. "I'm not doing anything."

"You're here. You're watching. You're letting me show you all this, things no other man has been allowed to."

I felt near to fainting, my breathing as labored as Didier's. "Let's go to your bed."

He stood at once, erection tucked behind his shorts. He held his pants by the belt and took my hand in his free one, leading me back to his room, where the candles still burned.

I sat on the edge of the mattress and watched the shirt drop from his broad shoulders, watched as he stripped naked. I moved to the far end of his bed and patted the space next to me.

He sat. "How are we doing so far?"

I laughed. "You're doing just fine...not sure about myself. I haven't kissed many guys. And I haven't kissed those few guys very, um, extensively."

"I could not tell."

"Really?"

A fond smile. "Really. I like the way you kiss. You kiss as though you are nervous about it, but curious. It's very sexy."

I reached for his face and he did the same to me, cupping my neck. It felt so intimate, his palm on my pulse point as explicit as fingers on my clit. We kissed deeply and I gave as much as I took, tasting his mouth then welcoming his tongue, like a dance. We must have made out for ten minutes, until I felt woozy and rabid and ravenous, ready for more.

I freed my mouth, lips and chin tender. "Touch yourself. Please."

We paused as he adjusted his legs, spreading his thighs and fisting his neglected cock. I watched with open fascination as he grew, as his skin went from tan to deep pink, as his erection lengthened and his foreskin receded to expose his smooth head.

CARA McKENNA

This was the closest I'd ever been to a bare cock, and the experience was nothing like I'd feared. He didn't look silly or scary. Everything about him was right. Everything about him made my body ache the way it was designed to, and I felt normal and functional, dry adjectives that are nothing less than miraculous to me. "Lie down."

He reclined, head on a pair of pillows, clasping his cock. I lay on my side, propped on my elbow, thrilled all over by how close we were, close enough for me to feel the damp heat of his freshly bathed skin and hair. I breathed in the scent of his covers and pillows, the old wood and the candles and his sex.

I brought my mouth to his ear, speaking softly. "Tell me how you think it might be, if you took me." It would be right here, I thought, in this bed. We were so close. All it would take was his strong, slow hands stripping my clothes away, the shifting of his body to cover mine.

He ran his fingers lightly along the underside of his shaft. "We would do nothing, until you were ready. Wet and trembling for it. Then I'd go slow, sinking inside you, holding back each inch until you asked for more."

I swallowed. "You're on top?"

"Yes."

Good. That was how I'd imagined it, too.

"Then when you told me to, I'd start moving. Still slow. Until you were right there with me, wanting it."

I watched Didier's powerful arm, the elegant twitch of his tendons as he stroked.

"Do you touch yourself?" he asked. "When you're alone?"

"Yeah."

"I would have you do that, while I made love to you. It would feel so exquisite, your body tensing around me as you took pleasure from both of us. Not just to be the one who had you first, but to know you enjoyed it. That's what I want. To give you the satisfying experience so few actually get their first time."

"Does it turn you on, being my first?"

"Yes, it does." His hand seemed to speed at the thought.

"I'm afraid it might ruin me, to have someone as beautiful as you. I'm not sure how I'd be able to date anyone, even after I got my first experience out of the way. I don't think anyone could ever measure up."

"I'm only a man."

Oh, but you're so much more than that.

"And you said, getting this experience 'out of the way'. If it were up to me, that's not how it would be. I would want you to feel that all this waiting was the right decision. Utterly worth it."

"It will be. But I am eager to finally, you know. Join the club, I guess."

Didier smiled, an odd tweak of his lips. His hand paused and he looked straight into my eyes. "You make it sound so ordinary."

"No, if it really were just ordinary to me, I'd have done it years ago. But you know. I'm nearly thirty. I want to have a lover, like everyone else seems to."

His smile deepened. "And you chose me?"

I nodded, feeling shy. I looked back to his hand and he resumed the show.

Didier's voice softened and his eyes shut. "I want to spoil you, if you decide you want me. Anything you wish to do with me, you only have to ask."

"Your other clients…" I thought it would hurt, to remember that so many women had had this man and his extraordinary body, but it only filled me with hot, antsy curiosity.

"Yes?"

"What sorts of things do they like to do with you? Do they want romance, like being seduced? Or are they aggressive?"

"Every woman has different needs and desires and secret cravings. Some want it to feel like a date, and to be seduced, yes. Others want to be in complete control."

"Do you ever get tied down or anything?"

"Yes, I've done that. I will do nearly anything. Anything but physically hurt a woman, or be hurt myself—enough to scar. But I've been tied. I've been spanked, and done that for others. I've had clients who want me to get them drunk and take them to bed against their seeming wishes, so they can imagine letting a man take advantage of them. So they won't feel guilt over having desires. And I have clients who like to treat me as their slave, order me around and demean me."

"And you don't mind?"

Another mysterious smile. "I love indulging a woman's fantasies. No matter what they are."

"Even being demeaned? What do they do to you that's degrading?"

"Well, it's not degrading, because it's all an act. But sometimes they talk down to me, call me a whore, reduce me to a hard cock, a servant. I love to be whatever a woman wants, so it turns me on. Some want the opposite, to be the one who's ordered. But I've done many things. I've been bound and gagged and sodomized."

"Oh. Whoa." I tried to picture such a thing but stopped, not enjoying the image. Didier to me is masterful, not overbearing but certainly not made to kneel in silence and submit to anything, least of all penetration.

"Whatever a woman's fantasy is, that is what I want to become. That is what gets me hard."

"When a woman wants to be the one who's degraded, what do they want you to make them do?"

"Suck my cock, perhaps. Or have me take them, rough and selfish."

I imagined trying all of those things, sampling a dozen other women's desires for this gorgeous man.

"Whatever you decide you want," Didier said, "I'll love that too. What I'm doing for you right now..." He looked to his hand, drawing my attention there as well. "My cock is aching, I want this so much. You want to watch and so I want to show you everything." He sat up and I did the same, letting him bring our faces close. "Do you wish to touch me?"

"I'm not sure. Not yet." I didn't know which of us I wanted to taunt with the anticipation, I only knew it felt right, waiting.

For a minute we both watched, and I sensed his gaze darting all over in my periphery.

"Does my body please you?"

I nodded.

"I'm glad."

Disbelief gave me a second's pause as I realized anew that the most beautiful man on the face of the earth was close enough to kiss and smell and touch, and that he wanted to make me happy.

"I hope that whatever you've waited to find with a man, you can find with me," he said.

"If it's not here, it doesn't exist."

I brought my lips close and he took the hint, kissing me. A couple of innocent nips, then back into the deep, rousing caresses that had steam filling my head, clouding my doubts. I let myself wonder about the other things his tongue might be able to make me feel, and imagined surrendering to such acts. As the kissing grew more explicit I felt his strokes turn aggressive, until his mouth faltered and our rhythm broke down. I stole a glance at his arm, his fist, his dick.

"Say my name," he murmured. "I like how it sounds, in your accent."

I thrilled at the notion that he might find me in any way exotic. "Didier."

He replied with a soft moan and his hand sped. "Carolyn."

"Caro-*ly*. *Oh, el, egrec*," I said, impressed to realize I could spell in French without thought, even lightheaded from arousal.

"Apologies. Caroly."

"Didier."

"I'm close," he muttered. "I need to stop, if you're not ready for that."

"I'm ready." How long had I waited for proof that I was capable of reducing a man to this state of desperate need? "I want to see."

"How?"

I watched him, thinking. "On your back."

He lay back against the pillows. I shuffled to kneel between his legs. I'd never felt a rush quite like that, the strangest kind of equality. Strong, handsome man on his back, uncertain guest looming above. He spread his thighs wide, gripping his cock, other hand stroking his belly. I reached down to touch his shins and calves. I realized this was how he might be when he takes me, this hard and needy. The thought had my body buzzing, and I slid my palms up his thighs, recording his firm contours, his soft hair. As he stroked, the muscles of his chest and abdomen and arm stood out.

"Is this how you normally are, when you..." I trailed off.

"On my back? Yes."

"What do you think about?"

"About women I know. Experiences I've had, or would like to."

I wondered what those things might be...the things he wanted but couldn't demand of a client. "Like what?"

"I imagine a woman I've been with, and the things I know she would never ask me for. I imagine the moment she lets me take her to those places."

"What kind of places?"

His hand slowed. "It depends on the woman. I have known women who think themselves above pleasuring a man with their mouths. I imagine how it might be if they gave in and asked me for that. If I know a woman who only demands rough sex in the dark, I fantasize about taking her slowly in the daylight, face-to-face. It's not my job to challenge my clients, only to obey. But I imagine what could be, if they let me push them just beyond their boundaries."

I wondered what my own boundaries were. Anal, certainly. Anything that reeked of lad mags and thongs and the tacky *Girls Gone Wild* culture of woman-as-porn-star.

"What are you imagining now?" I asked.

"I don't need to. You're right here, already testing your limits. I love that I'm showing you these new things."

"What things do you think I'd be afraid to do with you?"

"It is too soon to tell. And there are too many things you want but have denied yourself. I want those, first. What does it mean to you, to watch me now?"

"I guess... I've never seen this in person. I never thought I might have anything to do with a man being this excited. It makes me feel sort of...full of myself."

Didier smiled. "I like that. I want you to feel that way. When I come, I want you to know that it's from you, only."

"Show me."

He nodded and looked to his hand, drawing my attention down with his.

"You're so big."

"I haven't felt this way in ages, this hard. You've kept me so close, for so long. It hurts, I want to come so much."

I swelled with pride to imagine this was true.

"Do you like that you've done this to me?" he asked.

"Yeah."

"I wish you could feel how hard you've made me." His strain was audible, the uttered words harsh and hoarse. "Fuck."

I squeezed his broad legs and slid my palms higher, mere inches from his cock. I gasped as his free hand covered one of mine, holding it tight against his warm, damp thigh.

All at once, he lost control. I could see the unraveling of him, in his jerking arm and twitching hand, his clenching muscles and wild eyes.

"Caroly." His breathy voice matched his disbelieving face.

I shuffled closer, my arm brushing his as I reached out to touch his stomach, to feel that most coveted landscape of male beauty.

"You're so strong."

"No," he groaned. "I'm helpless." The hand covering mine clasped my fingers, the muscles beneath my other palm clenching. His perfection ripped apart at its seams, mouth trapped in a silent gasp, gorgeous face contorted. He let go a final moan, and his hips bucked as he gave in. I took my hand away as the come streaked his belly, white against his flushed skin, more with each body-quaking spasm. I wished he might draw my trapped hand up to touch it, but his intuition was long gone with his composure. His body went slack, arched back relaxing against the covers.

He let my hand go and reached for a cloth on the side table, wiping himself clean. He folded it neatly and set it aside, closing his eyes. For a minute our breathing was the only noise.

"Thank you," I finally said.

He swallowed, blinking hazily. "And thank you. For asking me to be the first man who showed you that."

"You're very different when you're like that. All worked up."

"I'm sure."

"It's fascinating. You're so... I don't know, graceful, I guess. I liked watching you come apart."

"Just as I like fantasizing about a woman, aroused by the things she denies herself. So much of taboo is in the contradictions."

I smiled at him. "That's very philosophical."

Didier laced his fingers together atop his ribs, gazing up at the canopy.

"I'd like to stay a little longer," I said quietly. "Unless that's awkward now."

"Not at all. I'm yours until the dawn. Just give me a moment to collect myself."

"No rush."

No rush indeed. I reclined a few inches to his side and we lay in companionable silence for a half-hour or longer. Eventually he dressed and we returned to the living room, along with the candles. We finished the wine and chatted for another hour, until I knew I had to catch the Metro before the real weirdos emerged from their holes.

As Didier bade me goodnight, my nerves returned. I opened the door to the hall, but more than I feared being spotted in a known prostitute's threshold, I was enlivened merely to be associated with this man.

"I'd like to see you again," I managed to say.

He smiled. "I would like that too. How is Sunday for you?"

Sunday was awful, as I had a staff meeting first thing the next day. But I also knew I'd be high as hell from whatever might happen that evening, and nothing would be able to touch me come Monday morning. "Sunday is fine. Seven?"

"Perfect. I will cook you dinner, if you like. And if you bring the wine."

I laughed. "I'm a bit terrified to pick wine for a Frenchman."

"And I'm a bit delighted to force you to be brave, so I insist."

"Okay, fine."

"You know the way out?" he asked.

I nodded.

"You have a safe trip home. It was a pleasure to meet you."

I was prepared to shake his hand, but Didier clasped my shoulder and bent to exchange kisses on each cheek. I waved lamely and headed down the hall toward the stairs, not hearing the gentle click of his door until I was well out of sight.

SUNDAY

The Second Visit

The wine was chosen at the urging of the pushy man who runs the liquor store near my flat, a dry red that cost slightly too much for my comfort. But I'm a simpleton when it comes to wine. The higher the price, the more adamantly I'll convince myself I like it.

Gone were my work clothes, for my second date with Didier. I wore a dress this evening, a patterned boat-neck more quirky than elegant, that forgave my broad shoulders and flattered my long neck and gangly arms. I felt positive, if not confident, as I walked up Rue des Toits Rouges. Excited if not prepared.

I rang Didier's bell ten minutes early, no longer ashamed of appearing eager. He buzzed me in and my nerves felt different as I mounted the steps. On Thursday they'd had me edgy and dry-mouthed, but this second night I was giddy, even bubbly, blood gone from my veins and replaced with champagne.

His door swung open at my knock and Didier was as tall as I'd remembered, even more handsome in his familiarity. "Good evening, Caroly."

"Good evening." I handed him the wine and followed him to the threshold of his kitchen, watching as he slid my offering from its twisted bag to examine the label.

"Very nice. You spoil me."

"I asked for a Portuguese one, and that's what the man at the store suggested."

"This is very fine, I've had it."

"Good."

"I have not started dinner, so I hope you're not starving."

I shook my head. "No rush."

"Have a seat." Didier beckoned me inside his small kitchen, pulling up a stool to the butcher-block-topped cabinet that served as a center island. He set a glass before me as I sat, and uncorked the wine. I breathed it in, that dry, warm aroma, and studied him as he filled his own glass. He was dressed in his understated but stylish way; a crisp, cream-colored shirt rolled up to his elbows and unbuttoned to mid-chest.

"Did you ever live in Portugal?" I asked.

"No, but I visited when I was younger."

"Which part?"

"On the coast, not far from Cascais. Very pretty. Very different after only having known Paris."

"You didn't leave the city much?"

He shook his head. "My mother detested the countryside, even the suburbs. She was very much addicted to Paris, all the noise and excitement and crowds and attention of it. Cheers."

I joined him in clinking our glasses and tasting my offering. "Oh, that is nice."

He nodded. "A very good choice. I only hope my cooking does it justice."

"You cook a lot?"

"Oh yes, though nothing fancy. Is there anything you do not eat?"

"I'll try anything."

"I was going to make pasta. A friend came by with sausage from a Sicilian butcher this afternoon, the best I've ever had. That with tomatoes and basil and bread."

"That sounds wonderful."

Didier prepped ingredients and sautéed onion and garlic and the meat in a pan, then gathered flour and other things, setting a metal, cranked contraption on the island.

"You make your own pasta?"

He nodded, eyeballing measurements. "It's not so hard. I enjoy cooking. It's the hobby I indulge the most these days."

"What else do you like to do?"

"I read a lot. Sometimes I take things apart and put them back together. Watches, clocks. My hobbies are quite simple."

I nodded, sipping my wine, watching this fascinating creature at work. "What did you want to be, when you were younger?"

"I always thought I might be a writer, but no matter how often I try, it never gives me the joy I expect it to. It never feels quite so romantic as it seems it should."

"That's too bad. I bet your memoirs would be very eye-opening."

He drove his fingers into the dough, flour puffing up to settle on his forearms. "What about you? What did you want to be?"

"I wanted to be an artist, but I never got very far beyond imitating other people's work. When I went to college I fell in love with art history, and that's what led me to curating."

"Who is your favorite artist?"

"I couldn't pick any one favorite. But I probably love Klee and Miró best."

He nodded. "Miro was fascinating. I heard he was an accountant, and that he suffered a nervous breakdown and that is how he came to art. Is that true?"

"I believe so."

"You must know the Louvre inside-out, after two years in Paris."

I nodded. "That's not where I work, though. I work at the smaller museum, just a couple blocks east. But I was lucky enough to get a summer internship at the Louvre when I was twenty. It was heaven, seeing all the works I knew from books in person."

"Yes, it's much different." He fed dough into the pasta maker and turned the crank, a nest of noodles gathering on the floury wood.

"In a book you can't move around, see the way the light hits the brushstrokes from all the different angles," I said.

"Or smell the wood or stone or paper."

"Exactly. It changed my life, that summer." I sipped my wine as Didier cooked, studying him in the cool dusk light, my very own work of art for the evening.

"What's it like, seeing yourself as other people's art in galleries?" I asked.

"It's humbling."

I smiled, unseen, liking his answer.

"It does not feel like me, in their photographs. Just some man I resemble. Though I've always been poor at reducing people to their outsides."

I pondered that, wondering if it was the willful habit of a man sick to death of being objectified, or perhaps one merely enamored with minds.

"Have you heard of that disease where a person cannot recognize faces?" he asked.

"Sure. That disorder Oliver Sacks had." I frowned. "Do you have that?"

"No, but I understand it. I've always been terrible with faces and names, even worse with places and buildings. I get lost very easily."

I smiled at that notion, at the visual of Didier's perplexed expression as he stared at a street sign, a dozen arrows pointing every which way.

"As a child," he said, "I only remembered how to get to places by counting the blocks. Three blocks straight, one block left, two blocks right. That was school."

"You couldn't just look at, I don't know, a fountain or something, and remember where you were?"

"It's odd, I know. If I passed the fountain I would ask myself, do I see that on the way to school? Or was that somewhere I went on the weekend with my mother, the post office, perhaps?"

"Weird."

"Indeed. I got better, if only at memorizing street names and writing notes to myself. And later I grew quite fond of taxis, letting directions be someone else's burden."

Didier switched on the lights as the daylight died, and before I knew it he was dragging over a second chair, clearing the island and setting dinner before me.

This was a date. A meal, drinks, the promise of foreplay if not sex. I didn't let myself diminish it, knowing I was paying for his company as surely as I'd purchased the wine we were enjoying. He was extraordinary, that way. He didn't trick you into believing this was something other than what it is. He merely made what it was a thing of substance. I was buying Didier as I might a gourmet meal or an evening of live music, a fleeting indulgence. Did it really matter that I paid for any of them, that I didn't prepare the food or compose the music; that others could enjoy the pleasures if they too were willing to pay for them? Was it really all some New World hang-up, the demand for permanence and ownership and exclusivity? I hoped so. My parents were such a cautionary tale against two people staying together, it's no wonder I'd never pined for commitment.

Didier spoke after a long silence. "You look rather thoughtful."

"I feel rather thoughtful."

"You are not sad, I hope."

I shook my head. "Not at all. I'm having a lovely evening. Everything is delicious. Thank you."

He lifted his glass. "And thank you, for sharing it." Didier was as smooth as I'd expected a Frenchman to be, but not in the cloying, coercive way I'd feared. His seduction puts you at ease, like a slowly sipped cocktail or a hot bath.

Didier is a fine cook, and the bite of the tomatoes brought out the tang of the grated cheese, the sweetness of the onions, the tartness of the wine. I will never be able to eat linguine again without thinking of him, his hands and mouth and voice.

"What else would you like to do tonight?" he asked.

"I hadn't thought too much about it. Just drink and talk, like Thursday. See where that goes."

"That sounds perfect. And if you are interested…if you enjoy music and you grow weary of my voice…"

Fat chance.

"I have a phonograph and some records. I know that's old-fashioned…"

"No, that's cool."

He smiled. "Good. I love old things. Typewriters, gas lamps. Those things that are trapped between history and the present. What we used to call technology, now antiques."

"That's interesting. What other sorts of things?"

"Toys fascinate me, like wind-up tin animals, miniature railroads, slot cars, music boxes. When I was a child I would get lost for hours in my grandparents' attic. My grandfather had nearly all of the toys he'd grown up with, board games too, and so many photographs."

"Wow."

"Yes. I would fantasize about living in that time, between the wars. I have a cabinet full of things I've collected, if you'd like to see, after dinner."

"I would."

I watched Didier as he ate, marveling anew at him. Surely no one is perfect, and yet he seemed so. A large man, big enough to seem exceptional but not so big that he felt inaccessible or overbearing. I adored every angle of him—his jaw, his strong nose, the dark, graceful arch of his eyelashes when his face was cast down. I remembered this face as it had looked on Thursday evening, seconds before he came. An entirely different strain of perfection.

When we'd cleaned our plates he took them to the sink and refreshed our glasses.

"May I see your cabinet?" I asked.

"Oh yes. Come."

We went through to the main room and set our wine on the coffee table. He turned on a lamp and I followed him to a corner, to an old china hutch I'd not noticed before. It contained no dishes, but a multitude of treasures. Beyond the glass stood tin toys, clocks, brass scales, metronomes. He opened a drawer to reveal a carefully spaced selection of watch faces. From behind them he withdrew a tied leather bag and unrolled it, taking out tiny tools to show me—a set of magnifying lenses, minuscule screwdrivers and the finest-point tweezers I'd ever seen.

"Wow."

"Thank you. It's not so astounding as art, merely taking apart others' inventions."

"It's still really neat." He'd taken out a jeweler's loupe and I put it to my eye, examining my fingernail. "You're quite the mad scientist."

"Not so mad. Merely curious. Many of these things came to me broken. It's very satisfying to understand them enough to make them work again."

I pointed to a pocket watch in the drawer. "May I?"

"Please."

I opened its face and peered at its insides through the monocle. Didier took it from me, just long enough to wind it so I could watch all its miniscule parts tick and snap and whir, like the X-ray of a marvelous little brass animal. "I can see how you might get lost in this."

"Yes. I find it very interesting, these tiny spaces, like little rooms. Microscopic factories full of gears and springs. I find the human mind very interesting as well, but these... I feel I can understand these."

I set the monocle down. "I think you understand people's brains just fine."

"Perhaps."

Didier put away his tools and I strolled to the couch. I watched his back as he adjusted his collection, fussy but not obsessive. When he joined me I asked, "Have you ever owned an ant farm?"

"I haven't, but I always wanted one. Have you?"

I shook my head. "I wasn't allowed any pets." Actually it was my mother who oughtn't be trusted with the care of an animal, but I didn't elaborate.

"We always had fish when I was growing up," Didier said. "They were the only pets my mother stood any chance of maintaining, she was out so much. Eventually I did all that, feeding and cleaning."

"Flushing."

His smile was grim. "Indeed. I remember when the very first fish died, how I found it and agonized over telling her. Then she came home and I said, 'Mother, I have terrible news. The fish has died.'

And she blinked at me and pulled a franc from her purse and told me to go and get a new one."

I laughed.

"I was devastated, but to her it was as if a light bulb had burned out."

"Did you get a new one?"

"Oh yes, we must have had twenty of them, at least, one at a time, one after the other. It did not upset me so badly after the first one died, because I loved the pet store. I would loiter there for an hour or more before selecting a fish, and then I would be so gentle and full of pride as I carried it home six blocks in its bag."

"Six very carefully memorized blocks."

"Indeed. If the latest fish died in the winter, I would keep the new one inside my coat, wrapped in my scarf as I walked home. I gave myself a cold once, doing that."

"That's sweet."

Didier's smile faltered. "They are nice memories, the fish. Until the last one."

"Oh. Why?"

"The last time I was given a franc to buy a fish, when I was perhaps thirteen, it was taken from me."

"Taken?"

He nodded, eyes cast down at the glass in his hand. "Older boys from my neighborhood, mean boys, pushed me down and took the bag."

"What did they do?"

"I do not know. But it was one of the worst days of my life, as dramatic as that sounds. That stupid little creature was in my care, and I thought I was rescuing it from the pet store. But I didn't keep it safe and who knows what became of it. Stepped on or tortured or who knows what. I felt very weak, very worthless for weeks."

"And you never got another fish?"

"No. I tried to go back to the pet store, but the guilt hurt so badly, I was sick."

"Oh my."

"That was the first time I truly understood how unsafe the world can be. And how unfair it is for the gentler creatures trying to make their way in this land of bullies."

I wondered if Didier meant the fish or his thirteen-year-old self. "That's very sad." I surprised myself, setting my hand on his forearm. He smiled at me, most of his melancholy seeming to lift.

"Would you ever get a fish again?"

"No, I don't think so."

"I'm pretty sure no one would try to take it from you now." I pictured Didier's bare body, wondering if he knew how to exploit that physique for violence as well as art.

"I think my time for fish has passed. I would enjoy its company, but I would always think, what kind of a life is this, living in a tiny bowl with no other fish, your only purpose in life to be a living trinket for some other animal, in exchange for food?"

I shifted in my seat, knowing too well that, to some, this man must boil down to nothing more than a six-foot-something trinket.

"I am too sensitive now for the pet shop," Didier concluded. He smiled suddenly. "And I am too depressing a date this evening. Forgive me."

"I don't mind. Everyone's allowed to feel sad now and then."

"I am carrying on about goldfish when you are here for romance. So come, let's leave all that behind us." He took my hand and put it to his lips, a gesture I'd imagined before but always skeptically, always as a stereotype of the cheesiest ilk. But in reality, I liked it.

He stared at my fingers and squeezed them gently, one by one. "Have you any idea what you would like from me, this evening?"

"No. I'd like to kiss you again, but beyond that, I'm not sure."

"Whatever you wish."

I looked to him nervously and he got the hint. He took the glass from me and set it aside. His hands were warm as he cupped my neck, his mouth bold, lips tart from the wine I'd purchased with exactly this in mind. Just as his kisses grew deep and my head grew cloudy, he pulled away.

"May I tell you something?"

"Sure."

"I thought of you, Friday afternoon. I touched myself and I imagined it was you, pleasuring me."

Every inch of me tightened and released, heat dropping over me like a sheet. Our eyes darted, his dark ones mesmerizing in the warm light of the lamp.

"Really?"

"Yes. I bathed and I remembered how it felt to have you watch, and before I knew it my hand was wrapped around my cock. Your hand, in my mind."

I conjured the scene, thick lather dripping from his fist. "I've thought about you as well." But strangely enough, I hadn't come since meeting Didier on Thursday. I'd been wound up beyond reason, but each time I thought I might touch myself, misgivings gave me pause. Had I known he'd still thought of me after I disappeared down his stairs—that he'd *come*, thinking about me—I'd have given myself permission to indulge in my own memories. But as it was, I'd been afraid as always that my lust was laughably one-sided.

Yet for some incredible reason, despite that fact that he was the finest man I'd ever seen and miles out of my league... I believed him, just then. And I realized something I never had before. Deep down, I wanted to be seen as an object too. I wanted to be coveted and sought after. I wanted to be taken apart and understood, reassembled, filed away in Didier's cabinet. I didn't even need to be pretty to have this. I only had to allow him to open me up.

After more kissing I said, "You told me that what women want from you is different, depending on who they are."

"Of course." I loved how rough his voice sounded then, and knowing it was partly my doing.

"Well, what do *you* like? If the woman had no preference and it was all up to you, what do you like best?"

"I cannot divorce the two that easily. Even in my own head, by myself, what I imagine has everything to do with the woman in my thoughts."

"Even if she was just a totally neutral, up-for-anything woman?"

He smiled. "As much as I love clockwork, I would never want to fuck a woman as soulless and without preference as a robot."

I sighed, pretending to be outrageously exasperated.

Didier laughed, a glorious noise. "Do you really want me to have some singular need? Do you want some secret key to pleasing me? Because you don't need one. You're doing just fine, right now. What excites you excites me."

"I just want to know who you are, I guess. By yourself."

"I can't give you some simple answer. It all depends on the company. I love wine," he said, "but I won't drink it with ice cream. I love coffee but I do not want it with mussels, you see? I may adore two things, coffee and mussels, a certain sex act and a particular woman, but all are ruined when they don't go together."

"Fine, I submit to your logic. What am I then? What would you pair with me?"

Didier offered me a mysterious smirk and laced his fingers between mine, a gesture that triggered a rush I cannot adequately describe. "I do not know all of your flavors just yet."

I squeezed his hand. "Guess, then."

"Because you're cautious, I think we should keep everything equal, no one the aggressor or the passive one. Slow explorations, to start. And when I get a better feel for you, I'll know what beyond that to offer." Another smirk. "But I suspect you are like shellfish, meant to be coaxed open and savored. I would pair you with a dry white wine. Something sharp, not dark."

It may not be the most likely poetry, comparing a woman to shellfish, but I felt warmth burst in my cheeks and chest, outrageously flattered to be reduced to food and drink to this man. Something to be consumed.

"But again," he said, "I have so much yet to learn about you."

I gazed down at his fingers twined with mine. I had much to learn too, but perhaps that evening I'd find another lesson or two to check off my list.

A finger crooked under my chin, brought my face up, a tender bit of pushiness I adored. I let Didier kiss me and what had felt romantic before turned carnal, deep and insistent. I let his hand go to stroke his neck, his shoulder. I felt his hard arm through his shirt, touched the bare skin and soft hair at his open collar. He didn't touch me back beyond my face and neck, and I wasn't yet sure if this was a relief or a disappointment. But my own hands were bold, running down and over his front to feel his abdomen. As I traced the waist of his pants with my fingertips, he freed his mouth to sigh.

I leaned close to open his buttons, one, two, three, until I spread his shirt open and feasted my eyes on his body.

He slid his fingers from my hair, bringing them lower not to touch me, but himself. As I roamed his chest and stomach, he cupped a hand between his legs.

"Are you hard?"

"Yes." He traced his erection with his thumb and forefinger, pulling the fabric tighter to show me. I know if he'd asked me to touch him, I'd have clammed up. He didn't. He made no requests, only fondled himself, illustrating what I was missing out on, what I could have.

"I want to touch you," I whispered.

"You can do whatever you like with me."

"I know. I'm just afraid I'll be lousy at it."

"You've never done this to a man, no?"

I shook my head.

"Caroly." My name on his breath short-circuited my brain. "Tonight, with you... Your cautious hands on me, unsure what they are doing, will be more exciting than the touch of the most masterful woman on earth. I don't need to be served, only explored."

"Oh," was all I could think to say.

"I want mine to be the first cock you ever know."

His words hit me hard, making my light head lighter, my pussy hot. "I want that too."

"Here." Gently, impossibly slowly, he took my hand, sliding it from his belly and over his belt to cover his erection. He held it there for a long time before guiding me, coaxing my palm up and down, a faint graze over his hard, hidden arousal.

"That is not so bad?"

"No," I mumbled. "That's very nice."

His hand abandoned mine to its clumsy devices. I measured him with light caresses, loving how tense the rest of his body had grown.

"You feel harder than I expected."

"This is how I felt when I thought of you the other night. Thinking of you made me hard then, just as your touch does so now." He was quiet through several strokes, save for his labored breaths. "Do you like it?"

"Yeah." Bolder, I wrapped my hand around him as much as possible through his slacks, squeezing to discover how thick he was. He moaned and I felt different, as I never had before—powerful and beautiful and wild.

"I'm the first," he murmured.

The idea that he was fetishizing this experience gave me permission to do the same. I'd already grown quite fond of Didier—

surely fonder than was rational, given our perhaps six cumulative hours of acquaintance—but reducing him to a stiff, suffering cock was electrifying. I'd always loathed this idea, openly lavishing a beautiful man with my admiration. As if such a fortunate specimen deserves more validation. But of course it felt nothing like that with Didier. I adored this glimpse into another side of him, a darker, cockier version of the man I was just coming to know.

"Kiss me," I said.

He did. He turned and kissed me as no one ever had before, urgent and demanding. I ached for his hand on top of mine again, dictating—perhaps even *forcing*—the friction. But I was in charge. I imagined teasing him this way until he begged to be taken out and given release. I imagined denying such a request, degrading him with my refusal until he lost control, quaking and pleading and erupting beneath my hand, inside his clothes, perspiration shining on his forehead.

But of course I wasn't ready for that. Indulging the idea was breakthrough enough. Having a hard cock against my palm and Didier's mouth on mine, the sensations feeling so natural... That was enough.

Everything was different now. More real. He was as horny as he had been controlled our first night together. And here I was, pursuing his body instead of having it offered. The fact that he was still dressed was a change in itself. Wicked fantasies aside, he felt alarmingly like my boyfriend, and the idea turned me on far more than it should have.

"What do you want?" I asked. I realized how backward the question was as it came out.

Didier surprised me with his answer. Our first evening he'd have turned it back on me, asked what I wanted, but this evening...

"Want to touch you."

I'd been nervous about such a thing, but far more potent than my anxiety was the pleasure of being at the heart of Didier's desperation.

"Okay."

His eyes met mine, and the neediness fogging them was the sexiest thing I'd ever seen. "Show me what I can have," he murmured.

I shifted, still stroking his hard cock through his soft pants. I took his wrist with my other hand and placed his palm on my collarbone. His skin was warm, and though he'd touched my face and neck before when we kissed, this felt very intimate, only a few inches lower.

"Touch where you want to," I whispered. "If it's too much, I'll stop you."

He kneaded my shoulder and stroked my upper arm, raising goose bumps. I could sense the tension in him as he held back. I gripped his shaft tightly and he repaid me with a sharp grunt.

"You're different tonight," I told him.

"Is it too much?"

"No, I like it."

"The way you're touching me... You feel different as well. It finally feels as if you own me. That you know you can take, instead of requesting."

"Do you like that? Feeling owned?"

"I do. Especially with a woman who arrives here so uncertain."

I imagined pushing him back against the arm of the couch, opening his pants and taking him with my mouth. How he'd moan and pant, and the weight of his strong hands on my head or shoulders. Then I recalled what he'd said, about oral being more intimate to him than intercourse.

But if I couldn't rush that act, I'd at least taunt him with it.

"I keep wondering what it would be like to taste you."

His hand clasped my arm tighter and he made a noise, as though a gasp had gotten lodged behind his tongue.

I let his erection go to free his belt buckle. His hand slid to where my shoulder met my neck, and the pressure was exquisite, a taste of plaintive aggression that lit me up. I freed the clasp of his slacks and lowered his zipper, his thick cock already straining at his shorts as I spread his fly open. It was *my* cock tonight. Mine to take, not his to offer.

"I love this," I said, stroking him. It was far more explicit now, one thin layer of silk between us. I could feel his skin sliding, feel his heat and the contour of his shaft and head. A damp spot darkened the fabric and all I could think was, *I did this to him.*

He whimpered. "Anything you want from me, you can have."

"I want you to be the first man I ever take inside me."

I gasped as his hand covered mine, squeezing his cock through the silk. It would have scared me only a few nights ago, but it felt amazing now. This polite, poised man, driven to bossiness by what I could make him feel.

He put his mouth to my throat, nearly kissing but not quite. His breaths were heavy and hot, as fast and rough as the strokes he made me pleasure him with. After half a minute he released my hand and pulled away.

Through a gasp he said, "Forgive me."

"No, I liked it."

"I did not mean to be so rough."

"It's good, really. I love that I've managed to make you that...worked up."

"You have. I feel crazy, I want you so badly."

"What do you want, when I touch you that way?" *So often, we're asking one another what we want...*

"Everything. I want to feel like the biggest, hardest cock you've ever had. Ever *will* have. I want you on top, using me. I want you on your knees before me, possessing me with your hands and eyes and your mouth. I want to hear you beg for me to take you, to come for you. Everything."

I shivered to realize again how in tune with me he was. I wanted such a messy mix of things too; to be both aggressive and passive, cruel and helpless. Everything, indeed.

I had always kept myself so separate from men, now that I'd found one I was willing to be close to, I wanted to be so close to him that everything jumbled, our roles mashed and swapped and switched, two bodies twisted in a frantic heap of sweat and mangled, modified kinks. I wanted his weight on me, his voice in my ears, his cock inside me. Behind me, above me, beneath me, even beside me, once the sex had its way with us.

I liked who Didier was turning me into. I liked who I was with my armor stripped away. Stronger in my defenselessness.

I felt so thankful and energized, I wanted to spoil him. Without a trace of fear, I pulled his underwear down to free him. His cock looked new again in the lamp's weak glow, bigger now that it was bare. He watched me, watching him. As I traced a finger along the ridge his flesh twitched, as though pleading for more. For *me*.

He slid his thumb under his waistband, holding it down for me. Something about this, about him presenting himself, exposing himself... His other hand palmed my shoulder. As I wrapped my fingers around him, his touch slid lower, lower, until he glanced my breast. The sensation made me buck and he took his hand away.

"It's okay," I said. "You're fine. It's just intense, having someone do that."

He cupped me softly and my racing pulse slowed.

I glanced down at my hand, his cock. "I'm not quite sure how to touch you. Beyond just exploring. How do you do it, when you're...you know."

"Here." He wrapped my fingers around him, just below his head. I clasped him tightly as he directed, easing my fist up and down, up and down, at a steady, sensual pace.

"Then when I am close, I go faster. Harder." He squeezed my fingers tighter and sped my pulls, rougher than I'd have ever done, taking my own liberties. He took us back to the slower caresses.

"Is that the same as when you're inside a woman?" I asked. "Slow, then more frantic at the end?"

"Typically, yes. You tease me for long enough and my body grows impatient and greedy."

A greedy Didier intrigued me greatly. For a long time I stroked him, liking the heat of his palm on my breast. I didn't want to feel *fiddled with*, and I didn't. I felt comforted. As my confidence with touching him grew, my mind wandered to what else I might do with this cock. What might bring him to that greedy, frantic state…

"I know you said oral sex is more intimate than intercourse."

"You do not agree?"

I laughed. "I'm not one to ask. But I've never had a man before, either way. And actually losing my virginity feels like a bigger deal. I mean, I might still be intact, down there."

His brows rose, curious. "You think so?"

"Maybe. Possibly." The science behind hymen preservation had always struck me as murky. Tampons, sure. Horseback riding, minimal and non-vigorous. Could I have made it to thirty, my seal unbroken? The curious look on Didier's face made me hope so. Such an old-fashioned notion of purity and ruin seemed fitting in this old-fashioned place, with its old-fashioned objects. Didier and his timeless, classical beauty.

"You do not use any toys by yourself?" he asked.

"Not inside me. I always thought I should save that. Since it's been so long already."

"Well."

I nodded. "So that kind of feels like, I don't know. The grand finale."

"I understand."

"But you do… You like going down on women, right?"

He grinned and released my breast, propping an elbow against the back of the couch and leaning back. "Very much. Perhaps that is why I save it for last."

Heat trickled down my neck through my chest and belly to my cunt. I'd happily be Didier's dessert, if that was how he felt about the act.

"You're blushing."

"Yes, I am."

"Was I too bold?" he asked.

"No, I like what you said."

"If I can make you blush just talking about this, I cannot wait to know what the actual caress will do to you."

"I'd like to find out. Some night."

"Some night?"

"Yeah. Maybe tonight… I'm not sure." All my clothes were still on and I wasn't certain if I was ready to go to the same base Didier had allowed me to take him. But I was here to find out.

"Could we go to your room?"

"Of course."

I let him go and he stood to refasten his pants.

"Candles?" he asked.

"Please."

The card table was in its place behind the couch and he carried it with us to his room. I sat and watched him light the many wicks, his exquisite face golden in the multiplying glow.

He turned to me as he shook the match. "More kissing?"

I nodded. "And could you maybe take your clothes off? Except your underwear."

He slid his open shirt from his shoulders and dropped his slacks. He was still hard from what I'd done to him, erection curved to one side behind the silk. More of that sticky, self-satisfied pleasure filled me, banishing the nerves.

"Could you sit here?" I patted the center of the mattress.

Didier did as I asked, facing the head of the bed, and I arranged his long legs as I wanted them, in a V. Mindful of my dress, I scooted close, also in a V, with my legs draped over his. Mirrored this way, I felt vulnerable but equal. I edged even closer, enough that my hem gathered against his straining cock, our crotches still two or three inches apart.

Didier ran his palms over my calves and knees, smiling. "I like this. Feeling your body against mine."

I liked it too, my smooth legs pressed to his coarser ones. I imagined more, both of us naked. I kept the idea in mind as I touched his face and his mouth lowered to mine.

Every time we kissed, it felt different. New, exciting, dangerous, sweet, and now fond. I'd never before felt mastery over any of the men I've kissed, the sort of confidence that practice and familiarity breed. With Didier I was beginning to. He dominates just enough for you to kiss him back, but to also feel without a doubt that *you. Are. Getting. Kissed.*

I hope it's exactly how he fucks.

I fumbled our rhythm to scoot even closer, finally near enough for my dress to ride up and for his erection to press the crease where my thigh meets my hip. It was harder to kiss now, because he's tall and we were so close, but the fascination of having my thighs against his waist and my chest brushing his… Further than I'd meant to go, but so exactly where I wanted to be.

Strong hands slid down my arms to my lower back, kneading. Punctuating the gesture were tiny movements from his hips, the faintest thrust of his cock against my bare skin.

I needed more, but I wasn't sure what. Against his neck I whispered, "I want to go further."

"You want me to take you there?"

I nodded.

"Everything now is fine? You just want more?"

"Yes."

With no further preamble, Didier took hold of me beneath each thigh and pulled me against him, my legs wrapping around his waist. All at once, a hard cock was pressed to my pussy, where no man's hand had even ventured. Our mouths were level once more and I'd found paradise, our bodies so perfectly enmeshed. He reached between us to center his shaft against my lips.

"Good?" he asked, our noses touching.

"Yes."

"Nice for me as well." He stroked my back and waist, my butt. I hadn't expected that area to be so loaded with nerve endings, but the weight of his palms there took my breath away. When his hands moved to my hips, I felt the request in their gentle tugging. I wrapped my arms around his shoulders for support and adjusted my legs to kneel, and began to move.

I was awkward at first, grinding too hard. But he was patient, and before long I found my way, softly grazing his cock with my pussy. This was heaven, surely. Even better than sex, the perfect torture of anticipation. He held my ass, following the rhythm I set.

Didier's breath went from deep to shallow to heavy to harsh. I leaned back to see what I'd done to him, his brows gathered in a tight line, eyes shut, mouth open. There's no way to make that face anything less than stunning, but whatever I was making him feel, the results were ten times more handsome than any smile. I could imagine him tied down now. I couldn't yet imagine actually inflicting his pleasurable suffering, but the thought of him submitting suddenly made sense.

His eyes opened. "Feels wonderful." His hands left my butt and he braced them behind him on the bed, leaning back. It tensed his chest and arms and stomach, and gave me more freedom to explore this act. So unlike the old Caroly—who would never dare look directly at a shirtless man in the park, lest she affirm his vanity—I *stared* at Didier. His body was mine for the evening, every inch of hard muscle, the spray of dark hair trailing from his navel to his cock, all that bare skin, his scent and his face and his voice. His pleasure. He stared at me in return and I felt no judgment, only awe.

I paused to surprise myself once more, peeling my dress up and over my head.

I didn't need his hands on me; his eyes were more than enough. I wondered what gave him that look… My skin, perhaps, far paler than his. My small breasts in the laciest bra I'd ever owned, purchased with a racing heart for this exact occasion. I didn't feel like any of the adjectives I usually do, being seen in a bathing suit or suffering the harsh light of a dressing room—*gawky, pasty, bony*. His gaze turned all those words on their heads. I felt rare and graceful. Electric.

I wanted something that hadn't actually occurred to me before. I wanted to come tonight.

Before, my thoughts had been nothing more than a carnal menu of unknowns—the proximity of a naked man, the feeling of his flesh against mine, the surrender of my moldering virginity…perhaps to kiss a man and actually take pleasure from it, as a bonus. But never had I bothered to wonder if I'd have an orgasm. How much of my life had I wasted, opting out of experiences? The thought sobered me and my hips slowed.

"Is everything all right?"

I hesitated before answering, long enough for emotion to take hold. Tears came, just a few. Didier sat up and wiped them from beneath my eyes.

"We can stop."

"I'm not upset, not from this. I just feel sad."

"Sad?"

"This is all really wonderful, but it makes me realize... I don't know. I wish I hadn't wasted so much time and energy, avoiding being this way with someone."

"You're here now, with me," he murmured. He kissed my cheeks, my ears, my neck.

"I am."

"So enjoy that this is all still new to you. That all this, these thrills most people can barely remember at twenty-nine, they're still ahead of you. Right in front of you."

I smiled, tears drying up. "You're a very smart man. And I am, I'm here with you, right now."

Didier smiled, something mischievous in his narrowed eyes. "You're very pretty when you cry, though."

I laughed, and Didier kissed me again, to the left of my lips.

"Better?"

I nodded.

Another kiss, on the other side.

"You're sweet," I said.

One more kiss, square on the mouth. It was a relief—a release—to allow him to lead. I welcomed him inside, the sweep of his tongue against mine. It was in that moment that I knew for certain, I'd have him. Not tonight, perhaps, but soon. I hoped he would feel just like this, intuitive and easy. As bold as I so often felt lost and unsure.

He spoke against my lips. "Lie back."

Excitement surged as my head found the pillows, all my sadness reduced to a figment.

Didier knelt between my legs, palms on the bed beside my ribs, bringing our centers back together. "Tell me if I'm too forward."

"I trust you."

He locked his forearms tight to my sides and the unexpected possession of the contact shifted everything. His hips began to move, the ridge of his erection teasing my clit with short, faint strokes. *Faster*, I thought. Fast enough to burn away the last scraps of our clothes.

He looked strong and solid, felt just as good as I laid my hands on his shoulders. I wondered how many women had been taken on this bed, head against these pillows… It sounds like an ugly, sabotaging thought, but weirdly enough, it only thrilled me more. I wanted to be that sort of woman, the kind who took what she wanted. I wanted to be with Didier, a man so skilled with his body that he'd made a craft of sex.

I watched his hips, fantasizing we were actually having sex. I pictured his cock surging as he fucked me, gleaming wet in the candlelight. I glanced to his bedside table as a thought tugged at me.

"Yes?" he asked.

"Do you have any water in here?"

He craned his neck and I spotted it—a pitcher and tumbler on his deep windowsill. He left me to fill the glass.

I suppose he expected me to drink it, but I sat up, pouring a bit into my cupped palm. I felt his gaze on me as I brought my hand to his abdomen, letting the liquid slip down his skin to darken his shorts. Another palmful, dripped right against his bulge, underwear becoming translucent. Even sexier than I'd hoped. I could see nearly everything, only the most explicit details obscured, as though behind fogged glass. The camera of my memory clicked madly and I pictured him kneeling in the ocean surf, pummeled by waves… Dirty-poetic; how I imagine a pornographer might shoot a cologne commercial. A decadent marriage of sleaze and luxury.

"I love the way you look at me," he said.

I drew my palm across his cock, side to side, reveling in the contrast of his hot flesh, the drag of wet silk. If I'd thought for even a second, the next words would never have fallen from my lips. "I'd like to feel you...in my mouth."

"You know you can have whatever you want."

I nodded. "I want that. And I have no idea what I'm doing."

"That's fine. That's very exciting, in fact. But do you know how you'd like to *feel*? In control?"

"Just free to...experiment, I think. Maybe you could tell me what feels good to you, give me instructions. Nothing too aggressive." I traced my thumb and finger down his shaft. "I'd like to be the one doing everything." I imagined the scenes that turn porn from exciting to *ick* for me—gagging and ears-as-fuck-handles are not my idea of *sensual.* Not that I could imagine Didier cast in any such sloppy imitation of the erotic.

"How would you like me? Lying down, or standing before the bed? Something else?"

Less intimidating on his back, but perhaps more exciting towering above me... "I'm not sure."

"I think you will feel most in control if I lie down."

I nodded. "That sounds wise."

Didier and I swapped places, and as I set the glass aside and knelt between his legs, the reality of the moment set my heart racing. He was the only man I could imagine doing this to. Beautiful beyond reason and aware of his looks, even profiting from them...but no smugness. No *getting his way.* This was my way, pure and simple. I don't care if that makes me selfish or cowardly. It feels safe. And I need *safe* to get off as surely as others merely need *horny.*

Below me, Didier cupped his cock through his wet shorts, the touch patient and seductive. I touched him myself, running my hands over his hard belly with its exceptional muscles, then his broad thighs.

"Let me see," I whispered.

He tucked a thumb inside his shorts and pushed them down.

"I'm nervous."

"And I'm just a man," he said. "I want only what you do."

I was tempted to correct him, to tell him he's more to me. He was my fantasy, maleness in its near-unattainable, ideal state. He was the one I'd waited for, even if my delusions of once-in-a-lifetime, breathless romance wound up mutating into the more two-dimensional courtship called prostitution.

I stared down at his bare length, needing a push, the tiniest shove past hesitation.

"It excites me to be the first," he said.

My body melted at the notion—molten, not gooey this time. Lava, not chocolate. I could smell him even before I brought my face closer. I held his thighs as I lowered, letting the scarier sensations wash over me, nothing but initial icy waves to endure en route to submersion. Submission.

"You have my word that I'm clean," he said. "But if you want a condom I'm more than happy."

I was torn… The good girl in me wanted to do everything right, but I also wanted the real deal, the taste of his skin and perhaps his come, not latex and lubricant. And God help me if it makes me a fool, but Didier's word was enough.

"I want you bare."

"Then that is how you'll have me. Get comfortable." His directive was kind, though also a touch devious if I wasn't mistaken.

Reclining on my hip, I propped my elbow beside him, sliding my hand under the small of his back. Heat seemed to roll off him, hot enough to ripple the air. Didier took my other hand and wrapped it around the base of his cock, holding it there gently. His head no more than three inches from my lips…

He waited while my dramatic pause turned to hesitance, hesitance to misgiving.

"Too much?" he asked. "Too soon?"

I met his gaze. "No, I don't think so. Just at the edge of the diving board, you know?"

"You need a push, I'm sensing?"

I laughed faintly. "Probably."

He let my hand go, smoothing a rogue curl behind my ear before resting his palm on my neck. "Taste me."

Ah, blessed nudge. I brought my mouth to him, the smooth, hot skin of his head grazing my lower lip. He smelled like sex—a scent so exactly its own, I could never have guessed it. His soap, his sweat, his sheets, beeswax, the kiss of wine still lingering on my tongue. It was as unique and raw as hide or soil or grass, perfect and potent.

Warm fingers traced my jaw. "Open your mouth, Caroly."

Oh, that was it. The push, the plunge, all my stalling swallowed by the blessed deep.

I parted my lips and kissed him. The tiniest sweep of my tongue, then a bit more. A glorious noise brightened the dim room, the involuntary sigh of an excited man. *My* excited man, for the evening. Until that sigh I hadn't been sure who all this was for, but suddenly it was about more than me and my checkboxes and lessons. I wanted to pleasure him. I didn't want to know merely how to suck cock, but how to suck *his*.

"Tell me what you like," I murmured.

"Many things. Stroke me, and learn what feels right in your mouth. Learn how far is too far."

I did as he said. I gave his shaft slow, artless pulls as my mouth found its way. It was harder than I'd expected. I knew to keep my teeth covered, to suck but not too hard. I was learning to swim—the rhythm, how to breathe, how to coordinate my hand, my tongue, my lips, my lungs. It was frustrating. But high-schoolers can do this, for better or worse. Surely I could too.

"Don't be afraid to rely on your hand, if you need to rest."

I nodded. My throat felt tight from disappointment, because I had always hoped that if I found a man I deemed deserving of this, I'd discover I was a phenom.

I wasn't.

And I didn't feel what I'd so hoped I would, with the right man— comfort. I felt small and fearful. I felt I was failing, and for the second time since we'd entered this room, tears were percolating. My jaw ached, as it always did when I was about to cry.

He gently drew my face away and coaxed my fingers from him, letting his underwear ride up to hide his cock.

He patted the covers beside him. "Come here."

Already crumbling, I complied. He urged me onto my side, facing the wall, and wrapped a strong arm around my middle. Kisses peppered my neck and ear, unspeakably tender.

"Sorry," I muttered.

"Nothing to be sorry about."

"Everything's been easier than I'd hoped, until just now."

"What did you feel?"

My airway was so closed up, I could hardly swallow. "I don't know. Panic. About failing."

"You thought it would feel different?"

"I thought... I hoped I'd be better at it. A natural, I guess. As dumb as that sounds."

Another sweet press of his lips, just behind my ear. "For whose benefit?"

"Yours. And for my ego, probably."

"What you can offer me is more intimate and special than discovering you are some great talent at this. There is no one else I know of, and will likely ever meet again, who can offer me your uncertainty. Your innocence, to perhaps risk patronizing you. I do not expect or want you to be perfect. So take me out of that equation, if it helps."

A huge tear rolled across the bridge of my nose, dropping onto his pillowcase. "I think it does. But I don't know... I wasn't expecting to panic. Not with you."

"I'm no magic spell," he whispered. "There's nothing about me that should make you think we're more than what we are."

His words perplexed me, *scared* me at first.

"We are two people getting to know each other," he went on, restarting my heart. "Two people who are fond of one another, attracted to one another. I like you vulnerable." I heard the smile in his deep voice. "I don't want to upset you by any means, but it touches me, to be here as you figure these things out. If you have any fear that I'm seeking perfection from you, and that you stand any chance in hell of ever disappointing me, please dismiss it. You can only be perfect in your intentions. Do not worry about the performance."

"Really?"

"Really. I may be your teacher in some ways, but trust me, there are no marks. No exam."

"No pop quiz?"

A tiny laugh. "No, no quiz. Just two people in this bed together. Two new friends, on their way to lovers. Okay?"

I nodded.

"Let's give that a rest, though, for tonight."

"Probably wise. Maybe you're on to something, saving that for last."

I felt him shrug. "Maybe. Or maybe this simply was not the night for it. When you want to try a second time, that is when we try a second time."

"Right." Bless him. If not for that lazy philosophy, I'd surely have stigmatized myself, let the act grow to looming proportions in my mind. But he was right. Some other night, that's all.

"I'd still like to…do things. I'd like to make you come," I mumbled. "Or watch, at least."

"Not because you feel you should, I trust."

"No, because I want to."

"Good. Whenever you're ready. Do you want another glass of wine, a break from this room?"

I twisted myself around to face him, our noses glancing. "No, it's nice in here."

He kissed me, soft to start. It told my pulse to slow, my breaths to deepen, my mind to quiet. He reduced us to two mouths, two bodies in this tiny corner of Paris. He fit us together like gears in a pocket watch and shut its shell, hearts ticking in time, safe in the dark.

Before long, my nerves were gone. Excitement came back and just as he'd promised, my earlier shortcoming was nothing but a slip, a case of the wrong moment. This new moment eclipsed the lousy one and my body warmed through, itchy to be nearer to him. I lay my thigh over his, thrilling as he held me close by the hip. His body felt hard, almost excruciatingly male against my softness—chest to chest, belly to belly.

I spoke against his lips. "You feel good."

"So do you… I'd like to touch you. If you'll let me."

The gentle request made me shiver, hot as a barked order "We can try that."

"Turn over."

I did, settling my back against his front, only the slightest bit embarrassed to feel his erection against my butt. He palmed my breast first, filling my chest with stifling warmth and quickening my breaths. It's a peculiar erogenous zone, for me at least. It can go either way, sexy or unnerving, but I liked how his touch felt, the faint squeeze of his broad palm far nicer than pinching or tweaking or some such. The lace had gone damp with perspiration from one or both of us, and my nipple perked, exquisitely sensitive. He brushed his palm over it, soft as a whisper. The friction lit me as I hadn't known it could, connecting my breast to my pussy like an electrical impulse. It sizzled. No other word for it.

"Wow."

"Good wow?" he asked.

"Yes. Very."

For a long minute he spoiled me with the caress, until I was flushed all over, actually, literally panting.

"I would like to go further," Didier whispered.

"Go ahead." I was so fever-stricken, he could have done anything and I'd have been helpless to resist.

As his hand slid down my ribs, he kissed my ear. I'd never understood how that could be sexy to anyone, but *fuck*. I'd also never known the heaven of a man's deep breathing so close, of his hot exhalations, the tiny noises of his lips moving as he tasted my skin.

He slid his thumb under the side of my panties, pushing them down my hip. I got them the rest of the way off and he coaxed my legs open, slipping his knee between mine. The air was cool and dry against my swollen sex. For a few moments he touched my thigh and hip, then my lower belly, my mound.

I'd been torn about the state of things down there, annoyed by the idea of waxing or shaving but not so adamant that I'd been willing to go completely natural. A trim in the privacy of my bathroom was what I'd settled for, and as his palm grazed me, the contact prickled. I muttered his name.

Two fingers slipped lower, glancing my clit. I tensed against him, from pleasure alone. Another touch, another, then lower. He traced my lips, already slick. It filled me with pride for him to find me this way.

"More?"

"Yes."

He teased my clit with a few light strokes then parted my folds. The edges of his fingers to start, then deeper. The most I've ever been penetrated, outside the doctor's office.

"No man has touched you this way before?"

"No, never." All his questions…before I'd thought it was mere courtesy. But he knew the answer to this one. He wanted to hear it again. He was objectifying me the way I did him, and it was a thrilling sensation.

"You're so soft." He slid his finger out, then deeper, the pad of his hand rubbing my clit. I bucked, earning a happy noise at my ear. I knew his cock would feel nothing like this, but I let myself imagine it. He could so easily have me, right now. Push his shorts down and slide his cock between my thighs and be my first. Tempting. I thought of his mouth, his tongue.

"Didier."

"It feels good?"

I nodded.

"I am imagining how it would be, taking you."

"Me too," I said.

"So warm." Drenched from me, his fingers slid back to my clit and I gasped. "Do you think I could make you come?" he asked.

"I think so."

"May I try?"

"Please."

"Like this?" He moved his fingertips in tight, light circles.

"A little harder."

More pressure, and in seconds I felt the blood pounding, that gorgeous, angry, desperate feeling mounting against his touch. He fidgeted behind me, erection brushing my butt. Jesus, the things I'd do to that cock if he let me come… I pictured it from Thursday night, shining with oil, dripping with lather, erupting against his stomach.

The frenzy doubled. "Oh fuck."

His hard arm locked tight to my side, muscles tensing with his strokes. "You're close?"

I grunted a senseless, "Yuh."

"Caroly, please." Fuck, those lips on my neck. "Please."

I reached behind me, grasping for any bit of him I could get and finding his shoulder. I rubbed maniacally at his damp skin as the pleasure crescendoed, rising, rising, rising until I lost my mind. I think I kicked. I'm sure I groaned, perhaps even swore. The climax was like none I'd ever had, because I wasn't controlling it. The first orgasm I'd been *given*, and it reduced me to mush, a pile of wobbly woman trembling against his still fingers. My lungs heaved as though I'd sprinted a mile, chased by a lion.

Didier moved his talented, wonderful, miraculous fingers to my ribs, kissing my jaw. I could feel his happiness and pride, nearly as pleasurable as my orgasm.

"Thank you," I sighed.

"Thank *you*."

A wicked, selfish idea struck. "I want to watch you again."

"Of course."

"In front of me, on your knees."

I took his place against the center pillows and he did as I asked, straddling one of my calves. He pushed his shorts to his thighs, and as he gripped his stiff length, I touched my clit. His lips parted, a look of dark excitement passing over his face. He stroked himself as I rubbed myself, and it felt like nothing I could have predicted, having his eyes on me. My pleasure rose anew, my second release nearly always a given. Plus I wasn't done hypothesizing... He'd drop forward, bracing his arms at my side. One clean, gruff push and he'd be inside me, and I'd feel... Full? Ecstatic? Drunk? Complete? I'd be the thing making him moan, not his fist, certainly no other woman, not until he was done with me. He'd hammer his body into mine until he came apart, push so deep we'd fuse into one sweaty, happy whole.

In the end, it was that last thought, the most romantic of the bunch, that tipped me over. I came with my eyes wide open, locked on his naked body. *He's the one*, I thought idly. I wasn't sure for what, but he was the one.

Didier's strokes had sped right alongside mine, and by the time I recovered from my climax, he seemed on the verge of his own.

"Caroly."

"You close?"

He nodded. "Where?" His gaze flickered over my thighs, belly, breasts, and I knew what he was asking.

"It's fine," I assured him. "Wherever you'd like."

"Your hand. I want your hand."

I sat up and he took my wrist. I let him cup my palm over his head, the warm, slick heat of his pre-come yet another first for me. Watching him masturbate, watching the way his arm trembled as he lost control... I was dizzy.

"Come," I said.

He answered with a gasp, his back arching. His free hand held my shoulder and I stared at his biceps, his chest, the flush in his neck. I thrilled from the way he held me—tight and frantic, possessive. I wanted that hand on my shoulder when we finally fucked, tugging me into his thrusts.

"Caroly."

Our gazes locked. I didn't look away as he came, just stared straight into his dark eyes and memorized them. Hot come filled my palm, coated his knuckles, and I felt dirty and happy and honored to be a part of this mess, with *this* man. I smiled up at him.

With a final weary groan, he released my shoulder, leaving me to grab a towel from the bedside table drawer. He handed it to me first before tidying himself.

"Well," he said as he lay beside me.

"Yes, well."

He turned to grin at me. "So many new things tonight."

"I was thinking that too."

"And the night is not over."

As he said it, I felt a yawn rising. "I think it may be over for me. That was plenty for my second evening."

"I suppose… My, look how far we have come from the other night, you watching from behind that changing screen. At the rate we're going, we'll be married by morning."

Though I laughed, his words upended me. Being teased about such a thing made me both giddy and sad. Such a wonderful but impractical, impossible scenario. This man could never be mine for keeps.

I sighed, suddenly exhausted. "I wonder what time it is."

"Not very late. Perhaps ten, maybe earlier."

Wow, not even my bedtime and look how much I'd accomplished! Being seen in sexy, matching underwear! Inaugural cock-touching! An orgasm at a man's hand! Then another, just as the thrill of watching me triggered the same in him. Fellatio, if barely. I deserved a gold star.

Didier leaned close, resting his chin on my shoulder. *Oh, melt.*

"Are you staying the night? You're always welcome to sleep here."

"I know, thank you. I hope you're not offended if I don't. Not yet, anyhow." I was already stripped bare emotionally, and I knew I'd wake up whiplashed by the memory of everything that had happened. Better to do that alone and not have the worries of my greasy morning complexion and nasty breath casting an anxious shadow on the moment.

Though perhaps if one evening I did sleep over, I could convince Didier to come out for a coffee. Didier by my side, in the broad daylight…

After twenty minutes' murmured fondnesses, we dressed in easy silence and he walked me to the door.

I patted his arm. "I had a wonderful time."

"I'm so pleased. I'll see you again?"

How I fluttered, that he thought he had to ask. "You will."

"Would you like to choose a date now?" He touched my ear, a fond, teasing gesture. "Since you seem allergic to the telephone?"

I laughed, blushing. "Not allergic, just shy. And sure. What evenings are you free this week?"

"How about Tuesday? Or is that too soon?"

I nodded, liking the notion—an otherwise boring day, but oh, how I'd float through the rest of my work week... "That sounds fine. Seven?"

"Whenever you arrive. I'm always home."

"Okay, great."

I waited for the cheek-kissing, but he surprised me. A warm hand on my neck, hot lips pressed right to mine. The goodnight kiss I'd dreamed of since junior high, the one that had never hit the mark at the end of an actual date. My face burned with pleasure as he stepped back.

"Goodnight, Caroly. Have a safe journey."

"I will. See you in a couple days."

That roguish smile. "I will count the seconds."

I rolled my eyes at him and waved, heading for the stairs.

He called after me. "How come you never take the lift?"

"I'm afraid of it." Glancing over my shoulder, I saw his eyebrows rise.

"So am I."

"Great minds," I called.

"Indeed."

A final wave, and I turned the corner. I counted the steps as I descended—sixty-eight. I tapped each mailbox on its glass window, smiled at every person I passed on my walk to the Metro station through the wet, good-smelling spring air.

Everything is beautiful in Paris, when you're a young woman in lust.

TUESDAY

The Third Visit

I arrived at Didier's flat late, having gone home to change after a long workday. It was blustery out and I'd stupidly gone with a skirt, one I had to fist at my side to keep from flashing the whole of the Latin Quarter. My bobby pins lost the war with the gusting wind.

Yet when Didier answered my knock, my lateness and wild hair seemed not to register. His smile was like a door shut on a gale, calm dropping down around me, warm and easy.

"Good evening, Caroly. Come in." He took my purse and a paper shopping bag I'd brought and set them on a table by the door.

"Evening. How was your day?"

He shrugged as he led me into the living room. "I did not wake until nearly two, so I could not tell you yet. Ask me again at the end of our date. I'm sure I will say it was just lovely."

"I, um, brought you something."

He turned. "Did you? What is it?"

I went to my bags and came back with the gift, swaddled in striped tissue. I handed it to Didier and watched him unwrap it, praying he couldn't tell how much of my heart was folded inside that gauzy paper, how long I'd stood obsessing in the antique shop, debating whether or not to buy this for him. He set the tissue aside and to my great relief, his face lit up.

"A clock." He turned the brass box around in his hands, twisted its winder and opened its glass front. "This is fantastic, thank you." He smiled right at me, a new smile I'd never seen from him before. No mystery now, only delight. My heart felt hot and swollen.

"You're welcome. I'm glad you like it."

"I do." He pressed it to his ear.

"It doesn't work."

His smile deepened. "Even better. I'm sure I'll spend many hours with my silly monocle and my tweezers, dissecting this."

I watched him examining it for a few moments longer, overwhelmed by how potent my pleasure was. The thought that he'd busy himself with the gift in my absence, perhaps even associate me with whatever fascination it brought him... It felt better than any physical touch, any carnal indulgence.

He set the clock on top of his cabinet and fussed with the angle. "Wonderful."

I was inclined to agree. "I wanted to buy you a fish, but I know you said that might depress you."

He returned to me, taking my elbows in his hands. "You're very kind." He leaned down and kissed my forehead, dissolving all my bones.

"Well, you're very welcome."

"You've spoiled me, and now I hope you will let me spoil you."

"I suspect I will." I suspected, too, that tonight was the night. The new knowledge that I wasn't a natural-born cocksucker only stung the tiniest bit, and I was ready to jump back into my education, head-first.

Er, make that sex-first. Head some other night, perhaps.

"Are you hungry?"

I nodded. "Are you cooking?" I held my breath, waiting for a no—for an invitation to go downstairs, to grab dinner at a restaurant and be seen with Didier by the world.

"I am."

A mental sigh. Not that being catered to by this fine man was anything to feel disappointed about. Plus knowing my luck, Ania or Paulette would walk by the restaurant window and spot us, and my reign as the demure, gossip-proof member of my small social circle would come to a dramatic close.

Didier made us a delicious meal and shared with me an extraordinary bottle of…cabernet? I can never tell. Some kind of hard-to-pronounce dry red. We spoke about my workday and a new exhibit that was opening next week at the museum, and when the conversation lagged in its comfortable way, my mind wandered.

Didier was wearing a thermal-type knit top with a generous neck, not quite a scoop; a look only a European male model can pull off. Though I wouldn't have minded pulling it off myself, right up over his head. The sleeves were pushed to his elbows and I studied his bare skin and his collarbone, his dark stubble. This man with all of his extraordinary nuances… He could be above me, before the night was over. I could leave here calling him my lover.

"You're very quiet," he said, tapping my forearm. "What are you thinking of?"

"About tonight."

"Me too. Come."

He says that a lot—*come*. A very interesting order. Or in the case of Sunday evening, a plea. Whatever its meaning, I'm happy to comply. I took our glasses and he grabbed the bottle and I followed him to the living room. As we sat on the settee, the wind rattled the old panes behind us.

"So you think tonight may be the night?"

I nodded. "I'd like it to be."

"I would like that too. Have you thought about how you might wish it to feel? Aggressive, gentle? Romantic?"

I think it's fair to say I'd given it a *ridiculous* amount of thought, easily a hundred hours' theorizing in the past week. The previous evening I'd lazed in bed for ages, fantasizing about Didier and running through every scenario, sweet and nasty alike, that crossed my overheated mind.

"Whenever I imagine it," I said, "I think about you. What you're doing. More than I need it to be, you know, satisfying, I want it to be *hot*. I care about that more than I care about coming, I guess is what I'm trying to say."

"You'd like a show?"

I laughed. "Sounds that way. Sorry, I'm not explaining it very well. When I fantasize about sex, it's usually just about the man. I'm not usually there in my fantasies."

"Really?"

I nodded. "That's always how my brain has worked with sex."

"You really do fear rejection."

"I really do."

"Well, we are not in your mind tonight. Before you know it we'll be in my bed. I don't know what you're picturing, but usually for two people to have sex, they both need to be present."

I rolled my eyes at the tease. "Of course."

"But I think I understand what you're saying."

"That makes one of us."

"And how do you want me?" he asked.

"Really…worked up. And aggressive, I think, but not mean. Just sort of desperate. Does that make sense?"

"Absolutely. I can be that way."

I sipped my wine. "How do most women like you to be?"

"They like many different things. Sometimes they wish to order me around. But far more often, they want to be the one who's dominated."

"And you like doing that?"

"As I said, I like pleasing women. I can be cruel, if that is what's desired of me."

"Does anyone ever just want to pretend you're their boyfriend?"

"Yes, sometimes. That is how many dates begin. With a meal or a drink, just as you and I have done. Talking leads to kissing, leads to bed."

"Do you… Are any of your clients married?"

He nodded. "I imagine so."

"Oh. How do you feel about that?"

"I don't."

His answer gave me pause, but he went on.

"My world is very small, and when I'm with a woman, I think it is my job to reduce that even further, to the space between her and I. It is my job to be someone's fantasy. And unless they, like you, wish to question me about reality, I give it no thought. For as long as someone is here with me, reality is just whatever happens between our two bodies."

"You aren't bothered that you might be helping a woman cheat on someone else?"

"That is not my job, to be bothered. And to be frank, that is a very American kind of guilt." He smiled at me.

"I know. I was just curious."

"It is not my job to ask these sorts of questions."

"Does it bother you that I ask so many?"

He shook his head. "It's a nice change, to have someone so interested in what goes on in my head. I so often play the role of the seducer, it's flattering to think that maybe I'm interesting to you beyond all that."

"You are. Very much." A thought I'd turned around in my head the past few days popped through my lips. "Has a woman ever asked you to get her pregnant?" He's certainly the man I'd turn to if I needed some genes.

"That has happened."

"What did you do?"

He laughed. "I said no. How on earth could I say yes?"

"Of course. That would be complicated."

Didier took a deep breath, gaze focused on the table or our empty glasses. "I'm not capable of being any woman's husband, certainly not a child's father. Even if my presence weren't desired, I would not be able to live with the anxiety of knowing such a child were out there, and that should I one day be needed, I wouldn't be able to do what is required of me. Of a father."

"Because you're not willing to be that emotionally invested, or...?"

"It's more complicated than that."

For the first time, I could sense that Didier was not eager to answer my questions, so I let it drop. I felt torn about the idea. On the one hand, what a waste that such a passionate and beautiful man would never be some lucky woman's husband. A shame for both her and him, because I truly believe he's a good person who deserves happiness...not that happiness can't exist without marriage or family. My father could attest to the miseries marriage can reap.

On the other hand, Didier's insistence that he could never commit to someone means I can't feel jealous at the idea of him belonging to anyone else, for keeps. A prettier, smarter, warmer, worthier woman than me. I frowned as my ugly, familiar thought patterns intruded.

He leaned close, pulling me out of my head. "Have I said something wrong?"

"No, I was just thinking about things. You're fine."

My heart raced as he put his fingers to my temple and drew his thumb across my forehead. "I do not like to be the reason you wrinkle your brow this way."

I laughed. "You're not. But I suppose we're a little bit the same, the way we think about commitment. I don't think I'm cut out for it either."

He swept his lips against mine, whisper-soft. "Then it is very convenient that this is where we find ourselves, for now."

"Yes."

He kissed me, brief and tender.

"I'm ready to have sex with you," I mumbled. "Tonight."

"It will happen if it is meant to happen."

I nodded.

"Would you like to go to my bed and kiss?"

"Yes, that sounds nice."

He stood and took my hand, led me to that wondrous dark room. *Our* room, for the evening.

"Candles?" he asked as I sat on the edge of the bed.

"Please."

He came back shortly with the table and its many pillars, and lit them one by one. Each flame exposed more of the room. The texture of the bedspread I'd lose my virginity beneath or on top of, the glint of bottles, the face of the man I'd chosen for this occasion.

Once the room was aglow, Didier took a seat beside me on his bed. No more questions. He kissed me, neither timid nor forceful, with perfect confidence and ease. The simple fact that I knew how to kiss him back was thrilling beyond words.

Soon we were on our sides, legs tangled, hands grasping. I remembered the moments from Sunday when I'd had him on the brink, graceless with desire. That was my only requirement. I needed Didier half-insane with lust when he took me.

I slung my thigh over his hip, and just as I'd hoped, he was hard. I rubbed against him and the reaction I earned was unexpected—a deep moan, a fundamental shift in how he felt. He rolled me onto my back, breaths harsh, eyes wild.

Things started happening very quickly. Shirts were wrestled away, my skirt stripped, his pants kicked aside, belt buckle jangling to the floor. Socks and underwear and my jewelry were shed until it was just two panting animals atop his covers.

Awareness set in. Not panic—clarity.

I was naked. He was naked. There was a naked, gorgeous, aroused man braced above me, knees between mine, hard cock at the ready. I'd always dreamed but never quite dared to hope that such a man might be the one to do this with me for the first time. Now that it was happening, I felt such a potent flash of gratitude I thought I might cry.

Everything about him was right—his chest hair, the smell of his skin, the weight of him, his soft voice and hard muscle. This was how it was meant to happen. I'd waited just shy of thirty years to arrive here with this exact man, and if the tenement blew down before he took me, I'd wait another thirty for such a perfect moment.

With a warm, possessive palm on my hipbone, he swept the head of his cock along my lips, slicking wetness over my clit.

"Ready?" he asked.

"Can we go really slow?"

"As slow as you wish."

"Then I think I'm ready."

He nodded and leaned over to take a condom from the bedside table, sat back on his heels to open it. The scent of latex was out of place in this drafty garret, with its pretty glass bottles of oil and carriage clocks and carved bedposts.

I watched him roll the condom down his thick length, slow and practiced. It was a far sexier moment than I'd have guessed, less a sobering intrusion of etiquette than a gesture of affection. Respect. It didn't detract from the atmosphere at all, only made it more real.

"This is how you want me?" he asked. "Above you?"

"Yeah."

"This is how I imagined it too." He lowered again, bracing his arms tight against my sides, just as I'd fantasized.

"You've thought about it?"

He smiled. "Of course. It's exciting, being your first. This is special for me as well. But if that feels too personal, I won't make a big deal of it."

"No, I don't mind." I didn't mind at all. The only thing that could've made losing my virginity to Didier any better would've been believing the act meant something to him beyond another greedy woman in his bed, another night's work.

"Bring your legs up," he said softly.

I hugged my knees to his thighs and he reached between us to grasp his cock.

"Ready?"

"I'm ready."

The head of his cock pressed at my entrance, feeling far different than his fingers. Scarier and sexier at once.

"Breathe," he whispered, backing off.

Right, yes, that. I did my best to relax, knowing it might be the key to a pleasurable first time versus a painful one. I stared at the cock intended for the task. Ambitious. I imagined him disappearing inside me and the lust grew, crowding out all nervous thoughts.

"Good." Didier's knuckles brushed my clit as he guided his crown between my lips once more.

A push. A twinge, but not the one I'd anticipated—too deep to be my hymen, and more like a cramp than anything being torn. I held Didier's arms, needing to feel grounded in him. "More."

Another inch and a strange new sensation. *Fullness* is too stupid a word. It felt like *violation*, only nicer... A lovely, stark intrusion. He gave me more and the pain arrived, a mean cramp and the small, unmistakable sensation of something surrendering in my body, welcoming him deeper.

My sharp "Ooh" gave him pause.

"It's okay," I said. "Just a cramp. It'll pass."

He was still and steady as I waited for the pain to fade. I watched him, the swell of his abdomen as he breathed, the patient, dark expression on his face. And his cock, half buried in me, obscured by his hand. Jesus, what a man.

"It's going," I said.

"Good. Whenever you're ready."

I stroked his arms, sinking back into the mood of this moment. "How does it feel for you? How do *I* feel?"

A grin—shy, if I wasn't mistaken. Cute. "You feel wonderful. Warm... Your body feels hesitant," he added, "just like your heart."

I smiled at that.

"More?" he asked.

"Yeah."

He withdrew first then slid back inside, infinitely easier than before. "You're very wet."

"Because I want you. And this." I aimed my gaze between our bodies.

Didier pushed again, another inch intensifying that feeling of intrusion. No cramps came and I relaxed further. The exotic slide of his body inside mine as he withdrew, the intoxicating pressure as he claimed me again...

Oh my.

I was having *sex*.

"Bring your knees up, if you can." He urged my calves higher and I raised them to his waist. When he thrust again it felt entirely different—smooth and easy. His muttered "Yes" sent a happy shiver all through my body.

He set a slow pace, taking me a little deeper with each push, until at long last our bodies met, utterly. He dropped to his elbows, burying his face against my neck and letting me wallow in him. This strong, big man momentarily weak. I combed my fingers through his hair, suddenly the reassuring one. I felt his cock…the heat of his skin against my lips, even the faint pulsing of his hard flesh inside me. Tick, tick, tick, a clock counting down to whatever was to come.

His head came up and he stared into my eyes. Something burned there. Something male and primal that made me high. Fuck feminism. I'd stay monogamous to him the rest of my life if it meant I might get to see this look again, be made to feel I was his sole possession. His territory. Whatever might make his eyes narrow at another man who wandered too close, whatever set a growl humming in his throat.

Enough with the gentle deflowering. I wanted to get *fucked*. "Take me."

He straightened his arms and edged his hips closer, spreading my thighs even wider. Still slow, he began to thrust again. For a minute or two I merely watched, recording it all in my mind, these new sights and scents and feelings. I hesitated before sliding a hand between us. I didn't want this to be about me coming, or to stress myself out by trying too hard to make it happen. But what if I *could*? And not just for my own pleasure, but for his… How smug could I make this man?

I circled my clit with the pads of two fingers, and it was extraordinary. Far different with Didier inside me. Everything felt taut and intensified. I glanced to his table.

"Yes? Do you need something?"

"Just a little of the oil."

"Not with the condom. Here." He pulled out, leaving my body cold and hungry as he grabbed a smaller bottle. I put my hand out and he dripped slippery liquid onto my fingertips.

I waited until he'd replaced the bottle before touching myself. As he slid deep, I teased my clit with the lube.

His dark eyes took it all in.

"Caroly." Brows drawn, cheeks flushed, a vein rising along his neck. Didier is even more perfect when he's a mess. "Do you think you could…?"

"Come? I'm not sure, but I'll try."

He nodded.

"You feel wonderful," I said. "It doesn't hurt at all. Feel free to take me however you want."

His lips parted with words that never came. If he felt as I did, he held those thoughts back because they were too loaded, too tender for people in our position to share. I ached to tell him any number of inappropriately earnest things. Our bodies would have to express the feelings too risky to utter aloud.

He took me faster. Not rough, not yet, but the speed was enough to tell me I'd like that…a forceful man. I abandoned my clit to wrap my thumb and finger around his cock, at my lips. I measured him, objectified his heat and stiffness. As I went back to touching myself, his thrusts grew harsher.

"Didier."

"Okay?"

"Yes, very."

He sat back on his haunches, candles drenching his torso in warm, wavering light. He held my hips as he pumped and the vision was…*gah*. Those tight, hard muscles were gorgeous at rest, but *fuck*.

Surely this was exactly what God had in mind when designing the male body.

As I watched him, he watched me. His tongue wet his parted lips, his nostrils flared, his throat twitched with a deep swallow.

"Let me," he muttered. My fingers were pushed aside as his larger, rougher ones took over.

So much of sexual pleasure comes from the spasms of the brain, not the flesh. His fingers worked wonders but it was watching him that brought flares of pounding heat to my clit. His touch merely stoked the fire, kept it glowing. A glance at his eyes, his chest or hips, a moan in that deep voice...those bits of evidence were what had me tight and antsy.

"Do you like it," he asked, "my being rough?"

"I do."

Again, his lips taunted me with words they wouldn't share.

"What?"

"I want... I'd like to take you from behind. If you're willing to try."

How about that? I'd driven Mr. Whatever-You-Wish to dirty requests. "Sure, I'll try. I'll miss the view though," I teased.

"Would you like a mirror?"

"Oh." I blinked. "If you have one."

"I do." He left me to cross the room to his tall mahogany wardrobe. He opened one side to reveal neatly hung shirts and a full-length mirror on the inside of the door. He angled it, glancing at me.

I got to my knees. "There," I said, when the bed was centered in the reflection. Studying his naked body as he returned to me, I was suddenly beyond intrigued by the idea.

"The way you look at me," he said, climbing onto the bed, "made me think you would like to watch."

To watch *him*, yes. My only fear was that my own reflection would distract me, that I'd not like how I looked paired with a man so breathtaking. Too much reality, too much chatter from my head...

I needn't have worried. I dropped to my hands and knees, facing the headboard, our bodies reflected in profile, but all I truly saw in the mirror was Didier. The shape of his hip, the curve of his ass. The shadows playing on his arm and back, his handsome face. And the way he *looked* at me, looked *down* at me. Hungry but patient. A predator.

And heck, a nervous glance told me I didn't look too shabby myself. Pale gold in the candles' glow. We made a rather pretty portrait of hunter and prey, I decided.

The weight of Didier's hand on my hip took my attention off our reflection and back to our reality, here on this bed. He edged forward on his knees until the fronts of his thighs touched the backs of mine. His thick, hot cock slid between my legs—not taking me, but brushing my lips and clit. My eyes shut, not opening until I felt his head at my entrance. I looked to the mirror and the sight of his face cast down, hand guiding his dick, muscles flexed.

"Didier."

He sank deep, the angle smooth and natural. As his hips met my butt, the contact electrified me. I reveled in this helpless feeling. He took me again, again, and the force that accompanied each thrust was honest-to-Christ the hottest thing I'd ever felt.

Before long he was fucking me as fast as before, and I was high.

In the mirror I watched my fantasy come to life in his pumping, greedy body. His moans started low and shallow, growing deeper and harsher by the minute. He became more than the man I'd paid for, more than the one I'd honored with this privilege. He was hot and strong and selfish, all things male, personified.

"You're wet." I loved the way he said it, as if he were accusing me of something. "I want to feel you come on my cock."

I gasped as he stooped to wrap an arm around my waist, fingers on my clit. His touch matched his driving shaft, fast and masterful. After a dizzying minute, he stopped.

"Forward." He nudged me with his legs and I shuffled closer to the top of the bed. "Up," he said. I braced myself on the headboard. The view of the mirror was ruined but something better took its place. Didier leaned into me, damp chest and belly against my back, free arm curled around my ribs. I felt everything a woman should— owned, spoiled, protected, exploited. I didn't need to see him. The most gorgeous man on the planet he may be, but I had everything I needed from Didier in this union.

His fingers knew exactly how to tease me and it wasn't long before a miraculous realization dawned. I was going to come. I was having sex and I was going to have an orgasm, be given an orgasm, by Didier. The world's biggest sexual fusspot was getting laid and, how do you fucking like that, it was hot.

"Didier."

His arm tightened around my waist, thrusts short and rapid. "Are you going to come for me?"

"Yeah. Just keep doing exactly what you are."

"Yes. Please." Oh, when he begs…surely no drug feels that good "Come," he whispered. "Come for me." He said it over and over, plea morphing to a command as I began to shake. My sweaty palms slipped along the headboard, arms trembling.

"Make me come."

"I will. I will."

And he did.

No crashing waves, no ripples of ecstasy. Violent pleasure tore through me, a whiplash at my clit that bloomed and radiated through my belly and chest, down my arms and legs to my fingers and toes. I felt possessed. I felt like *his*. And goddamn, I felt like a woman.

He'd slowed everything when I came, and as the mania faded I heard him. Heard his crazy breathing, smelled his sweat and the sex we'd created. I craned my neck to see what my climax had done to his face. One glimpse at his wild eyes was all I got before he kissed me.

As we broke away, I knew what I wanted.

"Sit back."

He let me go and did as I asked, and I shuffled around to face him.

He'd made me feel a million things, and being dominated by him physically had taught me what had been missing the previous time I'd tried to suck him. We'd made it too much to do with my comfort, and now I knew that wasn't what the act was about. It was about service, and I wanted my second chance, my "some other night". He'd shown me the commanding, merciless man he could be, and I wanted to worship him.

I settled between his legs, and after some slippery fumbling he intervened and took the condom off for me. He didn't ask if I was sure, if I was ready. He just held his cock as I brought my mouth to his head, groaned as I slid my lips down his shaft.

It wasn't a beautiful show, I'm sure, but my enthusiasm couldn't be faulted. I took him, embracing everything inelegant about it—the acrid taste left by the latex, the ache in my jaw, the stilted breathing. I felt a little demeaned, a little helpless, a little used when he gathered my hair, smoothing it away from my face for a better view. But those things were so much nicer than *comfortable*.

"That's good," he whispered.

Keep talking, please keep talking.

"Suck me. Suck the cock you waited so long for."

Perfect, filthy words. I sucked him as hard as I could, welcoming the bump of his fist on my chin as he stroked himself.

"Oh, Caroly."

I hoped he was watching us in the mirror. I hoped he was memorizing all of this and that five years from now he'd still remember me, doing this to him. Wherever each of us was, I hoped he'd wonder what had become of the weird American woman who'd come to him to be corrupted and got exactly what she was after.

"Fuck. Yes." Barely words, soon lost to gasping grunts. His strokes turned rough as his hips begged for me to take him deeper. I granted the wish as best I could, and that strong man unraveled to a frantic, quaking animal from what I was doing to him. The hand in my hair became a fist, his other palm pressed to my neck, trembling.

He went still as stone as he came. A hot spurt, a gasp, another taste. After three spasms his hold fell slack and he slid his cock from my lips. I swallowed what he'd given me and stared at the beautiful wreck I'd reduced him to.

I wanted to dance around the room and sing, "I did it, I did it, I did it!" but instead I watched him recover with a silly grin on my face. After a short while he dragged me down to lie with him, cupping my head to his chest and planting kisses on my hair. I listened to his heart and willed mine to beat at the same pace. It worked.

No one said anything for a very long time, not until my body grew cool and sleepy against his.

He cleared his throat.

"Well," I said.

"Well. We never finished our wine."

I laughed. "No, we didn't. Guess we got distracted."

He pushed onto his elbow to stare down at me. "You did not bring an overnight bag."

"No."

"If you won't stay the night, after all this, at least stay and help me finish the bottle."

"Sure."

We dressed, and everything I felt was right. Shy, relieved, energized, proud. Even sore. The tenderness in my sex was welcome, because it was Didier who'd given it to me.

He carried the candles back to the living room and I fetched the wine, then I lounged against the arm of the settee, my bare feet on his thigh. I turned my glass around in my hands, so completely, simply happy.

"You have a very mysterious smile right now," he said. "Like a certain Italian woman who lives in the Louvre."

I pursed my lips but they soon blossomed to a grin. "I'm very content, that's all."

"Oh?"

I nodded.

"So it was what you'd hoped?"

"It was fantastic. And it's just nice to… I don't know. Not 'have it over with'…"

"To be a member of the club?"

"I guess. Or just to feel like, yes, I'm a woman now. I'm okay. I used to worry and wonder, will it ever happen? And if it did, would it be because I'd get desperate and settle for someone I don't really like?"

"That would be a shame. It's sad what a burden some people make of their virginity these days, a defect. They are so eager to have it done with they'll sleep with whoever's willing, far too young. Sex is not as sacred as I would wish."

So says the man-whore…but of course, he has every right to say such a thing. I'd expected someone in his position couldn't help but be jaded about sex, yet this man speaks of it with the reverence of a monk.

"How old were you, when you lost yours?" I asked.

"I was young, sixteen I think."

"Was it with a girlfriend?"

Didier nodded. "It was love…or what passes for love, at such a stupid age." He smiled faintly.

"Since you, you know…came into your profession. Have you had any relationships? Or do the two just not mix?"

"I have." He nodded slowly, eyes unfocused, as if a videotape were playing in his head. "It's not easy."

"I'll bet. She'd have to be like, jealousy-proof."

"You have to be careful, that's true. I have dated two women since I became a prostitute, two very different women. The most important thing is to establish primacy, I think. When I've dated I cut down on how many clients I saw, and how often. I wanted to make sure my girlfriends got more time with me than my clients. I did my best to prove they came first."

"Did it work?"

"One relationship did not work so well. No matter what we tried, she could not get over what happened when she was not with me. We had a no-speaking policy about it, pretending it was not happening, and of course that failed. We had two hopeful months and another very painful one, then we went our separate ways."

"What about the other one?"

He smiled in a fond way and bit his lip. "The opposite. She asked to hear about the other women. It excited her. I respect my clients' experiences and I like to keep them private, aside from the most general details, which frustrated her, I think. She mistook my confidence for secrecy. But overall, that went quite well."

"Why did you break up?" My heart froze. *Had* they broken up? Yes, yes, of course they had. Past tense. *Calm down, Caroly.*

"We broke up after perhaps six months, when she became interested in a colleague of hers."

"Were you sad?"

"I was. But I had seen it coming. She was wonderful in some ways, very free and exciting, but also I knew no single man could keep her attention forever."

"Did either of them ever ask you to stop, you know…"

"Only the first woman, the jealous one. She offered to help pay for my flat and expenses, if I gave it up."

"But you wouldn't?"

He sighed. "It's hard to explain why I wouldn't. Why I still won't. Part is pride. I'm not willing to be a kept man. But more so—and I fear it sounds like a lie—but this work is important to me. It sounds as if I am trying to elevate it, pretend it's more than the thrill of sleeping with a lot of women and getting paid for it. But I really think what I do is noble, in its seedy way."

"I believe you."

"I also do not know what else I might do, for money. Modeling is nice, but the wages aren't comparable."

"No, I'm sure they aren't. But could you see things ever changing? Like you meet a woman you want to marry and all that? Someone who changes your priorities? Sorry, I'm not saying you should—"

"No, no, I did not think you were." Another sigh, and his forehead wrinkled in frustration or bewilderment. "I do not think that will happen. Not the way things are now. I have not organized my life in such a way that there is any room for a wife. I can't offer that."

"Can't or won't?"

He met my eyes, smiling an apology. "That depends on whom you ask, I suspect."

I nodded, ready to abandon my interrogation. I could sense I was putting him on edge. Like earlier in the evening when I'd asked him about fatherhood, a wall rose between us.

"I should get going pretty soon," I said, swirling the last swallow of wine in my glass.

"That is a shame. Will I be seeing you again?"

"Yes, I hope so. Maybe Friday?" I held my breath, wondering if Fridays and Saturdays were, I don't know, *reserved*. For premier clients.

"Friday is fine."

"Oh good. I was thinking…and forgive me, I don't know if you have policies about dates or anything. But would you ever be interested in maybe meeting for a meal or a drink somewhere? Or me, obviously."

His smile faded and my heart sank.

"Sorry. Are public things against how you…operate?"

"It's not quite that. And trust me, I would be happy to be seen with you at a restaurant or a bar, on a date."

"Oh."

Didier's lips quirked in the tightest, saddest smile. "My hesitation has nothing to do with you."

"You don't have to explain yourself. I was just curious."

"No, I owe you an explanation, for that question and others. And please believe me, I'd very much like to go out with you somewhere for one of our dates, but I can't."

"Okay."

Didier swallowed and met my gaze squarely. "I haven't left this flat in nearly three years, you see."

I stared at him for I don't know how long, struggling to make sense of what he'd said.

"I've lived in Paris for two years…" I trailed off.

"Then I was already a year into my exile by the time you arrived."

How on earth was that possible? The time since I'd moved here had been the most vibrant and exciting of my entire life. All those months and more, and he'd not set foot outside this apartment? I pictured him here, snow falling past the windows in the dark winter, sun beating the panes at the height of summer. Generations of pigeons marching past and Didier never leaving these walls.

"Really?"

He nodded.

I remembered what he'd told me about the pet shop and the fish. What was he really, aside from an isolated, pretty distraction, anyone's to possess for the right price? Was this flat just Didier's ocean, reduced to a tiny tank, his meals bestowed by kind acquaintances? Did he fear he'd die here, some routine inconvenience for whomever was in charge of handling such unpleasant inevitabilities?

"You look upset," he said.

"I'm... I'm surprised. Okay, and upset. It's a very sad thing to hear."

"Apologies."

"What set it off? Or was it gradual?"

"Gradual, throughout my life, but then all at once I couldn't leave at all. The last time I left, something terrible happened." He emptied the last of the bottle into his glass. "I was waiting to cross the street, a half a block from here, and so was a woman and her small child. Before the light came on to tell us to walk, a friend passed by and I started talking to her. And when the woman and her son crossed the street, they were struck and killed by a car that didn't stop for the red light."

"Oh my God."

"Yes. It was very...graphic."

"I'm sorry. That's horrible."

He spoke to his glass. "It was also barely a week after my mother passed away, and for a long time, checking on her had been one of a very few things that got me out of the flat. I've always been anxious about being outside, in big spaces, with traffic and busy sidewalks, in the Metro... The accident took everything I feared and avoided, and multiplied it so greatly, I simply haven't been able to leave. Even talking about it now…" He held up his free hand and I could see it trembling.

"How do you get the things you need?"

"I have friends and clients who pick up groceries and other things for me, and take my laundry out, go to the bank. On a good day, I can make it downstairs to collect my own mail. Every other day, perhaps."

"What if you need to go to the doctor?"

"I pay a steep surcharge to have my doctor come to me."

"No offense, but that's no way to live."

He met my gaze. "No, it's not. But if you don't have that fear, it's impossible to understand it."

I considered that, and my own fears. "I sort of understand. I mean, I've got social problems. With men, obviously."

"But you're braver than I am. You're trying to change." He smiled. "Perhaps that makes me your therapy."

"Actually, yeah. That is how I've thought about it."

We were quiet for a minute then Didier asked, "Do you pity me?"

I stared right into his eyes. "No. Well, maybe. I'm not sure. But is this what you want, to never leave these four rooms?"

"No, of course not. All the time, I try to leave. I make it halfway down the hall, maybe even to the front door, my hand shaking on the knob…then an idea comes into my head, of seeing someone robbed, a car crash, an animal being hurt, simple rudeness. All these injustices and disasters, things I have no control of. Though of course at the time, I think nothing so rational. I feel as frozen and terrified as I might with a train speeding toward me. But I don't even fear for myself, really. I don't fear death. I fear helplessness, of being in the midst of a bad situation, and being unable to do anything about it."

"And it doesn't make you feel helpless, not being able to leave?"

"Of course it does. But it's far worse feeling helpless in the face of other people's cruelty or carelessness."

I knew what he meant. Every balanced, empathetic human knows that frustration and shame and anger, witnessing assholery. The shame of not challenging it, or the powerlessness of knowing your actions won't change anything fundamentally. I tried to imagine multiplying that nauseating, worthless sensation by ten or fifty or a hundred, and having to endure it. I'd hide in my flat too. Probably under the covers. With a bottle of gin.

"Do you feel like the bad people are what keep you in here?"

He shook his head. "I know it's only me. It is my fear of experiencing those ugly feelings that keep me here. It's a terrible, suffocating fear that maybe I'm right. Maybe the world is as senseless as it seems, and if I go outside, I'll find proof of that. I fear the potential of what *could* happen, if I left."

"Oh."

"But of course, locking myself in this flat proves nothing. But I cannot explain it any better than I have."

"You don't need to." My goodness, how did he stay in such fantastic shape? Sit-ups? There was a rack of iron weights in the corner of the living room, but sex wasn't enough cardio for a man in his thirties, was it? So many questions… "Were either of your parents that way? Agoraphobic, or whatever it is?"

"It did not occur to me until recently that my mother likely was, but not the way I am. Like me, she hates the unknown. But the space she called familiar and safe was all of Paris, whereas mine is merely these few rooms. But yes, take her away from the streets she knew and loved, and she got very mean, very edgy and snappy. When I was growing up, I thought she was just spoiled and demanding. Selfish for not taking me traveling. Now I know better."

"Huh."

"And she always loved men from other countries. That must have been the only tourism she knew how to indulge in. Men and books and films, and her foreign language tapes."

I nodded.

"But I don't blame her for the way I turned out. This is just how I am. Who I am. I've always liked going inside, more than out, to explore. Inside objects. Inside people, in whatever manner you wish to take that—emotionally, sexually." He sipped his wine. "It feels safer inside."

"I'm sure."

"This flat is almost like my body now. The idea of leaving…it would feel like walking around without any skin holding me together."

"Yikes."

"Being exposed, outdoors… It's always done something to me Made me so poor with direction, because I can't focus outside. When I am out there, there is just *so*. *Much*. It is like being barricaded in a room with fifty televisions turned on, all loud, all on different programs."

I remembered my first visit to New York City and the anxiety attack the crowds in Times Square had given me. I'd wanted to run back to the Met and spend the rest of the trip hiding in the relative quiet of the galleries, where the frames and plinths and soothing-voiced docents herd you, guide you, instill order.

"I think I understand. It's an awful shame though. You're really quite an extraordinary man. It's sad so few people get a chance to know you."

Didier's nostrils flared with a tight, harsh breath, his gaze darting around the floor and our legs.

I leaned forward to touch his knee, offering a kind smile. "I'm glad to be one of the lucky few though."

"I'm glad you are too." He looked up, glancing around as though just realizing where he was. "Well, here we are again. On a date that I've dampened with my stupid rain clouds."

I laughed. "Not at all. You're far better company when you're imperfect. And much less intimidating."

"No one should be intimidated by me," he said with a crooked grin. "I am just some strange, broken man born with my mother's good genes. And her bad ones. I'm one of those watches, fine on the outside, but my gears..."

"Someone put you back together wrong?" I offered.

Didier covered my hand with his and gave it a squeeze. "Yes, I believe they did."

"It's okay. That's how my mother was too. How she is, I mean."

"She's still alive? The way you spoke about her before, I thought she was not."

"She is. But we rarely talk. On Christmas, basically. For a while she was doing well, living at a residence. But she left and went off her medications, and she's back to how she was when I was a teenager. She's living alone in New Hampshire, probably raising hell for her neighbors." I drained my glass.

"That's very sad."

"It is. I have an older brother who lives two towns away, where I grew up. If he wasn't keeping an eye on her, I'd be worried. But he's always been good with her. Plus he's a *gigantic* guy. He can handle her when she's in one of her really dangerous moods."

"You haven't talked about your brother."

"No, we were never super-close. He's twelve years older than me and moved out when he was sixteen, so I don't remember ever living with him. He's a good guy, but I don't think we'll ever have that bond. What about you? Any siblings?"

"Three half-siblings. Two sisters and a brother, who all grew up in Portugal, with my father."

"Younger than you?"

Didier pursed his lips.

"No?"

"Older," he confirmed. "I suppose you might say that my mother was my father's mistress for a summer, though I do not think she knew he had a family back home."

"Oh my."

"When she got pregnant, he told her everything. I do not know exactly why she had me... To spite him or perhaps to try to keep him, because I do believe he's the only man she ever loved. It's easy to forget sometimes, that our parents were ever as young as us, younger. She was even younger than you, when I was born. But needless to say, I was not welcomed warmly by my stepfamily those few times I went to visit. I did not even understand who they were. I thought this must be my aunt and my cousins."

"God."

He nodded. "It was all very confusing. But my father was a good man. I'm sure it was not his choice for me to be born, but he didn't keep me a secret. He did his best to make things right, though there was really no right to be found, in that situation."

"Well, my parents did everything the way you're supposed to. High-school sweethearts, engaged while my dad was in college, married, bought a house, had my brother. They checked every box in the right order, and it still fell apart."

"But they raised you, and you're successful."

"I guess I'm on my way. But the first twenty years of my life I was a real train wreck. If I hadn't fallen in love with art, who knows what I'd have gotten into."

"Well, I'm so glad you did. It's brought you here, to Paris. And here," he added, waving a hand to mean the flat.

I blushed. "I'm glad too. Everybody dreams of having some amazing love affair in this city. I did too. Then I started to think it'd never happen. But now it sort of has, just not quite in the way I'd imagined."

He held his glass out and I clinked it with my empty one.

"What's it like," I asked, "being with someone as inexperienced as me? Do you feel any different about it than you would a woman who's already had lovers?"

"Of course I do."

"How so?"

"Well, I feel a bit possessive of you, I suppose."

My body roused at the notion.

"And I do feel... What's the right phrase? Full of myself."

I laughed.

"I won't pretend it's not a thrill, knowing you waited so long, and that you picked me. And that I'm the only man you've known. I think that is engrained in a man, to wish his was the only cock a beautiful woman would ever want or ever feel."

"You really think I'm beautiful?"

"I do. You do not?"

"No, I don't. I'm less of a freak than I used to be, but I don't think I'll ever look in a mirror and see what's there now. Only what I grew up seeing."

"Well, I think you're very beautiful. You have very soft hair." He draped his arm along the back of the couch to smooth a curl behind my ear. "And this." He traced my jaw and cheekbones with his finger.

"I hated that when I was little. I was always mistaken for a boy, even when I had long hair."

"In the art and fashion worlds, interesting faces are treasured. Androgyny too. Are people surprised to find you're American?"

"Yeah."

He nodded. "I was too. Surprised to see you at my door, after your postcard said you're from the States. You look...I'm not sure. Dutch, perhaps. Pale and haunted."

I laughed.

"Americans are so robust, we think. Soft and pink-faced and smiling and loud. You are none of those things. Although I do occasionally see the pink in here." He leaned in and held my face, running his thumbs across my cheeks.

"That's your fault."

"Oh yes, such a scandalous man I am." He let me go to sip his wine.

"Can I ask how you started…you know. It started with modeling, I imagine."

He nodded. "It did. It always held much appeal, any money I could make at home. Even before the incident."

"Sure."

"It began as a favor of sorts. The line between posing for a photo for someone you're attracted to, someone you might sleep with anyway… They blended together. A woman who paid me to model for her drawings came here every week, and things evolved, as they do. But some sessions, we did not get around to the drawing." He bit his lip, his shyness charming me. "But she still paid me, those days. That's how it happened. And once such a thing happens a few times with a few different women, those women become clients, and word gets around. And I won't lie, I enjoyed the attention. Whether I'm wanted for a photo or a painting or in someone's bed, the excitement to me is the same."

"I see."

"I want to be whatever people wish of me. Perhaps because I'm so broken in other ways. And actually, you… You're the first client I've had in a very long time where I do not feel as if I'm playing a part. Maybe that first night, but even then…"

"Well, I have no idea what I want. That probably helps."

He smirked. "And here I thought perhaps you just wanted me, exactly how I am."

Never had a sentence filled me simultaneously with such sadness and delight. My lips trembled as I returned his smile. "Perhaps I do."

"I've gotten so used to modifying who I am for women, I lost myself a little. Being with you feels very nice. I feel very pleasantly naked, like a costume has been removed."

"I'm glad." I wanted to tell him so many things—how not only did I feel I'd rediscovered who I am, in this flat, but that maybe I never even knew who I really was until I met him. I was like one of his projects, busted and hollow until I arrived here, opened up and cleaned and put back together the right way, reanimated.

For a long time we sat in thoughtful silence, until Didier finished his wine and a deep yawn overtook me.

"It's time?" he asked.

"I think so."

I got my shoes on and he walked me to the door, as always. To the edge of his aquarium, as far as he could go without risking asphyxiation.

Didier took my hand. "Much has been said since we spoke about seeing one another on Friday. Do you need time to rethink anything?"

I felt my eyes widen. "What? No." I laughed. "I don't feel any different, knowing all that. Well, I do, but I certainly don't think any less of you."

"No?"

I shook my head. "I think you're lovely. I'd like to see you on Friday. Is there... Do you need me to bring anything? Wine, or anything else?" Anything, anything at all.

"Would you like to bring an appetizer, perhaps? It's supposed to be cold and rainy, I heard on the radio. I could make us soup, if you'd bring something as well."

"Perfect."

"Not so perfect as this evening." Didier stooped to kiss me, light and fond.

It occurred to me anew—I'd just lost my virginity. "Indeed. Thank you, again."

Another kiss and we bade one another goodnight, sweet dreams.

After I turned the corner to the stairs and heard his door close, I doubled back. For a minute or longer I stood staring at the brass panel beside the elevator, before I finally pushed the call button. The car rattled and clanged, every terrible noise a promise of my violent, plummeting demise.

At least I wouldn't perish a virgin.

But when the death-cage squealed to the fifth floor, I hauled the folding gate aside and stepped in. My heart hammered all the way to the foyer, yet when I wobbled down the steps and into the cold breeze, I felt lighter. Slightly nauseous, very shaky, but dizzy with pride as well as adrenaline.

I passed couples on my way to the subway, and though my chest ached to know I'd never enjoy even the illusion of such a thing with the man I adored, I couldn't feel poorly. I'd had sex tonight, and ridden in an elevator. I may not ever hold hands in the streetlight with a handsome man, but I would be okay. Every day, I was more okay.

And every day, I felt more and more like the woman I've always wanted people to think I am. The woman I want to be.

FRIDAY

The Fourth Visit

I spent forty-five euros at the deli up the street from my museum, on cheese and fruit and salty meats and fancy crackers. Easily enough money to feed me for an entire week, but the pretty packaging seduced me, as always.

I felt a bit inadequate, not having had time to make something impressive from scratch, arranged just so on a pretty dish. But in the end, showing up with a plastic sack full of deliciousness was best, as the rain Didier's radio had predicted touched down as something closer to a monsoon.

I arrived nervous and excited as always, if perhaps wetter than usual. We kissed and he asked me about my day. I felt strange when I asked him the same, knowing he'd been here, only here.

"It was a quiet day, until the storm arrived," he said, taking my dripping umbrella. "You look nice."

I laughed, looking to the leggings plastered to my thighs, the puddle forming beneath me. "Thanks. You too."

Didier looked far better than *nice*, of course. And that night he was wearing jeans, which appealed to me far more than I'd have guessed. Such an any-guy piece of clothing, when I'd grown so accustomed to this exceptional man verging on formal. But goddamn, he looked good. Cozy.

Which was perfect for what I had planned. I pictured my pajamas, folded in my overnight bag. Cozy, cozy, cozy.

"Wine?" he asked.

"Sure. And I have to get my half of dinner put together, if you've got a platter and a cheese knife."

He set me up at the butcher block and uncorked a bottle. The kitchen already smelled fantastic from whatever soup was in the pot on the stove.

"Wow," he said, watching me unloading the various goodies on the wood.

"I went a little crazy in the shop."

"And I was worried I would not have enough to feed us both. Here." He handed me a glass.

"Thanks. Cheers." We clinked. "I have a favor to ask you tonight."

He sipped his wine and set it aside. "Anything."

"Tonight…" I took a breath, petrified to utter my wishes. "I was hoping I could pretend you're my boyfriend."

Didier smiled in that way that exploded inside my chest, my heart a water balloon full of warm, squishy pleasure, bursting. "Of course."

"But I mean, I guess… Just be how you'd be, with a woman you've just started sleeping with. I trust you, sensing what my boundaries are. You seem to know what they are even before I do sometimes."

"Okay."

"So no asking me permission before we do anything we haven't before. Anything you want to initiate, please just do."

"Very organic."

"Exactly. I don't want to be reminded that I'm calling all the shots, you know?" And I didn't want to be reminded that I was paying to get whatever I wanted.

Didier didn't nod, didn't utter an agreement. Instead he skirted the island and took my jaw in his hands and kissed me, brief but forceful. He licked his lips as he stepped back.

"That was exactly what I wanted," he said.

Heat rose, flooding my cheeks. "Good."

"May I be frank?"

I nodded.

"I'm very attracted to you."

The blush burned hotter. "Oh?"

"And you're asking me to treat and approach you as if this was not all under your direction, everything done with your permission already tendered."

"Right."

"So please tell me, honestly, if it's too much. If I come on too strong. What you and I have done before... Nothing is an act with me. I'm a passionate man."

"I know. I just want to know what it feels like, hanging out with the man I—" I stopped, knowing the word I'd nearly used was *faaaar* too loaded. "The man I'm sleeping with. I don't want to drive, is what I'm trying to say."

"Very well. But don't hesitate to change your mind, if I am too fast for you. I would hate to sour our time together, just being myself."

I laughed as I spoke. "It would take a lot to undo the good you've done, but thanks for your concern. I'll tell you if it's too much, I promise." I turned my attention to the cheese.

"Right. That is all I will say about it for the rest of the evening. From this moment, unless or until you change your mind, I am just your lover."

My lover. I pursed my lips, a shiver giving me goose bumps despite the warmth of the room.

Didier clapped once. "But enough of this. You are my girlfriend. Let us worry about dinner first, before I make a panting fool of myself, yes?"

I nodded officiously. "Yes."

He started toward the stove then stopped short, turning to grin at me.

"What?"

"So you are my girlfriend tonight?"

"I am."

"And does this mean you are finally sleeping over?"

Oh, swoon. "I guess I could. I mean yes, I am. I brought pajamas and bathroom stuff."

His grin deepened. "Pajamas. That's adorable. Do you have little slippers with rabbits on them as well?"

Of course this man must sleep nude. I made my tone snotty. "They're very nice pajamas. Very sophisticated. And if you tease me like that you won't get to see them." Oh my crap, was I actually *flirting* with someone?

"Understood." He circled and came up behind me, wrapping his arms around my middle. I felt a kiss at the crown of my head, my temple, my neck.

"You're very good at taking liberties," I said.

More kisses, then gentle, silly gnawing at my shoulder. It seems the real Didier is far more of a goofball than I'd expected. Not a criticism.

He kissed my ear, a great barrage of noisy smooches designed to annoy.

"I'm armed, you know." I sliced the cured sausage demonstrably.

He straightened behind me. "You wouldn't dare castrate me. You know what it is I can do to you."

I smiled to myself. "Perhaps."

"Plus I am your boyfriend tonight. And that would make you a very lousy girlfriend." With a final peck on my cheek, Didier let me go, stealing a fingerful of triple crème brie as he went to check on his half of dinner.

"What did you make?" I asked as he lifted the lid.

"Onion soup, with mushrooms."

"Yum."

"I hope so." He stirred and tasted it, added a splash of sherry and a few shakes of salt. He replaced the lid and fiddled with a knob, then came to lean on the far side of the island. I rapped his knuckles with a nearby whisk when he tried to steal a strawberry from the carton.

"Wait 'til I've got it all arranged."

"You're a very abusive girlfriend."

"You love it."

He laughed then switched on the radio while I sliced the rest of the fruit and cheese and meat. I fanned them in arches, alternated with the overpriced crackers.

"This is a feast," he said.

"Yeah, I didn't know when to stop. They kept plying me with samples and my basket got heavier and heavier. Okay, I think we're ready."

Didier doesn't have a dining area, so we pulled up stools and ate at the island. Every last thing I tasted was exquisite and I ate enough that a stranger might assume I was in my second trimester. I didn't care. Didier was my boyfriend and I was happy. I told him some war stories from the museum, about the weird things rogue patrons try to get away with. It was more satisfying than the wine or the food, hearing him laugh and knowing I'd inspired it. And as another boyfriendish liberty, he lapsed into French now and again, and I let him bear witness to my abysmal accent and any number of improperly conjugated verbs.

As the nibbling wound down, my thoughts turned to other treats. What would be different, when Didier took me later? How different would his approach be when meeting my every delicate need wasn't the order of the night?

He set his napkin aside and sighed. "That was delicious."

"It was. I need your soup recipe now. I don't even like onions, but that was amazing."

"You don't like onions? I wish I'd known. I'd have made something else."

I shook my head. "Nah. I enjoy being converted. And I enjoy the idea of not telling you what I *think* I don't like, then you surprising me, and proving maybe I do like things. I like being proven wrong."

"You are talking about more than just onions?"

I shrugged. "Maybe."

He smiled at me and narrowed his eyes. "You're different tonight. You're very… I'm not sure. Cunning."

I laughed. It was an adjective I'd never have assigned to myself in a million years. But I supposed he was right. I did feel a bit devious.

"Have you started fiddling with the clock yet?" I asked.

He nodded. "It needs a new part, I'm afraid. I will look through my catalogues and see if I can find a replacement. But otherwise it is in very good shape. Very interesting construction. Like you, it is somewhat simple on the outside, and an intriguing, complicated mess when you open it up."

I tried to fake offense but was smiling too much to pull it off.

"But I'll soon understand you both, every tiny spring and wheel and pin."

"I'm afraid it'll probably take more than a replacement part for me to ever make any sense, but good luck to you."

He bumped my knee with his then stood. "Let me put away the leftovers."

I helped him with the food and the dishes. I will say this about Didier—he's quite handsy. Any chance that arose as we puttered, he had a palm on my ass. Again, not a complaint. With any other man it surely would've been, but with Didier it only reminded me how it might feel to be pulled hard against him as his cock sank deep inside me. Anything that tricked me into thinking I was his, for real.

"You're very frisky tonight."

He smiled, hanging up a dish towel. "Apologies. I assumed I was meant to be your boyfriend of four dates, not thirty years. But if not, we can brush our teeth and fall asleep reading by nine o'clock..."

"No, frisky is nice."

He backed me up against the sink and kissed me. "Oh good." More kissing, more handsy. He backed off at length to say, "Your clothes are still damp."

"I know. I better change before that hot soup wears off."

"Do you need something to wear?"

As unreasonably sexy as the thought of flouncing about in one of Didier's oversized shirts was, I declined. I'm not a flouncy girl. Maybe someday, but not quite yet. "No, thanks. I think I'll deem you worthy of seeing my pajamas."

I grabbed my bag and changed in the bathroom, into the new PJs whose price would give my father heart failure, considering it's basically a camisole and drawstring shorts. But come on, Turkish silk satin! And my exact favorite color, greenish-grayish blue—just like in Paul Klee's *Blick Der Stille*—and with tiny embroidered white-and-orange fish scattered all over. I know that sounds weird, but trust me, they're awesome. And since I bought them before Didier told me about his goldfish, it all felt rather serendipitous. So worth having to eat cheap pasta every night for the foreseeable future.

Thank goodness I didn't have any credit cards, lest my penchants for artisan cheese and Turkish silk and Parisian men tempt me away from reason. Which, sadly, they were on the verge of doing. I needed to talk to Didier about that, but not just then. Perhaps in the morning.

I found him in the living room, cuing up a record on his gramophone. He angled the old-timey brass horn and noticed me behind him.

"Oh. Those *are* adorable."

"They've got goldfish on them."

He smiled and approached to inspect my ensemble. "*Il te rehausse les yeux.*" *It brings out your eyes.* He rubbed a thumb over the shiny satin and one of its little fish. "You'll be cold, though. Do you want a blanket, or shall I turn the radiator up?"

"A blanket's fine."

And that's how the evening went. We sat on the couch, sipping wine, chatting and listening to the croony old records Didier had inherited from his mother. I pictured her as a French, brunette version of Marlene Dietrich, though that assumption was likely the fault of the music. Still, in my head she spent endless hours perched before her vanity, smoking and brushing her hair, lamenting the failure of a recent love affair, all in grainy black and white.

After an hour or so of lazy flirtation, Didier found us a deck of cards and taught me to play *piquet.* I did terribly, but he kept kissing me so I don't think my poor showing was strictly my fault.

Didier is very…playful. Off the clock, as it were. He's also very convincing, which would probably have worried me if the pleasure it inspired hadn't been so potent.

Rarely while I was with Didier—but often after I'd left, perhaps the following day—would it occur to me exactly what he was. I'd catch myself thinking of him fondly, then an ugly part of my brain would pop in. *Don't be an idiot. You aren't actually dating him. Plus think about it. You saw him Thursday, Sunday and Tuesday. Who was he with those other days?* I would wonder, *Does he like them more? Are they prettier or more exciting than me?*

But funnily enough, the thoughts always slip, like an egg off a greasy pan. For the first time in my life, I wasn't jealous of the other women in a fantastically handsome man's bed.

As we sat playing cards, I put my finger on the crux—Didier's body isn't sacred to me.

When all this had begun, that was all he'd been—a body, one I'd been prepared to suffer a less-than-stellar personality in order to enjoy. That he's kind and likeable was merely a bonus. But it took shockingly little time for his body to become incidental, and the thing I anticipated now went far beyond his physique or face or even his skills in bed. It was how he made me feel...like a woman worthy of his extraordinary company. And the glow from that lingered far longer than any post-orgasm haze.

It's scary, because I never expected any feelings I might develop for him to go beyond the sexual. I assumed the sheer fact that he's a whore would erect a wall and keep my heart safely on one side.

No such luck.

When yet another hand of *piquet* dissolved into a make-out session, he took our cards and tossed them on the coffee table. I was hauled onto his lap, back to his chest. Didier in boyfriend mode moves quite a bit faster than his professional self. His cock was hard from the kissing, impatient against my backside.

He put his mouth right behind my ear, breath hot against my skin. "I want you."

"I want you," I murmured.

His hand glided up my slippery top to cup my breast.

I fumbled and turned around, straddling his thighs.

He fondled me as we kissed. I felt one tiny strap slide over my shoulder, then the other. Satin slipped away, replaced by his palms.

His lips left mine to seek my ear. "I want to taste you."

"Okay."

A happy, cocky noise heated my skin.

I thought I could guess which words would come next—*where, how, in my bed?* Silly me. I'd forgotten who I was with tonight.

Didier leaned over to grab a throw pillow from the chair, tossing it to the far end of the couch. He ousted me from his lap. My heart beat fast as I leaned against the cushion, nerves and excitement stirred together, capped and shaken. Exactly as I'd longed to know how he looked naked, how he kissed and tasted and sounded in person, now I wanted to know how he'd feel, taking me simply as himself.

Just as I got my camisole hoisted back up, he was slipping free the bow of my drawstring. I lifted my butt and let him slip my shorts down my legs. He pushed the coffee table away, kneeling before the settee. A week ago I'd have been afraid of how I looked or smelled or tasted, but not tonight. Not seeing that gleam in his eye, that expression that told me I was far more exquisite a delicacy than any you could sample at the cheese shop.

I ran my fingers through his hair as he brought his face close. His nose glanced my clit, then his lips, his tongue. It felt nothing like I'd imagined. The opposite of sloppy. He indulged me with caresses, soft and teasing, deep and decadent, hungry and insistent. I felt imperious with this man on his knees before me. Utterly spoiled.

Spoiled felt wonderful…for ten minutes or more. Then my attention was drawn beyond his face to this room, the flat; his private world, where I'd learned far more than the mere mechanics of lust. As good as his mouth made me feel, I wanted more of him. At a gentle push on his shoulder, he let me go with a final deep lap.

"Stand up."

He got to his feet.

"Take your shirt off." As he did, I freed his buckle, brushing his hard cock as I opened his fly. When his jeans were kicked away, I clasped his erection through his underwear and gazed up at him. Marvelous. I've never before met anyone whose outside so matched their soul. You could drill clean through Didier and find nothing but layer upon layer of beauty, dark and strange and kind and prurient, but all of it perfectly, utterly pure.

I stroked him for the sheer pleasure of feeling his weight and heat in my hands, until his breathing grew labored and he spoke.

"I need to fuck."

"Good."

He pulled me to standing, pressing our bodies tight together, that bossy palm on my rear. "*À mon lit. Maintenant.*"

As ordered, I headed for his bedroom, his energy right behind me, tangible as echoing footsteps. No candles tonight. No patience. We tumbled across the sheets and my camisole went missing, followed swiftly by his briefs. Being trounced was as lovely as being seduced, perhaps even lovelier after so many nights of caution and gentle firsts. At moments I felt we were nearly wrestling, fighting to be the one touching, kissing, stroking. Kneeling, he pulled me onto his lap, his cock pinned against my pussy. His hands issued orders, drawing my wet lips along his shaft, friction so hot I scraped my nails down his back in retaliation and bit his ear.

He groaned and pushed me onto my back, leaning over me to open the bedside table drawer. With a smooth stroke he was sheathed, half a breath and he was at my entrance.

"Didier."

He sank deep, claiming my cunt with the smooth, sure thrust of a lover who'd known me for ages. No pause for reverence. He took me fast, not quite rough, until I was dizzy and frantic and high.

"Fuck me," he said.

One forceful flip and I was on top of him, no time to worry about my performance. No need. All I needed was to feel this hard, thick cock moving inside me. I gave my body everything it wanted from his, shutting my eyes and letting his moans and murmurs fill my ears. His fingertips grazed my thighs, my belly, my ribs, finally my breasts. The brush of his palms over my nipples set my whole body on fire. My clit was rubbing his base with each motion, and though I wasn't practiced enough to make myself come from it, just knowing maybe someday I *could*, that someday I *would*, filled me with giddiness.

"I want you like the last time," I said.

"On your knees?"

"Yeah." On my knees, with a rough, selfish man taking me from behind.

The moment his cock slid from me, I wanted it back. But first I got his hands on my hips and ass as I was turned over, his thighs nudging mine wider. When he took me again I sighed from the sheer, dirty completeness I felt.

"Make me come."

That voice, low and dark. "I will."

The sex was hot and fast and noisy, a flurry of slapping skin, his moans, my whimpers. I hadn't known I was capable of sex like that. Animal sex. There were a thousand things I hadn't thought I was capable of, not until I'd found the one key that fit my lock. I came hard against his taunting fingertips, the deepest, scariest orgasm I've ever experienced. When I recovered, he urged me onto my back.

"*Regardez-moi.*"

I did as he ordered, eyes on his laboring muscles in the dim light leaking from the living room. I watched the only man who'd gotten to know my body this way, watched him grow frenzied with lust until he couldn't hold on, then watched him succumb. He ground our bodies together as he came, so hard I thought my hip might bruise. If it did, I'd miss the mark when it faded.

He tumbled from me in a sweaty heap, stripped the condom and grabbed me around the middle. Powerful arms held me close, possessive and familiar, and after a few wordless minutes Didier whispered, "Spend the night."

"I will."

He sighed and released me, rolling onto his back. "Oh good."

"You knew that already. I brought my pajamas."

"Yes, but it's nice to hear it again. Perhaps I should hide all of your clothes and your shoes, in case you change your mind…"

I propped myself on my elbow and smiled at him. "You really care that much about my sleeping over?"

"Very much. I want to make you coffee. And see you with your wonderful curls, all wild against my pillows."

My grin deepened.

"I want to see you with your hair wet from the shower, and the morning light in your eyes when you wake."

I hoped everything he said was true. I hoped he wasn't just lonely, or that my company only felt so good because he'd forgotten what it was like having friendships and romances, out in the larger world. Then again, this flat was real. I'd had some of the most genuine and eye-opening experiences of my life inside these walls. And damn it, *I* was real, this night more than ever. Maybe I *was* alluring. Maybe I needed to quit letting my decades-old insecurities dilute every wonderful thing he said and just fucking believe the man.

I used the bathroom and put my pajamas back on. As I joined him in bed, the world felt lovely. He wrapped his naked body around my satin-clad one, and he was my boyfriend. I'd dreamed of sleeping with a man exactly this way for half my life, and here I finally was.

It really had been worth the wait.

I woke as the sun broke through the curtains, and I felt so much. Cool silk on my skin, Didier's warm arm cradling mine, a sweet soreness between my legs once more. I rolled over and stroked his chest until his eyes opened.

"Good morning."

"Hi. This is your chance to see me with my hair a mess, before I take a shower."

He tousled it, gaze taking me in. "Very nice. Thank you." He squinted at the window. "My goodness, I don't know when I was last awake at daybreak. Or indeed asleep by midnight."

"Keep sleeping if you want. Do you want me to go down to the baker's and get us breakfast?"

"That would be very nice, if you don't mind. Let me know when you're leaving, and I'll bathe and make us coffee."

I nodded and left him in bed, stealing a long look before I exited. This was exactly how Didier ought to be styled—stripped to the waist in the morning light, sage-green sheets wrapped around his legs. Click, click, click went my mental camera.

It was nine by the time we'd showered and dressed and pastries and coffee were served in the living room. I picked at my croissant. Worry had caught up with me at the bakery, right as I'd handed my money to the clerk.

"I need to talk to you about something," I said.

Didier set down his mug. "Oh?"

I shifted in my seat, addressing the hands fidgeting in my lap. "I won't be able to come by as often as I have. It has nothing to do with wanting to. Or from getting to know you better, or the sex, or any of that."

His brow furrowed. "All right…"

I laughed sadly. "I just can't afford to." My throat was tight, heart hurting to admit aloud what we were, what had brought us together. I'd let it become so much more in my mind. Even in my gut. But it had always been just checks slipped in his mailbox, hadn't it?

"I'm very sorry to hear that."

I nodded. I wasn't foolish enough to expect to be told I needn't pay, or that I merited some discount. I didn't want to hear anything that underscored what a transaction this arrangement was, behind the glittering veneer of romance.

"I would always welcome your visit, no matter how infrequent," he said.

"Thank you. I'd still like to come by, just not this often."

"Of course. And that's very normal. Usually when I meet a new client, we see each other several times very swiftly. Then soon enough it slows, one, two, three times a month."

It made me inexpressibly sad to be told I was typical. A typical *client*. I felt my heart retreat, like a little crab scuttling back inside its shell.

"Though I won't lie," Didier went on. "I've become rather attached to your company."

I looked in his eyes. "I think I've learned more about myself in the past week than I'd gotten figured out in almost thirty years, so thank you. I'm a better person for having met you."

A look of great melancholy transformed his handsome face. "This sounds very much like a goodbye."

Was it? Did he know what I ought to? That the time for deluding myself was over? "I don't know."

"Perhaps you're ready to go out and find a real man."

"You're real." I said it loudly, too loudly, panic hijacking my voice.

A weak smile. "You don't need to protect my feelings. You deserve a man who is capable of taking you out. Literally *out*. You come here and all I can give you is a few hours of make-believe. I can't walk you out that door and take you to dinner, see where you live and work. You deserve far more than what I can offer."

I was near to tears, because of course Didier *was* what I wanted, in enough ways to let me overlook anything he may lack, for better or worse. Plus he was the only man I knew how to be with, and I wasn't sure those skills were transferrable.

"But I do love your company," he said again. "And you're always welcome here."

I nodded, confused. Was this a breakup? Was Didier giving me the diplomatic brush-off with this talk of his inadequacies, our collective impossibility? He could probably sense how attached I'd grown. The notion that perhaps I ought not come back to this flat felt likely, and terribly heavy.

I supposed he was only ever my training wheels, an illusion of capability. Out in the real world, how badly might I fall and mangle myself, attempting an actual romance with an actual, available man?

I stood. "I guess I'd better head home soon."

"Would you like me to wrap the pastries up for you, or any of the cheese?"

"No, you keep them. Thank you for the coffee."

As I turned to begin gathering my stuff, he got to his feet and grabbed my wrist. "It feels as if everything changed just now. Did I say something wrong?"

I stared at his collar, afraid of his eyes. "No, you're perfect. I'm sorry. I'm just sad that I can't come as often as I have been. It probably sounds pathetic, but this has been the highlight of my life the last week or so, my visits here."

"I hope that is not pathetic, as they've been my best days as well. Though if it is, we'll be pathetic together."

Didier always knows what to say, but at that moment, nothing could neutralize the pain I was feeling. The grief.

"I, um…"

He rubbed my arm, waiting as I swallowed my fear and assembled words.

"I've had a wonderful time with you," I said. "More wonderful than is probably wise."

"What do you mean?"

"I like you, a lot. Enough that I probably need to step back for a while and remind myself, you know... About what we really are, I guess. Not to freak you out or anything, but if I keep seeing you this much, I'm going to fall in love with you."

A lie—I was already in love with him. Jesus Christ, give the frigid girl four nights with a French prostitute and what happens? Like I never drank a drop, then one pub crawl and I wake up with cirrhosis.

"I'm losing perspective, the more I see you."

"I understand." Surely it had happened before, with any number of his clients. Didier gave my arm a final rub and let me go to collect my things.

Neither of us quite knew what to say when we met at the front door, but he kissed me, soft and slow, fingers tangling in my damp hair. It morphed into a hug, and he whispered, "Goodbye, Caroly."

"Goodbye."

WEDNESDAY

Any Other Normal Day, Yet Not

Things sucked for a few days.

Once I left Didier's flat on Saturday morning, I felt lost. I felt unsure of who it was I'd said goodbye to, and unsure if I might see him again.

He'd cut me loose—I just knew it. I'd heard it in his voice. He'd cut me loose and I couldn't help but wonder which of us he thought it served.

The second I left him, the emptiness arrived. I missed Didier in a way I hadn't known it was possible to miss anyone, short of them dying. And I missed more than his body or company or the anticipation or the sex—I missed how I simply felt around him. How

I felt about myself, and the new person I'd begun blossoming into. I mourned her loss too.

Plus I'd made such a full-time hobby of fantasizing about him and replaying our time together, I was at a complete and utter loose end and nothing felt fun. Nothing sounded like the thing I ought to be doing. Nothing tasted or smelled or sounded very good anymore. My soul had the flu.

The arrival of the work week was a relief. And by the time I woke this morning, my symptoms had eased. My heart had quit actively hemorrhaging, but it still hurt. It simply hurt more quietly.

I shared an office with the head curator but she was busy elsewhere that day, so I had the cave mercifully to myself, free to mope without witnesses. Normally I grab lunch from down the street and eat with Ania and Paulette next door, but I wasn't feeling up to their energy just yet. There were plenty of pending emails to fill an hour and keep my thoughts from wandering into the dark, dreary corners of my head. I'd use them as an excuse for staying in, should my friends catch me walking by the gallery on my way back from the deli—

My phone rang.

"Caroly Evardt."

It was one of the girls from the front desk. *"Quelqu'un vous attend à l'entrée."*

A visitor? Ania, likely, with gossip that couldn't wait another moment.

I thanked the girl. I picked up my purse then put it back, lest my friend try to talk me into a so-called quick coffee.

But when I reached the lobby, my heart froze.

Didier.

Didier, in shoes. In the sunlight and the vastness of the building.

As I approached the front doors, he smiled and raised a hand.

I felt I could only half recognize him here. He looked like a picture of himself, those brown eyes Photoshopped brighter in the daylight As though he were a painting finally restored, a million long-lost details emerging to dazzle the viewer.

"Hi," I said.

"Hello." He bent to kiss my cheeks. I could tell he was nervous. That normally warm smile was tight and twitchy, jaw set.

I goggled at him. "You left. You left your flat."

He nodded. The lobby was especially chaotic, guests streaming in for the opening of a controversial new exhibit. I wondered if I ought to bring him somewhere smaller and safer, my office or the archives.

"Is everything okay?" I asked.

"It is. Is it okay that I've come here? I know some of your friends know what it is I do. You can tell them we know one another from a gallery event, if you—"

"No, I don't care about that. What's going on?"

He cleared his throat and stood a little taller. "I came to see what you're doing for lunch. If you're free to eat with me." He lifted a handled paper bag. "I made sandwiches. I did not think I was ready for a restaurant yet, but maybe the park…?"

Casual words, but this wasn't easy for him. All his typical ease was gone, his posture rigid, eyes alert, bag and hand shaking faintly.

"That's what got you to leave your place? To ask me to lunch?"

Another smile, slow and nervous. "Yes. So I hope you'll say yes."

"Is it a date?"

"That is my wish."

I felt… I felt like a pomegranate sliced open, all my ruby-red capsules spilling out, sweetness leaking everywhere. I felt like a beautiful, delicious, sticky mess.

"Like a regular old…date?"

Didier nodded.

"I'd like that. I'd like that very much. Let me get my purse."

I went back to the offices and I swear I was floating, walking two inches above the tile and wood and carpet. And there he was when I returned, right where I'd left him. How about that.

"Ready?" I asked.

He crooked his arm and I linked it with mine, and we strode through the automatic doors.

"How do you feel?"

His gaze panned the veranda and sidewalk, the intersection. "I feel better than when I first left the flat. But nervous now, letting you see me this way."

"I can tell you're nervous. But I don't mind."

The park was just across the street, and I watched his face as we reached the curb and waited for the WALK sign. His attention was trained on something in front of us, expression simultaneously blank and intense.

"You're doing great." I gave his arm a fortifying squeeze and to my relief, he looked down at me and smiled.

Parisians are kamikaze street-crossers, and businessmen streamed past us on both sides, happy to take their chances with the lunch-hour traffic. Our light came on and I was mindful to look both ways. I took Didier's hand, feeling a bit like a guide dog. But he'd led me to so many new and scary places, it was nice to return the favor and be the confident one for him.

People talk about hearts fluttering, and as soon as we stepped onto the opposite sidewalk, danger officially over, mine did. It absolutely did. I felt the opposite of that stupid, stubborn grudge that keeps me from making eye contact with handsome men. I was giddy, knowing I was so obviously *with* Didier. Lovers, hand-in-hand. Even if my lover was pallid and wide-eyed and trembling at the threshold of a panic attack.

We found a nice spot on the grass in the shade, sitting hip to hip, facing the fountain. The pigeons spotted us. They must live for that noise—the rustle of a paper bag. Beggars flapped and landed, eyeing us from a pushy, patently European distance.

Didier eyed our stalkers. "Oh dear."

"It's okay. I don't mind them. They remind me of your little nosy neighbors, on your roof."

"I worried so much about the people, I forgot about the animals."

"I'll protect you." I grabbed a stick and waved it at the birds, scattering them, if temporarily. "I'd hate for you to leave the house for the first time in three years and get some weird pigeon disease."

He grinned at me. "It'd be worth it."

I laughed, blushing. "That's very romantic. I think."

We unwrapped the picnic he'd prepared, and I didn't press him for more insight about his feelings, not just yet. We ate in silence, watching the children and shooing the birds.

I finished the first half of my sandwich and licked garlicky mayonnaise from my fingers. "This is delicious, thank you."

He laughed. "I made this lunch three times."

"How do you mean?"

"I made it on Monday and Tuesday, and again today. Today was merely the day I managed to get past the front steps when the taxi began honking for me."

He'd wanted to see me this way as early as Monday? Two days after we'd said goodbye? "And today you just…could?"

He smiled at me, eyes crinkling. "This morning I just realized it hurt more, missing you. More than it hurt to deal with the fear."

"You missed me?"

His grin deepened. "You look surprised."

"I am."

"I did miss you. Very much. More than I'm used to missing people, especially those I've known such a brief time."

"Oh."

He pursed his lips and squinted thoughtfully before going on. "I like the way you treat me. And the way you look at me. Like you're looking *into* me, not merely at me. I'm sorry, that does not make much sense."

"It does. I like that. And I do think that's how I see you. I mean, I came to you because of how you look, obviously. But I like the rest of you even more."

"The man who cannot leave his house?" he teased.

I raised my arms, gesturing at the vast blue sky. "But you did. Here you are."

He nodded and looked away, seeming shy. "Here I am. Two weeks and you've gotten me to do what no one's managed in three years. Without even asking me, or pressuring me. Begging me. I don't know how. It astounds me. Thank you, Caroly."

I mumbled an inadequate, "You're welcome," my cheeks hot with pride and pleasure.

We didn't speak again for several minutes, Didier taking in the action around us. "I forgot how it smells outside. When I first left the flat, it was the petrol. But here, the grass, the air...I gave all this up for so long. I forgot how a real breeze felt."

"Now you get to appreciate it more than anyone else in the whole city." *Like a parolee*, I thought.

"Perhaps. That is a nice way to look at it. I like the way you look at all kinds of things," he said. "You must gaze all around you, putting frames around different people and places."

I smiled. "Maybe subconsciously."

"Cataloguing beauty," he mused, watching me with a mysterious gleam in his eye. He sighed. "I wish we could go down to the river."

"We could."

"Maybe. But not today."

"Something to work toward."

"Perhaps this weekend," he said. "If you would like to spend the night on Friday or Saturday—as just, you know. Not as we have been. More as we are today?"

I nodded. "Sure."

"And then maybe you could help pry my hands from the front door so I may leave again."

"I'll bring a crowbar."

As he laughed, I read deeper into what he'd said. Did he not have clients to see on Friday or Saturday? And if not, was that incidental or because of me?

"I would like to see your flat sometime," he said.

"You're welcome to. Though I'll warn you now, it's tiny and stuffy and my bed's not really designed with guests in mind. But I live above a bakery, so at least it smells nice."

"Charming. I'd like also to see you again, this way. Out like this, though hopefully when I'm not so..."

"Shaky?"

He nodded.

"I'd like that too."

Didier opened a glass bottle of lemonade, took a deep drink then passed it to me. He seemed to hesitate before saying, "What I am is not so secret, in your crowd."

"No, especially not to my friend Ania from the gallery. She's got a whole fan-girl binder full of prints, just of you."

"I did not know I had fans."

"She's quite rabid. And she doesn't know I've been seeing you. I better have a talk with her, if it seems like we're all destined to cross paths."

"Are you sure you're comfortable with this? With us being so public?"

"Yes, it's fine."

"Really?"

"I don't care what people think. Do you?"

He shook his head.

"I'd only mind if you felt badly about it. I'd like you to be who you are. It doesn't matter what others think."

"It matters to me, what you think."

"Well, you're fine then. I like who you are. And I'm not going to waste my time worrying how I might feel about it in the future. In fact, at the risk of sounding shallow, I'm proud to be seen with you. You're the best-looking man I've ever met." I rubbed his back. "And I've spent so much of my life being boring, it might be fun to be part of a scandal."

Didier stared at the sky for a long moment.

"How are you feeling?"

"I'm...I'm breathing." He looked back at me. "I haven't slept very much since Saturday morning. It's beginning to catch up with me."

"Maybe once you get home you'll be able to relax, with this behind you."

He nodded. "I haven't been to my mother's grave since her funeral, and I thought after I saw you, I would try to do that. Then I suspect I'll take a taxi home and have a nervous breakdown. And after that, maybe sleep for a day or two." He smiled sheepishly.

"That sounds like a good plan. I wish I could come up with some excuse and get the afternoon off, but I have to help host a cocktail party for some of our donors. A new exhibit opened today."

"Yes, you said."

"You're more than welcome to come, of course."

Another smile, deeper and more reminiscent of the man I'd come to know. "You're kind, but I'm not there yet."

"I didn't think so. Just wanted to show you off."

He laughed.

"I'll settle for a coffee this weekend. Maybe the river. Whatever you're up for."

Didier tossed his crust to the pigeons and stowed our wax paper and bottle. "Lie down with me."

We reclined side by side on the grass and he laced his fingers with mine. I stared up at the sky. I was holding hands with the most beautiful man alive, watching the clouds drift past miles above Paris.

In a few days he might greet me at his door, take me to bed…maybe to breakfast. Perhaps in a couple weeks' time I could arrive and find him waiting for me on his stoop. At a bistro down the block. On my own doorstep.

We lay there for an hour at least, until I knew I was really pushing it. I squeezed his hand and sat up.

"Back to work?" he asked.

"Sadly."

We stood and brushed the grass from each other's backs.

"Are you taking a cab to see your mother?" I asked.

"I was going to, but now I think maybe I'll try to walk. It's not far." Didier dug a map from the bag and consulted it, murmuring street names to himself. The cemetery he traced a route to wasn't far at all. I was tempted to offer to escort him, but he must have felt naked enough already. After three years, he deserved to revisit his grief in private.

I walked him to the far end of the park.

As we reached the curb, he smiled down at me. "Here I go."

"You'll be fine. Three blocks straight, two blocks left. Three blocks straight, two blocks left." I repeated it a few times, making up a cheesy little tune and pumping my fists as if I were marching in a musical.

He laughed. "You tease, but I will use that."

I picked a stray blade of grass from his collar. "There's a florist's on the next corner. For your mom."

A slow, thoughtful nod. "That's a nice idea."

For a long moment we both stalled, then I took hold of Didier's shoulders and turned him toward the crosswalk. "Well, off you go."

"Off I go. I'll see you this weekend? Friday?"

I nodded. "You will. Thank you so much for lunch. You know, and for coming out to see me. It means an awful lot. Way more than I can say." And if I tried any harder to explain it, I'd surely start crying.

"Thank you for making me willing to. Really…" He trailed off. I could tell he wanted to say more as well, but it was too much on top of whatever crazy adrenaline high or anxiety attack he must have been mired in.

I stood on my tiptoes and kissed his cheek, stepping away as a large group of tourists began to cross en masse. With my gentle push, he merged into the safety of the throng.

He stopped and waved from the far sidewalk. I waved back. I watched him turn away. I watched him walk all the way down the block, until his sweater was just a dot of gray in the crowd. The most extraordinary man in a city of two million. In all of Europe or the rest of the wide world.

I hoped he'd stop at the flower shop, maybe do as I always do and spend far too long there, sniffing all the blossoms. All those scents and colors he'd left behind until today. I hoped they'd feel new to him all over again, as new as the excitement swelling in my middle.

A beautiful young clerk might flirt with him as he browsed, but she'd never see what I did. She'd see only his shiny shell, snapped shut to hide a jumble of secondhand parts, ticking not quite as they should, but ticking nonetheless. A bit rusty. A bit erratic, like my heartbeat in the moments before I press his buzzer.

As I aimed myself back toward the museum, I pondered what I'd wear on Friday. What I might bring as an offering, for our date.

I wished I didn't have to go to the party that afternoon. I wanted the workday to be done so I could walk to the shops and get lost, browsing the aisles for treats. Something fancy and overpriced from far away, that Didier would never have tried before. Something to remind him of the places that lay beyond the bricks that made up sixteen Rue des Toits Rouges. He'd opened me up inside those walls, and now I prayed I might do him the favor of helping knock them down.

The sun was hot on my hair, bright in my eyes. The breeze was cool with no promise of rain. The sky was blue as hydrangea, wide and high and limitless, and all of Paris belonged to me.

COERCION

THE CURIO VIGNETTES, PART I

I

Inside, my world is small. Safe.

Within the horizon of a curved boundary, everything is brass, steel, nickel. Air and shadows. The busyness of Paris fades, growing as distant as space, reality replaced by the movement of gears, the snap of springs. The rhythm and flow of the Métro, of WALK signs and traffic lights—all are gone, and I'm lost in the tick and pivot of cogs.

The only wrongs to confront are those of rust, dust, wear or warp. I solve them with tweezers, oil, a jeweler's monocle, a can of compressed air. I wander the dark geometry of my watches and music boxes for entire afternoons, entire appearances of the sun, until—

I jump when the alarm goes off, as I always do. And as always, I catch the monocle when it falls from my eye and press the knob of the clock to still the hammer assaulting its bells. The brass polish has left grit under my nails and a headache between my eyes from the fumes I hadn't noticed until now.

Outside my windows, the sunset is ripening. The pigeons have tucked their heads beneath their wings, seeming ripened themselves, soft and round with sleep.

It's nearly eight, time to abandon the world of my precious hobbies for the slightly larger realm of my flat.

I haven't left this place for two days, not since Caroly was last here. When she stays the night, she makes me come with her in the morning, just to the café down the street for breakfast. Then she goes to work, and I flee back to my safe little nest.

Before I met her, I hadn't ventured outside these walls in three years. Now I manage the feat as many as four times a week, for twenty minutes or maybe two hours, for a drink or a meal, or to sit in the park and listen to Caroly molest my language with her thick American accent. Such infrequent, brief excursions may sound pathetic, but to me it's no less profound than taking one's first steps following a car crash, having been told you'll never walk again.

Caroly is coming tonight, and tomorrow she'll make me leave. In the morning my heart will curl like a fist between my ribs, clenching as she opens the door and leads me to the stairs and down four flights to the street. It will stop entirely as we step outside, but halfway to the café I'll feel the warmth of the sun or the coolness of the breeze, smell flowers or bread, and forget the crushing hugeness of the sky and buildings for a breath or two.

But for tonight, I'll stay safe. Tonight we stay in my world, with its familiar walls and scents and sounds. Her body is familiar too, after these three months of acquaintance, and she'll let me get lost inside her, fascinating as any clock or watch.

I shower, scrubbing myself with a rough cloth in the hot water. Rub shea butter into my skin. Caroly likes my stubble so I forgo shaving, but smooth a measure of the good-smelling balm she bought me over my jaw and neck. I dress in my bedroom, stroll across the flat to select the evening's music. Something with cello tonight, I think. Dark and sensual. With her eyes and nose and ears catered to, I head to the kitchen to turn my attention to her mouth.

My bell rings just as I turn the heat down under a pot of pasta, and I jog to the intercom panel to unlock the foyer door and twist the deadbolt open. Sometimes, if rarely, I'll go down to meet her at the building's front door, to show her it's been a good day. But tonight I won't. She'll hand me my post, perhaps noticing the stack is thicker than usual, and she'll know that I didn't make it downstairs yesterday either. She'll give me a look—frustration, likely, but never pity—then the topic will be dropped.

As I check on dinner I feel her footsteps. My heart speeds to match them, the happy race of anticipation. Then she's at my threshold, haloed in the light from the hallway, and I couldn't hide my smile if I tried.

"Good evening." I say it in English. It's become our custom. English inside my flat, where she is still a tourist of sorts, French outside.

"Hey." She pushes off her shoes by the door. A green paper bag hangs from her hand, from the wine shop near the museum where she works.

I cross through the living room to kiss her cheeks. "What have you brought?"

"Something with a pretty label." She shows me the bottle.

Caroly likes pretty labels, beautiful objects, haunting, elegant music and rich food. She grew up poor, she told me, but her heart is an aristocrat's, beating for the finer things. It seems she counts my company among them. I watch her eyes sometimes, when she doesn't know I'm looking. When she reads, or studies a painting in a gallery, they're cool blue, distant. But when her gaze turns to me, heat burns there. Always.

I give the bottle a second's attention, far more captivated by her. She does things to me, as if she were magnetized, my hands made of iron. They reach for her face and I glance her smooth, fair skin with my thumbs, slide my fingers into her hair, dark blonde curls so soft they could belong to a toddler. Her lips purse in their bashful way, and I kiss them. My body would happily take things much further, but there is cream sauce to attend to. Besides, I have more planned for tonight.

"You smell awfully good," she tells me. "Is that the stuff I bought you?"

"It is." I smile when she presses her nose to my throat for another sample.

"It smelled different in the store."

"Oh?"

"Yes, it's even nicer on you." She kisses the spot, handing me a stack of post as she steps back.

"Thank you." Among the bills and rubbish is a plain, unstamped envelope with my first name written in cursive, inside it a check from yesterday's client. Caroly used to leave such payments for the pleasure of an evening. I can scarcely remember that dynamic, so much has happened since she ceased being my patron to become something more. I remember taking her virginity, every second of those first visits, but of us being strangers, client and whore—anything other than what we are now—it's as hazy and theoretical as a dream.

She's not coy about what I do, nor jealous. Lately she's asked more and more about my clients, wanting to know what they wish to do with me, *to* me. I tell her, compositing the details so they belong to no one actual woman. She used to ask over wine, before we took each other to bed. Now sometimes she asks *in* bed, and I know it excites her, eavesdropping on other women's fantasies.

She rubs my arms through my sleeves, and just that affectionate, innocent friction makes me wish the cotton would disintegrate. That everything would dissolve until it's just us in our bare skin.

"Something smells amazing."

"Only pasta."

"Works for me. I'm starving." She follows as I walk to the kitchen. "I like the music."

"I knew you would. How is your new exhibit?"

"Almost ready for public consumption."

I uncork the bottle and she sets glasses on the butcher block. I like that she knows where to find things, that she has a favorite mug. I like her secret basket of womanly accoutrements, hidden beneath my bathroom sink lest my clients see it and feel uncomfortable.

We toast to Caroly's achievements at the museum and sample the wine, as lovely as its seductive label.

She leans back against the counter, wrapping a slender arm around her long waist. I know every inch of the body behind her blouse and skirt, better than any man on earth. The thought stirs my blood as it always does, a hypocritical possessiveness. Though so much of sexual pleasure is rooted in the darker emotions, I long ago quit regarding guilt and envy and shame as sensations to avoid.

"What did you get up to today?" she asks.

"Very little, outside the brass." That is her term for my hobbies. *Going inside the brass,* as if I don special equipment and spelunk between the wheels and pinions. Which I suppose I do.

"Enjoy yourself?"

"I did." As much as one enjoys a deep dream. Once the trance of my hobby has been broken, it seems as though I've lost more hours than I recall experiencing. Often I feel as if I've only actively lived perhaps ten years of my life, many more lost. Not squandered, but dozed through. I wonder if morphine addicts feel this way.

Sometimes I suspect I ought to fret more about it, but the worries only draw me back to my cabinet and its clockwork curiosities, to hypnosis or meditation, to that world where my brain goes as quiet as the Buddha's.

"Can I help with anything?"

"No. You are only allowed to relax and be spoiled," I tell her.

"Sounds easy enough."

I tend to the sauce and pasta and we eat in the kitchen, tall chairs set close together at a corner of the island, facing the tiny window above the sink where a single ball of feathers sleeps. Caroly calls him the Sommelier, believing as I do that it's the same pigeon, night after night. Sometimes she'll hold up whatever bottle we're drinking from, as if seeking his approval. My flat is on the top floor of the building and other birds roost outside my bedroom window. She calls them the Perverts.

"Are you taking me out this weekend?" How that word sours my mouth. *Out.*

"I am. Not far, just down to the river again, if you like."

"I would." It will scare me white as bread dough, but I'll be proud of my effort once she's led me back home. And she *will* lead me. I have a terrible sense of direction, even in the city where I've lived my entire thirty-four years. As confounding as dyslexia.

"I'll pack us a lunch," I say.

"Saturday or Sunday?"

"I have a client Sunday evening, so Saturday is best."

She nods stoically. I hope she's noticed by now, I never take clients on Fridays and Saturdays anymore. Those are hers, the precious evenings without curfew, mornings when she needn't rise early for work and I get to study her face in the dawn light, placid with sleep.

Caroly toys with her supper. "Can I ask what she's like?" Again, no jealousy in her tone, only curiosity. Her question makes me smile, the perfect catalyst for my plans.

"You may." I assemble a female collage in my head, of this client and several I've known with similar appetites, constructing a fictional woman whose confidence can't be violated. "She's in her early forties," I say, picturing her. "Very successful, in a challenging field dominated by men."

Caroly's fork hovers, frozen above her plate, her expression rapt.

"She can never for one minute appear an emotional, vulnerable woman," I continue. "But inside she misses those things. She misses being able to let a man lead without fearing it undermines her professional façade."

"What does she like to do with you?"

"She likes for me to seduce her."

My clients like all sorts of things, and I enjoy being whatever excites them. I've always loved pleasing women. When I was a teenager and my classmates were concerned merely with *having* sex, I was determined to find occasion to become *good* at sex. To study and practice and master it, like the trade it would one day become to me.

Nothing turns me on more than seeing that wicked gleam in someone's gaze and knowing I've put it there. I see it in Caroly's eyes as she sips her wine, and I feel my cock grow warm and heavy and eager.

"How do you seduce her?"

"With wine," I say, tapping Caroly's glass with my fork. "And softly spoken words, and with pressure."

"Pressure?"

I nod. "She likes to feel the guilt, to feel as though I am talking her into my bed. She craves the regret as acutely as she might an orgasm."

Caroly's blue eyes are round. "She likes you to make her regret stuff?"

"She savors the shame." I sip my wine slowly and make a face of decadent appreciation upon swallowing.

"That's... Huh. I wonder what that feels like."

Finish your supper and I will show you. More than bedtime stories tonight. An entire play for us to act out, if she wishes to don another woman's identity, slip inside her skin and experience my body through new hands, new eyes, a new mouth.

"What else does she like?"

I smile. Sometimes I feel like a fine cut of meat, Caroly's questions asking what another woman's recipe might make of me. But her affinity for beauty makes her anxious, makes her worry she's shallow, and I've learned not to tease her about the topic. I understand anxiety as well as anyone might, so I hold my tongue, even as I find her objectification charming beyond reason.

"Finish your pasta and I will tell you what else she likes."

We eat in easy silence and leave the dishes to soak. I carry the glasses and she the wine, and we retire to the couch in my living room. Along the window ledges, pigeons we have yet to name are finding their spots in the day's dying light. Some bits of Paris are going to sleep as well, while others are only now waking.

Part of me wishes that one day this might be *our* living room, hers and mine. But much would have to change to make that possible. There would be no more clients, no more of the income I've grown so accustomed to.

I'm capable of change; I know that now. But only slowly. Someday Caroly might get me onto the Métro or out of the city, get me to sleep somewhere unfamiliar, to travel with her to Spain or England or beyond. All those things must happen before I could ever change something so great as my livelihood or invite her to share my home permanently.

This evening, however, I want to travel no farther than my bed. *Our* bed, hers and mine, until Thursday dawns.

"So." She tucks her legs beneath her bottom, cupping her drink in both hands. "Tell me about her."

"I would prefer to show you, if you'll let me." Hope flutters in my belly.

Long fingers drum her glass, ever-nervous creatures. "Show me how?"

"I wondered if tonight, you would like to *be* her. Do with me all the things she likes."

Her eyebrows rise.

"You're so interested in what my other lovers ask of me, perhaps we could begin exploring those things instead of merely talking. This woman's desires and any number of others."

"Like role-playing?"

"Like this storytelling you love so much, but more."

She purses her lips, nodding very faintly, very slowly. "We can try that."

She fascinates me, Caroly. Her body, long and pale as winter, her rich, smooth voice softening the edges of that homely accent. She arrived on my doorstep a blank canvas, at once terrified and eager to be transformed. At first so cautious, yet never once has she dismissed any lovers' game I've proposed. Each position and activity is a new delicacy to her, every one at least sampled and many deemed worthy of ordering again and again, and my pleasure to serve. At times she closes herself up, cold and tight as a mussel, but once you coax her open, she will let you swallow her whole.

"I am glad you're intrigued," I say, "but we've not played any games like this before. Do you trust me?"

"I do."

No hesitation, and I smile. "Then we have only one formality to discuss. Can you snap your fingers?"

She shows me she can, with either hand.

"The woman you are tonight may say things she doesn't mean. She may tell me to stop or slow down. And the man I will be may choose to ignore those words. But snap your fingers to tell me you truly want me to stop, and I will. In an instant."

"I know you would." Her face betrays her eagerness and I suspect she won't find occasion to use our little signal. She's excited to try on this woman's kink, to explore the places most women have ventured with their lovers by her age. To be "part of the club," as she's called it before.

"Always wine, with this client." I refresh our glasses nearly to the rims. "She likes to get drunk. To calm her nerves and so she may blame her desires on the intoxication." I give Caroly's blouse and skirt a mischievous looking-over. "She dresses not unlike you. Straight from the office, from all that pressure and power, all those men she fights so fiercely to make her equals, when she secretly wishes she could be off guard with a man. To surrender, if only for an evening."

Caroly adjusts her legs, crossing them primly and sitting up straighter. I smile to myself, because yes, some women like the fictionalized one I speak of do sit so exactly like that, ever alert. I lean closer, as I do with them, letting my nearness and the wine begin to loosen their shoulders, deepen their breathing, stir their pulses.

"When we are together," I tell her, "we are never client and prostitute. She is herself, but I am a handsome stranger who's taken her home against her better judgment." I am still Didier, but not the man I truly am. In those games I'm fearless and selfish, no sentimental whore with peculiar hobbies.

Caroly's gaze moves about the room, as though she's never been here before, never changed the records on my phonograph or played cards with me on the carpet, never laughed so hard she wept, sitting where we are now.

I move my wine to my right hand, laying my left arm along the back of the couch behind her, edging my hip closer. "Don't be nervous."

"I'm not nervous."

"Has it been a long time since you've let a man bring you back to his flat?"

She nods, and I wonder if the gesture's tight hesitance is acting, or her own shyness at taking up the role. She drinks deeply.

"Do I make you nervous?"

"A little."

"I want you. You can feel that, can't you? You've forgotten what it's like, to be wanted by a man. To be looked at like a woman."

Another nod.

"Let me remind you." I switch to French—seduction sounds best in French. I lower my face, speaking just above her ear. "Come to my bed."

"I shouldn't." Both hands clutch her glass, so accurate a gesture a shiver strokes cool fingertips down my back.

"What are you afraid of?"

"I don't move that quickly."

"I bet there are things you want that you won't even admit to yourself." I kiss her temple, then her ear, letting my breath steam against her skin, letting her hear the moan lurking in my throat. Between my thighs, my cock grows, a hungry animal rousing. I enjoy being this man, one with no crippling fears or cowardly compulsions, only confidence and simple, selfish wants.

I curve my arm around her, cupping her shoulder, kneading. I let myself become a seducer whose cock leads his actions, who feels lust so strongly he forgets courtesy and lets the predator inside him roam loose.

This close, I watch the color rise in her neck from desire and alcohol. This close, I see the pulse ticking there. I lean in and draw the tip of my tongue along the vein.

She pulls away, sipping her wine with trembling hands. I can read Caroly like a book, any fear and anxiety plain as letters spelling the names of her troubles across her face. But behind the shaking hands and the distance of her body, I find no true misgivings. Her fear is manufactured, and she wants me. So funny to think such a thing, knowing the man I'm playing feeds himself those sentiments, lies twisted into permission so that he may take whatever he wishes. We are not so different, he and I...except where I trust, he presumes

I scoot even closer, slipping the glass from her hands and setting it on the table along with my own. "Surely kissing would not be too much."

She lets me cradle her jaw and accepts a light brush of my lips against hers. I pull back and smile. "That was not so bad, no?"

"We can kiss." She's breathless, false nerves and true excitement. "But that's really all. I need to go slowly."

Leaning in, I caress her cheek with my thumb and speak against her temple. "If it is slow you like, I can make love to you for hours. Slow as honey. Just as sweet."

"No, not tonight."

"You're cruel, to make me want you so badly. To smell so good..." I breathe her in, that faint lavender scent of her shampoo, the amber and vanilla perfume she dabs behind her ears each morning. "Do you taste as good as you smell?"

She wriggles when my hand drops to cup her breast, and she plucks the offender away, moving it to her knee. I run it up her thigh, halted when I upset the hem of her skirt.

"Don't."

"I can't help it." Though she blocks me from reaching higher, I easily slide my fingers between her thighs. I have half a breath to marvel at her warmth before she pulls my hand away, setting it on my own knee this time. I cup my stiffening cock, leaning back so she'll see. "You make me so hard, I can't control myself."

"Just kissing tonight. Please."

The *please* reminds me of other clients I've known, with harsher desires still. So many fantasies to reenact with Caroly...and happily so many nights ahead of us to do so, for as long as my novelty lingers.

I stroke myself lightly, as a hesitant woman might, and in this game it heats me as no aggressive, appraising touch could. "Let me show you how much I want you."

"No. Just kissing. Really."

I sigh, the lazy sound of a womanizer's petulant, feigned defeat, and let my throbbing cock go. "Just kissing." I hold her face and sample her deeply, fingertips as possessive as my tongue and lips. The wine tastes ever richer from her mouth, as warm and dark as the secrets she keeps between her smooth, pale legs. Perhaps I'll kiss her there as well before the night is done, and feel her fingers in my hair, clutching in time with her moans.

I draw my tongue along her jaw, finding her perfume. Such a bitter flavor to offer so sweet a scent. The palm she sets on my neck is cool and unsure, and I shiver from how right it feels, how easily she's slipped inside this other woman's being.

Caroly disappears.

I disappear.

The people on my couch are strangers now, seducer and resister. I feel this man's desire rising from deep in my body, consuming me, a hot, growing force in need of an outlet.

I pull away, take her glass from the table and urge her hands around it. "Drink."

"I've had too much."

"I chose it for you. And the evening is still young. Plenty of time to indulge before the morning." The morning—the hateful pulse of a hangover, soured further by regret.

"I have to be at the office early…"

"You work too much," I tell her. "All this struggling only to keep your head above the water. Let yourself go under, just for one night. One glass."

"I'd drown."

"Drowning feels good, I promise." I coax her hands to her mouth, and she drinks.

"Good. In a minute you'll feel how fine an idea this is. Worry about work some other day, but not here. Not with me." There is a silk tie at the collar of her blouse and I slip its bow free, revealing creamy flesh and the shadow of her clavicle. Her hand covers mine, telling me to stop.

I fan my fingers across the bare V below her throat. "So soft." And so cool, the only thing that can quench the heat beating under my own skin. This torment would go if I could just be inside her.

"Don't."

"You've forgotten how to let a man be male."

"What do you mean?"

"You make us into your rivals, and forget what we really are."

"What are you?"

"Animals," I tell her, and slide my fingers under her shirt and beneath the strap of her brassiere. It slips from her shoulder when I push, her chest swelling with a gulped breath. I'll hold her this way in my bed, watch her breasts rise as her back arches, watch her flesh quiver, echoing the impact as my cock claims what it's owed.

"I don't need an animal in my life," she tells me, forcing my hand away and righting her strap. "I don't need any man, but if I wanted one, I'd pick a gentleman." She clutches her collar closed.

"A gentleman is nothing but a dog on a leash. Take away his tether and you'll meet the beast as he wishes to be."

"I should leave." As she rises, I grasp her wrist. She tugs. "Let me go."

"I'm sorry. Stay, just to finish your wine. I'll be good."

She doesn't move, and I tug again at her arm gently, once, twice, until she bends her knees, sits once more. I pick up my own glass, letting her think me well behaved for a minute or two.

"I'm sorry if I offended you."

"You have, a little."

"The way you looked at me at the bar, I took you for a different kind of woman."

"What kind of woman?"

I picture such a scene, myself a man capable of prowling so easily in public, among strangers. Her, a sophisticated professional longing to escape the cage she's made for herself, if only for a night.

"You looked so...hungry," I tell her. "So much fire in those eyes."

"I never meant to lead you on."

"It was your eyes that led *you* here, to my flat. Your eyes, and other forces..." I drop my gaze to her breasts, her lap, then smile at her. "I'd give you anything you desire, if only your mouth would admit what those things were."

"I just want to finish this wine and get home to bed."

"There is a bed here. A fine one, big enough for two."

"No. Really."

I walk my fingers up her forearm, careful not to cross a line and invite another flight. "How long since you've let a man be a man with you, and let yourself be a woman?" When she doesn't reply, I lean closer. "How long since you've enjoyed a man's mouth or hands or cock?"

She swallows. "I've kissed you tonight."

"With your lips, yes. I would kiss you elsewhere, even more deeply." The mere idea makes my mouth tingle and water.

She shakes her head.

"How long since a man has made you come?"

Another blush, but she doesn't rise to leave. "A while."

"I would give you that, with my tongue. With my fingers or my cock, whichever part of me you wished to invite."

She bites her lip, and I lean forward to splash the last of the bottle into our glasses. Her eyes widen as though I've served her blood still hot from a sacrifice.

I turn to her, my knee pressed to her thigh, and drop my face close to whisper, "I want you."

She exhales with a tight, sharp huff, as if she's been struck.

"I'm hard for you now," I murmur. "Let me show you."

"No."

I feel the need as such a forceful man would, desire careless as a tidal wave, eager for the thrill of the crash. Her body is rigid as I reach for her jaw, holding her face as my lips brush hers. Hands push at my shoulders, their pressure pleading, not fighting. They tell me to stop, but in such a *quiet* voice, so quiet I know it's not meant to be heard. I push too, gently, telling her to lie back and let me have my way. She doesn't obey. But it's my wine, my home, soon to be my bed and my needs. Everything within these walls is my possession, and she'll be no less. I will use her—as is my right, since the moment she chose to step across my threshold. In her body I find proof of the desires her lips won't admit to.

Some women will never ask for the pleasure they want, and they must be given it, by force if necessary.

Or so that is how I imagine such a man would think.

And though I am not such a man outside the bounds of this game, to borrow his greedy delusions ignites a lust, hot and coarse and cruel. It's chased by the shame—that spice too delicious to resist, yet nearly too strong to suffer. But why eat grapes when one can drink wine? Why behave when sin feels so natural?

Tar me with shame in thick, hot strokes, leave me blacker than midnight.

I suckle her lip, coax her open so that I may come inside and taste her. Against my mouth, I feel her soften. When I slide my hand across her throat and down to hold her breast, she covers it but doesn't move it away. Her flesh grows hot under my palm, her lips plump and likely tender from what I've demanded. It reminds me of Caroly's sex, swollen with desire, welcoming me into that slick sanctuary where only I have yet been invited. My throat is all at once thick, remembering how she tastes, how her legs tremble against my cheeks when my tongue teases her toward release. How thick I feel when I slip inside her.

This forceful man's urges tug at me, bullying me to guide her hand to my cock, to open her blouse, to push her down and feel the warm junction between her soft thighs against my hard sex. But her cooperation would make this seduction far easier, so I hold back.

She lets my hand go, moving hers to my shoulder. Yet she doesn't push me away as I expect—she squeezes, finding something of interest there. Then my arm. I wonder if she senses my triumphant smile as we kiss.

"You're so beautiful," I tell her, words tumbling straight from my mouth to hers. So beautiful and all mine. The man I play could never claim such a prize.

"Th-thank you."

I move my lips to her ear, letting her hear how my voice has grown deep and strained, as rigid and needy as my cock from the lust. "I want you. I wanted you at that bar—for everyone to simply see us together. To think maybe this stunning woman was mine." And for a night, she will be.

"I don't usually do this…"

Unseen, I grin sly as a wolf at the surrender in her tone. I nip at her neck and fondle her breast, and though she tenses for a breath, the exhalation leaves her soft and receptive.

"But I won't go too far," she tells me.

Good. I was not ready for the coercion to be done. There are walls yet to scale and locks to be picked, so much more fun than strolling invited through open gates.

COERCION

"Come to my bed," I say, letting my words caress her skin. Soon that steam will warm her elsewhere, and I'll feel her heat at my lips moments before I taste her sex. I will wait until I know I've coaxed a wealth of that honey between her thighs—and then I will feast.

"I shouldn't."

"But you should. I want your body in my sheets, so I can breathe you in after you've gone and remember everything we'll do tonight."

She's stiff once more, so I graze my palm across her breast, gathering all her attention into the contact, into whatever pleasure she feels as her nipple draws tight.

"You won't regret any of the things I'm dying to show you." I drag my teeth softly along her throat then kiss the same spot. "My body will please you, I know it."

I *do* know such a thing. I wasn't born with an extraordinary voice, but my body and face make women shiver as they might while listening to some divine aria. I've seen proof of this since I was perhaps fourteen and first realized that people look at me differently, that I am wanted in people's photographs and paintings and beds.

My caresses draw her out, and I feel her hand at the back of my head, fingers clutching my hair.

"Come to my bed, and I'll ask no more than just this, what we're doing now."

"I don't know."

"Please." I say it once more, then again, a kiss to punctuate between each word. "Just this, I swear."

She doesn't reply, but when I stand and take her hand, she rises from the couch willingly enough. I feel desire open inside me, uncoiling like a snake, tongue and tail flicking, a writhing mass of restless, predatory muscle.

Caroly's hand in mine is smooth and cool, and I imagine it on my naked body. She used to be cautious, lately far less so. But tonight, who knows? I will have to see how far she takes this wicked tourism.

II 〇━━

I lead her to my room, lit only by what glow the city has slipped through the crack in the curtains.

"We need light." I speak to both Caroly and the woman she plays. "I need to see you."

I gesture and she sits on my bed as I fetch a metal card table from before the window, a dozen or more pillar candles fused to its top.

I light them one by one, the room enlarging with each dancing flame. Her gaze drinks me in, telling me things she's uttered aloud, though only when a glass too many of wine has spurred her to. *You're so beautiful,* it tells me. A look I know well, warm as sunshine and mischievous as twilight.

Beauty is a queer and unearthly power.

I was born of my father's infidelity and my mother's consumptive infatuation. I'm a bastard and a prostitute, crippled by agoraphobia…but I *am* beautiful. My deeper flaws seem to go unnoticed, all cracks in the stained glass, lost amid the dazzling colors of the whole.

I inherited my father's dramatic Portuguese face, his strong nose and widow's peak, his dark hair, his cowardice. Like his, my eyes are deep brown, but they are unmistakably my mother's. She gave me her fine complexion, her romanticism and her fear of the unfamiliar. My parents' affair lasted only a summer, but they must have been a sight to behold—exquisite young lovers set loose in Paris, giddy with forbidden lust. Or in my mother's case, love. A love that stayed with her like a whispering ghost until the day she died.

Had I not been beautiful, who knows what would have become of me. I might be as I am now, shut away in some garret with my projects and my view and my wine, but no women would call on me, certainly none willing to pay for the luxury of sharing my bed. I might be forgotten, left in a cupboard to grow pale and soft and unmissed, unable to escape of my own volition. But I can never know, just as I may never know what it is like to not be beautiful.

Caroly, she is the opposite. I watch her pale gaze roam my bedroom in the multiplying light, pretending to regard all these familiar objects for the first time. She knows nothing of how it feels to be beautiful, though plenty of people might say she is. A beguiling, androgynous face worthy of a Dutch painting, high, rare cheekbones softened by those feminine curls. All of it even more enchanting in the candlelight.

Sometimes I see her touch her hips when she dresses, as though wishing there were curves there to accentuate. But with her angular body and her unusual face, she could buy the clothes off a couturier's rack and be mistaken for a model. So utterly photographable and yet so terrified of being photographed. True, she is no classic American beauty. She is a single black pearl in a strand of the expected white, and so much lovelier for her difference.

I blow out the match, staring at her over the flickering flames. There's fire burning in my belly as well, and I hope she can see it in my eyes. Sentimental thoughts leave me, darker ones taking their place. Our two bodies fucking on that bed, in this light, as we've done dozens of times. I've watched us in the wardrobe mirror and put myself to sleep nights later, recalling how we looked together.

More often I conjure other memories—moments of deep intensity, the two of us discovering what gives her pleasure. Her body is an exotic instrument in my hands, one I hope to never finish mastering. To never cease to find new, thrilling, heartbreaking notes to coax from her with my fingers.

But I push the romantic thoughts away. I've forgotten my role, lost in my head as I so often become.

"You look lovely," I tell this woman. "In this light. On my bed." I smile as the final word leaves my lips.

"Thank you." She runs her hands over the blanket, as though confirming the mattress is still there, supporting her.

I round the table and for a moment I cast her in my shadow. Our game clicks back onto its track, and the real Didier falls away like a shed garment. My gaze drops to the shadow between her legs, a reward that must be claimed at any cost.

"Lie down with me." I wave to the pillows and she reluctantly reclines, careful to keep her skirt in place. I join her. My face is shaded, hers golden in the warm light. Her wary gaze flits back and forth but her lips part when mine do, and she accepts my kiss eagerly enough.

I slide my hand lower to cradle her ribs, thumb tracing the curve of her breast through her blouse. With my other hand I graze the skin at the base of her neck, as soft as the silk collar that seeks to hide it. She is just as soft elsewhere—her belly, her wrists, the tops of her feet and her inner thighs. I nudge her legs with mine, edging my knee between them. Her legs clamp tight, stopping my mischief just as the hem of her skirt begins to rise. Her resistance triggers a change in me.

My arousal turns sharp and selfish, the sheer *challenge* turning me on as nothing has in months. We're competing, and one of us must lose for the other to win.

And I intend to win.

This man's borrowed desires burn hotter and darker than my own, and though they disturb me, I can't deny how intoxicating it is, to want a woman so badly all reason and civility abandons you. All empathy.

I push with my knee, quick and sudden, and I gain another inch before her legs tense once more.

Below the open tie, tiny fabric buttons trail down the front of her blouse. It is so tempting to savage them, but I know Caroly's tendency to spend so much on a piece of clothing that she can eat nothing but soup until her next paycheck arrives. After all, I used to be one of her indulgences. I smile to think that at least I always fed her well—she never went hungry the nights she treated herself to my company.

She grabs my wrist as I touch the topmost button. "Don't."

Her hold is a warning, not a restraint, and I ignore it, freeing the closure. Her hand tightens but her legs have let down their guard, and my knee pushes ever deeper between her thighs. My cock throbs as I imagine forcing my other leg between hers, rolling her onto her back, freeing my cock and taking her with no more than a gruff tug to move her panties aside. Will she go reluctantly? Or will she fight? I know Caroly better than any man can claim, but I don't know that— how coerced a victim she may want to play, and how cruel a villain she might wish to bait.

"I want you," I whisper. "You have no idea how badly."

"Not tonight. Maybe some other time, if we see each other again—"

"You came to my bed. You must want this too." I twist my hand free from hers, switching who holds who. Her body stiffens as I lead her fingers down my chest and side. "Touch me." My grip on her wrist is tight, her struggle meek. I draw her hand along my hip and she tugs it back, though not hard enough to escape.

"Just kissing, you said before."

"I won't ask for anything else," I lie. "But it hurts, I want this so much. Touch me. Just once. Let me show you what you've done."

Still she resists, limply. I pull her hand closer, closer, until her fingertips brush me through my pants, the contact like lightning. As I press her palm over my erection, every instinct begs to thrust against her, fast and greedy until the friction tears me apart. But I won't. I won't. There is too much fun yet to be had.

Her mouth is open, eyelids heavy. I know this look—it's Caroly. I'm charmed to find she's not such a fine actress that she can shroud those little cues I've come to recognize so well.

"See? You feel how much I want you?" She lets me squeeze her hand tighter, draw it up and down my ridge in short, maddening strokes. I can't imagine I've ever been so hard before.

"I can feel it."

"I could show you as well."

"No."

Rougher now, I guide her hand. "You don't want to see what you've done?"

"It's too fast."

"How long since you've seen a man? Touched his bare flesh?"

"A while."

"Let's change that." I let her hand go to slip free the button of my trousers, and suddenly it is she who holds *my* wrist.

"No."

"You don't want to see?" I rub myself through the fabric. "Don't you want to feel how hard you've made me? Find out how big I am?"

She shakes her head. "Not this soon."

"Very well. But here," I say, sliding my hand up to cup her breast. "Give me this, at least."

She doesn't speak, her throat flexing to gulp a breath. Her fingers rest on my side, uncertain.

"We will kiss," I tell her, kneading, "and any way you want to touch me, just know that you may." As our mouths reunite I squeeze her, stroke her with my thumb until her nipple stiffens under the whispering glide of her blouse. I feel lace as well, and I imagine what color it might be. I hope it's the navy one she sometimes wears, the shade of a stormy sea. She's so pale the blue highlights her veins, making her seem ethereal, some delicate creature with its very heartbeat painted across its skin.

She permits me to free the second button with little more than a sigh to mark her protest. Teasing her tongue with mine, I let her hear my ragged breaths. As I suckle her lip, I'm reminded of other things I've missed since our last date. I release her flesh. My mouth is poised to whisper how badly I wish to taste her elsewhere...

But I am selfish in this game, and I doubt such a man would preoccupy himself with an act that focuses so starkly on a woman's pleasure. He would take, not give, and so my craving must wait.

I've been a bad man before, for clients who wish it of me, though never with Caroly. It feels new and forbidden. Criminal. For the sake of our game, I muster a force I'm not entirely at ease wielding and pin her down, her shoulders pressed flat to the bed. I shove her legs apart with my knees, jerk her hem to her hips.

"Don't."

She grasps my shirt but I pretend to mistake the gesture. I peel the top away, and her hands are on my bare chest, pushing. As I cast the shirt aside, I grab an open a condom from the side table and set it on the covers, trying to ignore its presence. The man I play would not trouble himself with such a requisite courtesy, and I hope she, like me, is filtering it from the scene.

"I've wanted you from the moment I saw you." The lust makes me sound angry, and my arousal shifts to mimic that emotion—hot and urgent, in need of a target.

She slaps at my hand when I push her skirt higher. "Don't."

I abandon her clothes to attend to mine, opening my fly. My cock escapes from its prison, enveloped in cool air, the band of my shorts shoved down, out of the way. It binds my balls, the discomfort somehow perfect. Her sex is hampered as well, but only a strip of lace and cotton stands between me and my goal, and whether it's shed or ripped or yanked aside, it won't protect her. I stroke myself, wondering if I've ever felt this big.

"See what you do to me?"

"Stop."

In this instant I realize how vulnerable it must feel sometimes, to be a woman. In this position, your only weapons are the smallest of words, your strength only the volume with which you speak them. And the more dangerous a man, the more useless they become. An ugly, frightening thought, but like the anger, fear thunders in my heart, sends blood racing through my veins like a rushing tide. I search her eyes and see the fear there too, but veiled behind her arousal. I listen for the snap of fingers, knowing it won't come.

"Touch me." I grasp her hand and force it to my cock. Her protest is silent, just a jerking of her arm and a clenching of her fist, but I squeeze tighter and her fingers close around me. I clasp them there, drawing them up and down in brutal strokes. My lust mirrors the motions, a harsh and choking need that sets my entire body throbbing.

"You feel how badly you've made me want you?" I ask, slowing her forced caresses.

Her mouth is open, gaze on our hands. Her lips are flushed plump and dark. It dawns that this is Caroly's chance to sample other men—even cruel ones—within the bounds of our odd, one-way fidelity. She must like that, just another aspect of the education she was seeking when she came to me.

All at once I want to be a hundred different men for her, so many she'll never need anyone but me.

I free her hand, but only to push the violation further. In a breath I've clad myself in latex, and my knees push hers ever wider. Even in the candlelight, this act seems to cast us in shadows.

"Let me in." It's no request, and I tell her so with my actions, jerking her panties aside with my thumb. I can smell her, that scent that makes me salivate as no other delicacy can.

She grasps my wrist with both hands, pulling, pushing. "Stop."

"I can't. I want you too much."

They feel shockingly true, this man's words. Far more shocking is the absolute fact that I am stronger than her. She's holding me off with everything she has, but it's not enough, not even close. It's an ugly power to feel, and a shameful power to take even the slightest glimmer of pleasure in exploiting. She yanks and thrusts at the hand baring her sex, and with the other I guide my cock to her lips. Her heat kisses my crown, searing and slippery. It eases both my entrance and my conscience, this proof that the intrusion is a welcome one.

Her voice turns small, so small. "Don't." But her grip on my wrist goes slack. As though she, like me, is focused on this moment—on the hard, slow slide of my flesh claiming hers.

The penetration isn't enough. Normally I'm a blank page, an unmolded handful of clay, only as domineering or hesitant as my client wishes me to be. But now I want to feel strong, bossy. I want to be that thing I despise more deeply than anything I can think of— a bully.

I lower my body to hers and press our foreheads together. Her cunt is hot and tight, and mine. My territory, my possession. I tell her as much with my thrusts, pushing deep again and again.

"Now you know," I say. "Now you feel how hard you make me."

"Stop." The syllable sears my lips.

"Don't fight me."

Even as I say it, I feel an elbow jab my ribs, a palm pressing uselessly at my chest. I drive deeper.

"You made promises, the way you looked at me at that bar."

Silence from her throat and lips, though her pushing hands are screaming for me to stop. One moves to fist my hair, the way it has during our more frenetic couplings.

"Keep your promises," I tell her, drawing my length away then plunging deep, seeking a rhythm. "Admit you want this too, and you'll enjoy yourself. Or else make me take what I need and it will not go so easily."

It's all harsher than I'd expected. I've been rough before, though with the clients who ask me to seduce them, typically the force is less physical, the surrender far more coy. I pry them open with wine and words, but tonight there is more muscle, more implicit threat. So strange, the way lovers play at hurting one another. Strange but so nearly universal.

She lets my hair go. I hear my own sounds, disembodied. They're the curt, rhythmic moans of a desperate man. I've redressed in my own skin, the brute abandoned with my self-control. I try to clad myself in his cruelty but she's so warm, so soft...

The protest is gone from her touch. Her fingers are curious, assessing some contour or other, cataloguing whatever muscles flex as my body plunders hers. Caroly's hands, unmistakably. Her hips shift with mine, that private dance in which I alone have had the pleasure of being her partner.

Our little play has lapsed, but when I rise on straight arms, she finds her script. Those admiring hands stiffen and push, telling me she would not have her gentle teacher back so soon. I detach from the pleasure, letting only enough register to keep me hard.

Planting my knees wide, I grab her waist at each side and hold her in place. She claws my forearms and I answer with my thrusts, telling her I'll take anything she refuses to give willingly. We grapple until I seize each of her wrists, locking them at her hips, though careful to leave her fingers free to snap. Her back arches and her head mashes the pillow, hair a wild corona of curls. She writhes, electric, and I'm in awe. Does she feel the scrape of the clasp or zipper of my pants, as I feel the rasp of lace each time I plunge deep?

When I speak, my voice sounds like a stranger's. "Turn over."

This will be a treat for her, her favorite position. I suspect she likes the way it turns her elegant lover into a panting, growling animal, or perhaps merely the ease with which I can wrap my arm around to tease her clitoris. Perhaps both, some mix of the messy and the masterful. She loves contrast, she told me once, speaking of her favorite paintings. Hard lines over soft brushstrokes, murky mingling tones cleaved by slices of pure white canvas.

She resists still. I shift her bodily with gruff, borrowed hands, and desire pierces my composure. A mere prick to start, then cuts, a flurry of ragged slashes until my self-control lies in tatters. "Hold the headboard."

I've been treated to this view many times now, but never like this, with lace still framing her backside and her skirt twisted about her waist. Variety holds little novelty for me—it's never been a commodity I've had to labor to enjoy. But it excites me to see her this way, like a different person. The same woman I'm coming to know, but cocked at a new angle so a facet yet unseen leaps gleaming into the light.

Her back flexes as she braces herself against the scalloped wood of the headboard, and my hand shakes when I tug her panties aside and sink deep. The lace teases. I make her feel the slap of my skin against hers. The smell of sex hardens my muscles and draws moans from my throat.

She cranes her neck to watch. There is only Caroly in that curious gaze, and she sees only me. Our game is done and I do not mourn it. We have nights enough ahead of us to play, and right now, *this* night, I want what she does—just the two of us in this bed.

My arm or her hip is damp with sweat as I reach around and under her skirt, fingertips slipping beneath the lace to find her clitoris taut and swollen, as hard as my driving cock. Her lids lower as I stroke her, mouth falling open. I can bring her to climax twice, three times, until happy, lust-drunken drowsiness dulls her pretty pale eyes. Yet when the time comes for my pleasure, desire shines there, always. She likes whatever the need does to my face when I chase my release.

I smile to myself, arousal deepening, heating, tightening, to know how she must relish this. I curl the fingers of my free hand over her shoulder, tugging her into my thrusts the way she loves.

She murmurs my name and I say hers in return, rubbing her in tight circles. The world is no bigger than this bed, the only noise and scents those of our two bodies. There is no gravity, merely the friction of my fingers against her pleasure to pin me to the earth, no night or day or dusk or dawn, just the sweet, hot slide of my cock between her lips. I slow my thrusts but let my fingers race, wanting to make her feel each push and drag of the penetration. She turns her head sharply and I know she envies my view.

"Come now, and I'll let you watch," I promise.

A grunt answers me, then another, one to mark each moment my hips meet her backside. I echo the sound, my deep voice and her feminine one groaning together in time with our sin. The pace turns so slow and smooth. I can feel the change in her, the way her body grasps at me, begging for my come.

Just now, I want what my animal nature does. To do what our bodies were designed for and fill her with the spoils of this sex. To make a terrifying mistake, the kind that could bind me to this woman for the rest of our lives. I thank Christ for the condom, the flimsiest armor protecting me from such destructive impulses.

"Didier."

"Good." Unbidden, my hips rush to match the frantic strokes of my fingertips. "Come for me. Give me what no other man gets to have."

She presses against me and I grant her body what it wants, every inch buried deep in her pulsing heat. With each tide of her orgasm she squeezes tight. In its wake she goes limp, her stillness disrupted only by the swell of her breaths.

I lighten my caresses, recording the tempo of her blood in that most intimate pulse point. Her hip shines in the burnished light and I relish the coming summer, to see that sheen all over her body, feel her skin slippery against mine in the August heat.

At my urging, she releases the headboard and turns onto her back. I undress her slowly then shed my own garments. I ease the silver baubles from her ears and now we are bare, utterly. Well, nearly. I check that the ring of latex is snug to the base of my cock and I spread her thighs wide, finding her lush and slick.

Normally I find it difficult to override my programming, the voice that tells me to put off my own pleasure, to deny my release until the permission is implicit. But for the first time in years, I'm remembering how to simply be a man, my needs equal to my lover's, to be a partner and not a doting, selfless servant. I want to come, as badly as I would like to do the same for her a second time.

She strokes my arms, watches my cock.

"Touch yourself," I tell her.

She does, then offers an order of her own. "Lean back."

I sit on my heels, hugging her thighs to my hips and giving her the show she desires. The heat of her gaze fills me with a smug streak of pride.

"What do you want to see?" I've asked her this before, and she knows what I mean. What kind of man does she want to find in me? The picture of seductive self-control or a frantic wreck? Some other man altogether?

"Whatever you're feeling."

A frantic wreck, then. I grin, letting her see the madness behind my smile. "You will have to race me."

Her laugh gets me as hot as any caress or plane of bare flesh could, and I hand my body over to lust. I set aside her needs to indulge in a rare act, the singular pursuit of my own pleasure.

"Say my name. Tell me whose cock fills you."

"Only yours."

"Say it. Please."

"Didier." Those six letters are more to her than some man she's hired for an evening's indulgence. To me the sound is like clouds parting, warm sunlight spilling out. It's the sound of her beckoning me home, deep inside her body. I drop back to my palms, close enough to smell her sweat and perfume and the wine lingering in her throat. She says my name again, twice more until her voice is strained and words abandon her.

"Yes." I feel her unraveling, and when her body milks my cock, I do as it begs. My hips plow into her, too hard, but she only holds me tighter, nails clawing my back. The pleasure blinds and deafens, bright as a roaring fire. In the moment there is no *too hard*, no *too deep*, no groan loud enough to match what I feel. I push into her, so rough it could bruise, yet her legs hug me close, telling me it's a mark she might relish.

Even against my fevered flesh, my come is hot. I wish she could feel it too. If there were no condom, I could stay inside her as long as I liked, fall asleep there with my arms around her, our bodies joined.

Perhaps one day, in some foggy, hypothetical future where my bed is hers alone to share.

But here in reality, I hold the rubber in place and leave her warmth to dispose of it. For now it's too sticky to suffer the sheets and blankets, so we lie on our backs, breathing deeply and watching the shadows playing upon the canopy. I link her fingers with mine and squeeze. She squeezes back.

After a time, I ask, "Did you like it? Trying on another woman's desires for a little while?"

"I did. Sorry I lost the thread toward the end."

"Not at all. There's no shame in the thought that perhaps the pair of us, as we are, are still as compelling as two strangers."

Another squeeze. "Well said."

I turn onto my side to meet her eyes. "The more I get to know you, the more you fascinate me." It seems as though I navigate through one chamber of this woman only to find myself in a new and curious room.

"I'm different now than I was even a month ago," she tells me. "Even *I* feel like I'm meeting me for the first time."

"That sounds very exciting."

She bites her lip, cheek round with a stifled smile. "It is."

My skin grows chilled and I pull her close, wrapping my arm around to cup her shoulder blade. Her fingertips stroke my arm, as light as the fluttering of eyelashes. Thoughts gather in my head. They solidify to take the shapes of words, words I ache to say as deeply as they scare me. My throat constricts, so tight I know it won't let me voice my reckless realizations.

But no matter. We have other nights ahead of us, or so I presume. To presume is reckless as well, but without it I have no cause to hope, and hopelessness is a dark and lonely cell indeed. I hold her tighter.

Beside us, the candles burn. They will expire, whether one of us snuffs them now or we allow time to do the job. The light will go out all in one dramatic gust or a flame at a time, one by one by one.

And I hold her tighter still.

III

I love all of my clients—true and romantic love, though a breed without attachment or expectation, full of affection yet unhampered by possession. A love as one feels for a wondrous meal or a thrilling film, pure and resonant...but a love that ends, offering nothing lasting save for memories.

For Caroly I feel far more. More than I've felt for anyone, and I like to think I've loved deeply in my life, once or twice.

What I feel for her scares me. On fearful days I wonder, will she grow weary of playing my caregiver, once the newness of my body or our sex fades? Or once my beauty itself fades, should I manage to hold her attention for years, not weeks. She doesn't want children, so how long will she abide a man whose hand she must hold, leading him out into the noisy wilderness of Paris? A man who cannot drive her to a hospital should she get hurt; a man who can offer kindness and passion, but so little else...

She strokes my hair. "You're quiet."

I tug her close and pepper her face with kisses until she giggles. "You have emptied my head," I tell her. "I'm drunk from sex, and drowsy."

"A thousand apologies," she says, not sounding sorry at all for incapacitating me.

I run my thumb over her cheek and study her eyes, and kiss her a final time, a lingering press of my lips to hers. I could tell her now. Tell her I love her, but she's heard from my own mouth that I love each of my clients, and I worry I can't explain what about us is different. Special. I don't struggle often with words, but here I'm lost.

"What?"

"It is nothing."

She traces the line between my brows and those beside my lips. "Doesn't look like nothing."

I sigh. I swallow. I frown deeper, but ask what I need to. "What do you think of me as?"

"My lover. And my friend."

"Am I your boyfriend?"

"Sort of."

I nod.

"I guess I'm not sure what the definition of 'boyfriend' is," she says slowly.

"You're not the only woman I kiss or flatter or take to bed." This bed, where we lie now. My bed, hers, and yet so many others'.

"Yeah. Without that distinction... I don't know."

"You are the only woman I am with publicly." A flimsy, incidental distinction, being that I am so very difficult to drag out the door and down the street. There is another distinction, as well, one it would feel crass to enumerate—she is the only woman who gets me, gratis.

"You are who you are to me," she says. "I don't care if I can't say you're my boyfriend. I'm such a late bloomer, I don't think I'm really ready to start... I don't know, laying claims to anybody."

Her answer carves a pit in my middle, because I wouldn't mind such a thing. Perhaps I've grown too accustomed to feeling coveted.

She frowns. "Am I being too clingy?"

"Clingy?"

"Am I being too… Am I acting like you're my boyfriend too much, or…?"

"No. No no no." I kiss her temples in turn. "No. I would be happy for you to think such a thing. Though I understand why you can't."

"I just don't know how to yet."

"If I was your boyfriend, you could invite me places. To parties. To meet your friends."

"You're welcome to do all those things anytime you want. I don't care what my friends think."

It is a brave thing she says, because some of her friends know what I am. My reputation precedes me in the city's art circles, from the days when I sold my body for people's canvasses and photographs, instead of their pleasure. I'm touched she would say such a thing. I'm not ashamed of what I do, but many would be, including some who leave unmarked envelopes in my mailbox.

"You know why I can't," I say.

"Not yet, you can't. But a couple months ago you couldn't make it to the sidewalk. Now look at all the places we've been."

"Maybe."

"You're probably not ready to be my boyfriend any more than I'm ready to wrap my head around the idea. But I don't mind." She traces my jaw with her fingertips. "We make awfully good lovers. At least I think so."

I smile at that, knowing that only a few weeks ago she would never have flattered herself so. She's coming into her sexuality, slowly but unmistakably. I twine our legs together. "I think so too."

"If you're worried that I'm not satisfied with how we are, don't be. Really."

"I'll try."

"If you're afraid I don't feel special, don't worry about that either. I know I'm the only one who gets you, this way. I'm the only one who'd have this conversation with you."

"True."

She shrugs against the pillow. "It's enough for me."

"That is good."

A smirk twists her pretty lips.

"What?"

"Sometimes I feel like you're such an extraordinary man... It'd be a shame to keep you all to myself. Like having the only recording of some wonderful piece of music and keeping it locked up, not letting anybody else hear it." She pauses, blinking. "Sorry if that sounded like I was commodifying you. I do that a lot."

I grin. "That is your job, after all."

At the museum she spends her days cataloguing and ordering beauty. Of course she would think in such a way. At thirty-four, my beauty is a gift that will only fade with each passing season, but for as long as I have it, I will maintain and exploit it. It is what I was given, after all, and what I have to offer. What a pity it would be if our great writers and composers and painters had not exploited what they were born with. I am nothing so special as that, but I can be the statue, if not the sculptor. And I can fuck a woman so well she no longer mourns the husband who's left her or the youth that's passed her by. A muse to inspire or a shot to dull the deepest ache. Whatever a woman needs, I can be that.

I sigh grandly and roll onto my back, dragging Caroly with me so she lays her arm over my chest, head against my neck. I muss her hair. "I don't mind that you think of me so. And you're right. Maybe it is enough that we're lovers."

And yet…

Not so many years ago, I dated a woman. I cared for her very much—if not quite as intensely as I do Caroly—but her jealousy put an end to our affair. I'd have thought I'd be relieved to find a lover who keeps her envy at arm's length, as Caroly seems able to do. And yet part of me is hurt by how easily she shares me. It is a selfish hurt, though, as few emotions cut so deep and so ragged as jealousy, and I would never wish this woman such pain. And yet…

I stroke her back, thinking perhaps it is I who am jealous. All those hours she spends outside these walls, so many men she passes and meets who might smile at her, might ask her out. She grows more comfortable in her skin with every evening we share, more confident in her desires and her ability to give and receive affection and attention. A day could well come when she tires of her pretty tutor in his brick fishbowl.

I would have to upend my life to stand a chance at keeping her, making her mine. But as the weeks pass, it feels more and more as though losing her would be just as traumatic a change.

The worries gnaw at my bones with dull yellow teeth, but I press my lips to her hair so she won't see the evidence on my face.

My mother always said, "Show me a man who admits his love to a woman, and I'll show you a eunuch." She did not say this to me but to her friends, any number of times in my childhood. A grim gospel sung by a woman who still ached for a man, decades after their final caress. A man who never loved her back—a powerful man, by her philosophy. That notion always stayed in my mind, even as it depressed me. Keep a woman doubting your attachment and she will always work to earn it. Admit it, and your power over her evaporates.

I believe there is truth in that dismal mantra. It offers a power I've never craved, myself. A power I would never want to use against Caroly, if it meant letting her think I do not care.

I *do* wish her to keep wanting me, however, so I leverage the one power I'm comfortable wielding.

She smiles when I tip her onto her back and brace myself above her on my elbows. I part her thighs with my knees, one at a time. The worries fade as the promise of pleasure snakes through my body.

"Yes?"

"I like having you here," I say, and damn my mother's wisdom to hell.

"I like being here."

"Someday, you will outgrow this place."

"So you say. But I'd say the same to you." She has so much more faith in me than I do myself.

I lower my chest, drag my lips along her jaw. "You bloom wider and brighter each night we spend together," I murmur. "Someday these walls won't hold you anymore."

She doesn't speak, merely strokes my hair.

"But before that day comes, I will know your body so well, no other man will ever be able to make you forget me." My pulse quickens, stirring my cock.

"I wouldn't ever want to forget you."

A bleak but comforting thought crosses my mind. Should this be our last evening together, she will remember me as I am now, still young and handsome. Idealized in the most flattering snapshot. Perhaps that is the best way, for a man like me.

Her body has cooled. She's always cooler than I am, cool and smooth as a statue. When I hold her through the night I take pleasure in the way her skin warms, pressed to mine. There are so many things I cannot do for her, but I can do that. Warm her, please her.

I'm stiff and heavy against the crease of her thigh, and again I imagine a life in which I could simply push inside her, the formality of condoms forgotten. It's been almost a decade since I've enjoyed that intimacy with anyone, and the mere thought sets my flesh

188

throbbing. As always, we treasure the prizes that mock us the most cruelly.

I meet her gaze, then glance to the table beside the bed. "Would you?"

She knows where I keep the rubbers, and everything else in this room, things she's yet to request—toys, ties, oils. Those accessories only hold as much allure for me as the woman who asks for them, so with Caroly they are not missed. Though should she like to try on another woman's interests, some night not so long from now, I would be more than happy to introduce them.

She sheathes me with far more patience than I'd have mustered. When I sink inside her, I imagine the latex gone, nothing between our bare skin but her slickness. My hips want to race at the thought, but I command them to be slow and smooth, this sex as sensual and lazy as we've enjoyed on a Saturday afternoon once or twice.

"Are you sore?" I ask, setting a slow, easy tempo. Easy sex to hide the pain that tempers my lust.

She shakes her head, gaze focused between our bodies.

We are us again, Caroly and Didier—no roles. Merely two people enjoying one another's company and chemistry, a concept so simple, yet so miraculous.

The hands stroking my arms slide over my chest and down to my hips, urging. I let my body tell her the things my mouth isn't ready to voice, spreading my knees wider to own her deeply. Her nails graze my back, whisper-light.

"We're very good together, don't you think?" I look straight in her eyes as I ask the question. Sometimes she shies from such earnestness, but not tonight.

"I do." She smiles, and I can't help but mirror it. I bring my braced hands closer, butting them tight to her ribs. Those smooth thighs rise, hugging my hips. For these fleeting moments we feel like one person, and I think perhaps I could go outside just now. I could stroll barefoot through the bustle of a Paris evening without a care.

But in the wake of the sex I will misplace my courage, and when she coaxes me from the building tomorrow morning I'll be the man I know myself to be. We will order coffees and my cup will tremble as I raise it to my lips, clatter against its saucer as I set it down with a shaking hand. She will be sure to choose a table on the periphery, and though she'll make no announcement of it, I will know which chair is mine. I'll sit with my back to the wall, cataloguing each sudden sound, each patron, my temples throbbing with each of a million racing beats of my heart as I sip my way through twenty minutes that feel like a lifetime.

Here in bed, she is smiling up at me, her expression asking where I've gone—our bodies joined but my mind on worries still hours away. That will never do.

"Tell me how," I say.

"I'm not choosy."

"Tell me all the same."

She strokes my sides, gaze sweeping up and down my body. "Not fast or slow…just steady." She wants to watch, I know. And all at once, I want nothing more than to *be* watched.

As I find our pace, I think of how many years she spent getting herself off, imagining just this—a beautiful man in the throes of sex. She told me once how she rarely features in her own fantasies. Only men. Even in her head she fears she won't be desired. I hope now she conjures memories of us together, and that I've given her undeniable proof of how completely her lust is reciprocated. My cock turns greedy at the very thought.

Her breathing speeds with my thrusts and the nails begin to dig. I want them at my shoulders, or her fingers clutching my hair. I want her thighs at my ears and her heat against my tongue. I want to escape into her, to that fascinating realm between her thighs.

Her gaze is curious as I pull away.

"There is something I need."

I edge closer to the foot of the bed, dropping to my elbows to slide my forearms beneath her legs. Her lips gleam in the candlelight, and I'm high from her smell before I've even lowered my mouth to taste her. When I do, she sighs. The latex greets me first, but soon enough, only her. Juicy and lush as a peach from this evening's game, though her flavor never so cloying. The animal taste of sex, dark and alive, and I'm the man who made her this way. I lap it from her swollen folds with long, slow strokes, tracing with my tongue then suckling her clitoris. Cool hands on my neck, hot flesh pulsing between my lips.

"Didier." Nails scrape my scalp, but it's her voice that sets me shivering.

I kiss her deeply, excited to think no other man has tasted this. Unfair that a whore should revel in his partner's fidelity, I know, but I'm a man first, and selfish. With my tongue and mouth I tell her, *Just try to forget me. I won't make it easy.*

When she comes, I lap at her, drink her in until her legs twitch and the grasping hands on my shoulders plead for me to stop, the contact too intense.

She speaks through a hitching breath. "Come here."

So badly I want to be back inside her, to sink deep into the wetness I've coaxed…but I've no patience left for condoms. Her mouth is warm and wet as well, but I want to taste it more than I need to feel it around my cock. So I kiss her, leading her hand between my legs.

"How?" she asks against my lips.

I strip the rubber. "Slow and light, until I'm gasping."

She does exactly as asked, stroking my length with a whispering touch as we kiss. Heat and need and madness gather there, and I close my hand over hers, demanding friction. My mouth and fingers turn clumsy. Sighs become pleas then dissolve into moans as the pleasure finds its crescendo, until my release bastes her fingertips and belly. She kisses my chin as I catch my breath and reaches beside us for a cloth. By the time she casts it aside, I'm smiling like a madman.

She settles against my chest and as I stroke her hair I think, *I love this woman.* For her kindness, her oddness, for the way she looks at me. I love her for having come to seek me, and even more so for spurring me to seek *her*, out in the wider world. In the most literal sense, she has brought warm sunshine and cool breezes and the smell of grass and clover back into my life. And if that isn't love, I do not know what is.

I will tell her so…but not tonight.

Our bodies have already spoken the words in their carnal language. When I tell her, it will be outside. It's too easy to love inside this safe place, too easy to feel such things for most any woman who's invited me to spoil her rotten for an evening. I will tell Caroly someday soon. I'll tell her as I'm trembling, amid all those buildings and all those people, beneath that crushing sky. I will tell her when I am at my absolute worst, my least beautiful. And if she chooses to say it back, I will know she speaks the truth.

"Tomorrow," she says through a yawn.

"Yes?"

"We're not going to that café."

My heart seizes at the thought of leaving at all, then soars at the prospect of a morning's cowardly respite. A morning's safety, or perhaps a morning's pure and lazy pleasure, lolled away in bed with this woman before work calls her away. "Oh?"

She kisses my temple, then my ear, affectionate little gestures. "No. We're going to a different one."

"Oh."

"Farther away."

Another hitch in my chest. "How far?"

"Not as far as the museum, certainly."

The museum where she works was the first place I left my building to visit, to end my three years of domestic exile. It is halfway across the city, very far. But I took a taxi that afternoon, when the pain of missing Caroly trumped the comfort of the known. I shut my eyes and allowed another to ferry me.

Tomorrow we will walk. There will be crowds and noises, cars honking and rushing. Chaos, and a million opportunities for humanity to confirm for me how callous it is. Every shouted word will bring back a hundred catalogued taunts from my childhood. Every person streaming by who makes no eye contact, regards others as little more than obstacles. I'll see my mother in their detached, distracted faces. At every traffic light my memory will overlay the moment I saw a woman and child struck dead by a car. The world will prove itself as senseless and uncaring as I've always known it to be.

"It's not *super* far," Caroly adds, stroking my arm. "A kilometer, maybe. And a quiet kilometer, I promise. I picked it for all those reasons, with you in mind. And I'll walk you back, don't worry."

"That's very kind." Yet the frightened child in me does not agree. I'm being punished, he says. She wants to hurt and upset me, and when I fail she will mock me, abandon me and leave me out there in the city, no inner compass to guide me home.

I tell the voice to be quiet, because I *know* things, even if I don't feel them. I know she wants me to succeed at this. She wants me to be better. And though it stings my ego to admit I'm broken enough to warrant fixing, I've known that for years. I pull her closer and press my face to her throat. "We will go."

"Good. My treat."

"No, mine." Her elbow linked with my arm, her leading and reassuring me as one might an elderly blind relation…that is indulgence enough. I do not need my breakfast paid for.

"You'll do fine."

"I'll shake so badly people will think I'm having a seizure."

"You do that less and less every time we go out."

"Do I?"

"You do." She strokes my hair. "And you talk more and more."

"I hadn't noticed. I barely remember the moments of being out, once I'm home."

"Trust me, you're making progress."

I wait for words that never arrive, for gentle suggestions that I seek professional counsel, get a prescription and find normality in a bottle. But she never poses these solutions. After all, she treated her own anxiety regarding men by soliciting a prostitute. If I am her therapist, why shouldn't she be mine? I suppose that may be codependent, but I find my own inner workings far less enjoyable to diagnose and obsess over than those of my clocks and music boxes. She is welcome to make a hobby of me.

"You're progressing too," I tell her.

After a pause she murmurs, "Thank you."

I pull back to study her face. She wears a queer little smile, shy and proud at once. An ache rends my chest—so badly I wish I could say this was my girlfriend. My heart hurts as sharply as it does when I venture outdoors, only in slow motion. I press my forehead against her neck to hide my fear.

It is a strange sensation to lie in this bed, a woman's body against mine, and still suffer these insecurities. But Caroly's no longer my client, and when she's with me now I am only me, the faulty human, not the perfect man women pay me to be. It feels sometimes as though my skin has come off, as though she's peeled away my clothes and not stopped at exposing my mere nudity, but shed every layer straight down to my heart and nerves and bones. If she lets go, I might come apart.

The anxiety hurts, so I think of other things. I go inside her body in my mind's eye, and imagine all the places I might take her, within these walls. All the people we might become for an hour or two…women I've known and the man they wished me to play. There is no fear in these journeys, only excitement. I hold her tightly and, from the way her breathing hitches, I realize I've woken her.

"Go back to sleep."

"Okay," she mumbles, already slipping back into her dreams.

Dreams and clockwork and other people's fantasies, so many fascinating places to go without ever mustering the strength to open a door.

Tempting. Very tempting.

I keep a whore's hours, falling asleep late and rising around noon, but I can feel myself dropping off. Safe against her warm skin and beneath this sloping old roof, safe in my own dreams, if they prove kind tonight. The dawn will bring a stab of dread sharp as a knife, and I will be awake, so very awake. I will trade all this security for the tremors of bravery, led on halting feet like a kicked dog to some unknown destination. There will be coffee—decaffeinated, at Caroly's wise insistence, lest my heart jackhammer my ribs to dust. Its heat and flavor will go unregistered on my tongue, drowned out by the volume of the café, cranked to deafening levels by the echo chamber of my anxious brain.

Then I will look across the table, into those blue eyes. I'll find concern and patience there, but also pride. Pride in me for having come so far, and pride for being seen with me. Those eyes will tell me they're finding things in me I do not feel, like courage and potential and worthiness, and I'll try to believe in what they see. The noise will quiet and the activity will slow, if only for a breath or two. But a breath is all I need, just air in my lungs, blood moving through my body, proof that fear may hurt but it does not kill. Perhaps my shaking hand will find her slender, still one across the tabletop. She'll squeeze my fingers, happy somehow to be with this man, even at his worst.

I wonder if maybe that too is love—to feel fondness for a person's deepest flaws, to recognize beauty even in their least flattering portrait. It is what I see, looking back at me across those terrifying café tables, and suddenly, somehow, I'm looking forward to waking up tomorrow. To uncovering proof that someone might find my company worth keeping, even away from the candles and the calm.

I would walk a kilometer for that.

I would venture into the earth alone and cross Paris on the Métro, suffer the crush of a thousand strangers to believe that was true. To see it there, reflected back at me.

I may surprise her someday, show her exactly how far I might go.

Someday, I may even surprise myself.

CRAVING

THE CURIO VIGNETTES, PART II

1

"*Excusez-moi—quelle heure est-il?*"

It's twenty past seven, the young waitress replies. She eyes the empty seat across from me and the untouched second menu. I smile far too cheerfully as she refills my water glass. *He'll be here*, I tell myself. *He'll be here.*

He's late, but he'll be here.

Ten minutes later, the server gently asks if I might prefer to wait for my companion at the bar and let another party be seated.

He's nearly here, I tell her, praying it's true. I can't text him to check—he doesn't have a cell phone. He's not had use for one in several years.

The server walks away and I think, *I could go and find him.* There are only so many places he could be, a small area to cover. What if he's lost? What if he got hit by a car? What if he saw something that'll undo all the progress he's made?

No.

He'll be fine. If I went and got him it would undermine the entire design of this date. Worse, it would make him think I have as little faith in him as he does. Never.

Plus I made a reservation. I bought a new dress and set aside money specially for tonight's wine. Even if he keeps me waiting until midnight, I'm not leaving this table.

My waitress returns, her expression that mix of pity and contempt the French make look so stylish. Before she can suggest I'm a waste of space and free bread, I order a bottle of Grenache and two glasses. As she leaves, my date and I make eye contact across the restaurant.

My heart turns weightless and I smile, all forgiven in an instant. His own smile is tight as a sprung bear trap, but I knew it would be.

I stand as he arrives and we exchange cheek kisses, plus an extra one on the mouth. His hand trembles on my arm. He murmurs an apology but I don't even waste the energy to acknowledge it.

Normally I'd offer him the seat facing the room, with a clear view of every noise and movement that might unnerve him, but it's a table for two, the wall at our sides.

As we sit, I admire my date. I'm not the only one. People will be wondering, *Is that...?* But they'll fail to supply the name of a famous actor, because although Didier's too handsome to be plausible, my date isn't famous.

Infamous, perhaps, but only in small circles. A former artists' model, presently a prostitute. Also a severe agoraphobe, though no one looking would likely notice the menu fluttering in his quaking hands, the way he swallows too often, the taut tendons along his throat buttressing a clenched jaw. All they would see is a striking face, lush dark hair, seductive brown eyes, a pleasing frame filling out a crisp dress shirt.

Before we met, that was all I expected to find in him—that, and a sexual education. And when we did meet, it was I who was frightened and out of her depth, thinking him some perfect, confident creature.

He intimidated me just as the chaos of the outside world intimidates him, though I'm not naive enough to believe he'll find ease with his disorder in a matter of weeks, as I have with my inhibitions.

I let him settle in silence, knowing the journey was tough. This is the first time I've asked him to meet me somewhere, as opposed to us going together.

I chose this restaurant because it's only four blocks from his flat. A ten-minute stroll for most anyone, though Didier Pedra isn't most anyone, and he was nearly an hour late. I drew him a map and listed useful landmarks along the journey. *Turn left after the store with the beehive on its sign. Keep going straight at the intersection with the Métro station.*

I'm mindful to always be patient, because I know that when he ventures outside, the anxiety is so chemically intense he might as well be intoxicated. If you escort him, you have to speak clearly and calmly. You wait for a WALK signal at every new street, even if there are no cars in sight and pedestrians are slipping past on all sides, safely jaywalking. When a crossing doesn't have a WALK signal and you have to rely on cars to halt at stop signs, I swear you can hear Didier's heart beating, stark as a metronome.

The waitress returns, seeming surprised that a) I wasn't stood up and b) my date is so undeniably worth waiting for. Suddenly friendly, she pours us each a glass of the wine. I know Didier won't be very hungry, so I order three hors d'oeuvres for us to share, the waitress shooting my companion curious glances as she scribbles.

Part of me wishes he appeared a bit more enthusiastic to be here. From the outside we must look like a couple on the verge of a breakup, me the cheerfully oblivious soon-to-be dumpee. But fuck what people think. Behind closed doors in the safety of the familiar, he's warm and kind and wonderful. Not my boyfriend—his occupation doesn't allow such an easy label. But he's my first and only lover, my friend, and what feels more and more like a partner as the weeks pass.

Just now he's as comfortable as an arachnophobe crawling with tarantulas, but I look past the fear to find his beauty, and past his beauty to all the fascinating depths beneath his skin.

He stares at his glass and takes a stilted breath, then another, and finally one deep enough to catch in his chest, always a good sign. He blows it out, smiling weakly, and meets my eyes.

"Hello." I speak as though he's just arrived, because in a sense he has.

"Good evening." He nods around us, the gesture a flimsy imitation of ease. "This is lovely."

"I've never been, but my coworker says the food is amazing." Though as an American transplanted from a dirt-poor patch of northern New Hampshire, I trust everything I'm fed in Paris is delicious, as long as it's overpriced and hard to pronounce and comes with a cloth napkin.

"You said we have something to celebrate," Didier says.

I pick up my glass and he does the same, and for a moment curiosity distracts him from anxiety. That warrants a toast in itself. "I have good news. I got promoted."

Oh, that smile. He's forgotten the restaurant and its noises and sudden movements, beaming pure happiness at me.

"That's wonderful!" We clink our glasses. "Do you get a new title?"

I swallow the first sip, shutting my eyes to savor the tart, sharp red on my tongue before speaking. Setting the glass down, I say, "I do. I'm going to be the assistant to the director." It's a funny diagonal step up from assistant curator at the museum where I work, but it means that in another year's time, I may get to see my name listed as regular old unadulterated curator in an exhibit program.

"I don't get my own office or anything, but they're giving me a nice raise." A *very* nice raise, enough to move me to a larger flat if I don't blow it all on fancy food and fancy clothes and gifts for my fancy French not-a-boyfriend.

"That's excellent news. Congratulations."

"Thank you. And we've got something else to celebrate as well."

"Oh?"

I gesture at him, sitting here before me. "No taxi, right? And no escort."

He nods and I catch him blushing, a rare sight indeed. It makes my own cheeks heat in return.

"I was terribly late."

"But you're here. That's enough. Punctuality's a goal for the future."

"I froze at the postboxes." I picture him there, immobilized beside the bank of narrow brass doors in his building's foyer. "For twenty minutes. Maybe thirty. Neighbors came and went, and I pretended to be checking my pockets for something. And when I did leave I got lost, though I couldn't tell you how or where."

"But you un-froze, and you got yourself un-lost."

"I suppose."

"So *salut* to that," I say forcefully, and we toast a second time. "How do you feel now?"

He glances to his side, dark eyes darting at the activity all around us. "Better. Stable." His hands have stopped trembling, though now they're unnaturally rigid like his shoulders. Still, a good sign.

"What did you do today?" I ask. It's a Friday, and I wonder if he woke with another woman in his bed.

I try not to think too hard about his clients and, when I inevitably do, to not find them threatening. When I feel jealous I remind myself they've never crouched at the edge of the sidewalk, stroking Didier's hair until he stopped hyperventilating. Many know he's a shut-in—for years he's relied on his clients to run errands so he could stay inside. He's very easy to be kind to. But none of them have seen him as I do. They've seen him naked, seen him turned-on and watched him come, but I know him even more intimately. I've seen him so scared I swear I could hear his bones rattling, and I wouldn't trade the shivering baby bird for its pretty shell, never in a hundred years.

"I did laundry," he tells me.

I blink, surprised. "Did you?"

He nods and the food arrives. The second the waitress is gone I gape at him. "At the launderette around the corner?"

Another nod. It's scarcely a thirty-second walk, but when we met he was lucky if he made it downstairs to check his mail twice a week. This is *huge*.

"Wow. You left two times in one day."

His smile is full of shy pride. "I did."

"That's amazing. How was it, doing laundry?"

"Quiet. Nearly pleasant, I suppose, once I caught my breath."

He tells me about a little girl who was there with her mother, how she helped him pair his socks. The vision sets dangerous creatures prowling in my reproductive jungle. That never used to happen, but since I turned thirty and discovered I can interact with a handsome man without getting sick to my stomach… It's all very treacherous down there of late. But it's nothing. Biological insanity. A byproduct of my age and overexposure to Didier's pheromones or something.

Provided he never had to go outside, Didier would be a wonderful father—doting and patient and loving. Provided I… Well, in no scenario do I suspect I'd make a good mother. Karma would come collecting, landing me with a child as callous and volatile as I was growing up. I also worry it might be saddled with my mom's bipolar disorder, my social awkwardness or Didier's crippling anxiety, or his late mother's depression, or all of these things.

Plus it's only been a few months since I started seeing him without having to pay for the privilege. He's not my boyfriend. He's far from monogamous, exceptional as our relationship is. I'm stupid in love with him and not thinking straight, and theorizing about the children we shouldn't have is an exercise in extreme delusion. Stupid brainwashing ovaries.

We sample the various hors d'oeuvres and moan our delight. Sipping his wine, Didier motions frantically with a hand, as if he's remembered something important he meant to tell me. He swallows and blurts, "You look beautiful."

"Oh, thank you." I look down at my dress, all my guilt over its price melting away at his three little words. Three little words he needed to say so urgently he nearly choked.

"I noticed right away, but…"

"It's fine. Your head was someplace else. You look nice too."

He looks far better than nice. He looks as if he stepped out of the window dressing of a shop in the Rive Droite. I've grown so used to him barefoot and in jeans that seeing him in a dress shirt, open at the throat…I feel that same giddy excitement from the first night we met. He shaved today too. I love him all rumpled and casual, as if he's just rolled out of bed, so he usually skips on days when we have a date. But I like how dapper he's looking tonight. We both look nice, as if we belong in this fancy restaurant. I know we're only playing dress-up, but I also know that everyone else here is doing just the same. Everyone's a mess underneath, but it's fun to put on costumes and play tourist in elegant places.

I tell him about my new duties at the museum as we eat then the waitress corks and bags the half-empty bottle so we can take it with us. For what it cost we ought to be allowed to keep the stemware.

Didier holds the door for me as we leave, looking like six feet of well-feigned calm. The June evening is cool and smells of spring. I breathe it in, glad to leave the noise and warmth of the restaurant behind. But as my body relaxes, Didier's surely tenses. He told me once how the open sky feels like a smothering blanket above him, the buildings like fingers, poised to curl in and strangle him. I take his hand to begin the harrowing journey back to his place.

When we reach the first intersection, I ask him which way to go. He stares at the storefronts for an extraordinarily long time, like someone trying to makes sense of words written in a made-up language. As if he hasn't lived in this neighborhood for over a decade, or this city his entire life.

"Straight," he finally says. "Straight at the Métro station."

I squeeze his hand and smile, and when the sign tells us to walk, we follow his directions to the next busy block.

We pass innumerable people and some of their gazes linger. A couple months ago I'd have told myself, *They're staring because they can't understand why on earth he's with you.* But getting frequently and thoroughly laid has been good for my ego, and though those thoughts do still poke and whisper, I can shrug them off. If people stare it's because Didier's extraordinary looking. Being the one holding his hand makes me feel as though I'm wearing the most beautiful dress in the world. It makes *me* feel beautiful. Makes me walk taller, as if someone were filming us.

An elegant woman walking a dog smiles at me. *"C'est une jolie robe."*

I stutter a *"Merci"* and cast my dress another appreciative glance.

Didier's thumb rubs my palm. When I look to my side I find him smirking.

"Don't look so shocked," he teases.

I *am* shocked though. Everything pales next to Didier. This dress must be magical to warrant notice with him so close by. I try to remember if it came in any other patterns. If it does, I'll buy one of each.

The first dress I recall owning was a hand-me-down from a cousin, a swishy satin thing she'd gotten for a wedding. I'd thought it was the most glamorous garment ever made, and couldn't believe the shining lavender jewel of a gown was suddenly *mine.* I wore it on picture day in fifth grade, imagining it'd trick my classmates into forgetting I was weird and mean, white trash, that I shuffled through the halls in the same three faded, frayed outfits week in and week out. They'd see me in that dress and think I was bound for Hollywood. If only my parents could afford the cool laser background for my school photos…but that cost an extra four bucks.

My dad was a garbage man then, usually gone hours before I woke. He's a kindhearted guy. If he'd been there that morning, maybe he'd have gently asked if I really wanted to wear that dress to school. I don't remember my mom saying a word about it, though it wasn't rare to come home at three and find her still in bed.

At the time I was madly in love with Jeremy Fournier, the cutest boy in my class. He passed me by the lockers and said, "Nice dress, Aardvark." That was my nickname, a devilish bit of ten-year-old wordplay combining my last name, Evardt, and my general homeliness. Oblivious spaz that I was, I spent the day thinking he'd meant it. By sixth period, I'd already planned our wedding. It wasn't until I was home that night, undressing, that I gave any thought to the fact that all the other girls wore their coolest jeans and skirts and trendy sweaters for picture day.

Occam's razor cut me then, and I realized I'd been the unwitting victim of sarcasm. It became the first social cue I taught myself to diagnose, and as it turned out, I had many opportunities.

Didier's hand is damp against mine, pulling me from my old, dusty worries to his current ones. He breathes through his nose—it seems to help him avoid hyperventilating—and I can hear the odd inhalation, wheezy and desperate. I glance at him in the streetlights. His eyes jump everywhere, searching for danger. I know his mind is a half block ahead of us, already dreading the next street crossing.

But we make it to number sixteen Rue des Toits Rouges without incident, and though his keys jangle as he unlocks the inside foyer door, relief is written all over that stunning face. Being outside is like holding his breath underwater and now he's finally breached the surface.

Neither of us trusts the creaky old elevator in his building, so we hike up four flights, winded as we reach flat 5C. Inside Didier sheds his fear like a jacket, hanging it beside the door for the next time I make him leave. The surety returns to his posture and gait, and from the couch I watch him putter for a few minutes, in awe of the transformation.

He brings me a glass of the wine and sets his own on the coffee table.

"Thanks. Can I ask you something?"

"Always." He sits and unlaces his shoes.

"Have you ever considered moving out of Paris? To somewhere calmer, with less traffic and fewer people? It seems strange you've chosen to live in such a crowded and chaotic city, and so close to its center." Not that I want him to leave—quite the opposite. But I've always wondered what keeps him here, like someone who's afraid of drowning living on a houseboat. Maybe the thought of making a jump for the dock is just too terrifying.

He pushes off one shoe, then the other, blinking thoughtfully. "I suppose I never considered it a choice."

"No?"

"This city has always felt like a spider's web to me. This is just where I landed."

Where he got entangled. It's only fitting, considering what a struggle it is for him to move from thread to thread, always seeing shadows scuttling out of the corner of his eye.

"I wasn't always this bad," he reminds me. He was functional up until his mother passed away three years ago. "By the time I *was* this bad, I was attached to this flat. And to my job, and my routines."

"Of course."

"This is all I know." His mother was agoraphobic as well and rarely took him beyond the city limits. Paris constituted what a psychologist would call her "safe zone", and it sounds as though she managed well enough inside its bounds. Checking on her had been Didier's main outside obligation toward the end of her illness, and his safe zone quickly shrank to the size of his flat after she died.

He shrugs. "I've been to the countryside and the ocean, and to Portugal when I was young. But nowhere outside Paris since I was seventeen. And not outside the Latin Quarter since my mother's funeral. Except that trip to your museum."

"That counts."

He sighs, and I feel badly. I forced him into exposure therapy for the sake of our date, and now I'm grilling him about his life choices. We're in the only place where he gets to feel secure, and I'm opening a window to let his troubles blow inside and disturb the calm.

I remember something, a convenient distraction to take the edge off our conversation. "I got you a gift."

"Oh?" That brightens his expression, and I know he expects a clock or watch or some other broken refugee from a thrift shop. It's something a bit different, and I feel my chest tighten, hoping he'll like it.

I lean over the couch's arm for my tote and fetch a drawstring bag, heavy and lumpy, and a flat, wrapped box.

He accepts them with a raised eyebrow and I settle closer beside him.

"Open the bag first."

He tugs the bow loose and uncinches the mouth, draws out an old padlock, then another, and two more. He studies the final one and gives me a curious look.

"Now open the box."

He strips its paper and lifts the lid, taking out what looks like a thin leather-bound journal. He frees the tie, unfolding the case in quarters to reveal two dozen small, gleaming instruments, slender steel rods each in its own tiny pocket, and all with different heads—diamond shapes and circles and hooks.

For a moment he stares, then the warmest laugh tumbles from his mouth. He holds one of the locks up and smiles at me. "No keys, then?"

"I have the keys. I had to make sure none of them were rusted shut or broken. And I'm not cruel, so there's one more thing." I reach for my bag one last time to retrieve the book I had to special order, a slim guide to lock-picking.

"Yes, this would be useful." He flips through a few pages, his gaze catching on this diagram and that. He loves the insides of complex objects, queer little puzzles in need of solving. Hours a day he sometimes spends fixing broken things, and it doesn't take a psychiatrist to find the metaphor. He sees himself as broken, and I don't like that. There's no perfect shining part you can order that'll make him tick like a so-called normal person. I'd prefer he see himself as a keyless lock—a conundrum, but one that can be solved with patience and gentle experimentation.

He inspects one of the instruments.

"Do you like it?"

"I do." As he stares at the largest lock, I know what he's thinking. He wants to see inside and understand how it works.

"I bet they're really hard to take apart. To look inside, I mean."

"One would hope so. I will just have to work blind, I suppose. And see with my hands and ears and these little tools." He sets the items aside. "Thank you."

My face heats when he kisses me. When we part, I have to purse my lips to keep my grin from growing too wide and goofy. "You're welcome."

"You spoil me."

"I try to."

"It's I who should be spoiling you, to celebrate your good news."

"You didn't know."

"I know now." He smiles, slow and devious. "Perhaps I'll find some other way to treat you."

"Perhaps you will." I sip my wine, liking the way he looks at me. Liking *him*, just being with him. If this *is* my first boyfriend, our romance doesn't look like how I'd pictured it when I was that gawky mantis in Goodwill clothes. Our courtship is short on carnations and prom dresses, surprisingly heavy on the wine and antiques and orgasms. I missed out on getting groped in the cab of some redneck hockey player's truck, but here I am in Paris, about to be taken to bed by a man so good-looking and so skilled at sex women pay for the chance to enjoy him for a night.

My first love came half a lifetime later than I'd hoped, and though it may look a bit twisted from the outside, I wouldn't trade it for anything.

Didier takes a deep drink then asks, "Would you like to play another game tonight?"

I nod, suddenly shy. It's been a couple weeks since our first such game—exploring the sorts of things other women come to him to experience. I know he fuses past and present clients together, composites them into anonymity so he can indulge my desire to eavesdrop on their fantasies. Two weeks ago we went further than just storytelling, acting out the scenario. It was exciting, trying on another woman's kinks. My own sexuality is still forming, and before it gels I want to sample as many people's appetites as I can.

"What sort of game, do you think?" he asks.

"I'm not sure." I cuddle closer, pressing my arm to his and taking another sip. I wish we had a fireplace, just now. I wish we were in some tiny stone vacation cottage in Provence or somewhere, with a hearth and stars and crickets. I wish lots of things, but I know not to hold my breath.

"Tell me about some of your clients. About the ones with the most unusual requests."

"I find very little unusual, when it comes to sex," he murmurs, but there's distraction in his tone—he's already browsing his memories for stories I've yet to hear.

He swirls his wine, speaking to his glass, it seems. "I had a client for a while who only wished to come here and do what we are now." He drapes a warm, strong arm behind my shoulders. "For hours we would just sit or lie together, and I'd hold her. We would kiss, very softly, but for so long my lips would grow tender."

"Never anything more?"

"For hours we would do that, and sometimes I would tell her how much I wished we could do more. Be naked together. Touch each other. Make love. She wanted me to say these things, but she would never go any further. Then she'd tell me she had to go home, and we would say goodnight and she'd leave me alone in my bedroom. She would pretend to go, but stay just outside my door, watching from the darkness while I masturbated."

"Oh." I hadn't seen that coming.

"We would pretend this was what happened after she left, that she had me so excited and frustrated I couldn't wait for relief."

"And that was it?"

"That was it. I would give her the show she wanted, and after I came I would hear her quiet footsteps and the front door would click shut for real. That was all she ever asked of me. And after perhaps a dozen visits in as many weeks, she never made another appointment."

"Wow." Here I'd thought *I* was the repression poster girl.

"And ages ago I had another client, a violin teacher. When she was a few years older than you, she'd had a student in another city, a young man of about fifteen, the son of a close friend. She spent two years so infatuated with him and so disturbed by it, she ended up moving to Paris, where she wouldn't have to see him. It hurt, she wanted him so badly. And the feelings didn't go away. She came to me many years later, wishing to pretend I was her old student."

"To pretend you were a teenager?"

"Sometimes. Sometimes to pretend she was giving in to her attraction. Educating a young man in far more than the violin."

"Ah."

"More often she wished me to simply be the age that I was, roughly as old as her student would have been. She would have us pretend to have met after those years of separation, me finally a man grown, and one who'd secretly pined for her with the same ferocity and heartache that she had for him."

"Gosh. That's kind of romantic." And kind of heartbreaking... Mostly heartbreaking. But all the best romances are tragedies, I've always felt.

Didier smiles suddenly, melancholy lifting like a blind. "And I used to have a client whose only appetite was to baste my cock with honey or sweetened cream and suck me clean, again and again."

A shock of pleasure contracts deep in my belly. Didier raises a playful eyebrow at me, one that says, *I have a very strange job, don't you think?*

So many women he's been with, with so many tastes I've never even conceived of. And I have a good imagination.

I picture the chest that sits at the foot of his beautiful old bed. It's not off-limits, but I've only ever peeked inside when he's in the shower, and afterward wondered if he noticed my acting shifty and shy upon his return.

The chest is full of toys, as he readily told me. I was his client then, after all, and those toys were as much for me as any other visitor to flat 5C. I was also a virgin at the time, though I owned a vibrator. An unassuming, minimalist thing with a few speeds that I only ever used to stimulate my clit. Now I never use it, too spoiled by what Didier can do to me. Kind of like how I used to love Kraft Singles, but now that I've tasted fresh chevrotin from Haute-Savoie, it's painful to imagine going back.

It took me a long time to work up the nerve to look inside the chest, and I hadn't found what I'd expected. Garish stuff—that's what I'd imagined, but actually many of the items look like art objects. No neon colors or veiny rubber dicks of frightening proportions. Beautiful things. There was a paddle made of beech and honey-colored leather, silk scarves as nice as you'd find at a boutique, a glass dildo swaddled lovingly in a soft towel. There were quite a few rolled towels, but I had a vision of snooping too clumsily and Didier walking in from the shower to find me blushing with shards of cock littering the floor at my feet, so I hadn't peeked inside more than a couple.

The only thing in there that's truly haunted me is what I know must be a strap-on. Given that he has a perfectly serviceable cock of his own and all his clients lack that apparatus, I can only assume it's for… Well, for stuff I don't entirely get.

"You know the chest, by your bed?"

He smiles, a weird little smile I've only rarely seen him wear, all mischievous, like he ought to be licking his lips. It makes me want to smile myself.

"Yes," he prompts.

"What do your clients like to do with…you know. The stuff in there."

"Their tastes vary as widely as the objects. Have you looked inside?"

I nod, blushing.

"Did anything spark your curiosity?"

The strap-on springs to mind, but that's more confusion than curiosity. "I only saw the stuff on top, really. I was afraid I'd put things back messily and you'd know I looked."

"Did you think I'd be upset that you looked?"

"No, I was just embarrassed. Or afraid you'd think I was interested in something I wasn't ready for."

"But now you bring it up, so does this mean maybe you're interested?"

Pandora's box, my brain whispers. What if we open it up and I find out I'm some crazy kinky woman, with weird fetishes no regular man will ever abide? Or worse, find out I'm utterly, incurably vanilla and be stuck worrying that for this man who probably maintains a rotation of a dozen or more regular lovers at a given time, no one woman could ever provide enough variety?

But I didn't come to this flat—not tonight or that first evening, back in March—looking to maintain my sexual status quo.

I drain my glass, nodding as I swallow. "I think I am."

II 🔑

In the bedroom, Didier lights candles and draws the curtains, blocking out the twinkly skyline and the round shapes of roosting pigeons. I sit cross-legged at the edge of the bed, fidgeting with my nails.

"I will show you what I have," he says, setting a chair before me then hefting Pandora's sex-toy chest onto the chair. "If something sparks your interest, perhaps you would like to hear about the sort of woman who requests it?"

"Sure."

"And if our bodies end up being all we need from each other tonight, then we are not so very unfortunate, no?" He gives me a teasing look, quieting my buzzing nerves some.

"Sounds good."

He sits, leaving room between us, and leans forward to open the lid. "Here. You choose, my little curator."

I smile at that. It does feel a bit like opening a crate of new arrivals at the museum, and my anxiety turns to giddiness. I choose a rolled towel, unfolding the soft terrycloth to reveal the same smooth glass dildo I'd peeked at weeks ago.

"I saw this one. It's beautiful." It's crystal-clear save for a ribbon of deep blood-red spiraling through the core. There's the vague suggestion of a head, but other than that it's pretty innocuous, an eight-inch cylinder, slightly curved and slightly tapered. I turn the gleaming glass around in my hands so the candles' glow lights it from within. Knowing Didier, caring for these objects goes far beyond the chores of sterilization. I bet he polishes this glass reverently with a soft cloth, oils any leather he owns, buffs any brass or copper rivets the way he dotes on his precious watches and clocks. I bet he wraps them in the cleanest, fluffiest towels and stows them gently, as if putting them to bed.

I pass him the dildo. "Do lots of your clients like that one?"

"They do. I like it as well. If I'm in charge of choosing, I often pick this one."

I hadn't thought of that—surely many of his clients would leave the decisions up to him. I remember what we did the last time we pretended to be other people. He's perfectly capable of taking charge. He's perfectly capable of being whatever a woman wants.

"Do…"

"Yes?"

"Do any of your clients ever…" I stare at the dildo. "Have any of them ever used it, you know…"

"On me?"

I swallow, nodding.

"They have."

"Do you like it?"

"If it excites the woman I'm with, then it excites me."

Of course, that old refrain. I've heard it a dozen times or more, and I don't know why it rubs me wrong. I suppose because it makes me feel incidental, wrecks any starry-eyed belief I want to hold that he and I are perfectly suited.

"But it feels good?" I ask.

He nods. "Physically, yes, with the right preparation. And psychologically… It's a bit like a drug, I suppose. Not that I have very much experience with such things."

"How so?"

He eyes the glass. "You start to tinker with dynamics as basic as who is penetrated…you feel a bit out of control, but also uninhibited. It's like Halloween, perhaps. It feels awfully wicked, modifying your identity for a little while. Shunning what society expects of you."

"What does the woman get out of it, do you think?"

He looks thoughtful. "I think for some it is simply a kink, picked up from who knows where."

I nod. I'm not a stranger to gay pornography. In fact, it's the only kind I've really watched much of, since the men tend to be far nicer looking and there aren't any women for me to compare myself to. And I'd be lying if I said it didn't turn me on, beyond the mere presentation of naked, aroused men. The idea of a guy getting sodomized doesn't turn me off, but…

I glance at Didier, the man who embodies my entire non-solo sex life. He's always been my teacher in this, the one who knows what he's doing, and me the vessel. I'm not ready to see him as a vessel, so I reach for another object and a change of topic.

"What about this?" I ask, turning the paddle around in my hand. Its blond wood grip is perfectly weighted, full of authority, the business end made of thick leather, flaring out like a fish tail. It's not too big, only as broad as a spatula. Not too scary. "Do you use this a lot?"

"Fairly often."

"On your clients *and* on you?"

"Yes, both. Typically the former, if only because typically women's appetites tend to lean toward the submissive."

It's weird to hear him talk about bondagey things. I always knew he must dabble in that, but he and I have always been so…basic. All at once I feel very naive. "How hard?"

"Depends," he says, taking the paddle from me, studying it as though he's never seen such a thing before.

I imagine him using it on me. I've felt his palm before—not very hard, but a sharp little slap on my hip once or twice when he was behind me. I liked how it felt. Like a kiss of pain and heat, but even better because I never asked him for that. It was proof he has desires that don't hinge on a woman's express request.

"I'm interested in that one," I say, and set it elsewhere on the bed. "And maybe these." I draw a pair of silk ties from the box and set them beside the paddle. It's liberating, choosing things, admitting to being curious. And it's fun, like shopping. I'm good at shopping.

The next item that draws my eye is a fabric box, not unlike the kind that a pair of steel meditation balls might come in. I undo its brass latch and metal does indeed wink at me in the candlelight, though it takes me a second or two to realize what the objects are.

There's a glass one and several in copper and steel, different sizes. In this felt-lined box they seem like chess pieces, but even a sexual neophyte like me knows better. I wish I knew whatever the French term for these is, as anything is bound to sound more elegant than "butt plug".

I turn one around in each hand, liking the weight of a copper one particularly.

"Do you know what those are?"

"Yeah."

"Are you curious?"

"I think so." The idea of heterosexual anal sex makes me cagey. It used to strike me as a misogynist's appetite, though since Didier began educating me, my old prudish opinions have softened. Plus, I think, studying the plug, these don't scare me. "They're pretty."

"My little magpie," he teases.

"Do you use these too?"

"I do."

"Because a woman asks for it, or just because it feels good, or ..?"

"Both."

"Huh. Which size is good for, you know. A beginner?"

He reaches over and draws a shiny steel one from the box, handing it to me. The base is spherical, the insertion end shaped like the kind of oversized Christmas bulb you put in a fake window candle. It has a pleasing heft to it, and I set it with the paddle and scarves. "What about for yourself?"

He sorts through the choices, as one might deliberate over a sampler of chocolates. I'm handed a copper one—a bit bigger, but nothing crazy.

Didier eyes my pile of goodies and smiles. "Ambitious."

I suppose it is. But as well as I've done keeping my jealousy at bay, knowing the man I love fucks other women... Suddenly faced with a chest full of things he doesn't get to enjoy with me, a competitive female gland has grown enflamed.

I doubt I'll ever be some wild, insatiable nympho. I've got much too noisy a brain for that. But I'd like to be adventurous, open to things, and Didier's very easy to be open with. Deep in my insecure heart, I want to be as good a lover to him as I can be, so if by some astounding feat of witchcraft he should ever want to be mine, just mine, I can feel confident that settling for me doesn't mean he's giving up anything he likes in bed. Though that's impossible, since he's probably done just about everything, short of some real Marquis de Sade-level shit. Still, I want to aim high, and yes, I *am* feeling ambitious.

I close and latch the box and set it in the chest.

"Anything else?" he asks.

"I think we've got plenty to start with."

"I'd add two things, if you would permit me."

I raise my eyebrows, curious, but he doesn't lean forward for the chest. Instead he leaves the bed altogether, disappearing from the bedroom. I hear him in the kitchen, the faucet running, then the clicking of a gas burner before it lights. Perhaps he's boiling water to sterilize some special toy?

He returns empty-handed and rifles through the chest, setting a satin sleep mask beside me with a smile. The chest is shut and returned to its place, and he leaves again. I toy with the mask's elastic strap, faking patience while he putters in the kitchen for another two or three minutes. There's the low whistle of the kettle, a crinkling noise, then silence. Finally he returns, though the steaming mug in his hand doesn't do much to solve the mystery.

I squint at the tag dangling from its rim. "Is that some kind of aphrodisiac tea or something?"

"It's peppermint."

"Oh."

Without explanation, he sets it on the table near the condoms and tosses a clean towel on the foot of the bed. He sits, hands clasped atop his shins, and I shuffle around to face him. His smile is slow and warm, melting away my lingering misgivings. He's excited. My calm, unflappable lover looks like a boy ready to open his presents and a grin hijacks my lips too.

"I have no clue what I'm doing," I remind him, gesturing at the pile. "Do you mind leading?"

"Of course not."

I expect my sensitive sex coach to preamble our game with his usual reassuring wisdom, but he doesn't. Instead he gets to his knees and crawls to me, urging me to lie back.

My heart swells, growing heavy and hot between my ribs. There's his familiar weight and warmth above me, the gentle shove of his legs spreading mine and driving my dress up. Somewhere in my body I'm excited, but another sensation is stronger. He tucks his forearms to my ribs and it occurs to me, as it so often does, that this is my man. Maybe he's not my boyfriend, maybe he's not only mine to kiss and caress and sleep beside, but he's the one I want, and the one I get, strings or no. The most handsome, elegant, kind man I've ever met, and he wants to be with me.

I hug my calves to his hips and accept his kiss. He feels so right, I actually could cry. I feel the sting behind my nose. I spent my entire adulthood terrified of good-looking men because the pain of wanting one—of loving one—and being rejected or discarded would surely destroy me. Now I have one, and he wants me back. It'll hurt when things end. It'll hurt if he's the one to end them. The pain will be as terrible as the pleasure has been exquisite, but I don't want to spend my life missing out on pleasure just to avoid pain. It's no way to live. Like never feeling the sun on your face because you can't bear to risk getting rained on.

Rain dries. Heartache fades. The sun shines, whether you're outside or not. You may as well tilt your head up and enjoy it while it lasts.

Inside my body, the warm sun is setting, a mischievous moon rising. Our sweet kisses deepen and darken and Didier presses close, brushing his erection against my pubic bone. I cup his face and welcome his tongue, dig my heels into his ass in time with the thrusts I want. He gives them, rubbing me through my panties and his slacks, long drags that remind me how big he is, how hard he gets, how it feels when I welcome him inside. How he sounds and smells and tastes. How much he wants me.

He wants me.

I slip my hand between us, letting his stiff length stroke my palm as he keeps his hips working. When I squeeze, the softest moan interrupts our kiss.

He speaks against my mouth. "Let me undress you."

He drops back on his knees and I sit up, arching so he can draw the zipper down my spine. I lay back and his dark eyes dart as he eases the dress over my shoulders, down my arms, exposing my bare breasts. His lips part. The stretchy fabric skims my belly and he slides it from my hips. I tuck my legs up and he strips it away along with my underwear. They were cute panties, new ones, but he'll see them some other night.

He covers my naked body with his clothed one, teasing my skin with a whisper of cotton, the kiss of buttons, the cool press of his belt buckle. The hot, hard insistence of his cock behind his fly.

His lips and tongue trace my throat, his moans hot and low. In French he tells me, "I want you. So much."

"I want you." I've never *not* wanted him. Even in the moments when he frustrates me, I would never wish I were elsewhere. He's a hundred things to a hundred women, a different pretty bauble reflecting their unique tastes. But he's my kaleidoscope. I want to keep turning him, discovering new patterns, seeing him through new eyes.

"Show me the things other women want from you." *And what you want from them, so I can be everything. So I can maybe, just maybe, be enough.*

Without a word he leaves the bed, standing before me in the low light. I sit up. A button is freed, exposing a slice of his chest, then another. Two more and the shirt falls away. My hearts speeds as it always does in the face of beauty, how I imagine a hunter's pulse races when he spots a buck, how a wine lover's mouth tingles as she twists the corkscrew. Didier opens his belt with those deft, capable fingers, sheds his trousers and kicks them aside. His cock is hugged in the boxer briefs he favors, a single spot of wetness darkening the cloud-gray silk.

He's more perfect than any man has a right to be. I suspected as much the moment I laid eyes on a photo of him. Now that I've made him laugh, kissed him as he slept, soothed him as he trembled in a crumpled, heaving heap…now I know it.

There's no show tonight. No teasing strokes of his hidden cock to make me crazy with impatience. He strips his shorts and joins me on the bed, guiding us onto our sides and locking our legs. He's stiff and ready at the crease of my thigh, but we touch each other's faces and hair, taste each other's mouths for five minutes or more. The space between our chests grows warm and damp, and he breaches it to graze his palm over my breast. My nipple draws tight, my breath coming short. He tugs me closer by the hip, belly to belly, then his hand cups my butt. He kneads me there, traces the cleft softly.

"Do as I do," he says.

I stroke his ass, as firm as mine is soft. When he rubs, I rub. When his nails rasp, mine rasp. When his fingertips slip between my cheeks I do the same to him, and it smoothes the edges of the anxiety I knew I'd feel. He's touched me there before, just casual glances as he gave me head. I've never touched him that way, but when his fingers find the spot, I mirror them. A warm sigh heats my lips and the last of my nerves dissolve. We're two people, two bodies giving and receiving equally.

His caress turns firmer, more focused. I mimic it. Because he's taking pleasure in this, I can relax and do the same. His hips flex, stroking his cock against my belly and guiding my touch. His moans are deep and needy, and I let myself imagine the things that unnerve me. I picture how his face might look as someone violates him, eyes shut tight in the pleasure-pain of taboo, mouth open, brows drawn.

It's not so wrong, I think. Or maybe it *is* so wrong—so wrong it might be hot.

He stops us suddenly. I study his cock when he peels our sweat-sticky bodies apart, and it looks as hard and flushed as I've ever seen. His muscles clench as he twists behind to grab a bottle from the table. With its eyedropper he drips mineral oil onto my fingertips, then his. He's lost his grace, setting the bottle down with a sharp knock and pulling me close, rougher than before.

"I want more," he breathes. I'm unsure which he wants more of—touching me there or being touched, but I don't care. I love when his civility cracks and I catch glimpses of the animal prowling underneath.

I wait for his lead. I feel embarrassed and intimidated by his slippery fingers, roaming in such a *personal* place. But only for a moment. I do the same to him and there's no spotlight on me anymore. I'm not having things done *to* me. What we do, we do together. When I feel the pressure of his fingertip, I take as deep a breath as I can and give him the same.

I'm grateful my lover's no roughneck with raspy palms or ragged nails. Didier's calluses are small and few and peculiar from his watchmaker's tools, but the pad of the finger seeking entrance is smooth, as dutifully manicured as every other bit of its polished owner.

He drives his thigh deeper between mine, opening us both a little wider. There's cool air where there shouldn't be, and a slick, demanding fingertip. But there's also Didier, breathing heavily, moaning softly. He's composed for all those other women, a master performer, but for me he's just a horny, needy man. I flush at the notion, feeling drunk, and drive my own finger a bit deeper.

My breath catches when he starts to penetrate. It feels…strange. It doesn't hurt, but it doesn't feel good either. Just…bizarre. He doesn't push in any farther but moves his fingertip gently with the tiniest of twists.

"How is it?" he whispers.

"Different."

"It's a better garnish than a main course, I find."

"How does it feel to you?" I ask.

He smiles deeply and kisses me. "It feels wicked."

We kiss more, heavy and hungry and thorough, and he's right—when it's not foremost on my mind, the things our fingers are up to aren't nearly as unnerving.

After a few minutes of play he asks, "Ready?"

For what, I'm not clear. But I've learned that he often knows before I do what I'm ready for, so I murmur my consent.

He turns away, then hands me the bottle to hold while he grabs the two plugs from my pile. I watch as he oils the bulb of the small one, and I do the same to the larger copper one. He sets the oil aside and brings us back together in our tangle of legs.

The metal is cool between my cheeks, eerie in its perfect smoothness. I press when he presses and our breathing hitches together. Still no pain, just cold, hard, alien weirdness. He makes a sound, a sharp moan of surprise or discomfort.

"Okay?"

His sigh tells me I misread. "Yes. Keep going."

He's more relaxed than I am, and more aroused. With a final push, his body welcomes my intrusion.

"Good," he murmurs. His hips begin to shift in small thrusts, rubbing his cock against my mound and belly, sliding the sphere at the plug's base against my fingers. His reactions distract me, turn me on and take me out of my own body. With a sudden, subtle popping sensation, I accept his entrance.

"Ooh."

His turn to ask, "Okay?"

"Yeah, I think so." The anxiety of the penetration's done and now it's just a curious presence back there. I feel vaguely as though I need to use the bathroom, but I don't share the thought.

"Now put it out of your mind," he tells me. "I'll show you how it's meant to be enjoyed."

He pulls away, coaxing me to lie on my back. With a hand towel, he wipes the oil from his fingers and passes it to me to do the same. Next he gives me the sleep mask. The satin blocks everything but the faintest corona of candlelight.

"Now hold out your wrists for me."

I do as he says and more slippery silk glides across my skin.

"We're only playing tonight," he tells me. His voice sounds different somehow, with my eyes covered. Deeper. Closer. "I'm only tying this in a bow, so you'll have no trouble freeing yourself if you wish to."

I feel a tug as my wrists meet.

"Put your hands above your head and pretend I've tied them down."

I do, my knuckles resting against the headboard. I fist a bit of the bedding to feel anchored.

For a long moment, there's perfect stillness and silence. I know he's there. I'd have felt him leave the bed.

"Didier?"

"I'm just looking at you." I hear awe in his voice—reverence of the dirtiest sort. For a breath I tense, intimidated. Then his warm hands are on my ankles, calves, my knees, then spreading my thighs. Without sight, every sensation echoes.

"You look like a present," he murmurs. "Wrapped up for me." His palms slip beneath my butt and I feel his weigh shift on the bed. The forgotten plug asserts itself as he nudges my thighs wider. In the isolating dark, I feel his breath as starkly as I do his hands. It warms my sex in steaming bursts.

He makes a sound, a small grunt of decadent disbelief. My legs twitch at the first lap of his tongue, and when my inner muscles clench from the arousal they find the toy there, with its odd but admittedly exciting resistance. He kisses my clit just as he might my lips. Gentle, fluttery caresses to start, then more aggressive. He moans as he lowers his mouth to my folds. He loves doing this as I'd never guessed a man would, as though it's his absolute favorite thing. Twice he's begged for nothing but this—me on my back and he on his knees, his mouth between my legs, his weight braced on one forearm as he strokes himself into a frenzy with his free hand. For some men I imagine it's a means to an end, an admission fee for access to the main event. For Didier it *is* the main event.

Suddenly he's gone—cool, dry air where his warm mouth and hands had been. He doesn't leave the bed, but there's movement. He's getting another toy, I think. The paddle? That scares me a little, not having a visual warning before it lands.

But then he's between my legs again, and when his tongue laps my labia it's *hot*. I gasp and his lips wrap my clit in the same heat. It fades soon enough, and in its wake my sensitive skin tingles. *Peppermint.* I shiver.

"Do that again."

He makes a smug noise and I can picture his smile perfectly. "I'm going to set the mug on a book, beside us. So try not to thrash."

More moving around then finally that scalding kiss again. Jesus, it feels good. A pause, another treat. My thighs tremble and I can feel an orgasm growing with every searing swipe of his tongue.

"You like that," he whispers between sips.

I start to reach down to hold his head, but I've forgotten the scarves that bind my hands.

"No," he tells me. I put them back down. I can hear the blessed impatience of arousal in his voice and the next time his mouth spoils me, the slick strokes come harder, faster. There's a cruelty brewing in him, one I trust implicitly.

"You like that," he tells me again, in a meaner voice than before. "I like that too." More moving, then, "Tilt your head up."

I do, and I feel the warm rim of the mug. He tips hot tea past my lips, a bit running down my chin. I hold the rest in, warming my mouth. The mug is gone, more movement, unseen body parts at my armpits. Knees, I imagine. When he speaks, his voice seems to come from high above.

"Open up."

I swallow and do as he says. The crown of his cock feels cool against my hot lips and I can feel the groan as it vibrates through his body. The headboard creaks under his braced weight, and he cradles my head in one hand, pushing inside.

"Oh. Good."

He gives me more, though not too much. Not enough to gag me or obstruct my breath, but plenty to trigger a dark, exciting rush. I felt it a couple of weeks ago, when he pretended to force himself on me. It makes me wish my hands really were tied.

He draws his cock from my mouth, panting. "You're hot for me elsewhere."

"Yes."

The warmth of his body leaves me, and I hear things being set aside and the crinkle of plastic. I picture how he rolls the condom down his cock. I've watched it dozens of times now and it never fails to thrill me. His hands on his own body in the candlelight… The very first night we met, he spoiled me with such a sight, the realization of years of theorizing.

More than anything else, I fantasize about men masturbating. It imprinted at first because it was safe, detached from me in every way. I could imagine watching any handsome man I wanted, aroused and aggressive, without ever painting myself into the scene. Until Didier, I'd never touched a cock, never seen a hard one in person, never smelled that curious smell. What he let me watch that night made every speculative show I'd ever entertained pale in comparison, and now it's his hands, his cock, his excitement and no one else's, branded forever onto the pleasure center of my brain.

His thighs spread mine, rougher than before. One hand clamps to my hipbone, the other guiding his erection—I feel his knuckles as his head sweeps along my lips. I'm wet from excitement, from his mouth and the tea, everything. My body welcomes him in a single deep push and a gasp flees my lungs. As his length fills me, the plug makes itself known again. The weirdness of it has gone, and as he thrusts it massages something inside me, intensifying the pleasure of his driving cock. I wonder if he can feel it too.

"Do you wish you could see me?" he asks.

"Yes."

"Do you wish you could touch yourself?"

Fuck yes. I nod.

"Too bad." He hooks his hands under my knees, urging my legs up and hugging them together, my ankles over his shoulder. His cock plunges deep in long, rhythmic strokes, teasing my lips and inner thighs. My clit is screaming for attention. My brain is screaming for my hands to lift the mask so I can see him, see his body strained and his face mean and focused.

"I can do anything I like with you," he tells me.

"Yes."

"Turn over, then."

He helps me move to my knees and elbows, both of us still pretending my wrists are bound to the bed. He sinks deep with a ragged sigh.

"Have you ever fantasized about two men?" he asks me.

"Only a little." Now and again, a passing curiosity.

His weight shifts against me as he leans for some item or other. I hear a familiar clink—the crystal stopper of the lube bottle. His cock resumes thrusting and his arm is at my side, then the smooth, slippery touch of something at my clit. He draws the glass along my fevered flesh, letting me feel each inch of the dildo.

"You've imagined having two cocks at your service? Two men wanting you?" He doesn't wait for my confirmation. "One man fucking you." He owns me for a flurry of thrusts. "While another waits his turn?" The glass strokes me. With a long, slow drag, his cock leaves me empty, then the dildo is at my folds. He finds the right angle and I'm filled with that too-perfect smoothness, cold after the heat of Didier. His thumb teases my clit each time he pushes deep. He positions his erection along my cleft, thrusting to toy with the base of the plug. Too many sensations. I'm blind and bound and the pleasure is too much, too many places at once.

"Imagine another man," he tells me.

I do, and the effort grounds me amid the chaos, giving me focus.

"One man beneath you," Didier says. He pumps me with the glass. "Another behind you. *Me* behind you, waiting for my turn."

On a whim, my brain supplies the image of the baker who works at the *boulangerie* below my flat. An intense, handsome man, leaner than Didier but with an intriguing face and sinewy forearms always dusted in flour. I imagine him below me and wonder how it would feel to have a wall of male heat on each side, two different voices, Didier's hands on my hips and this other man's holding my breasts.

The dildo slips out, Didier slides in. As he strokes my clit with the glass, I try to keep the baker under me but his face blips out. I'm too far gone with the man behind me. The reality of what he's actually doing is hotter than any ménage fantasy. I may be stuck sharing Didier with other women, but I don't care for the idea of him sharing *me.* I've done too much coveting in my life. I want to feel like the coveted one for a change.

"I'm only thinking about you," I tell him, my words jumping with his thrusts.

He slows. "Oh?"

"I don't want another man here." Everything we do, I want it between us. I won't make room for another, not even in my head.

His hips stop completely, and I feel his palm grazing my waist down to my thigh then back up, the dildo now warm against my mound.

"What *do* you want?" he asks quietly.

"Just you. You doing all this to me. And to see you." And to see the dark wood of the bedposts, the weave of the covers, the glint of the candlelight on the bottles. Familiar sights to anchor me while his body leads mine into these uncharted territories.

"Take off the mask, Caroly," he murmurs.

I do as he says, fumbling with my tied hands, and seeing again is like a drink of cold, quenching water.

"Look at me."

I crane my neck and take him in, that body I know better than any other man's, yet as exciting as the first time I laid eyes on him. His expression is dark, as dark as his pupils or brows or the shadow of hair between his legs. As dark as the far corners of the room.

"Just me?" he asks, drawing his length out languidly, sliding back inside just as slow. He feels thick and hot and impossibly hard, so explicit I shut my eyes.

"Just you."

"What about this?" he asks me, and I feel his fingers between my cheeks, manipulating the plug.

"I don't mind that. I think I like it." Sometimes it feels funny and distracting, but more often it feels good.

"And this?" He rubs me with the glass.

"It's nice, but you're plenty." It's always been quality for me, quantity not a particularly strong draw when I'm looking to spoil myself.

The dildo is gone and two powerful hands knead my hips. "You don't want to be shared," he says softly.

I don't want you to want *to share me.*

Of course I don't say that. "I like when you're possessive."

A warm noise, neither laugh nor sigh, opens my eyes. He's smiling that bone-softening smile, little lines around his eyes and mouth etching wisdom across his face.

"I'm more possessive than you know," he tells me.

My heart squeezes, hard.

"You have no idea how often I think about how all this…" He pumps me deeply for a few strokes and trails his fingertips up and down my spine. "How all this is only mine. How no other man has ever had you."

It's no love proclamation. It's more male ego than anything else, but I'll take it. I open my eyes.

"I can be very greedy," he tells me with a smirk.

"I like when you are."

He reaches beside us and picks up the paddle. "Let me show you how greedy."

III

"Keep your hands as they are."

I clutch the blanket tight, reminding myself I'm meant to be bound.

He draws the edge of the leather paddle up my thigh, over my butt, along my waist and back. "Here are the rules. You want me possessive?"

Yes yes yes yes yes. "Yeah."

"Then I want your eyes on me. If you turn away or shut them—"

Whap. I yelp as the slap lights a fire on my thigh.

"Understood?"

"Yes. I understand." Bossy *and* possessive, check. As always, Didier's brilliant at this contentious stuff. He's merely the mechanism for the pain. He delivers it, but only when my eyes tell him to. And though my neck's already growing sore from strain, I won't drop my head and give the order until the first sting fades—he's not fucking around with that paddle. I keep my attention locked on his undulating body.

"This is what you like to see?" There's cockiness in his tone and in the way he takes me—slow, sure thrusts, presenting every inch for my appraisal.

"Yes."

He grazes my back with the paddle, slides his free thumb between my cheeks to circle the plug's base. I huff a breath and shut my eyes, not realizing my mistake until—

Whap.

"Ow, fuck." I lock my attention on him, wincing until the second strike fades to a pulsing fever.

"Only I get to have this." He drives deeper, faster, his stare demanding my confirmation.

"Just you."

His gaze rakes my body like fingernails. "I'm the only man who's tasted you or smelled you. Made you come."

"Yes."

I turn for just a second, needing respite from his intensity. Another stinging slap, another yelp. I look back obediently.

"Mine is the only cock you've ever touched or sucked or welcomed inside you."

My arms shake from shoulder to elbow, weak from his words. "Only you." The ache in my neck sharpens and I hang my head, knowing the consequences.

The leather burns my hip and I buck. Another slap, the exact same spot. It stings so badly tears glaze my eyes, but I welcome the fifth strike. By the sixth, Didier is moaning like I've never heard, trembling behind each measured thrust. He mutters, "Fuck," and I see in my periphery as the paddle lands on the bedspread, abandoned. He holds my waist with both hands, letting his dick do the punishing. Another curse, and he slaps my searing skin with his palm.

"I'm the only one." It sounds as though he's speaking through his teeth.

"Just you," I tell him again.

No more strikes, but his fingers bite the flesh at my hips, holding me right where he wants me. His cock owns me in rough, long strokes.

"Tell me," he begins, but a groan interrupts the thought. "Tell me you'll never be with another man."

If only you could ever reciprocate that vow. But he's not asking me to reply with the truth, simply the next lines in our little carnal play.

His hips speed, his skin slapping mine with each mean stroke "Tell me."

"I'll never be. With another man," I huff. "I don't want. Anyone else." He didn't ask for the truth, but deep down I'm so scared it's exactly what I've just uttered.

His grip relaxes, pace slowing. Fingers whisper a circle around my hipbones. Damp palms drag along my waist and over my ribs, back down. Each thrust still lands with a jarring bump, but his possessiveness is shifting. He strokes my back, and I can feel his gaze as tangibly as his hands. His thumb traces the furrow of my spine, the gesture tender with affection or awe.

Unsure which incarnation of my lover is behind me now, I crane my neck.

Dark eyes lock with mine and he swallows. For a second I see uncertainty in those perfect features, then his aggression returns, casting any misgiving in its shadow. His cock speeds and his hands grow bossy once more, anchoring me tight by the waist. I drop my head and shut my eyes, wanting to memorize this feeling.

You're mine, his cock tells me with each push. *You're mine. Mine. Mine.*

And I am. I wonder if he knows that, in his heart. I wonder how shoddy my resolve to act as if this is all just casual—just for as long as it lasts—looks from the outside. How it looks to a man who's made a craft of stripping away pretense to expose women's deepest desires.

The mysteries of what goes on in that unusual mind are too daunting, so I get myself lost in the demands of his cock.

He grunts with each smack of his hips against my butt. I wish I could see us from the side. I wish I could float out of my skin and just watch, like a ghost. It's safe, just watching. Here in my body, I feel so much. *This is what it feels like to be wanted.* All these props and games have made him wild and needy—the things I feel from merely picturing his face. *Take what you can get.*

Unsteady fingertips circle my waist to find my clit, sparking pleasure in harsh bursts, shooing my worries away. Excitement takes their place. Heat builds against his touch. His full weight presses into me and he's never felt so big before. Never this rough and never this exciting, not even when we played at him forcing me. That wasn't him, after all. Not really. But this man, right now…this is the Didier I know, and this is what I've done to him. I don't know which of us is more powerful.

"Let me feel you come," he says, a plea dressed as an order.

His fingers are frantic, nothing like the masterful instruments I've come to expect, the ones that know the precise tempo and pressure I love. It doesn't matter. Anything will do, coupled with his surging cock and the deep, strange, pleasurable murmur of the plug. I feel a head rush coming on and abandon my acting to slip one hand free from the silk scarf. I grab the headboard as I have so many times now. His thighs urge me forward until I'm nearly upright, and there's the hot, firm press of his belly at the small of my back, hard arms bracketing my waist.

His free hand cups my breast. I feel a kiss on my shoulder, then a nip, the gentle scrape of teeth and the heat of his moans. I turn my head so we're cheek to cheek, sharing the same air. Sharing the same body, it seems, sealed together. His groans voice everything I feel—

CRAVING

desperate, violent, this pleasure bordering on pain, I want to come so badly.

He puts his mouth right to my ear and whispers, "Come for me, Caroly. Please. *Je t'en prie.*"

My arousal spikes. It drops deeper, grows harder, constricts like a fist gathering cloth, binding me tight tight tight until I can't breathe and then…bliss. The hottest, neediest, angriest bliss. His hips slow to the beat of my spasming body, riding the orgasm with me. Joining me? I couldn't say. I can barely think.

I hear gasping, surprised to discover it's me.

"Good," he murmurs, and kisses my neck. "Good."

His cock's still hard as stone, its pulse ticking inside me.

I could pass out now, but I crane my neck a final time and he takes the hint, brushing his lips to mine.

"Thank you," I mutter.

"You're so very welcome. I hope I didn't hurt you."

"No more than I'd hoped you might."

He laughs at that, and when I turn around there's mischief in his expression, poorly veiled arousal.

"You've earned some spoiling," I tell him.

He turns me and pins me to the bed, straddling my hips with his erection beating softly against my navel. Suspecting I know what he wants, I reach around, finding the plug between his spread cheeks.

His moan tells me I guessed right.

I tease him for a minute or more, but the touch seems so intimate and he seems so far away, towering too high above me… "Here, lie down."

On our sides, we lock our legs like before and my fingertips seek smooth copper. With a grunt, he grinds his cheek against mine. "Fuck me."

I ease the plug out slowly, push it back in. Another groan.

"What does it do for you?" I whisper.

"It's you. It's feeling like you own me."

I think I'd always assumed that if we went here, it would undermine Didier as the strong, masculine figure I've come to see him as. But it does something I never expected. It makes *me* feel strong, giving this man pleasure in the most literal, active sense possible. For the first time in my life, I envy men their cocks. Even when a cock's passive, it's a thing of aggression. I like being the aggressor, a little bit. The one *doing*. I'm timid when I'm on top and not a confident head-giver. But this...this I can do. I'm the active one, but the attention's not on me.

I stroke him slowly, in and out, recording how he trembles, the way his hips flex to meet the intrusion, rubbing his cock against my belly each time he pulls back. I could do this when we fuck, maybe. I could...

"I could do this when I go down on you sometime." I could spoil him *so rotten*.

He moans at the idea.

After a few more languorous strokes, I ask, "Would you like that?"

"Yes. With my hands tied."

A shiver trickles through me, a chill chased by heat.

He nips at my lip and makes a happy, devious noise. "I'd like to be at your mercy."

I imagine such a thing—being in charge of everything he feels. An intimidating goal for another night, but a worthy one.

"Yes. Fuck me."

My hand had sped without me realizing. I give him what he wants, watching rapt as he gets hotter and hotter, his cock all but ignored. I imagine he could come from only this, but finally he stutters, "Straddle me."

We flip over and I do as he says without any hesitation. He's too far gone for me to fret over my lackluster skills on top. Turns out I needn't have worried.

"Hold there." His hands freeze my hips with a few inches between our pubic bones. He guides himself to my lips and pushes up with a pained gasp. "Just stay. Right there."

His chest and stomach clench with his rolling thrusts, tendons rising along his throat. His hips move with the exaggerated, rhythmic purpose of a dancer, the motion surely designed to deepen whatever pleasure the plug is giving him. He kneads my thighs, nearly rough enough to bruise, but I'd suffer far worse for a chance to see him this crazed.

"Fuck," he says, then again. I grin, unseen, ever thrilled to think I'm to blame for this sophisticated man's descent into prurience. He lets go of my thighs to fist the covers, knuckles bleached bone-white.

"Fuck, Caroly."

And he's gone. He grabs my hips and forces them down, cocks his own up, locking us tight as he rides what looks like the most violent, perfect orgasm ever felt by man. His head mashes the pillow, mouth open in silent agony as tremors tense the length of his body once, twice, three times. His ribs work like a bellows as he lowers, and I rub his sweat-damp chest, waiting as he calms. I know we shouldn't linger this way, not with the condom, but I can't bring myself to break our bodies apart. Not yet.

He sighs grandly and drops his head to one side.

"Yes?"

He blinks as though he's just regained consciousness after a head injury. "My goodness."

"We should probably…" I ease up and he takes the cue, securing the rubber as I move to the side. He strips the condom, folding it in a towel along with the plugs. I feel a little empty with mine suddenly gone.

We take turns in the bathroom. I change into the pajamas I keep in his underwear drawer. They're crisp and sweet-smelling, freshly laundered by his own hands this very morning, I can only assume. Remarkable.

As we lay down facing one another on the covers, he gives me a deep, shameless, *filthy* smile. "I enjoy visiting these new places with you."

Of course he does. A vacation that takes him no farther than the bounds of the mattress. Any excuse to go inside, rather than out. But I agree. "Me too."

"It's like doing these things for the first time again, experiencing them alongside you."

My heart grows big, too big, pumping too hard, making me blush. My voice is a weak whisper. "I like that. A lot."

He trails kisses along my jaw and between them he asks, "Why do you sound so shy?"

Because I want so badly to be special to you. Because I'm in love with you. "It's just nice to hear. It's nice to think I make you feel that way, that the stuff we do feels new to you, since you've made me feel nothing *but* new things since we met."

A kiss below my ear, another, another. So many I know he's caught on some thought, trying to decide whether or not to give it voice. My swollen heart clenches tight with irrational panic. *What if he wants to break it off? What if he can sense how attached I've become?* But it's stupid. He just told me lovely things about us, and he's the last man who'd clam up or run away, faced with sentimentality.

After a very long pause and countless idle kisses, he finally speaks. "Thank you for my gift."

"Oh. You're very welcome."

He pulls back so I can see his smile. "You like the idea of me opening things, don't you? Locks. Doors."

"I hadn't thought about it, really." But yes, of course I want the world to open for him. He deserves the entire ocean, not just some lonely shell. "You like puzzles. Mechanical puzzles. And the tools are very you. That's all."

"You would have me become some master lock picker, so every door in this city would be mine to step through. Until I could go anywhere, Paris growing bigger and bigger and bigger, one door at a time."

"You know I want that."

"And you'd be at my back at every threshold, ready to push me through."

I cool under his gaze. There's something intense and unknown in that look. Is he angry? "I hope it never feels like I *push* you. I only ever want to encourage you…"

Another smile banishes my fears. "I need pushing, Caroly."

"I'd never want to bully you, though." He suffered enough of that as a kid.

The intensity returns to his eyes and he kneads my shoulder with fierce affection. "You're the only person in my life who pushes. I have wonderful, kind clients and friends who run my errands, bring me groceries, do a hundred things for me so I can feel safe. But you're the only one who cares enough to say, 'Fuck your precious safety, Didier.'"

I blush deeper. "I don't think I've ever said *that*. Not even in my head."

"No, of course not. Even when you push, you're gentle. But you care enough that you're not afraid to upset me. Everyone else, they love me as some pet. They want me fed and happy and warm, safe in a pretty cage, always waiting right where they expect me to be. But you would make me into one of those pigeons." He nods to the window, where his little gray voyeurs doze beyond the drapes. "Maybe a little worse for wear, maybe skittish and dirty, but you want me free to fly, I think."

I nod. "I do. In your own time."

His soft laugh warms the room. "My own time kept me inside for three years. I'm grateful for the pressure." He pauses. "No, not pressure. For the baiting. For giving me the incentive to find my balls and go outside with you. Or meet you somewhere."

"What incentive?"

He bites his lip, but I can see how broad his smile would be from how his eyes crinkle in the candlelight. "To impress you."

My turn to laugh. "To impress me?"

"To make you proud. And to be honest..."

"Yes?"

"Because it's a relief to let someone see me so helpless. To admit my problem to people is one thing, but to actually let someone see what it does to me... And you've seen that, and you're still here." His voice goes strange and thin, and he clears his throat. "Anyway. For a hundred reasons, you make me want to be a stronger man."

"Oh. Wow."

He presses his lips to my forehead, seeming ready to put the topic to bed.

When he rises to blow out the candles, I feel all funny and overheated. I spent forever worrying I might never even find a man I wanted who wanted me back. To imagine I'd find one I cared for as much as Didier, to believe he *does* want me back, that he wants to be stronger for me, *better*, as if he thinks I deserve more...

The thought should make me giddy but it scares me as well. It's terrifying, feeling so much for one person, and after waiting so long for it. There's so much to lose if they change their mind and leave you, if they're taken from you...

I'm sure I'm not the only woman who's in love with Didier. Half his clients might easily feel as deeply for him as I do, and I suddenly understand why they might want to keep him in this pretty cage, as he called it. To keep him polished and nestle him on a cushion in a beautiful box, and store him where they can always find him. If he hadn't left this place to seek me out... If the moment we ceased being client and prostitute and became something more hadn't happened how it had, I'd probably do like all the rest. Hoard him here for my own enjoyment.

We climb under the covers together in the dark.

I kiss his temple. "Turn over."

He rolls onto his side and lets me hug my body to his. I breathe in the scent of his neck and hair, feel his ribs rise and fall under my arm. I find his hand and twine our fingers and squeeze. He squeezes back.

I love you.

I think the words I'm afraid to say. If I say them it'll make all this real, and real things rarely last. They get lost and broken and worn, and you look back and try to remember the time when this faded object meant so much to you. If I say them he'll know beyond a doubt I'm his, and we never yearn for things as deeply once we know they're ours to keep.

But then I picture Didier's cabinet full of curiosities and I realize newness isn't his currency. He's attached to the old, the discarded, the broken and fixable. He wouldn't leave a woman simply because her novelty faded. I hug him a little tighter, thinking of how very many objects live in that hutch. I'm special, maybe even the most special, but what does that warrant? A central space on the top shelf perhaps, but I'm still just one among dozens. Maybe I'm greedy, wanting more than that.

You knew what he was before you met him. You knew *he wasn't yours alone.*

But I hadn't suspected then that he'd become this much to me. He was only ever supposed to be the handsome, expensive solution to the issue of my loitering virginity. I gave him that, and so much more. He holds a great hunk of my heart in his hands, so big it feels like I'd die if he took it away.

But it beats now, steady thumps against his back. And here he is, solid and warm. He's already real, and I'm already in love with him. I slip my fingers free to rub his chest and feel his heart thump too.

"Tomorrow is Saturday," he murmurs.

"Yes. I'm excited to sleep in."

"Where are you taking me?"

"Let's not worry about that now." He'll never fall asleep if he starts stressing about leaving the flat. Anticipating the route doesn't calm or prepare him—it only makes his thoughts race faster. "We'll figure it out in the morning."

"It's supposed to be warm."

"I heard."

"Let's go to the river. Let's find a café with a terrace, overlooking the water."

"Outside? Really?"

"Yes," he says, and he *yawns*. He's speaking about going outside and *staying* outside and he *yawned*.

"Okay, sure. Whatever you want."

"What I want is to sit with you and listen to the water, and feel the sunshine warm my hair."

In all likelihood he'll be too anxious to register anything so subtle as the shush of the river or the heat of the sun, but far be it from me to remind him of this. "That sounds nice."

He turns over, knees finding mine under the covers, our legs locking. "You know what else is so good about Saturdays?"

"What?"

"Did you notice that I never take clients on Fridays or Saturdays anymore?"

I'd noticed, though I hadn't let myself hope it was anything more than a pleasant string of coincidences. "No?"

"No. So unless you have plans, maybe I could see you tomorrow night as well?"

"Sure. I'll need to go home for a change of clothes at some point, but yes, of course."

"And maybe I could take you out for a glass of wine, and stop at a market and find things to make dinner."

Again, out. *Markets are full of people*, I want to say. And bars are full of people, as are all the streets of the Latin Quarter on a Saturday evening. "I'd like all those things. If that's what you want."

"Those are things I *want* to want. That's the sort of man I'd like to be, so I'll go through his motions, again and again and again, until they feel like my own."

I kiss him between his brows. "That sounds like a very good strategy."

"Now *you* turn over."

I do, savoring the shifting of his body as I'm enclosed by strong, warm maleness. So many years I missed out on this embrace, letting fear guide my decisions. I hope Didier finds his payoff too, all that warm sunshine on his hair. If it feels even half as wonderful as his chest at my back or his breath on my neck, it'll be worth the work, a hundred times over.

"Good night, Caroly."

"Good night." *I love you so.*

REVERSAL

THE CURIO VIGNETTES, PART III

I 🗝

The deadbolt clatters in my shaking fingers, twisting into place with a click.

Click, and my heart slows, if only by a fraction.

Still it hammers, a thousand beats for every footstep as I cross the room, moving so quickly I startle the pigeons into flight from the window ledges. I tell myself, *don't look beyond the glass,* but I sense the city all the same, the labyrinth of Paris spreading out boundless as a sea.

One set of curtains shut, then a second, finally the third. Panic left me faint but gravity's returning to my limbs, focus settling my jumping gaze. My head throbs with every heartbeat, white light pulsing at the edges of my eyes.

I hurry to the bedroom and shut those curtains as well, drawing darkness across the room. Not dark enough. With their ties freed, the drapes hanging from my bed's canopy fall into place. I crawl between them and lie on my side, hugging my knees. I'm a child in the womb, in the warm, safe darkness. I imagine the slow, calming thump of an omnipotent heart, its rhythm telling my own pulse to calm.

There's no soothing heart. Only the harsh wheezing of my breath, the faintest tick of a clock on the other side of the wall.

Clocks.

I could go to the clocks, to the cabinet in my living room, once my panic has eased. I could take that brass carriage clock apart, the one Caroly gave me in the spring. I picture it, March seeming so very long ago, the time when she still paid to enjoy my body for an evening. Years ago, surely, yet mere months.

I could take the clock apart. Putting it back together would take me days—days I would happily sacrifice if it meant I could stay in one place, making sense of the wheels and springs, hunched over the coffee table with a magnifying loupe at my eye, so relieved to let the world pass me by.

It's safe inside the belly of that clock. Its bounds are so finite, the order of things so precise. I can make sense of things, inside...

Tick, tick, tick, comes the murmur through the wall. The time. What time is it?

Caroly will be here at seven. It is seven now? I haven't any idea, but my compulsions have me thrusting the curtain aside and swinging my feet to the floor. Perhaps it *is* still early. Perhaps I have as much as two or three hours before she arrives—

But no. When I hurry into the living room the whispering clock tells me it's twenty of seven.

I should have started dinner long before now. I don't even have time for a shower. All because of that stupid, stupid notion. And that awful parade. Yes, the parade is to blame.

I shake my head at the thought. *It's not the parade, you idiot.* No normal man would seek a scapegoat in that.

No normal man would go out for an hour's errand and get lost for four. Not in broad daylight, not in the only city he's ever called home.

Now dinner will be late, and my beloved guest will find me white and trembling from my own failure.

No normal woman would put up with a man like you. Your brain is a knot of frayed wires, too much bother to untangle. Be grateful anyone's deemed your body worth buying for an evening's distraction—

The buzzer jolts me like a shock. She's early, and I'm too late. Too late to pretend I'm at all prepared to see her, too late to dress myself in the trappings of a functional man.

I press the button to let her into the building. For a minute I stand still, counting my flaring breaths. My mouth is dry and tastes of old coffee.

Soon I feel the faint echoes of her footsteps coming down the hall. I twist the deadbolt back open, that click again, but this time it feels dangerous, as if I've freed the city from its cage and welcomed it into my flat to prowl and sniff.

Yet when the door does open, all that slips inside is Caroly. Her wide lips smile, her soft curls bounce as she turns to lock up.

Another turn, another smile. "Hey, you."

Her face alone calms me, that pale skin and those cool blue eyes. A real calm, unlike the artificial safety of my cabinet. My shoulders drop and the stitch in my chest loosens. I don't know that I've ever been so relieved to see someone, not since I was a tiny child, lost in the supermarket and rescued by the familiar tattoo of my mother's heels on the tile floor.

I wrap Caroly in my arms, so tight I hear her huff with surprise against my shoulder. She strokes my back, realizing how desperate an embrace this is. "Didier?"

As I let her go she rubs my arms, gaze making an inventory of her broken lover. "Is everything okay?"

I take a deep breath, swallow, clear my throat. "I had a scare," I admit. Simply speaking English is a comfort, a tiny taste of security, hiding behind the affectations of a different man.

"I can tell. Here, let's sit down." Her eyes dart to my shoes. They tell her I left the flat, the state of me inferring it didn't go well. "It's awfully dark in—"

I rush to flip on the lights before she can suggest we open the curtains. She heads to the couch and I follow. Seeking walls wherever I might find them, I wedge my hip against the armrest. Still I sense the city behind me, hear it growling, feel its hot summer breath on my neck.

Caroly scoots close and takes my hand. Her purse is still slung over her shoulder. "What happened? Did you go out?"

I nod.

"Did you get lost?"

"Very."

She rubs my knuckles with her other hand. "For how long?"

"Four hours."

Her eyes widen "How awful. No wonder you're all shaken up. When did you get back?"

"Minutes ago. I'm sorry—dinner's going to be late. And I didn't have a chance to bathe or—"

"Shush. I'll pick us up something from down the street in a little while. You can shower while I'm out."

She says these things to fix the situation, to make me feel better, but in truth it only triggers more shame. It's my job to be a perfect host, to be ready when a visitor comes calling. It's my craft and livelihood to please and spoil women, and I've failed.

I fail Caroly constantly. She's the only one I care for deeply enough to put myself in a position to fail.

This afternoon I'd gone out in search of a token, some trinket from a store my mother used to take me to when I was young. She would browse the jewelry while I mashed my face against the glass case full of watches.

CARA McKENNA

I was going to buy Caroly something—a bracelet or a ring or a pendant, something shiny to excite her inner magpie. She always brings me gifts. I was going to get one for her, and tonight I was going to tell her I love her. I was going to go out into the city on my mission and nothing would keep me from it, and I'd return home triumphant from the longest walk I've taken by myself in years. I'd prove myself a recovering agoraphobe, not a terminal one, and tell her I'm in love with her.

Fool.

I never reached the store. I made it six shaking, sweaty blocks in the July sun, only to find my meticulously plotted route blocked by metal gates, partitions corralling a parade. Any chance I had to find my way back was swept away in the streaming crowds, my brain wiped blank by the music and shouting and the squeals of children. Just remembering, I feel panic rising inside me, tasting of bile.

"Where did you go?" she asks, still rubbing my hand. The contact smoothes the roughest burrs from my nerves, but my voice comes out thin and brittle.

"I was going to visit a store my mother took me to years ago. But there was a parade blocking the streets, and I lost my way."

She frowns her sympathy. "Four hours, huh?"

I nod. At least one of them I spent locked in a café restroom. "I found a cab eventually, but..." I shake my head. Surely men get stranded in the wilderness for days on end and are less traumatized than this. Useless.

How had I ever thought I was ready to present myself as a man worth loving? Of asking this woman to consider me her boyfriend? She could have any number of men, and some day her self-consciousness will fade completely and she'll realize that. She'd be a masochist to saddle herself with the likes of me. She's smart enough to know she deserves a whole man, not some mess chewed half-hollow with the worm holes of his own anxiety.

"Well, you're home now," she says, patting my hand and sitting up straight. "Why don't you take a shower, and I'll get us some dinner." It's a statement, not a query. She's already on her feet, checking her wallet for cash.

Her brusqueness has nothing to do with being weary of my breakdown. It's merely her telling me that it's no big deal, this change of plans. She doesn't like for me to wallow in my disappointments, to give them as much power as I do.

"Okay," I finally say, and stand. She kisses my cheek. As the door shuts behind her, my cabinet calls to me. But I turn my back on it and head for the bathroom. I brush the coffee taste from my mouth, feeling settled by a tiny measure. I'm tempted to shower with the lights off, as I sometimes do—warm water, calming dark, the steady shush drowning out my ragged breaths. I shudder to imagine what a psychiatrist would make of me, of all these artificial wombs I seek when the outside world becomes too much to bear.

But I feel better as I dry off. I groom, reassured by the familiar rituals. Perhaps it's only a costume I wear, pretending to be this sophisticated man, but it often feels far better than the skin I was born in.

Caroly buzzes again as I'm uncorking a bottle of wine. When she meets me in the kitchen I see her overzealous shopping tendencies have gotten the better of her. She sets far too much food on the butcher block—half a baguette, soup containers and several steaming carry-out boxes from the corner bistro.

I've calmed enough to see her properly, take in her clothes. She came from her museum, dressed for work in a striped silk skirt and a plain black top. The latter hides all but her slender neck and the grooves above her clavicles, the little well between them at the base of her throat. The most opportunistic bits of my manhood return as I wonder if I would taste her perfume if I drew my tongue along that skin. I feel arousal glowing pink, deep in my belly, embers coming alive if not yet crackling bright. Soon, though. It will feel good to get lost inside her, lost in a mission I can't fail—pleasing her. Pleasing a woman will always trump fixing a clock when I'm in need of comfort. I can be a worthy lover to her, if not a boyfriend.

We dole soup into bowls, bread and beef and roast potatoes onto plates, and I pour the wine. We toast, speaking for the first time since she left, I realize.

"To the weekend," she announces.

"Indeed. To the weekend." To waking with her in the morning—

The morning. In the morning she'll make me go out again, for coffee somewhere. The notion drives a knife between my ribs, I'm still so rattled from the day's fiasco. The wine tastes acrid from the toothpaste and I drink too quickly.

My distress must be as plain as my prominent nose, as she says, "It's much too early to worry about leaving."

Then tell me we don't have to leave tomorrow. She won't, though.

"Plus you'll be fine. Everything will go smoothly, and it'll wash away the bad taste this afternoon left in your mouth."

"Perhaps." But it still sours my stomach. We eat in silence for a little while, though I'm not hungry. I feel her gaze flitting from her plate to my face. She'll catch my worries like a cold if I don't snap out of this mood.

"Tell me about your day," I say.

"Nothing special. Though I did find out one of the curators is pregnant."

"Oh?" I imagine Caroly pregnant and for a split second an intense curiosity eclipses my anxiety.

She nods. "I'm hoping I might get to fill in for some of her duties while she's on maternity leave in the winter. It'd put me in a good position the next time a curator position opens up."

"That's excellent."

"How about you? Before you got lost, I mean. What store were you going to?"

I can't tell her the truth, not in its entirety. She needn't know I was so deluded as to think I was ready to present her with jewelry and a love proclamation.

"It was one of my mother's favorite places. They sell antiques. Clocks," I add, the perfect alibi, and the truth.

"Ah. Run out of patients to operate on?"

"Something like that." I eye the little crystal droplets dangling from her ears, wondering what I might have chosen for her at that shop, in some alternate universe where I'd found myself capable of the mission. I'd have enjoyed choosing. I'd have taken her up to the building's roof this very evening with the box in my pocket, told her how I felt with that sky looming, those buildings sprawling. Shown her I felt for her, even surrounded by the things that scare me most... My chest would have swelled with pride to know I'd made that trip by myself, walked those twenty-odd blocks on my quest and come home victorious.

But quests and prizes are for knights. I'm no knight. Just some self-exiled wretch barricaded in his lonely tower.

I look to the woman so hell-bent on rescuing me.

"Yes?" she asks.

"I'm calming," I say, though my voice is melancholy.

"Good."

"What would you like to do tonight?"

She shrugs. "Play cards for a bit?" She's gotten quite addicted to *piquet*. And quite cutthroat.

"Sure."

I'd happily adjourn us to the bedroom and shed my worries alongside my clothes, turn my mind over to the delightful task of exploring her body. But I can survive a few hands. We stow the leftovers, refill our glasses and wander to the living room.

I put a record on—viola, but nothing too sad. As Caroly shuffles, I think again how nice it might be if this place were ours, hers and mine. Her things in the medicine cabinet and around the bedroom, not secreted in cupboards and drawers, lest my other visitors see. In that alternate universe where I'd managed the day's mission, maybe I'd have asked her to come live with me. She wants to move this autumn, out of her current flat. If we split the rent, I could afford to stop selling my body, find another job.

All these years I thought this must be my calling, but lately…

Arranging my cards, I wonder, what else could I do? Go back to being an artists' model, perhaps. Tutor people at French or English or Portuguese. Anything but continue being a kept man—kept and shared by a dozen or more women, but kept all the same. I've long fancied myself lucky to have succeeded in my vocation, but what used to strike me as decadent has begun to feel cloying. I'm anyone's pretty pet for the right price. I could be Caroly's alone, not a pet but a partner.

But that universe is so very far away. I realize that now.

"Making any progress with the locks?" she asks. Earlier this month she gifted me a bag of antique padlocks, along with a set of tiny tools and a book on how to pick them.

"Yes, I've fiddled two open so far. It's harder than I expected."

She grins, clearly pleased to hear her puzzle is proving difficult. "Good."

"It's rather satisfying, that sound when you've succeeded and the shackle snaps free. Though it comes after quite a bit of blind frustration." My clocks are kinder. Like a jigsaw puzzle, you can see your progress. The padlocks do nothing but taunt, and until I get better, picking them is more a battle of wits than an art.

"When your birthday comes around, I'll be sure to put your present in a box with at least four locks."

I shake my head, smiling. "Cruel creature." I imagine it, though—Caroly still a part of my life when January and my birthday arrive. Snow falling outside. Picturesque, the two of us here in this room, sharing a hot meal, perhaps playing this very game. So bleak and lonely should she move on before then. Me still here. Always here.

"Did you have any interesting clients this week?" she asks, discarding a queen. I warm to the change of topic. There's no jealousy in her tone. She likes to hear the sorts of requests my visitors make of me.

"I've had two since the last time you were here."

"Anything unusual?"

"You know I can't tell you anything so specific. So recent." A woman's desires are as intimate and vulnerable as her sex, entrusted to the man she exposes herself to.

"Of course not."

"But I can tell you that neither visit was peculiar in any way." My Wednesday evening guest was a typical one, in that she prefers to simply treat our appointments as dates, dressing up to be catered to first with food and wine, then with my mouth and hands and cock. Thursday was much the same, if a bit more...vigorous. The only difference was which man I was expected to be.

"I got to play very different lovers," I tell her.

Her cards immediately lose their interest. She sips her wine, eyes wide. "What sorts of lovers?"

Ones very unlike the coward I truly am. "First, the perfect seducer. Warm and clever and shameless." I can feel his skin slipping over my shoulders like a cloak.

"Forceful?" she asks, meaning a different sort entirely.

"No, nothing like that. A beloved scoundrel, not a selfish one. A persuasive gentleman. A slow-burning candle between the sheets."

"Who else?"

"A rougher man, with a foul mouth and punishing hips," I say with a smile. "The sort who'd never bed a woman beneath a stitch of covers."

She purses her lips then brings the glass to kiss them.

"I could be either of these men for you," I tell her, eager to do so. Eager to be anyone but myself until the sun rises again.

"Do most women want you to be nice or mean?"

I hadn't thought about it before, but the answer needs no pondering. "Nice."

She nods.

"It's not just any woman who pays a man to make love to her," I say.

"Are most of them weird, like me?"

I smile, leaning forward to curl a dark-blonde lock behind her ear and trace her jaw. "None are so special as you." I speak a Lothario's words, but they're my words as well. True down to each letter.

"But a lot of your clients must be...I don't know. 'Damaged' sounds mean."

"Many come to me needing a sense of safety or distance. A prostitute is a man one can't get too attached to—"

"Oops," she says, teasing herself. Just a little joke, but her meaning floods my chest with heat and pride.

"I'm not your prostitute any longer."

"That's true."

"You're welcome to get as attached to me as you wish. Though it baffles me why you might."

Her gaze falters. "Some of them must get attached, though. Despite how impossible the circumstances are."

"Of course."

"What do you do?"

"I end those relationships."

"Just like that?"

I nod. "It's the kindest way."

She swallows. "How close did you come to doing that with us? Ending it?"

The question startles me. But she told me perhaps four visits into our arrangement that she had to stay away for a while. I was proving too expensive, and she... How had she worded it? She'd been in danger of falling in love with me.

"You were the one who wanted distance," I remind her. "You had the self-awareness to understand how worrisome your feelings ought to be. I didn't need to scare you away. You did that job yourself."

"I suppose."

I clear my throat. "In truth, it would have been hard to draw that line. I'd grown attached to you as well."

That draws a pink stain to her cheeks, a sunrise to banish my gloom.

"You must know that by now, having seen what it takes to coax me out of these walls." That had been my first time in years, leaving this flat—going out to seek Caroly after she'd told me she needed to stay away, to protect her heart and her bank balance. It took me days to manage it, but the gesture had to be made.

I picture the twinkling cases of that old jewelry store, of gestures needed and unmade. I failed once. Perhaps that doesn't mean I'll fail the next time. Though the thought of a next time twists my guts into a fresh nest of knots.

Setting my cards on the table, I give her a dark, familiar look. I want to escape into a costume—any identity but the one I was born with. I want to be whatever man she has a taste for tonight.

She lets me slip the cards from her hand and scoots closer when I tug softly at her waist.

I graze my lips across hers and smile. As I toy with her hair I murmur, "I've missed you, since Sunday."

"I've missed *you*."

Five days we've been apart…five days and two other women stacked between this visit and the last. It's selfish, but I wish my infidelity hurt Caroly more. I wish she'd make demands of me, need more of me, refuse to share me.

I love this woman. Yet a man in love would cross a desert for the object of his affection, swim an ocean, scale a mountain. I can't even walk to Gobelins for mine. What exactly makes me feel I'm someone worth suffering jealousy over?

Anxiety is tugging at my sleeves with its tiny, insistent hands. Such a waste. I waste too much—entire days' worth of sunshine. I won't waste this too-short time I get with Caroly.

Her cheek is velvet against my palm, lips tart with wine. My fingers seek her hair, my tongue her tongue. I feel her stiffen with excitement then soften in a breath. Her mouth welcomes mine and cool, slender fingers slip inside my sleeve to cup my shoulder. Blood pulses through me, its quickness nothing to do with fear, finally. My cock wakes, eager. Hungry.

I whisper against her lips. "Let me take you to bed." *Let me get lost in you, in a place I could navigate blindfolded.*

She doesn't reply in words, but stands and takes my hand. I let her lead me to the dark bedroom, but I won't be led for long. Not tonight, when I need so badly to feel capable.

As we cross the threshold I push her toward the bed, a firm hand against the small of her back. She shoots a mischievous glance over her shoulder then pauses to tie one of the curtains to the canopy post. I peel my shirt away as she sits, and we push our shoes off. She reaches for an earring.

"Don't," I say. Anything that's to come off that fascinating body, I'll be the one to remove it. I tell her as much with my eyes, and she laces her fingers obediently in her lap with a little smirk.

Heat fills me from my toes, rising upward with licking flames. I've left Didier outside the door with his precious disorder. Here in this room I'm a different man, a better one. One deserving of that smirk, those hands, that mouth, the secret place between her legs where only I've ever been allowed. That final thought swells my cock so hard and hot it hurts. Just the brush of my hand as I open my buckle sucks the breath from my lungs.

Socks and pants are kicked aside, and I join her in my underwear, my readiness surely plain even in the faint light that leaks in from the hall. She's eager as well, palms roaming my sides and hips as I roll her onto her back, drive up her skirt with my knees. I slide my arms beneath her, bury my face against her neck, breathe in that vanilla-amber scent and her skin underneath it, her hair, her sweat. The July heat's made her warm and soft and ripe. I'll tease her with my mouth, taste that juice no other man has ever sampled. I'll drink her down for as long as she'll let me, feeling her fingers clutching my hair and imagining she owns me.

I brace myself on my elbows and bring my hips low, grazing my erection between her thighs through two taunting layers. Nails scrape softly over my shoulders and down my arms, and she leans up just a moment to nip at my lower lip. I reward her eagerness with an explicit stroke, drawing my length along the soft cleft of her sex. Approving hands seek my backside, kneading. Begging.

Already I can feel her growing wet, the way the fabric catches between us.

"Tell me what you want tonight," I say.

"I want to make you feel good."

"Then let me do whatever I like." Before the words are even out I'm moving down her body, already anticipating her taste, the pulse of her swollen flesh between my lips. I sit back on my heels and trail my fingertips over her top, her skirt. Her inner thighs are soft as the cotton, as smooth as the satin. My thumbs find the border of her panties, a tease of lace. A hand cups my heart, squeezing, coaxing the blood through my veins in heady bursts. I crave the same treatment for my cock, from her actual fist, but it'll have to wait.

I hook a finger under the strip of fabric between her thighs, draw it up and down so my knuckle strokes her lips, making promises. Her own hand moves to join mine. I expect her to push her panties down, but instead her fingers close around my wrist.

"No," she says.

A word I've rarely heard her utter in this room, curious pupil that she is.

I move my hand to her hip and meet her gaze. "No?"

Sitting up, she shakes her head, smoothes her skirt over her legs, strokes my hair. "I know what you want." Her voice is thick with arousal. "To please me."

"Always."

"But I know what it does for you. I don't want to be one of your clocks, Didier."

I frown.

"I don't want to be some space you escape inside to get out of your head. I don't..." She sighs and looks around. After a long moment, she rises to tie the other three drapes to the bedposts. Then she's at the window. She flings the curtains aside, revealing all those buildings under the darkening sky, the sunset winking pink and gold from their west-facing windows. My pulse races as I remember how it felt to be lost in that maze mere hours ago. My role dissolves and I feel like myself again—an ugly sensation.

She takes a seat on the edge of the bed. "When you shut the curtains or go inside a hunk of brass or between some woman's legs...you're not fixing anything that's upsetting you." The words are forceful, but her tone kind.

"It soothes me."

"But it doesn't heal you any. You have to feel that stuff. Distracting yourself and hiding just puts the pain on pause. It doesn't actually go away."

My cock goes limp. In my rational brain I know she's right, but the frightened child in me resents her for it. This room is the single place I can rely on to make me feel capable and in control. The safest corner of my tiny world, and she wants to take that away?

No no no no no.

Why does the woman I care for the deepest insist on causing me the most distress?

I speak slowly, feigning calm. "I could wallow in how anxious I feel for hours but it won't fix me, either."

"It will. Over time."

"Letting the pain become familiar won't lessen it. It'll only numb me. Why not numb myself with pleasure, instead?" I reach for her, but she moves farther down the bed, stretching her legs to build a moat between us.

"I don't want to be treated like an alcoholic's drink," she tells me.

"That's not fair—"

"And the pain *will* lessen, if you make yourself feel it. It's like…it's like a storm. It can't rain forever. You have to ride it out."

I crawl to her, uninterested in being swayed by any logic outside the carnal. "It can rain all it likes, but I don't see why I should stand outside and be miserable. Not when I can be warm and safe. Inside." I nudge her knees apart with my own, but she braces her palms against my shoulders.

"Fine. Not a storm then. But it's homework. It has to be done if you're ever going to graduate to what's next. And ignoring it won't make the pile any smaller. Don't give it the power to make you hide."

I sit back on my heels and sigh, relenting.

"I won't pretend we're the same," she says, "but you know how I used to be. So anxious about being with men I nearly turned thirty still a virgin."

"Not such a terrible crime."

"Maybe not, but pretty cowardly. It wasn't easy coming here, to be with you. I stood on your doorstep for ages, too nervous to ring your bell. But I did, and I did the work, and the reward's been worth it. So worth it," she says again, and rubs my thighs in gentle concession. "I know it's not the same. But find a reward. Something to make the work bearable. A place you want to visit. A friend or a relative you've had to shut out of your life, who you could see again."

A woman whose respect I want so desperately to earn. Whose body should stay here, wrapped in mine each night, under these covers. But the pain hurts so badly and there's no guarantee she'd want the same, even if I could become functional again.

I let a long breath rattle from my throat then meet her gaze. "Do you not want me tonight?"

"No, of course I do." In a near-mumble she adds, "I always want you."

Relief loosens my back.

"I just don't want you to medicate with me."

"That's never my aim."

"I'm sure it's not. But I don't want you all…"

Weak? Pathetic? Exactly as I am?

"I don't want you all worshipful."

"Oh."

"Not when I know it's to help you get out of your head." She looks thoughtful a moment, staring past my face toward the window. Slowly, a smile curls her lips and she meets my eyes.

"Yes?"

"Why don't you let me seduce *you* for a change?"

My brows rise. This is unlike Caroly indeed. If sex is a Sunday drive to her, she's perfectly happy to come along and see the sights—but she's never once asked to steer. And I don't know how I'd feel, not having my hands wrapped firmly around the wheel. Even with clients who wish me to be passive, I always feel in charge of the experience. The performance.

She's not after a performance, though. Already my mind is racing. It feels as though I've drunk several espressos, anxiety buzzing at the edges of my head, drying my mouth. Tonight of all nights, I want to fall back on what makes me feel competent, in control. Tonight of all nights, I want to be the one *doing*.

"I don't know." I stroke her calves. "I like to please you. It would make me feel better to be that way. To feel...capable." It's hard to say these things. It's been my job for so long to give women no reason to doubt my manhood, my skills, my command and reverence for their sexual experiences, inside my home. It occurs to me that the woman here with me now knows me better than anyone has in ages. She knows the veneer and the mess it hides. I suppose she must like the mess, but it scares me—being known.

"I know you're capable. You don't need to prove it to me."

"I want to *feel* it."

She sighs, seeming resigned for just a moment, before a fresh wave of determination straightens her spine and she sits up. "Let it be my turn to feel capable. In bed."

I hold her stare, waiting for more.

"If the past few months have been my exposure therapy, with sex and men and all that, let's test me then. Let's see if you've trained me well enough to seduce a hot-blooded Frenchman." She grins. If the idea intimidates her, she hides it well.

I hide something well—a heated, painful pang in my gut to imagine her going to bed with another man, eager to share with him the sexuality I've helped to foster.

You have her now, but you won't keep her, not if you don't get better. I think this woman loves me, but she's not a saint. Her patience will wane sooner or later.

I mirror her wicked smile, faking the enthusiasm I wish I felt. "Is that what all this has been? Your training?"

"In a way."

"And you're ready to earn your certificate, now?"

She smiles again, softer this time. "I'd like to find out."

I nod, surrendering. And surely not for the last time tonight. "All right then. Let's see how well I've taught you."

II ⊙═══

"Let's stand," Caroly says. "And start this properly."

We do, and I shiver as she runs her hands and gaze up my belly and chest, over my shoulders, down my arms. I reach for her waist but she catches my wrists.

"You don't get to do anything except be spoiled," she informs me.

"Not even touch you? What a cruel deprivation."

"Just let me be in charge."

"Very well." Worries nip at me. Will my cock respond, with all my precious control castrated? If it doesn't, will I hurt her confidence as well as mine?

The questions drop to the back of my head as she strokes my sides, then my back, her small breasts under her soft cotton top glancing my chest.

Plenty of clients have requested this one-way breed of contact, women who crave a man's body but fear his touch. It was different all those times. I simply embodied that role, became that obedient man for an hour or two. But Caroly wants *me*, just Didier, and I'm fidgety when asked to be still. If my hands aren't kept busy, all their wasted energy goes directly to my hyperactive brain. I could take on a pleasing part, put on a show, make myself into the perfect submissive man...but then it wouldn't be the two of us anymore. Not the way she wants. Not the way I want, either, in all honesty.

"May I speak, or shall I be mute as well as limp?"

She smiles up at me. "You can speak all you like. Just don't bother making any demands."

She looks strange to me. New somehow. There's a gleam in her eye, a wicked glint to match her smirk. She rises on her toes, holding my jaw as she kisses my mouth. It feels odd to accept a kiss, rather than give it. Like writing with my left hand.

Dropping back on her heels, she lets me go and nods to the bed. "Have a seat."

I do. Caroly does what I might have next, moving the card table iced in half-melted pillar candles closer and lighting a dozen or more wicks. My fingers twitch, wanting to be the ones busy with the task.

She turns, still wearing that funny little grin. Still wearing everything but her shoes, but she remedies that, removing her jewelry, peeling her shirt up her long, long waist and over her head. Her pale skin is opal in the moonlight, cream in the cool dawn, golden now in the candles' glow. Her brassiere is a shade darker, caramel satin edged in the same lace that minutes ago tickled my fingertips between her thighs. She's full of interesting angles—the dip of her collarbone, the points of her elbows and the bones of her wrists, the strong lines of her jaw and cheeks. You might find this body on a runway, if never the cover of a men's magazine. She's a heron, at once graceful and awkward, long and rare and startling.

Her skirt drops in a whisper of silk. I've never watched her this way before. In fact I can't recall a night when I wasn't the one to undress her. My mouth waters. I'm a hungry man forced to watch a feast laid out, not yet allowed to taste. She steps out of the garment, standing between my knees at the edge of the bed. She strokes my hair with lazy distraction, traces the outline of my face. I stare up into her eyes, the angle reminding me of every succulent minute I've spent between her legs, kissing her sex. Her thumb follows the curve of my lips.

"Lie down."

I do as ordered, head on the pillows and arms draped behind in a gesture of obedience. She nudges my legs apart and kneels between them, gaze roaming my body like a landscape.

"You're so handsome."

So often, her lust is framed in awe, but tonight there's something predatory about her. It quickens my pulse.

Smooth palms stroke my shins, my thighs, skirting my cock to slide up my abdomen and chest, then down my ribs. My breath grows short. My fingers curl, arms tense from wanting to move, to touch her in return.

Her attention is at my hips, thumbs following the contours of the muscles there. She slips her fingers under the band of my shorts and draws them back and forth, back and forth along my belly. She does the same to the hems at my thigh, a thrilling tease against the sensitive skin.

Take them off, I want to say. *Take them away and touch me. Suck me. Make me so hard it hurts. Take my cock inside you and use me until the ache is so sharp I'm begging, and say my name when you come.*

But I don't get to make demands.

Instead I let my breathing grow shallow and loud, let her hear what so few do outside those frenetic final moments of sex—my helplessness. My need. I groan softly, the sound saying, *Touch me. Please.*

Her taunting hands edge closer, closer to the ridge of my erection, close enough that I can feel the pull of the silk against my pulsing skin, and that alone is enough to make me moan. My hands twitch and rise, ready for more. Ready to push my waistband down and do what she won't, stroke my flesh and end this torture. But I stop. I lay my palms flat to my stomach, willing them to behave.

Oh, she's mean. She toys with the fabric, drawing it taut—to outline my shape or purely to torment me, I don't know. I shift my hips, intensifying the sensation.

"You want more," she murmurs.

"Yes."

Her thumbs trace me, their nails drawing fiery-hot stripes down the sides of my cock.

"Please." I shut my eyes and my hands curl into fists atop my middle.

She touches me—a soft sweep of her knuckles or fingertips over my balls, then another, lower. There's tenderness as she cups and fondles, but I want more. More intensity, more of everything. The silk binds my cock, maddening. Everything I've trained myself to suppress in aid of spoiling my lovers gnaws at me, greedy and impatient. I want callous, tactless male things. To expose myself to her like an animal in heat, ease the skin down until I'm completely bared. I want her eyes on my hard flesh. I want her hands, her mouth, her cunt. Want her on her hands and knees. I want to punish her for teasing me this way, remind her which of us does the fucking, which takes what they're given.

But all that aggression dissolves the second she touches me. I tremble as the pads of her fingers run up along my ridge, gasp as they brush my head. Cool air caresses that fevered skin, and she's inching the band down. I open my eyes, draw my knees in so she can strip my shorts completely. Suddenly I have what I wanted so violently moments ago, to be exposed to her. But on my back I feel a shiver of vulnerability. Not an unpleasant sensation, I admit. Being at her mercy is taboo—an enjoyable twinge, unlike the paralysis of being at the mercy of my compulsions and fears.

She draws her palm along the sensitive underside of my cock. "Better?"

"Yes."

I watch her hand and the sight draws my desire into a fist, hot and tight in my lower belly. Her touch grows steadily gruffer, until I'm stiff as steel in her hand, until my skin and her palm grow damp, the strokes dragging with exquisite friction. My back arches, hips seeking more. She pushes me flat with her free hand.

"Just enjoy." *Just suffer,* her tone tells me, a happy hint of cruelty glimmering.

I obey. I watch her extraordinary face, lips parted with mischief or lust, and it's laughable that I ever worried I wouldn't rouse for her— with just us, just Didier and Caroly. I doubt I've ever felt so deeply, utterly naked. Stripped of clothes and control and the safety of roles.

She moves to my side, propping herself on her hip and one hand, the other free to explore my body. The position presses her breasts together, the softest, palest flesh I've ever known, clad in lustrous satin. I reach for her, wanting to feel the weight of her, the warmth.

She plucks my hand away. "You're not allowed to do a thing."

But I violate this rule without thinking, not even a minute later. She catches my fingers as they glance her skin. "The maestro's very bad at sitting back while someone else conducts."

"My hands won't listen to me. Or to your rules. Tie them down if you don't wish them to wander." I say it with a smile, body flushing at the notion. Perhaps I'm not so terrible at passivity as I'd imagined.

Caroly calls my bluff. She leaves me to go to the chest at the foot of the bed. I admire the curve of her hip outlined gold in the candlelight, the trail of her spine, all the shadows of her. She straightens with silk scarves in her hands.

"Those will never hold me," I say, a touch cocky. "Keep digging."

With a curious look she turns back to the chest to rummage, eventually finding what I hinted at. Two thick, tan leather cuffs, connected by a foot-long strap. The buckles jingle as she holds them up. "These?"

"Yes. Those may stand a chance at keeping my hands out of trouble."

She returns to the bed, scanning for something she might secure me to. The posts rooted in the headboard are too high, and too awkward, being at the corners of the mattress. *She doesn't know all the secrets of this room yet,* I think, smiling at the notion.

"There's a spot at the foot of the bed," I tell her. A decorative scalloped cut-out in the footboard big enough to slip a fist through, which I fitted with a metal post for just these wicked purposes. Caroly finds it, and since she's driving tonight, I let her fumble with the logistics and discover the best way to squeeze one cuff through the gap, around the post and back. If she's nervous, it doesn't show on her face when she turns to me. I think back to the woman I first welcomed into this flat a few short months ago. A startling transformation indeed.

"Come here," she tells me.

I lie as she directs and rest my wrists above my head. The leather feels stiff and smooth, buckles cold, the bed foreign with me lying backward and without a pillow.

"Tighter," I say as she threads the first cuff. "One more notch." If I'm to feel helpless, we'll do it properly. No chance I can slip free. This may be just the sort of therapy I can get behind.

When the task is done, she smiles and tells me, "That's the last order you get to issue tonight."

"This is less a seduction than a hostage taking."

"This is whatever I feel like," she says, smug and playful.

I tug at my restraints. In an emergency my hands could unbuckle one another, though it would take some effort.

Caroly leaves me for the chest again. What else does she want, I wonder?

It all feels very…different. I've had the odd client ask to tie me down, but I've let none of them do it quite so snugly. And those few times, I knew if I was to fight or tremble or beg. I knew what I was expected to be. But I know Caroly wants only me, and unadulterated Didier hasn't ever been restrained quite this way.

Without a part to play, my hands are antsy as ever.

They want a job. They need a watch to fix, a lock to pick, a meal to prepare, a woman to excite. They've always been that way. As a child I was a nail biter and a skin picker, whapped soundly by my mother whenever caught. Like me, her beauty had been her power, and she proclaimed my anxious habits tantamount to self-mutilation. Desperate, she had my grandmother teach me how to knit, and I took to it so obsessively it's a wonder I didn't develop arthritis at age eight. I made great long useless rectangles, only to unravel them when I ran out of yarn and start again. My mother said she always knew where I was in our flat from "that incessant clicking." But I never again bit my nails or savaged my skin.

I moved on to tinkering by adolescence, turning an unsightly compulsion into a rather useful hobby. I sometimes wonder if I could have been a musician, had my fingers found keys or strings instead of a tool set. But I will settle for being a master of the female body. No instrument feels so good in the hands or makes so fine a sound.

But now my restless fingers have only leather and air to occupy them. I grasp the strap that links my wrists, rubbing its worn edge with my thumbs and letting the texture distract me.

After a minute's perusal, Caroly says, "Shut your eyes."

I hear and feel as things are set at the foot of the bed, near my elbow. I try to guess from the sounds what she has in store for me. Was that the clink of glass or metal? The smoothness that touches me a moment later is merely her fingertips. Her weight joins the bed and she strokes my chest, throat, arms.

"You can open your eyes."

I do. I swallow.

The woman I love is above me, and not in any context I've ever experienced. Her face is half in shadow, curls lit by the flames behind her. The way she stares, she looks beautiful and dangerous, an angel gone rogue. An exciting stranger in familiar skin.

Her fingers play along my side, drawing a line from my hip to my shoulder and back again. Her touch teases, but her gaze burns. Hot desire in those cool eyes, that huntress look she gives me so often, one that strokes my vanity and arousal equally. Finally the setting matches that stare. I'm no lesson tonight, no tour guide, not even a partner.

I'm her plaything.

"What will you do with me?" I ask.

"Whatever I like." She reclines again on her hip and elbow at my side. Her gaze and fingertips trail from my throat to my chest, my belly, down to my thigh and up again. And again. Just the lightest touch but fire rises in its wake. My cock envies the attention, stiffening, but she ignores it. It's my mouth she wants next. She traces my lips with her thumb then slides it inside. I shut my eyes and close her in my heat, sucking. She draws her thumb away, replaces it with a finger, then two. I spoil them as if they were as sensitive as her clitoris, lavish them with my tongue, remind her what I can do.

She takes her hand back and I open my eyes. Her hair brushes my cheek as she leans in, her warm breast settling on my chest. I've grown used to being the initiator of our kisses, and I have to ignore an urge to lead when her lips brush mine.

Her kisses excite me—deep and confident. How long has she known how to kiss this way? How long have I gone not realizing, always so busy dictating?

The questions fade as her palm glides down my chest and belly to close over my cock, drawing a moan from my mouth into hers. She coaxes my thighs wider and I obey. Her touch roams, stroking, cupping, squeezing. My hips flex, wanting more. That firm hand pushes me flat to the mattress, and I feel her smile through the kissing. A fond smile of amusement at my eagerness? Or the smirk of a woman keen to torture? Her hand closes around me and I lose the will to care.

Her strokes are slow and decadent, long pulls from the root to just below the crown. I feel spoiled. And measured. Taunted. I feel hard and needy and helpless, powerless and virile at once. A predator, fettered and hungry.

When my hips rise again, she allows it. *Faster,* I tell her, thrusting into her fist, willing it to tighten. But she only indulges me for a dozen beats, then her hand is gone, my arousal left to throb in the cool air. I'm abandoned next by her mouth as she sits up. I watch her tongue trace her lower lip, imagining her servicing my cock. She kisses differently when she's in charge. What other tricks might that mouth reveal tonight?

Alas, I'm not to find out. Not yet.

"Turn over. On your hands and knees."

A shiver whisks through me. In part it's the uncertainty, not knowing what she has planned. But more intimidating is that wide-open curtain, being made to look out across the rooftops and the glittering city.

I do as I'm told, getting to my knees and palms. The strap of the cuffs twists, drawing my wrists a bit closer, a bit tighter. Now I see the items she's chosen for tonight's reversal—the smooth glass dildo and the smallest of my paddles.

The last time we used either, *my* hands wielded them. I'm no stranger to being their target, but the idea tenses me more than it normally might. The city is watching tonight. No human gaze could chance upon me, not in this dim light and not so high above most of the neighboring windows. But Paris is watching. That great brick bully's twinkling eyes are on me, witnesses to my powerlessness.

My heart is a rock, my throat a length of cloth wrung dry and taut. A soft, slow hand strokes my back, and I sense Caroly reading my thoughts.

"It's a beautiful city."

"From afar, perhaps."

"It's your home," she tells me.

No, I think. *This building is my home.* These walls are my entire world some days, the flat my island nation, its rooms familiar provinces, all of it suspended in a cold, chaotic sea—Paris. Paris, with no up or down or left or right, where I'll be swept away and lost if not tethered, where I'll drown. My lust withers to limp shame with those electric eyes blinking, staring. Mocking.

That city is my jailer, but I love my cell so very much.

I fidget, needing to feel the leather around my wrists. Captivity is as soothing as a blanket to a mind like mine. Paris has a willing prisoner in me. It's Caroly who keeps digging tunnels, keeps sawing through my bars and inviting me to make my escape. Always her hand, reaching out.

Everyone else is content simply to visit, to believe I'm happy as I am. To let me believe it. With their help I stayed locked inside for three years. With their help my tender feet grow blistered after two blocks' journey, it's been so long since I've laced them into shoes. Their love has turned me pale, left my eyes sensitive to the sunlight and made me forget what a garden smells like. They love my costume as much as I do. Only Caroly seems to prefer the naked actor trembling inside.

She loves me best, I realize. And all at once, I sink with perfect surrender into my body.

"Okay?" she asks.

"Yes, I'm okay." *Take me out of my head,* I want to beg. Let me suffer this vulnerability in my body, where everything is simpler, where misgivings morph to kinks.

She shifts behind me, knees nudging my calves apart another inch or two. Her hands stroke my skin in perfect symmetry, seeming to memorize. The fins of my shoulder blades, the chute of my spine, muscles in my back that I can feel but never see. She kneads my hips, my thighs. The briefest, cruelest tease of a touch tells her my cock is still hard—some parts of me won't be bullied by the disparaging nonsense that haunts my head, at least.

Her hands round my hips to my ass, circling my flesh, tracing my cleft. I sigh when she grazes that most intimate spot. My arms shake and I drop to my elbows.

"You like this, don't you?" The cockiness has left her tone, and she wants reassurance she's welcome to cross this line, and the next.

"I do." Her fingertips stroke up and down between my cheeks. I've done this any number of times over the years, with a generous handful of clients. But it's different tonight. Caroly's going somewhere I know she never expected she would, and it makes the act feel new to me as well. Everything feels new with her.

"It's intense," I say, "but that's good. It pulls me out of my head. Without numbing me, I mean."

She doesn't reply, just keeps drawing her fingers up and down.

Fuck me, I think. *Dominate me. Push me so deep inside my own helplessness I find its pitch-black, frozen center; so deep it can't hurt me anymore.* "I'd love for you to do that to me," I whisper.

It's the nudge she needed. She leaves me, shuffling to the other side of the bed, to the side table. I know that in a few breaths she'll return with the mineral oil. The lover I've coaxed and molded these past few months, the one always so eager for my guidance… A novice no more. The master tonight.

III ⚷

As Caroly sets the oil on the floor beside the bed, I hear her mutter the faintest, "Okay," to herself, a breath's pep talk.

A cool hand holds my hip then slippery fingertips glide between my cheeks. A shiver runs through me, chased by a fever.

At once I wish my hands were free. I wish I could brace myself higher, against the footboard, turn my head to watch. Instead I drop my forehead between my fists and submit to the powerlessness.

I moan each time she brushes my entrance, letting her know I want this. And that it's okay if she wants it too, this act that used to furrow her brow with confusion. She's asked about it often, wanting to understand why other women would request it of me.

She preps me well, with more oil and the slow, thrilling ventures of a single fingertip. Circling to start, then inside, just a millimeter. Deeper, deeper, by the tiniest measures. My entire body is on edge, that exotic mix of excitement and shame I know well, dark and rich as caviar. I ache to know what she feels—if she's nervous or turned on, scandalized or fascinated. All I get are her heavy breaths behind me.

Then her finger is gone, and both hands. The dildo disappears from beside my elbow, and my arousal spikes in perfect counterbalance to my nerves.

As the tip glances me, a desperate, helpless sound falls from my lips. Caroly draws it over my entrance in short sweeps and the pleasure sharpens.

It's by no means my first time in this position, not my first time with my hands bound, even. But it's been a long while, six months or more since I had a client request this. It's never a natural sensation, not for either sex, but that's what makes it exciting. That and the sinfulness of the inversion, of a man letting a woman penetrate the most intimate depths of his body.

The glass leaves me only to return in seconds, slippery with a fresh drizzle of oil. She doesn't push yet, only strokes between my cheeks, the contact explicit and scary and forbidden.

There's hesitance as she whispers, "You can give me instructions. If I do anything that doesn't feel right."

"Get me wet." Such a female request—the words send a chill through me. "Get me ready, just as you are." With that said, I suddenly don't want my precious control. If we're doing this, I want to submerge myself utterly. "Do as you want. I'll say if it's too much." Though too much may feel perfect.

Pressure. My lids squeeze shut. I force myself to keep breathing, calm my body and invite this experience. I wish she could feel this moment as I can, when I sink inside her sex. All that slippery, tight heat wrapping itself around my flesh, sensations wasted on a rigid length of unfeeling glass.

"Oh." The first surrender, that sudden, strangely gentle breaching

She's good—doesn't press further, just moves the dildo with subtle twists as my muscles adjust. I gasp again when the pressure suddenly leaves, and when the glass returns, slick again with oil, I welcome it easily. The room feels so quiet, though. My thoughts so loud.

"I want to hear what you're thinking," I tell her. Neither an order nor a plea, merely a request. She grants it.

"I'm just admiring your body." She runs her free palm down my back. "All these little muscles that tense."

Lovers' Braille, I think. She reads my body as I so often do hers. The notion flees as the pressure returns. I clamp like a fist but only for a breath, willing my body to calm. To peel open the violation and find the pleasure wrapped inside. She holds back until I've relaxed then puts her palm to my hip, and pushes.

I shudder, tiny hairs rising along my arms and back. The anxiety has finally fermented to excitement, and I shift my hips, wanting more.

"Does it feel good?" she asks.

"Yes. It's beginning to."

"How does it feel, exactly?"

I take a moment to explore the question, settling into the intrusion. My muscles have adjusted and I find subtler sensations now, the smooth caress of the glass against those secret, private spots. I feel used and spoiled, resistant and eager. Should some stranger see us, I'd be flooded at once with shame and brazen pride. "It feels like many things. Dirty, above all else. Sinful." I clear my sticky throat. "What does it make you feel, doing this to me?"

She eases out the dildo and I groan. She doesn't reply until the head returns once more, cool from the air and the oil. It slips inside with only the briefest twinge, lighting up a million neglected nerve endings.

"It makes me feel...powerful, I think." The dildo creeps deeper, another inch or more, its progress seeming to darken the room. My body wants this—faster than she's giving. I roll my hips to show her, but she stills me with a firm hand.

"I'm driving, remember?" The confidence is back in her voice.

"Yes, of course."

"Do you ever…" She trails off. I let her assemble the thought, lost for a few beats in her physical demands. My head's grown light, my breathing fast and reedy.

"You've done this before," she says.

"I have."

"Do you ever think about… Do you ever imagine it's a man doing this? You know. Not a dildo."

"No. I don't."

It's an obvious thought, a natural question to ask, but I've never been at ease around men. Certainly not ones in a position to make me feel weak. Imagining opening the most vulnerable realms of my body to their graceless, sweaty male appetites is the last thing that would have me panting this way.

"It's far more exciting to me—and taboo enough—just being fucked by a woman." I'd do anything for a lover, be anything she wanted. A hard cock to own her, a tight vessel to swallow her aggression. Just want me, and I'm yours. Just look at me with hungry intention in your eyes and I'll slip into any skin you hand me.

Caroly takes me deeper, deeper, so deep I feel the brush of her knuckle. She eases back and there's the clink of the glass stopper of the oil bottle, the soft rustle of a towel. She fills me again, again, finding a pace. Every push, I gasp. Every withdrawal, I shudder. Every worry dissipates, swallowed in sensation.

"Oh. Fuck me."

The strokes quicken as she learns to intuit how deep to go. Her free hand squeezes my cheek, the way mine has done when I've taken her from behind, the way I've clasped her hip when she's beneath me. I straighten my arms to rise and crane my neck, savoring a glance at her feminine body, the slender arm flexing as she takes me. I wish I could see the dildo in her hand, see the cock she's wielding to make me feel this way. I shut my eyes and imagine it strapped about her hips, both hands free to grip my waist or pleasure my own cock, to feel her thighs touch mine as she took this role-reversal even further. I'd watch in the mirror. Watch that willowy female body fucking my larger male one. The image draws a moan from my lungs.

She strokes my back. "Tell me what you're thinking."

"About watching you, doing this to me. How beautiful you'd look. How strong you'd look, owning my body."

"Is it just you here with me, now?"

"Yes, just me." I open my eyes, turning my head to meet her gaze. "Just us." Just me, stripped of everything, stripped of my maleness, even.

The motions slow, turning deep and focused. "Good," she murmurs. "You're all I want."

Her words caress me far deeper than any physical touch could. They cradle my heart in cupped hands. She can have that, that and so much more. Whatever she believes this malfunctioning man has to offer, it's hers.

And I'll tell her so. Soon.

Overwhelmed, I squeeze the strap tight. I feel even more exposed this way, weak and degraded, utterly naked. Each time the dildo slides deep, a fearful noise falls from my lips, chased by a groan as the glass glances that electric, unseeable spot. My cock twitches with every pass.

Her palm circles my hip, then my cheek, a light caress but blazing with heat, coupled with the penetration.

Touch my cock, I want to say. A plea or an order. A pull or squeeze or the whisper of her fingers. To drop my hips and feel the brush of the covers. Anything. The intrusion is sweet, but so intense. If she'd only rub my hurting cock. I might come in a single stroke, but at least it would end this exquisite torture. I keep my wishes to myself, begging only with my moans. Suddenly, she slows.

"I want…" She's hesitant again. Shy.

"Whatever you want, just ask."

"Can I use the paddle on you?"

Fuck, yes. "You can do anything to me." I've let this woman take me outdoors, after all. There's nowhere we can go inside this bedroom that will test my boundaries more.

The paddle disappears from my periphery, and I feel the edge of the leather whisper along my thigh.

Hit me. Punish me for liking this. Deepen the shame that has me panting like a dog.

Her hand stills, holding the dildo in place. "Show me how you want it."

Edging my knees a bit wider, I ease my hips forward and back, the strokes growing longer and quicker as I master my thrusts. It's the same motion as when I'm fucking, and the mechanics tighten that pleasurable knot in my belly, reminding my cock all the more acutely what it's missing, how backward all of this is.

"That's sexy," she whispers.

The first night we met, she watched me masturbate. I conjure the memory of her gaze and her parted lips, of the curious, fretful woman who came to me in search of an initiation. I can't see her face, but I know what her expression must look like. Just picturing it triggers a pang of arousal, clenching my body around the glass. I falter.

The paddle lands with a *whap*. My body bucks from surprise more than pain, and I feel fire collect on the spot, seconds before the leather brands me again.

"*Oh.*"

"Keep going," she says.

I do as I'm told, eager for everything—the sensation, the orders, the threat, and the correction if I fumble. The pleasure grows wild, too hot and frantic to control. My hips lose the beat and the second I take to recover is enough—*whap*.

My moan is a pure sound, encapsulating every contradictory thing I feel. I defy her just long enough to earn another slap of leather on my ass, then comply with the strike still stinging.

That burn on my skin. The trespass of smooth glass inside me. The fucking motion of my hips but with no warm flesh welcoming my cock. Too much. My thrusts are frantic, and the penetration in turn. I'm edging close to that most frustrating of mistakes—coming without my arousal even being touched. If she'd only stroke me, I'd die of pleasure. So intense I'd go blind, with the dildo filling me, if only she'd *touch me*.

"I can't…" I begin, but the words abandon me.

"You need to fuck?"

Yes yes yes. "Please."

"Okay." So, so slowly, she eases the glass free. "You on top, then."

She's read my mind. If I don't get a turn to be the one doing, I'll die. I'm sure of it. But I want the dildo, and that makes it tricky. She leans over me, hands shaking as she fumbles with my buckles. I hear her labored breathing. She's excited and I haven't so much as warmed her sex against my palm.

Who are you? I want to demand, but discovering is more fun than being told.

Finally, I'm free. "Lie down," I say, sitting back on my heels.

I nearly come just getting the condom on, and for once I'm grateful for the dulling latex. I'm clad and above her before she's even got a pillow and settled herself.

"Keep your legs together." I straddle her hips, guiding my cock between her thighs and finding her lips, pushing inside at a sharp angle. I have to ignore how she feels—hot and slick and snug. It's not the easiest position, but this way she can still reach to give me what I want.

"Give me the glass." It's exciting to issue orders, to feel my aching flesh pulsing inside hers.

The arrangement has me spread wide open and the dildo slips inside, smooth and swift. I groan like a beast, the primal sound roaring from my lungs. I doubt I've ever worked so hard to suppress an orgasm. It's a battering ram, every beat of my cock splintering my defenses anew. "Don't move," I mutter. "Don't move."

We're frozen for a minute or more, as though posing for the most lecherous sculpture ever commissioned. I feel the climax inching back, control returning to me one breath at a time. "Okay. Just hold it still."

She does.

But I'm back at the edge in an instant—one push and I'm losing it. My head swims. I can let go and fuck hard and come so fast and deep I scream. Or I can hold back for her sake. Try to ignore the ache and risk neutering one of the most violent climaxes of my life.

As lousy as I am at it, I have to be selfish.

I fuck. I fuck with every thrust, get fucked each time I pull out. Rampant and filthy. My appetites have left her with nothing but a clumsy left hand to pleasure her clit and too many tasks to bother, it seems. Even if she could, I won't last. We've been teasing my body inside-out for the better half of an hour.

Suddenly, fire—the mean scrape of her fingernails where the paddle stung my cheek.

"Fuck." My hips race. The climax is rising, rushing, boiling. Any second. Any second.

Caroly's eyes are wild and bright, darting like lightning bugs. "Jesus, you're hard."

Any second. "It hurts," I tell her through a gasp.

I need to come.

Why can't I *come?*

I buck with another drag of her nails. Years now, I've been trained to wait for permission—begged or ordered or implied with the tug of eager hands on my ass, my hips, my cock. Hard as I am, as much as I'm suffering, I need to be told.

"Please," I moan.

"Come."

I do. I drop to my elbows, press my sweaty forehead to hers with a thump, jam our bodies together. I come like a dam bursting, the most violent, frightening relief. The pleasure in my cock feeds the sensation from the dildo and back again, doubled, deepened. Each wave of it tenses me anew, each flash surely the last, until I feel the next on its heels.

I lost myself, but now there's her hand gripping my arm, the twinge of pain where my thigh grinds against her hip bone.

I push up onto my palms and she eases the glass out, drawing a final shudder from my throat.

"Oh fuck."

I'm drunk.

I've died, surely. The orgasm killed me.

Caroly combs her fingers through my hair, strokes my neck. She smiles.

She hasn't come. "I'm s—"

Two fingers still my lips. "Don't you dare."

I nod and swallow my apology.

Her smile sharpens to a grin. "Wow."

"Oh?"

"Yeah. That was… I've never seen you like that. So nuts."

I get control of my legs and flop down alongside her, peeling away the rubber. "Come here."

She does as my hands ask, letting me pull her close, her back to my chest.

"It's your turn." I can't even be bothered to strip her. I just push my hand inside her panties, finding her as wet as I've ever felt. She gasps, the softest, sweetest noise.

"All this for me," I mumble, "and I haven't even touched you."

My fingers slip against the hard nub of her clit, and she gives a thrash from the shock. I'm not the only one who suffered, it seems. I rub her in slow, light circles until she stops jolting, until her hips flex with greedy motions, rubbing her backside against my cock. I put my lips to her ear, still high from my release.

"I love the way you fucked me tonight." I say it in French, a whisper. She tenses, stroking my knuckles with frantic fingertips.

"I don't think I've ever come so hard," I tell her.

"Didier."

"It felt so good, being at your mercy. Taking whatever you gave me." Even thinking about it, I'm growing stiff. I'm too spent to bother with the rigmarole of a condom, or to much care about coming a second time, but I slip between her thighs and thrust, just to make her feel what she does to me.

She draws a harsh breath, lets it out as a groan.

"Already you have me hard again."

"Take me."

"No. I've been spoiled quite enough for one night. Just feel what you do to me."

I want the tease now, and the ache as I fall asleep. I want to spend the next morning wound up from wanting her. Hurting. Then in the afternoon perhaps I'll take my turn at being the demanding one.

Her hair smells of lavender, her skin of summer and sex. I kiss her ear, nipping and suckling the lobe as my fingertips stroke her clit. I can nearly taste her. "I'll spoil you tomorrow," I promise.

"Sure," she says, though the panting ruins her quip. "Because tonight was—such a hardship."

"Shhh." I kiss her ear again, imagining baubles I might find to decorate that soft skin. With my lips at her neck, I try to conjure a pendant she might prefer. A bracelet or ring or pin, or some other unexpected offering. I'll discover soon what that gift might be. Very soon. I'll find some pretty, inadequate object, just a token to punctuate what I really want to give her. My heart. Perhaps my hope.

Her sex is hot against my fingers, body antsy. The hand on mine has grown frantic and I give her thrusts of my cock to match, stroking her lips through the damp fabric.

"Tell me what you're thinking."

"About what we did," she mutters, squeezing my wrist.

"You liked it?"

"Yes."

"How did you feel, fucking me?"

She doesn't answer at once. She gulps a few breaths, squirming under my hand. "Strong," she finally manages.

"Powerful."

She nods, curls caressing my face.

"That's how you felt to me, too."

I intensify the teasing and she moans, coming apart, stitch by stitch.

"Come, Caroly."

Her cries fill the room, sweet, ragged sighs and gasps. I feel when she releases, her thighs squeezing my length as her pussy so often has, fingers rubbing my knuckles before she suddenly stills my hand, pressing it hard to her clit, forcing only the faintest motions until she lets go for good.

"Beautiful." I say it again, burying my face in that soft, soft hair. "So beautiful."

With a spent shudder, she flops her arm along mine. I hug her tightly.

She shifts, surely feeling my cock still beating hard between her thighs. "Do you want me to—"

"No." Let it suffer.

For twenty minutes or more I hold her, listening as her breathing goes from speeding to steady, to calm, to sleepy. My erection softens and our sweat cools, though the night is still balmy.

I rouse her, excusing myself for a quick shower, to wash away the oil and the stickiness of July. My body feels tender under the cold spray, but it's nothing to do with the sex. There's a thinness to my skin, a persisting nakedness quivering in my very cells.

I submitted to her. There's that. But I'll do anything in the pursuit of pleasure. No, this naked feeling tells me I've nothing left to bare to the woman in my bed. No secrets, not a single shadow of my body, no state of emotional crisis short perhaps of tears—and I haven't shed those in years.

There's only one thing I've held back. Those two little words— three, should I utter them in English. All just sounds in the end, just my soul tumbling from my lips into her ear. A trifle.

But I can't tonight.

Not from a place of weakness, no matter how willing and pleasurable the deconstruction was. I'll tell her outside as I'd planned, standing under the sky she reintroduced me to, with my hands trembling but my confidence steeled. I'll pick the caretaker's padlock with the very tools she handed me and take her to the roof, stare out over the city I love and hate so deeply, and tell her then. Whatever gift I find for her at that shop, I'll fold it in her palm, and wonder if she can feel my heartbeat wrapped in her slender fingers.

I shut off the water, towel myself dry. The bedroom is dark, only one candle left burning and the night sky black. I shut the curtains, but not for fear of the city's mockery, this time. Only to feel closer to the woman in my bed.

It's too sultry for sheets, and she makes room atop the covers. She changed into pajamas in my absence, the ones she wore the first night she slept over, tiny embroidered goldfish scattered across stormy blue-gray satin. I leave the candle to burn itself out, wrap her in my naked body once more and kiss her long neck.

"So," she sighs.

"Yes?"

"How did I do tonight? Driving?"

"How did *you* do tonight? You were a natural." I squeeze her tighter. "What other women are you hiding behind that novice act?"

"I dunno. I didn't even know about that one you just met."

"I like her. She's welcome in this bed." I slip her hair behind her ear and press my lips to her jaw. "Though perhaps not until I've had a chance to be conductor again, for a performance or two."

She goes still in my arms for a few tight, thoughtful breaths. Her body's cues are a mastered dialect to me now, and I wait patiently, knowing she's choosing words.

Soon enough, she frees herself to turn over. She blinks at my chin and rubs idly at my collarbone, assembling a thought.

I smooth an errant lock. "Yes?"

"I told you tonight, I don't want to feel like your medication. Something you numb yourself with."

"And I agree."

"How do you feel about the opposite, about my treating you like...I dunno. A project. A patient."

"I've never thought that, about your intentions."

"No?"

I kiss her nose. "You treat me like a friend. You soothe me when I'm upset, but push me when I need pushing."

She softens. "Okay. I just don't want you to wind up resenting me, for putting you in all these positions to *get* upset."

"I could never resent you."

It's a soft, kind lie. I resent her in tiny, sharp flashes, but only in moments of deep panic. Even in the midst of those pangs, I know my anger is misplaced. It's me I resent, that I can't move through this world the way other men can. I accept her invitations to remind myself of this fact, but to blame her would be cowardly.

"I only want..." She trails off, not liking whatever words she found at the end of that sentence.

"You only want what?"

"I was going to say, I only want you to be happy. But that's not entirely true. I want all this for myself too. To be able to see you, outside. Go places with you. Not that going to bed with you isn't wonderful, of course."

I kiss her for that, liking her guilty smile. "I know what you mean. I want those things too."

All at once she moves, slipping a bit farther down in my embrace so she can rest her cheek against my shoulder. "I think you're very brave."

"Even when I'm shaking, breathing into my collar to keep from passing out?"

"Especially then."

I press my lips to the crown of her head. *You'll see me shaking soon enough.* I glance at the ceiling, imagining the roof above, standing there with Caroly and fumbling through those words that must be said.

"What are you thinking about?" She reads my signals as easily as I do hers.

"About going out."

"Tomorrow?"

"Yes," I lie.

"Let's just go to the usual café. Nice and close."

"Sure." If she stays over tomorrow night, we'll likely do the same on Sunday, before she has to head home to her flat. I'll kiss her goodbye, wave as she turns the corner. Let her think I'm going home as well, but I'll unfold my careful directions and map, and set out for Gobelins again. Back at my quest, lest I give her any more cause for doubt. Lest I let the prize go unclaimed for too long, and allow some other man to prove himself worthier in my stead.

I picture my hutch, lined with its watches and clocks and other wind-up treasures.

They glitter like liquor bottles, I realize. I hide inside them as an alcoholic might, numbing and procrastinating and telling myself *tomorrow*.

Always *tomorrow*, I'll be a better man.

But I've let tomorrows gather like bricks, three years' worth. If I keep going that way, I'll wake some morning and find this garret stacked dark and tight and airless as a crypt, no room for Caroly, no room for anything but me and that cabinet. Give it enough time and no one will come knocking anymore. Or if they do, my walls will have grown too thick to hear.

My heart is thumping, my mouth dry. Caroly stirs from the edge of sleep. "Everything okay?"

"I'll be back."

I let her go and leave the bed, finding my pants and yanking them up my legs.

"Where are you going?"

"Out."

"Out where?"

"I don't know. Not far. Just to the pavement."

She sits up. "Really?"

"Yes. I won't be five minutes."

A long pause as I pull a shirt over my head.

"Okay," she says. "I'll be right here."

My legs are already weak as I stride through the living room, fingers clumsy as I unlock the door. I grab my keys from their hook and pocket them.

The hall tile is cool under my bare feet, the carpet on the stairs worn and gritty, the railing smooth in my grip. The air seems to grow thin as I descend, an alpine climb in reverse. More tile as I reach the ground floor, and that dreaded rectangular slice of street at the end of the corridor is growing closer, closer. Through the first door and past the postboxes. Usually they trigger me, with their tiny knobs and hinges, miniscule windows. *Come back inside,* they say. *You like it inside.*

But I think, *fuck you all.*

Fuck you and all the times you've witnessed my paralysis at this very threshold. Fuck you and every check slipped between your cold brass lips to keep me here.

The front door handle is cold in my sweaty palm, but it turns. It turns and I pull, and Paris spills in from the street, its sounds and smells and its breezes, a living, breathing beast, jaws as wide as the sky.

The warm granite steps are under my soles, then the brick and pebbles of the pavement. I stand before sixteen Rue des Toits Rouges and jam my shaky hands in my pockets.

Motorbikes and taxis fly past, shuttling simple people to simple places.

A Friday night. I used to go places on Friday nights, fancying myself a simple person. I used to drink and laugh and loiter on thick summer evenings like this one, and count myself lucky to bring a woman home. I took cabs then, to quell my anxiety, and smoked like a foundry. But my mother had been alive still, and visiting her kept me outside, in regular circulation. My refusal to ride the Métro and need to stand with my back to the wall were quirks to my social circle—to me, too—not symptoms of a disorder. My curious hobbies were merely that, not yet vices to self-medicate with.

He's eccentric, my friends said.

The beautiful are forgiven their shortcomings too easily. My looks brought me attention and the odd modeling job, kept my sheets warm and my ego stroked. I didn't depend on my beauty then, as I do now. Now it means income and groceries, the simplest of errands run by my admirers so I needn't suffer.

I draw my hands from my pockets, open and close my fingers, feel the grass between the bricks tickling my feet. My body is sore in the most private places and the seam of my trousers caresses my naked sex. There's sky above me for miles, a jungle of streets stretching in every direction.

Two young women, clearly drunk, are swaying down the pavement toward me, and I move to the stoop's bottommost step to give them room. My heart pounds as they near, as it does whenever another human is about to cross my path.

"*Salut,*" says one brightly, not seeming to notice my bare feet, my pale face, the way my hand trembles as I raise it in a little wave.

"*Salut.*"

Her friend giggles, tugging her more quickly down the street.

My heart still thuds, but I smile to myself, remembering how it felt to be this man. To leave girls giddy from having mustered the courage to even address me, as if I were someone special.

Someday they'll even pay for the chance to fuck you, I want to tell that man. *Don't let them. The ones who coddle you now will pity you in time. They'll pull the shades down and you'll tell yourself it's safer that way. It's better. Don't believe it. Wait for the one who presses your face to the glass. The one who makes your heart pound so hard, in so many unexpected ways.*

I sigh, surprised to find I can take a deep breath. I gulp another, another. I glance at the sky, beyond the haloes of the streetlights. The moon is elsewhere but perhaps I'll see it soon, see it from the roof where it can't hide, Caroly's hand in my clammy one.

My gaze drops to the windows of the tenement across the street, the building a twin of my own, only in tan brick, not red. There's a human shape in one frame, silhouetted by a flickering, unseen television. Perhaps he's watching me in turn. He backs away from the window and disappears into the private shadows of his own little realm.

You could leave too, I think.

He could be outside, smelling summer's heat in every vehicle and body that passes, feel it rising from the street, hear the urban pulse in the music of far-off clubs and thumping from cars.

I feel it all, hear it, smell it, taste it, everything beautiful and ugly and vital that feeds this city. It feeds on me too. I feel bare naked out here, skinned and split open, but I *feel*.

I let the city drink from me a minute longer, then turn and mount the steps on watery legs. No threats leer at my back as I unlock the foyer's inner door, only promises of what lies upstairs beckoning me. A soft body in my bed, soft lips ready with soft, sleepy questions about my absence. I mount the steps two at a time, as eager as I am anxious. Four flights, but five soon, perhaps next week.

Five flights, all the way to the roof, her hand in mine. And I'll tell her, with all of Paris watching.

CONFESSION

THE CURIO VIGNETTES, PART IV

1

I beat the rain, if barely. The sky went from silver to pewter between the Métro station and number sixteen Rue des Toits Rouges, but I'm spared, dodging a headful of frizzy curls and a ruined silk skirt.

I trot up the stone steps and into the elegant old foyer, and press the brass button for flat 5C. Smoothing my top and hair, I wait for the buzz—for Didier to unlock the foyer's inside door. Normally it takes a matter of seconds, but not this evening. After a minute I ring the bell again and check his mailbox. Empty.

A smile overtakes my lips.

It blossoms to a grin when I spot him through the glass door, appearing at the end of the hall from the stairwell. He waves, striding to let me in.

"Hello," I say. "Well done." Perhaps one visit in five he'll come down to meet me. Sometimes he has food on the stove, a ready excuse, but in truth it's his agoraphobia that keeps him upstairs. But not tonight, it would seem.

"Caroly. Good evening." He kisses my cheeks and takes the overnight bag from my hand. We head for the stairs and I save the chitchat, knowing he'll be edgy and distracted until the deadbolt's snapped shut behind us, four flights up in his garret sanctuary.

Ah, blessed Saturdays. Nowhere to be in the morning and my lover all to myself for the evening. Usually I get him both Fridays and Saturdays, but yesterday I had a friend's engagement party to attend, a girls-only affair.

Other days of the week…

On weekend nights Didier is all mine, but he's anyone else's for the right price come Sunday evening. I used to pay that price myself, but not since March, nearly five months ago. Now the price I pay is having to settle for whatever leftover weekdays haven't been booked by his clients.

Sometimes it's a pittance. Other times, not such an easy pill to swallow. But he's my lover, not my boyfriend. I'm a total lost cause— drowning in terminal love-lust for him, though I haven't told him in so many words. In gifts? Yes. In heated glances and physical gestures and emotional support—loud and clear.

I watch his back as we climb the stairs, wondering if he knows exactly how bad I have it. He's the best-looking man I've ever seen, as if you shook a copy of *Vogue* and a swarthy, elegant model from a Brioni spread magically tumbled out. Add to that the fact that he's so good in bed, women pay for the experience? Yeah, wobbly-kneed infatuation probably isn't a noteworthy reaction to him.

What does make me special—aside from my being the only woman I'm aware of who doesn't have to shell out to enjoy his company—is that I'm the only one who makes him leave his flat. Every time I visit, I drag him out with me, down the street for a coffee, occasionally to dinner. It's the equivalent of taking someone who's deathly afraid of the ocean and pushing them overboard into a choppy sea, so I must be special for him to keep letting me torture him so.

We reach his flat and when the door shuts behind us, I smile up at him. "Good job."

"Thank you."

"And your mailbox was empty."

"Yes. It was a good day." He pushes off his shoes. He hadn't bothered with socks, and he's just as I prefer, barefoot in slacks and a tee shirt. A shirt I bought him, a cotton-merino blend as soft as a baby's cheek and the dark green-blue of the Seine, with a price tag that would make any sane person snort with derision.

I lean my umbrella against the wall and breathe in deeply. "I smell potatoes. And chicken. And something else."

"*Romarin*." Rosemary.

"Yum."

The living room feels already set for seduction, a single lamp switched on in the corner, its soft glow all but swallowed up by the deep red walls. The curtains are drawn back, but the clouds offer little more than a view of the birds roosting on the ledge, gray as the fog. Except for one.

"The white pigeon is back," I say, excited. He showed up last week, and has a mottled black and gray marking on his breast partly obscured by one wing, which I think makes it look as though he's holding a painter's palette. Perhaps I'll name him Gauguin. Gauguin was a Parisian transient with unsavory diseases too.

I follow Didier into his warm, cozy kitchen and watch as he checks on the roast.

"Wine?" he asks, his voice still a touch tight from the journey downstairs.

"Please."

He pours us each a measure of white. "*Salut.*"

I echo the toast and we clink our glasses. "Oh, very nice." Clear and sharp.

Didier nods stiffly. He feels...far away tonight. It's just from the trip downstairs, I assure myself.

But a week ago I arrived here to find him mired in the aftermath of a panic attack, triggered by a disastrous solo excursion out in Paris. He's nowhere near that upset now, but there's definitely something going on. Something that's stolen the ease from my normally graceful lover's movements and words, and made his steady dark eyes dart nervously.

"So. What did you get up to today?" I ask, hoping I sound casual.

"Not very much. Tidying up. Reading."

"That sounds relaxing."

Another nod.

"How soon 'til dinner?"

"Fifteen minutes."

"Want to go sit down?"

He gestures for me to lead the way.

I settle on the couch and Didier switches on a second lamp, lifting some of the shadows. He sits beside me, but he feels so distant he may as well have stayed in the kitchen.

His anxiety's nothing new—it's a cloak I've seen him wear dozens of times, though rarely inside these walls. Usually here, sitting as we are, it's only him and me, easy as breathing.

He sips his wine. I sip mine, unsure where to look. I've caught his nerves and there's a knot forming in my chest. I take deep belly breaths to try to loosen it.

There's something undeniably not right with him, and it's getting worse by the minute. He's as stiff and quiet as he gets in the moments before we leave for the corner café, but we're not going anywhere tonight. Only to bed.

Or maybe we aren't going to bed tonight.

My stomach turns over.

Usually by now he's flirted with me. Asked about my day. At least given me that hot little look, the one that makes promises about what will happen between us later. So far, nothing. Evasiveness or nerves. News he needs to share...bad news.

I watch him as we drink but his eyes are on the wine, the floor, his hands, the far side of the room. Everywhere but my face, it feels.

If we're not going out, then the stress is coming from inside his head. And now it's inside *me*, a black viscosity rising from my gut, chilling me to the bone.

"Is everything okay?" It hurts to even get the words out, my throat's grown so tight.

A long pause. A very long pause, then a deep breath. "I need to talk to you about something." His voice is heavy—heavy with dread, not lust—jumpy gaze watching the wine in his glass.

My heart twists. My feet are heavy, like huge rocks pinning me to the bottom of a river, cold water rushing by, wrenching my limbs and filling my mouth.

"Okay," my lips say, detached from my brain.

Didier swallows, and I know now it's over.

We're over.

No one looks like that, so sad and broken and scared and disappointed, unless someone's died.

Or some *thing*. A relationship, if that's what this has been.

My chest aches so badly I want to rub it. My lungs shrivel like pricked balloons, and I can't seem to gulp enough air to stir them.

Didier leans closer, eyes narrowed at my face. "Are you all right?"

"Yes, fine." I drink deeply, gaze glued to the middle distance beyond his shoulder. "Are you? What did you want to talk about?"

He stands. "I don't want to tell you here."

"Here?"

"Not in the flat."

Pardon? Is this place too sacred, too sensual to be soiled by a breakup? I set down my glass. "Where, then?"

"Follow me."

He offers his hand and I take it, numb.

We stop in the kitchen so he can crack the oven door and switch off the heat. Already my palm is clammy, and I want to run. I want to run away from what's coming, and from this delicious roast I surely won't even get a chance to taste.

He leads me to the front door, not bothering to put his shoes on.

"Should I get my stuff?" I ask.

He looks confused. "No."

"Okay."

Back to the stairwell we head, Didier marching with more purpose than usual at this moment. But his hand shakes in my damp one, undermining the show.

"Where are—" I don't finish, too surprised when we turn left in the stairwell, heading *up* the steps, not down.

He drops my hand as we turn a corner, climbing another half flight. It's cramped and dark, with just enough light for me to watch him draw a padlock from a latch. The door opens with a creak, a sliver of gray sky widening to a rectangle. Didier helps me over a high threshold and out onto the narrow, tar-papered roof, caged on all sides by an old wrought iron latticework rail, topped with posts like spearheads.

Paris is all around us, above and below, in every direction, its tallest spires hidden by the heavy woolen cap of clouds.

I've never been dumped before. I've never even had a boyfriend before, and Didier's the only man I've gone on enough real dates with to warrant such an official conclusion…but I don't think this is right.

People don't get taken to rooftops to get cut loose. They get taken to roofs to be murdered, perhaps, but even panicking as I am, I know that's not why we're here.

I look up at his strained face. "What's going on?" *Why have you brought me to what must be the most unpleasant spot an agoraphobe could imagine? What on earth are you trying to prove?*

"I need to say something to you." He swallows one, two, three times. He falters, gaze darting all around us, at his worst nightmare. When he switches to French, the words seem to come easier. "I wanted to tell you here. When I'm terrified, so you'd know I meant it."

My shriveled lungs swell a bit and my aching heart gives a weak pump. "All right."

He clears his throat and takes my other hand, holding each gently, running his thumbs over my knuckles, eyes on the task. He clears his throat again. I look everywhere—at our hands, at his face, at the first beads of drizzle clinging to his dark hair.

"A few months ago," he begins, slow and shaky but clearly determined, "I hadn't left this building in three years. I hadn't taken my laundry out or collected my own groceries, sat and had a coffee in a café. Or smelled the grass or felt the sunshine."

A fat raindrop smacks me on the temple and slips down my cheek.

"I hadn't passed an evening with a woman—just her and I with no money exchanged—since before my exile. I haven't felt I had much to offer, besides my talents, in all that time."

I give his hands a squeeze just as another drop lands, slipping between our fingers. The breeze flings my curly hair all over and threatens to lift my skirt.

"You've made me feel things again. Made me *want* to feel things again." His gaze jumps to mine for a second before dropping shyly back to our hands. "Difficult things, not easy ones like lust. The things I work so hard to numb, like fear and helplessness and…and attachment."

My brows rise.

He laughs, the sound like a huff of frustration or disbelief. "I don't know why you think I'm so worth fighting for. But I'm grateful you do. And I'm grateful for whatever it is about me that keeps you coming here, dragging me out that door every morning we wake together."

My throat is swollen, sore and tight; the pain is *so* sweet, nothing like the way my heart hurt a few minutes ago. My eyes are already glossing with tears, my lips quivering.

"I'm going to tell you something," Didier says in English. "I wish I could claim I've never said it to anyone else. I have, but if I'd known that it felt like this, I would have saved it. I'd have known better."

My first tear rolls free, tracing the edge of my nose. Didier lets my hand go to wipe it from my chin. He smiles and the second falls, the third and fourth and more. I laugh out of nowhere, emotions short-circuiting. It hurts to laugh, my throat's so constricted. It hurts to cry, my sinuses burning.

He releases my other hand to cup my jaw, thumbs wiping at my cheeks, where tears and rain are mingling. He looks right in my eyes. The breath before he speaks again lasts for ages, long enough for me to record the texture of his irises, every radiating brushstroke blending a rainbow of rich, deep browns, molasses and chocolate and espresso and every other decadent flavor.

"I love you." He strokes my cheeks. "I'm in love with you."

My lips part but nothing comes out.

It feels…

Oh God, it feels so scary.

It feels like the breathless, slow-motion instant when you realize you've tripped, but you haven't hit the ground yet. Free-fall. The pain in my throat and heart is gone, and I'm blissfully numb. If I take my foot off the ground, if he lets go of my face, I'll tumble weightless up into the rain clouds, never to find gravity again.

My mouth opens, and words I've never said to anyone out loud tumble past my lips like soap bubbles, so faint they're nearly lost in the wind. "I'm in love with you."

Just a shadow of a smile, a perfect, unsure little gesture, gilded with hope.

When he kisses me, I think, *he's not shaking*. His hands are strong and calm, his lips steady against my trembling ones. I wrap my arms around his neck, needing his solidness to anchor me to the roof.

He tastes like Didier, like wine and seduction, like the salt from whatever sauce he made to baste the chicken.

He loves me, I think.

He loves me.

When he releases my jaw, I slide my hands down his shoulders and hold his arms, unwilling to let him go. I feel more naked than I ever have, letting him see every messy emotion contorting my face. I want to hide, but more than that, I want him to see. If this is love, it's sloppier than movies and pop songs let on. It's wonderful, and I need him to see what a wreck it's made of me.

"I'd like to ask you something." His voice is deep and confident, the way it sounds in the dark of his bedroom.

I sniffle and clear my clogged throat, nodding. "Anything."

"Can I consider you my girlfriend?"

I laugh. I hadn't had the time to guess what his question might be, but this one needs no deliberation. "Yes, of course you can."

A broad grin, another kiss—fierce and brief.

"I got you something," he says, reaching into his pants pocket. "Open your hand."

I let his arms go, honestly surprised when I don't float off into the stratosphere. He holds my wrist and silver pools in my palm, along with a pair of heavy raindrops.

It's a bracelet. A charm bracelet, made of delicate double links. Three baubles dangle from it and I have to peer close to make them out, the sky's grown so dark. I hold my whipping hair out of my eyes.

There's a tiny, ornate key. A Tahitian pearl, big and dark as a ripe blueberry, threaded on a simple sterling post. And a little bird.

"A dove."

He smiles. "A pigeon, I decided. They're doves, technically. Doves with bad publicists."

I laugh again. Of course a pigeon. And the key needs no explanation. The pearl doesn't hold any symbolism for me, but it's beautiful all the same. I close the chain in my hand.

"Thank you. I love it. I love you."

He wraps me in his arms, kisses my temple, whispers, "And I you."

For a long time we stand that way, until the breeze becomes wind and rain is running down my collar, plastering my skirt to my thighs, gathering in my flats. The last time rain filled my shoes this way, we were strangers. I was standing on his stoop, so scared to ring his bell...

I laugh for no good reason at all and step back a pace to stare up into the sky, just as lightning flashes in the distance.

"Maybe we better not ruin all this by drowning," I suggest, glancing at his bare feet. As if some greater force agrees, the thunder arrives and the door slams against its frame with a rattle.

He holds out his arm and I precede him down the stairwell, water squishing around my toes with every step. My skirt's clinging to my legs, trying to trip me. Didier shuts the door on the shushing rain and secures the lock with a snap. We trail puddles all down the tile corridor.

Back in his flat, I gape at everything in wonder. The last time I smelled that roast, I thought I was about to get dumped. When he'd flipped on that lamp, when he'd led me to the door, when I'd last set that glass on the table...

And now he loves me.

I'm his girlfriend.

I'm someone's *girlfriend*. And not just anyone, and not even just someone I love back. Someone extraordinary and kind and so handsome it breaks your heart, someone lovely and...and unlike any man I've ever met.

Didier heads to the phonograph in the corner and puts on a record, something soft and classical. Unlike me, he doesn't bonk his head on the garret's sloped ceiling when he straightens. He knows this place too well, could navigate it in the dark as easily as he does my body.

I excuse myself to change into the plain ivory shirt-dress I'd packed, draping my skirt over the door of his wardrobe to dry. The silk will probably never fully recover, but I'll love it all the more for its wrinkles.

I glance at myself in the mirror hung inside the wardrobe's door, at my wild, wet hair and the smudge of mascara beneath one eye. I wipe it away, thinking for the first time that I can remember, *I'm beautiful.*

I'm sort of *off*, too long in places, too pointy in others, but so is the *Girl with a Mandolin*, and now she gets to live in the MoMA. Maybe Picasso designed my figure too.

I grab my new bracelet and find Didier in the kitchen, setting the roast pan on the butcher block.

"Would you...?" I ask, holding out my hand.

"Of course." He clasps the links around my wrist, and I wonder, *Is this what it feels like when a man slips a ring on your finger?* If it felt any better, every woman would surely die of pleasure overload the second she got engaged, just crack into a million gleaming pieces from her smile outward, leaving a heap of empty clothes and happy shards where she'd stood.

I admire my bracelet under the kitchen's bright bulbs. "Thank you." The light glints off the little pigeon charm and I glance to the window. The Sommelier is there on the ledge, a gray ball pressed softly to the glass. He's asleep, but I hold it up to show him all the same.

"Let's give this ten minutes, then I'll carve," Didier says. He's quiet again, but not like before. He's spent, I can tell—from the exposure or the proclamation or both, or perhaps the same tenderness I feel, this deep nakedness with the words said and heard.

He excuses himself to change into dry clothes. I refill our glasses then wander around the living room, glancing at everything through these new, intoxicated eyes. He returns and I sit on the couch, leaning my back against the arm with my knees bent. Didier does the same, interlocking our ankles. He looks so sexy with wet hair, I blush and bite my lip.

He loves you, I think, floored anew. I always felt it but never dared hope it was special, just for me.

I sip my wine and it tastes brighter, like liquid gold, little effervescent stars bursting on my tongue. I can't believe it's the same wine I tasted a half-hour ago. It pairs with everything—the rain on the windows, the earthy beeswax scent of Didier's home, the phonograph crackling like a hearth and its music warming the room.

Didier reaches between us, rubbing the top of my foot. "I'd like to live with you. Someday."

I blink, falling down to earth with the gentlest plop. "Really?"

I imagine us eating dinner, kissing each other goodbye—and me going out to blow a few hours while a client borrows my bed and my boyfriend. *Yeah, no.*

"But you'd…"

"Yes, I would. I'd have to find a new job."

Another dumbfounded pause. "You love your current job." And truth be told, as amazing as it would be to hear he suddenly craved monogamy, for the sake of him and me... Can I handle the pressure of Didier giving up all that variety to settle for only me?

"I have loved my job, yes. I've loved it like I love my clocks and these walls." When hiding inside the flat isn't enough to quell his fears, he takes the immersion a step further, losing hours to his meticulous, obsessive hobby of fixing broken clocks and pocket watches. "All my job asks of me are things I find very easy to give. But lately..."

"Yes?"

He sighs. "Lately, I don't know. This job is what keeps me here, inside. Safe. And I'm starting to resent that, strange as it seems."

"Well. Wow."

"Indeed. I don't have any grand plan at this point. Only desires and intentions."

I squeeze his hand. "There's no rush, not for either of us. I'm floored to even hear you say so."

He smiles. "And here I thought my attachment must be shockingly plain."

"It is...but I always wondered if maybe you treat all your... You know. That way."

"Affection, yes. Not attachment."

Attachment. Holy crap. The most amazing man ever is *attached to me*. I'd worry I'm dreaming but he's too real, his eyes and his smell and his heat, his hand in mine.

"I'll carve the roast." As he stands, he pauses to kiss my temple, so tender. I watch him going, thinking, *this could be my life*. This could be my home, where my impossibly kind and sensitive and handsome boyfriend cooks us dinner and we drink wine and listen to music, in the heart of Paris.

It'd be different, of course. He'd work, presumably outside the home. His anxiety would lessen over time, but surely he'd have to suffer it far more frequently. And for me. All his safety, his routines, the novelty of a different woman in his bed every other evening.. He wants to trade those for me. What if I don't prove worth the price?

Stop it.

The most amazing man ever loves me. He just told me so. *Enjoy the glow, dum-dum.*

I grab our glasses and join him in the kitchen, where he's slicing the chicken at the butcher block, delicious-smelling grease gleaming on his fingers. The rain is a muffled din.

"You do know how to spoil me."

"You make it easy," he says with a smile, glancing up from his task. His ease has returned, utterly. "I hope this is special enough for such an auspicious night."

"It's perfect." I settle on one of the high chairs, cradling my glass in both hands. "You could've served me burned toast and I wouldn't have complained."

He shoots me a flirty glance, but in addition to the seduction I so often see in his eyes, there's an extra layer. Something delicate, vulnerability or hope or happy fear. A nudity that bares the very soul.

I bite my lip, stifling a grin.

"What?" he asks, carving.

"You love me, huh?"

He smiles down at his busy hands. "That I do."

"Even though I torture you all the time, and make you go out."

He sets a choice cut on each of two plates. "Especially because of that."

"Does that make you a masochist, do you think?"

He smirks at my tease then leaves me to wash his hands. I find a serving spoon and scoop carrots and potatoes from around the roast onto the plates, drizzling both servings with extra juice. He sits and we drape cloth napkins on our laps.

"We ought to toast again," he says, lifting his glass.

I hold mine up, suddenly shy as I try to think of the right words. I feel the pleasant, new weight of his gift at my wrist. "To…"

"To you saying it back?" he offers.

"To you saying it at all. I…" I falter, choked up all over. "I felt it ages ago. I never let myself think you felt it too."

His brows draw close, heartache etching a crease between them. "I won't ever give you reason to doubt it again."

My throat hurts worse than ever, clogged with tears. I sip my wine, feeling castrated of my voice.

"I've felt it for a while," he tells me, and his ankle rubs mine between our chairs. "But it's so easy to feel it when I'm inside. I didn't want to tell you here. And I promised myself I wouldn't tell you until I bought you a present, from that shop I mentioned, the one my mother used to take me to."

"Where is it?"

"Gobelins."

The thirteenth Arrondissement isn't so far, but adjusted through an agoraphobe's lens, even two or three kilometers become an epic journey. "That's a ways. Did you take a taxi?"

He shakes his head. "That was another rule. I had to walk there and back."

"Wow."

"Yes. You should see my blisters."

"Was it how you remembered?"

"Exactly. The same old man behind the display cases, even. And he remembered me. He remembered my mother, the second I said her name."

"Neat."

"He was much the same, only with white hair instead of gray. He said, 'I remember you. You were always staring at the watches. You always left your face behind on the glass, after you left.'"

I laugh. "Did you buy anything for yourself?"

"No. I have enough projects for now. Perhaps on Christmas I'll permit myself a new one. On special occasions… But they're my drug. I can see that now. I'll treat myself now and again, but not daily. It's not good for me, spending entire days stooped over, squinting. It's a wonder I'm not a blind hunchback."

"I thought for a while I wanted to restore paintings," I said between bites. "I took an internship one summer to try it out, but my back ached too much and the cleaning solutions gave me migraines. I'd much rather stand back and admire."

He smiles. "When you first came to me you were content to stand back and admire. But not for long."

I blush, immediately flooded with visions of that first night. Nervous virgin me, with all my clothes on, a check for Didier in my purse. Him, stripped naked, masturbating for my entertainment for what felt like hours, until he couldn't hold back any longer. I think I touched his bare back that first night, and we kissed. I didn't touch him intimately until our second date, though I'd paid for the chance to do far more. I let him touch *me* on the third date, and he took my virginity. All of that feels like ages ago. It's shocking now that I ever thought of him as just some beautiful creature to feast my eyes on.

Lately when his handsomeness strikes me, it's at unexpected moments—the time I swore in French without even thinking about it, and he laughed and smiled at me across the café table, his anxiety momentarily forgotten. The second his brown eyes open in the morning, their usual intensity blurred by sleep. The grumpy face he makes when I beat him at cards.

I've made love to Didier dozens of times, in dozens of ways. I've made love to the real him, my fond and frantic lover. I've made love to the men he plays for other women—seductive men, rough ones, cruel ones, obedient ones.

He knows me better than anyone else in this city does, and I suspect the reverse is true. He knows sides of me I'd never let friends see, and I'm in love with a man his clients will never meet. The one buried inside all the pretty packaging. The vulnerable, imperfect one.

And he's the one I want to make love to tonight. No games, no trying on other women's desires. Just me and the man I love. Who loves me back.

II ⚷

When the dishes are clean and put away, the leftovers stored, the wineglasses empty and the sky outside dark, the atmosphere shifts. All our tiny, playful touches have added up, leaving me stoked and hungry and wanting more. More intensity, more contact, more of Didier in every way.

After he dries his hands on a kitchen towel, I link my fingers with his and lead him silently into his dark bedroom.

Watching Didier lighting candles, I smile to myself, a thought filling me equally with happiness and fear.

If I hadn't had the ridiculous notion to pay a prostitute to put my virginity out of its misery…

If I hadn't made it to his door and found the balls to ring the bell…

None of this would be mine, now.

If I hadn't chanced upon portraits of him at the gallery next to the museum where I work, if my friend hadn't caught me ogling and told me who he was. So many ifs. Yet here I am. In love with a man I never could have met, not just waiting to pass him in the street. All of this so easily could have never been. I'd still be terminally afraid of the men I desire and he'd still be trapped in this flat, three years of imprisonment creeping steadily toward four.

And yet here we are. Together.

When he shakes out the final match, at least two dozen pillars flicker from the table, bathing the room in skittish shades of gold. Didier joins me on the bed, both of us still dressed. We lie down together, locking our legs at the knee. For a long time we don't even kiss, simply touching one another's faces and hair, watching each other's eyes. He feels utterly new. Yet it feels as if I've known him forever.

I run my fingertips along his jaw, up the curve of his cheekbone, down his nose and across his lips. The charms at my wrist jingle.

He asks, "What do you have in mind for tonight?" What sort of lover would I like him to be, what woman's appetites do I wish to explore?

"Nothing. Well, far from nothing—plenty. But only you. Only you and me."

His smile is broad, revealing his slightly crooked teeth, the only imperfect thing about the surface of this man...and even those hide behind his lips. He didn't shave today, and I love the brush of his stubble. The other women don't get to feel this soft scrape against their fingertips.

"We can do that," he says, and catches my wrist so he can kiss my knuckles.

I imagine other things Didier's clients don't enjoy—his bare cock, during sex. I don't enjoy that either, but maybe someday, if his intentions reap the real and major changes he claims to want. I know the thought excites him. Surely it's been years since he's done that.

"Do you really think..." I start over. "All those things you said you wanted. Just you and me, and no more clients."

"I meant all of it." He kisses me softly. "And I wouldn't say such things if I didn't believe them possible. That would be cruel to the both of us."

Shy, I stare at his chin as I say, "I want to feel you someday, inside me, without anything between us." And to be able to hold him tight in the wake of his surrender for as long as I like. He and I, completely and utterly stripped, on our bed, just ours. To know without a doubt I'm not sharing him any longer.

In a heartbeat his lids are heavy, lips parted, eyes glazed. Didier wears his lust like a heat wave, and I long to know what exact thoughts have him looking so sultry and hazy now.

He swallows. "I want that too."

I hug our legs tighter, tempted to reach between us and find out how hard the idea's made him. But I don't want to rush a thing tonight—

Lightning flashes. The curtains are open, and the window. The pigeon silhouettes of the three Perverts rise as one beyond the screen, thin with alarm. They're just settling back into fluffy drowsiness when the thunder rumbles. They confer in anxious coos as the rain picks up, falling with a great rushing sound, the odd fat drop pinging the metal fire escape.

I must have gone as stiff as the birds, as Didier strokes my hair, reminding me to relax. Reminding me that I'm in the easiest, most surrender-worthy place in the world. We kiss, and I melt. Everything we were speaking of bobs back to the surface of my consciousness, the storm just another atmospheric element in this two-way seduction.

"Tell me," I whisper against his lips. "About how you think it would be, without the condoms."

He kisses me first, a slow, sensual tease. "I want to feel you around me, with nothing in the way. And to be able to lie with you after, no rush to tidy up." Another kiss, deeper. When he speaks, his lips brush mine. "And to come inside you. More than anything."

Now I feel it, the heat wave. It's not merely from the notion, but from knowing the idea gets him so worked up. This man who's done everything in bed with who knows how many different women, yet there's still something left to him that's taboo. And I'm the one who might enjoy the chance to give him that gift.

"I know it's a small thing," he says. "But the thought makes my blood hot like nothing else."

We always want what we can't have. My nervous, noisy-headed self of a month or two ago would have extended that sentiment to Didier. Once he's mine, only mine, will I still want him as I have? When I'm no longer scheduled into his life, when perhaps I wake with him every morning and call all his things my own? But I'm not her, anymore. And I want Didier more now than I ever did when I was his client.

The more I get of him, the more attached I become. And though it's a revelation I never saw coming, the more attached I get, the less fearful I am of losing him.

Though perhaps I'm just high from the words he spoke, up on the roof.

"I hope I'll get to give you that," I whisper.

As we kiss, my mind races with to-dos that are still months off, surely. We'd need blood tests. I'd need birth control, who knows what sort. All that stuff most women are versed in by college. Soon maybe I will be too. How grown up.

His mouth turns needy, tongue seeking mine with deep, explicit sweeps. I grab his backside and pull him closer, feeling his erection at my thigh. I tug at his hip and he does as I'm asking, moving with me in small, subtle thrusts. In my head, I imagine the same moment Didier surely is. Only I see it from my perspective—that beautiful face strained at the moment of release, disbelief and excitement in his eyes as he finally gets what he craves. I'll draw it out, when the day comes, make him crazy and desperate, so wound up he'll come like his sanity depends on it. The scheme brings a smile to my lips, disrupting our kiss.

I reach between us, closing my hand around his cock through his slacks. Simply feeling his arousal spurs my own, drawing hot, dark energy into a ball in my belly. He covers my hand, squeezing. His moan warms my cheek.

"I'm thinking about it too," I whisper.

"Someday. Not so long from now," he promises.

"I believe you."

Another squeeze, another moan. "I love you. So much, you can't possibly know."

"I bet I do."

He rubs the tip of his nose against mine, smiling.

I let his cock go and turn my attention to his shirt, pushing the hem up until he helps me peel it from his chest and arms. He opens my dress one button at a time, spreading it like a robe. My underwear is still a touch damp from the rain, but it's his gaze that has goose bumps rising all over my skin.

"*Très jolie,*" he tells me, studying my bra. It's new, bought with his male approval in mind, like so many others. The only man I've ever let see me in my underwear and, unexpectedly, still the only one I'd want to. I never used to subscribe to the idea of a one-and-only, a Mr. Perfect. I only knew I wanted beautiful men and nothing less, despite the fact that I'm less than stunning myself. But now I want so much more than Didier's beauty. I want what he's given me—his heart—and greedier still, I want his fidelity. In time.

"You really want just me? Only me?" I ask. *Only me, for the rest of your life?* That's the question in my mind, but I'm too new at all this to voice the concept of permanence. As of a half-hour ago, I have a boyfriend. My first ever. What do I know about commitment and devotion and monogamy?

He says simply, "I do."

"When I first met you, you made monogamy sound silly. Some American delusion. Like a fairytale."

His grin is warm and sheepish. "We're all foolish enough to dismiss fairy stories, until we find ourselves face-to-face with a dragon."

I laugh.

"Forgive the man you met this spring for being so naive."

"I'd forgive him most anything," I say, stroking his neck and shoulder.

"He was a fool, and a coward."

"I loved him even then."

My mouth welcomes his, the kiss ripe and sweet and fierce, promising so much more. I want his hips pumping between my thighs, his hard, thick cock taking pleasure from my body. I want his grunts and moans in my ears, want his smell and taste and the fire in his brown eyes. Last weekend he let me do the darkest things to his body, let me see him crazed and whimpering from the most sinful submission. I watched his back muscles knot with pleasurable strain, watched his hips tremble, watched him welcome my penetration. Watched his profile as anxiety softened to surrender, and as surrender sharpened to the wickedest ecstasy. For days afterward I could fantasize about nothing else, but not now. Not tonight.

Tonight I want our bodies dancing—his leading, mine following, both moving together to the same beat. Partnered. Let the power play resume some other evening, but not now. Not with those words so freshly uttered and echoed.

I reach between us to unbuckle his belt and draw the leather out slowly. Just as slowly, I free one of his trouser clasps, then the second, and ease the zipper down. His erection is at his open fly, eager behind cruel silk. I give it the briefest stroke of my knuckle through his shorts then turn my attention back to his clothes. It must be interesting to have a cock. Like a greedy, nagging, ill-mannered creature always begging to be let out of its pen and lavished with attention. I'll make it wait, for just a little while longer.

Didier shifts to let me push his trousers down his hips. I pause to admire the dip and swell of muscle there, possibly my favorite part of his body...aside perhaps from his talented hands. I strip his pants to his knees and he finishes the job, kicking them to the floor. When our kissing resumes his erection is warm and stiff against my belly. I can sense it begging for freedom from his underwear, and for the indulgence of my touch.

"When you have a night off," I murmur, "from clients and from me..."

"Yes?"

"Do you usually... You know. Relieve yourself?"

"Yes."

I'd always wondered that. I'd wondered if it was like working at a bakery and losing your craving for sweets, or if he just...saved it up, I suppose. The way you fast so you'll enjoy Thanksgiving dinner all the more.

"I have a strong libido," he says. "And professionally it behooves me to keep it under control. For longevity."

"Oh, right."

He smiles. "I often would do that before you came over."

"Really?"

"After that first night, I didn't know what superhuman feats of endurance you might demand of me."

I laugh. "I like watching you lose control as much I enjoy an impressive performance."

"Good to know. I've had clients who've ordered me not to, however."

My pleasure deepens, darkens, the way it so often does when he tells me stories.

"But you asked for only you and me tonight. Forgive me for mentioning it."

I rub his shoulder. "No, tell me."

His smirk is wicked and he smoothes my hair back, tracing my ear thoughtfully before he grants my request.

"More than one client wanted to dictate when I could come. Or enjoy the illusion of that power. We would pretend I didn't come unless she was present, and when I could, I'd schedule our dates with a day or two off beforehand, so I really could deny myself. If I felt particularly inclined to suffer, I'd touch myself, but stop before I lost control."

"You're a very dedicated lover," I say with a smile. "You could have just lied and acted extra wound-up."

"Sometimes I had to, as scheduling demanded. But I liked that game. It was my pleasure to make it real, when I could."

"We'll do that someday. We'll do everything."

He kisses my lips. "I suspect we will. We have so much time."

"And so many stories." I could choose to feel insecure about Didier's exploits, and to resent those patrons for what they enjoy with him. Or I could continue to borrow their tastes and appreciate this man through the fantasies of a hundred different women, and view his experience as an enrichment, not a dilution. People are afraid of what a lack of variety will do to their attraction when they settle down, but Didier is countless lovers in a single body, all mine to peruse and sample without even so much as ogling another man. I hope I'll be the same to him.

But tonight… Tonight I still want nothing more than the two of us.

The lightning flashes again, but a soft, tardy grumble of thunder tells me the storm has moved off.

"You told me once, after I'd just started coming to see you, that you thought about me," I say. "When you touched yourself."

"And I still do."

The flattery heats me like a gulp of brandy. "What do you think about?"

"Often, whatever it is we last did together. And this week, knowing my plans to buy you that gift, and say those words to you... I imagined you saying them back and us going to bed, as we are now."

"Has it happened how you fantasized?"

"It did not rain in my fantasy."

I laugh.

"But reality has been better in every way. Including the weather."

"What was the sex like, in your imagination?"

"Tender. And passionate."

"Oh good. That's exactly what I want."

"And without condoms."

"Darn. Well, soon, maybe. And we can always pretend."

Didier replies with another kiss and our conversation is done, drowned in desire. I'm pushed gently onto my back and he eases the dress from my shoulders and halfway down my arms, pinning them slightly, and not unpleasantly. His mouth lavishes my neck and collarbone, my shoulder. I feel the sweet drag of his lips over the sensitive skin of the top of my breast, and his warm exhalation there. His arms look strong, braced as they are, his shoulder blades cocked.

He widens my legs, getting to his knees between them and dropping to his elbows. Warm lips on my breast, the feel of satin growing damp. The soft scrape of his teeth against my tightening nipple and a spasm of pleasure curls my spine like a wave. I fist his hair and whisper his name, the sound lost as his lips close over the point of sensation.

He turns his attention to my other breast, then my navel, my hip bone. I know where he's headed—toward an act we both love, but tonight I want perfect equity. I need his face near mine so I can see his eyes and hear his every breath.

"Not tonight," I say as he hooks his fingers under the band of my panties.

He stares up at me with raised eyebrows.

"I want us equal. No one serving the other."

"Very well." He sits up. "Come, stand with me."

He takes my hand and we get to our feet before the candles. Behind the thin silk of his shorts, I can see the outline of his ready cock. He slips my dress from my arms then reaches around to unclasp my bra. The damp satin drops from my shoulders. Slowly, almost cautiously, he tucks his thumbs beneath the sides of my panties and pushes them down my thighs.

For a long moment he stares, gaze making an inventory of me. "You're the most stunning creature I've ever seen."

My blush is hot as a fever, my smile goofy. I step close, cupping his bulge. I run my palm along his length a few times, and he eases his underwear down and kicks it away. Now we're just two naked people—friends and lovers, boyfriend and girlfriend. Partners, I suppose, or on the way there. Whatever that means.

I picture Didier still in my life in ten years. I picture his wavy dark hair streaked with gray, the lines beside his eyes and lips deeper and all the more striking. I picture his intense beauty fading as he relaxes into a dignified and handsome middle age, and I want him all the more for it. We're in the summer of our lives now, but I welcome the fall and winter too—cool black nights warmed by bright fires.

The day's been humid, and the soft skin of his cock drags against my palm as I stroke him, light as a whispered fondness. He does the same to my shoulders, arms and breasts, faint caresses echoed by the awe in his eyes.

"Come to the bed," he says softly.

I let him take my hand and we sit together on the mattress, me between his spread legs, my thighs over his, chest to chest. We touch lips and noses, nearly kissing.

I never knew love would feel like this, before I met him. I never knew how right it could feel, simply being this close to a man's body, seeing him and smelling him, touching and tasting and feeling his warmth, knowing his mind. I want so many things. To wrap myself around him and keep him from harm, and have the same done for me. Make him laugh. Soothe his worries. Turn my body over to the desires of his.

His cock is hard, glancing my belly. I reach between us and stroke him, filled with wonder to realize I know the exact speed and pressure and angle he likes. My hands are as confident now as they were clumsy and nervous the first time I touched him. I've learned so much in this room, well beyond the physical mechanics I'd come in search of.

The tiniest moan vibrates against my lips, and he whispers, "I love you."

"I love you."

"Let me make you feel good."

"Okay."

"You on top," he says. "If you don't mind."

"Whatever you like."

Didier shuffles backward, sitting upright against the headboard with a pillow behind his back, legs stretched in front of him.

The condoms are in the bedside table drawer, and I open one and straddle his calves, sliding it down his length. *Not for long,* I promise him with my eyes. *Soon it'll be only you and me.*

I settle on his lap, and he angles his cock. He slides inside with only a breath's friction before he's wet and deep and welcome. He bends his knees to cradle me, holds my hips tight, guiding their motions until I find my way. His dark gaze wanders my body but his cock is hard and steady and still, the shaft stroking my clit each time I take him deeply.

"Good," he murmurs.

Usually I'm awkward on top, but tonight I feel fearless. I have everything to gain and revel in, nothing to lose. He's mine, and in more ways than just this time we've set aside. His cock is still a shared commodity, but not his heart. Not that look in his eyes, not the thoughts he bared to me, under that blanket of clouds.

"You're mine," I whisper.

"I am."

I smile, wrapping my arms around his neck and falling into the rhythm. He strokes my back and hips and butt, cups my breasts between us.

"And you're mine," he breathes.

"I always was."

He grazes my nipples with his palms, lighting me up. He pinches them gently, rolling them between his thumbs and fingers. The sensations seem to go from monochrome to full color, my body connecting, sizzling with electricity. Inside me he's stiff and thick and so fucking close, so familiar.

For a long time, our bodies dance. His moans are quiet, thighs strong and warm, hands possessive. We kiss deeply, slowly, languidly. Desire simmers inside me, hot but calm for minutes on end. Then I sense a shift in him, a sharpening in his excitement that I can feel in his touch and hear in his throat. My pleasure changes too, dropping lower, drawing tighter. Our mouths lose the beat, so we press our foreheads together and concentrate on our bodies.

I'd been thinking only of us for so long, but now I feel his cock explicitly. My hips grow needy, my sex owning him more roughly than before.

"Yes." His hands slide to my waist, urging each motion.

I lean back, and the look in his eyes sucks the sense from my head. There's awe in that stare still, but lust too, and mischief. There's possession in his touch and urgent male need throbbing between my legs each time I claim him.

I do as his hands dictate, feeling a pang in my hip growing from mild to sharp in time. The discomfort is welcome. Sex is physical and visceral and impolite, and I'm coming to savor its challenges as much as the moments of perfect delight. Even now I feel my focus shifting, rhythm and coordination losing their primacy to the baser elements. The slick slide of his flesh inside mine. The smell of his sweat.

Someday I hope we fuck so hard it feels like fighting, setting aside the tenderness and letting our bodies' most animal impulses mingle, until sex becomes violence and vice versa. Things I'd never wanted, all from this man who makes holding back the only shameful act there is in bed.

My limbs grow sloppy and selfish, desperate. I feel foolish. I feel exposed, using his cock this way, my pleasure so obvious and my pursuit so physical. Only infrequently do I take, preferring to have pleasure given to me, and now I'm greedy and graceless. All that matters is his arousal stroking mine. His hands on my body in ways I couldn't have imagined those short months ago.

"You feel so good," he says. "So warm and soft."

Warm and soft, when I'd been thinking of much rougher things.

"No other man's ever done this with me."

He reacts just as I'd hoped, with a groan of filthy disbelief. I love when he gets riled up. Anything that strips away his perfect control and lets me glimpse the helpless side of his sexuality.

"And you're the only man I've ever touched. Or tasted."

"Yes."

He releases my waist, tucking my wild, damp hair behind my ears before scooting us down the bed a few inches so he can brace his palms behind him and join the motions. He meets every roll of my hips with a short thrust, his mastery as hot as the friction.

With each push he moans, the faintest sigh to start, soon loud and deep and shameless. I peek between us to watch his clenching chest and abdomen and admire the sheen of summer sweat on his skin.

He's so beautiful. I still objectify him sometimes. Often. But my awe runs deeper than his face and physique now. It worships his tender heart and his unusual mind. I love him this way, so in control and at home in the sex, but I love him just as well when he falls apart. More so, maybe, to know he wants me. And trusts me. That maybe I excite him as much as he does me.

Need claims my body like a possession. The need to feel him close, to own him. I rest my forearm on his shoulder and clutch his hair, so tight it must border on pain. Whatever he feels, it spurs his hips.

"Are you going to come on my cock?"

"Yes. But I'm not in any hurry." I run my hands down his back and drag my nails back up. He moans against my throat. I rub his skin, cradle his head, clutch his hair. I can't hold him tight enough, can't possess him fully enough.

"I thought I might never find this," I whisper, stroking his shoulders, his arms, his sides.

He shifts between my legs, letting me feel his excitement. I want him so badly it hurts. Inside me, above me, his voice in my ears and his mouth on my skin.

"Neither did I. I didn't know what I was even missing." He ravishes my throat and shoulder, hot breaths flaring between nips and kisses.

There's one request I want to make, one trick I know he must be capable of. "I want to come when you do."

"Then you will."

"I'll tell you when I'm close."

He leans back to smile at me. "I'll know."

Of course he will. He can read me like a map. Which is funny, as he's useless with direction. But whatever compass he lacks in the outside world, his prowess here says my body's a landscape he's memorized, down to the last blade of grass and wrinkle of tree bark.

I say, "I want you on top."

He holds me tight to his waist with a strong arm, never breaking our bond as he turns me onto my back and plants his knees between mine. I hug my legs to his sides, eager for him to lead, thrilled to be cast in his shadow. I stroke his back as his hips begin to pump.

"Like our first time together," he says.

I remember it perfectly, us in this bed, him on top, the first time I felt a cock push inside me. And still only one man's gifted me that sensation.

"You excite me now as much as you did then," Didier tells me.

The thought thrills me in turn. I fist his hair, holding his head. The possessiveness goes both ways, it seems, as his rhythm grows quicker, fiercer.

"Take me."

He locks his arms against my ribs, edges his knees wider.

"Touch yourself," he says.

So often that task falls to his capable fingertips. But he must feel, as I do, that no one is being spoiled tonight. We're catering to each other, as equals.

I slip my hand between us and rub my clit with two fingers. He watches, fascinated by my hand or our point of penetration, or perhaps even by the silver bracelet he clasped around my wrist. The charms brush my belly and tinkle softly.

"Yes." His voice sounds deeper and shallower at once. Strained, just as his handsome face has become. His brows have drawn tight and his eyes have narrowed, nearing that expression he wears when his role for an evening has been wrapped and the moment for pursuing his own pleasure has come. So many times I've glimpsed that look over my shoulder, when he owns me from behind. My favorite position, because of how commanding he looks and feels. But tonight's not about that. Only us. Only this.

I've gone kinky places with this man—kinky to me, anyhow—but tonight is hotter than any game we've played, his hands and mouth and eyes more arousing than any toy or tie or borrowed persona. What I feel for this man magnifies my awareness, so I feel every slick inch of his cock claiming me, hear every breath at his lips, feel every thump of his pulse.

My pleasure is gelling, going from a promise to a looming reality. It's gathering in my core like a tangle of heat and muscle, growing mean and demanding.

"I'm close."

"Good." He takes me harder for a flurry of thrusts, reactivating my fantasies of harsh, adversarial sex. "Good."

I watch his chest and face, his arms. I watch Didier, the most extraordinary person I know, giving me all this. Everything a man should be—kind and sensitive and passionate and dripping with lust.

He groans each time his body meets mine, the noise more ragged and rough with every push.

"Didier."

"Yes. Come for me."

My hand is a blur, his hips racing to match. The bubble of my pleasure grows bigger, bigger and I tease my clit, aching to burst. I say his name again, and one last time, just as the orgasm arrives. A long, harsh, exquisite release, drawn out by my fingers and his slowing thrusts. For sweet, endless seconds, the world is just his skin and mine. Two bodies brought together by unlikely circumstances, kept together by affection. By love.

As I come down, I realize something. He smoothes the hair from my face and I stare into his eyes, feeling the pulse of his swollen cock.

"You didn't come."

"Not yet," he says.

"You promised you would when I did."

A cruel little grin, chased by a kiss. "I did not say exactly *which* time I would be joining you for."

I shoot him a look full of false disapproval. "Tricky."

He drops to his elbows, claiming my mouth. Fondly at first, the kiss turning starker as my bliss steadily evaporates to make room for a fresh wave of desire.

This is my man. This is our bed, for tonight. Someday this will be our bed for keeps, and no one else's. This will be my man, for my hands and body and eyes and mouth alone.

I free my lips to say, "This time."

"Yes?"

"This time," I say again, and start to move my hips beneath his. "You're joining me."

"As you say." He pushes back up onto straight arms, sliding his hot, hard cock out with the slowest withdrawal. Back in, a bit faster. Soon we're racing once more, and I know this time he'll make good on his promise. I can tell from his voice and the tendons rising along his throat, he's not far from madness. It would be mean to make him wait too long. And yet...

I make the fingers on my clit grow sleepy, touching myself with the laziest caresses and letting my orgasm draw back a pace or two.

"You're not done?" he asks, confused.

"No, no. Just don't want to rush the show." I eye his laboring body.

"You have me on a hair trigger," he says with a smile. "I hope you're not planning to make me suffer."

"Certainly not." But I *would* like to wind him up as tight as possible and blow his fascinating, fractured mind. "I just don't see any need to rush things."

His smile turns ominous. "You try my patience."

"You shouldn't have tricked me."

His eyes narrow, and he rests his weight on one arm, sliding his other hand across my belly, knocking mine aside.

"Hey."

His thumb is on my clit, rubbing. Rubbing in those perfect, tight circles that have made my toes curl so many nights before. I push at his wrist, but that hand won't budge. In a few breaths' time I don't care. I don't care if my chance to torture him is through, or if our equanimity has been replaced by this smug little game. All I care about is how good his cock feels taking pleasure from my body, how skilled his touch is. How his face looks when his desire is stronger than his self-control.

My clit is a match, his thumb a striker. Each practiced stroke brings a brighter spark, tiny little bursts of pleasure.

"Didier."

"Yes. Again." His thrusts grow mean. "Come for me."

As my release mounts, I watch his arm. Strong, draped in trim muscle, locked and hard from the physicality of this sex. Tendons flex and I realize what a remarkable machine the body is, and how Didier's is so perfectly maintained and polished for exactly these deeds.

Soon I'll be the only woman allowed his services. I came here looking for the shiny machine, but if he should grow softer when it's just the two of us, me the lone woman he has to please... If he sacrifices some of his rigorous calisthenics and lifts fewer weights in favor of walks with me... I won't mind. His smile will stay the same, and his sweet words, and his beautiful heart.

I came to him seeking startling, rare beauty in a context that couldn't hurt me. But now it's the rest of him I want, so badly I'm only happy to take the risk.

I never knew I could feel all this, and even the fear of losing it won't stop me from tackling it to the ground and rolling around with it, feeling every ounce of this happiness until the time comes to say goodbye. Next week or next year or when I'm a bony old lady. It doesn't matter. All that matters is the present, and the present is without a doubt the most wonderful place I've ever visited. I'll pack my bags and move in for an extended stay, if it'll have me.

"Caroly." There's a plea in his voice. *Get out of your head. Get back to objectifying me. Come, so I can do the same before I lose my mind.*

"I love you," I tell him.

"I love you. So much." It's hotter than the filthiest words he's ever uttered to me under this canopy, and I'm a goner. My back arches so sharply my nipples brush his chest. I wrap my arms around his neck and shut my eyes, thinking of nothing but the friction of his thumb on my clit and the hard, thick length of him driving deep.

"Didier."

"*Yes.*"

I come, shuddering and gasping, and I hear him right there with me, a serenade of low, pained moans punctuating each wave of his orgasm.

If there was no condom, he could make such a perfect, sticky mess of me. The first man to do so. That would excite him so much. My gift to give him—not as pretty as a bracelet, but somehow I doubt he'd complain.

For long, labored breaths, he looms above me. I feel his thighs shaking ever so subtly and see his arms doing the same when he scoots both palms close to my ribs.

I stroke his face, flushed and gleaming with sweat, lids heavy as lead, hair a tumble of damp waves. He's a wreck, panting and pained. And he's never looked so handsome.

III ⊶

For ages we lie in silence, Didier letting me spoon him from behind and stroke his chest with lazy fingertips.

He clears his throat at length and covers my hand with his.

"Yes?" I prompt.

"Nothing. Nothing at all. I'm just happy to have you here, this way."

"This is nothing new."

"It feels new, with the words said."

I agree, but want to hear him explain. "How so?"

He rubs my knuckles. "I don't know. It just feels very…real. Like I know for certain now that all these little moments are building to something. Something permanent."

I kiss the back of his neck. "You're right." These embraces were always lovely, but they felt fleeting before, something to cherish in the moment but no promise of anything more. I've poured so much affection and concern into this man, and finally it feels like an investment, not an indulgence.

"What are we doing tomorrow?" he asks.

"I hadn't thought about it. What would you like to do?"

"If it's not sweltering, I'd like to show you that shop. Where I bought this," he adds, jingling my bracelet.

"Okay."

"It has so many memories of my mother. And pretty things, which you love. And I want to show you exactly how far I went, to buy you a gift. And to show myself I was capable of the trip, after the first try proved such an utter disaster. To prove myself worthy of saying those words to you."

"You were always worthy. But yes, I'd love to go there. Maybe I'll find another charm to add to the collection."

When the conversation lapses he rolls over, prompting me to do the same so he can do the spooning. I feel his cock against the back of my thigh, stiff. I laugh. The hazards of dating a sexual savant. And such a hardship, woe is me. "Again?"

"Always. And tonight, especially."

His arousal excites me. He always excites me, but my first two orgasms have left me sluggish and heavy-limbed, and I crave his pleasure far more than I wish to chase my own again.

"I'm spent, but I'm happy to grant any requests you might have."

"I've always wanted you in the shower with me."

"Oh?"

"From your very first visit. So many times I've put myself to sleep, replaying that evening but imagining watching you strip away your clothes, surprising me. Joining me. Your curious hands soaping my cock. Your hair wet. The two of us so close, in such a small space. All that white noise and warm water and steam."

All at once, I'm hot. The embers of my spent desire crackle and catch, flames rising all over again.

I get to my feet and take his hand, lead him into the little bathroom. It's such a mundane space now. I try to think back to that first night, when everything here was new, when I looked at the glass cubicle and marveled to imagine this was where the most beautiful man I'd ever seen got naked and washed his extraordinary body—a spectacle I was allowed to witness for myself, that evening. This is the space where I first glimpsed his shampoo and razor and realized he was a real, mortal man, silly as that sounds.

"How hot do you want the water?" I ask, opening the shower door and turning on the tap.

"Hot, but not too hot. Same as that night you watched me."

Soon steam fogs the glass, and Didier steps inside first, offering his hand. We face one another with the spray at our sides. I gather water in my cupped hands and let it cascade down his hair. He smiles, a gesture so pure my heart hurts.

"I love your teeth," I tell him. He offers a broad, cheesy smile and lets me run the tip of my thumb across them.

"I could stand to get braces," he says.

"No. Never. Then you'd be too perfect, and I'd wake up and find out I dreamt you."

"I'll keep them crooked then. It'd be a shame to find this was all a figment."

Words abandon us, and it's just him and me in this aquarium, us and the vapor and heat and nothing else.

Two baptisms in one night. I think as the water streams through my hair and over my back, as warm as the rain was cool. It slips down my breasts, belly, arms. Mutes the tinkling of my bracelet.

Didier takes the soap, turning it around in his hands, lather building. His gaze explores me for ages before those slippery palms even touch my skin. He laves my neck, shoulders, back, around my waist to my hips and belly. Finally my breasts. He lingers just long enough for my desire to stir, though it's still his gratification that's foremost in my mind. I stare up at him, the thick, dripping locks of his hair, the lips I've kissed a thousand times, dotted with beads of water.

"I don't think you ever look as sexy as you do in the shower," I inform him.

"No?" He reaches for the bottle of shampoo, and I let him lather my hair. "You're quite beguiling yourself, with your curls tamed and dark. And that look in your eyes."

I shut the eyes in question as he guides me under the flow to rinse away the suds. I do the same to him, but he kisses me before all the shampoo is gone and I can taste it on his lips. We pass the soap back and forth next, stroking each other's shoulders, necks, backs, bottoms. Between us, his cock is stiff and ready but I save it for last, not slicking my soapy fist down his shaft until I know he's on the edge of madness. When I do, his moan fills the cubicle, a throaty echo.

"Is this what you imagined me doing, if I'd joined you that first night?" I ask.

He nods, mouth open but no words arriving. His eyes are half shut, gaze aimed at my stroking hand. I pause to re-lather my grip.

"I didn't imagine this," I admit. "I was still too nervous to fantasize about being an active part of anything. Back then."

He smiles. "You've come a long way. You're perfectly capable of being the active one now. Especially if my hands are indisposed."

A pleasurable shiver courses through me, as I conjure the memories he's speaking of. If someone had told me that first visit that in a few months' time I'd be tying this gorgeous man to his bed and violating him, I'd probably have fainted. But I've changed so much. Grown so much. And I trust him so, so much. I want to know my desires as completely as he does his. I want to know his desires as intuitively as he knows mine, better than any woman ever has. A tall order, but a pleasurable challenge to rise to.

Without my meaning them to, my caresses have grown aggressive. Didier groans, so excited he sounds angry. He slaps his palms against the tile behind my shoulders, leaning close, looming. He rests his mouth at my temple and I feel his moans as much as I hear them, like echoes inside my own head.

For so long, he's been my flawless lover. In control of his pleasure and always putting it after mine. Watching him rushing headlong toward a selfish, messy release feels forbidden.

He leans back a bit, wanting just what I do—to watch.

"Yes," he pants.

My rhythm is sloppy, nothing like the masterful show he offered that first night. I conjure the image, his cock gleaming with oil, his face still that of a gorgeous stranger. But there is no show this evening. Only him and me, frantic and familiar, no room for any performance.

"I'm close. I'm so close."

"Someday," I whisper, "you'll be inside me. As bare as you are now."

Grunts answer me before his words do, a half-dozen pained breaths. "You'll be as wet and warm as the water." He puts his slippery palms to my shoulders then slides them to my breasts, kneading and cupping with shaky caresses. We're so close, his smooth head glances my navel with every stroke.

"Tighter."

I do as he asks, earning a buck of his hips.

"Yes. Don't stop. Make me come."

My strokes grow crazed and clumsy, the gracelessness worsened by his trembling hips.

"Yes. Keep going."

He succumbs only seconds later, groaning his pleasure into my wet hair.

His release is long and generous, his come hot against my skin, making the water feel tepid. "*Oh.*"

I kiss his shoulder. "Good."

I pump him slower and softer. I watch until the spray has washed his come from my belly and fist, then release his softening flesh to hold his hip. His face is flushed, eyes nearly closed. His lashes are dark spikes, hair and brows drenched black. With my other hand I stroke his cheek and trace his parted lips. "So good."

All at once, he leans his head back, face overtaken by a gigantic grin. A dopey chuckle tumbles from his mouth.

I laugh too, just to see him so blissed out. "Yes?"

He opens his eyes to stare down at me. "I love you. That's all."

I stroke his wet hair. "That's plenty. I love you too."

"Do you think you could ever move in with me? Here?"

"Once you found another gig, sure. Why not?"

"I didn't know if you'd mind. I've had so many guests here, after all."

I shrug. "I've never been too bothered by all that. Maybe I should be, but I'm not. That's just how it's been from the start."

"At the start," he corrects. "Not for long."

I twist shut the taps and climb out first, handing him a towel. As we dry off I say, "The only thing that would give me pause about us living here is if it felt like a trigger for you. If this has been your safe place for so long, you couldn't feel like you were moving on, staying here."

He tousles his hair, looking thoughtful. "I think at first, I'll need the familiarity. If I find a job that takes me outside, coming home to a strange new place may be too much change, too fast."

"Sure."

"But maybe someday."

"As long as it feels healthy. I certainly don't mind the thought. I love your flat, and your view. It's so... *Paris*."

"We'll make room for your things, of course. I bet you have lovely photos and paintings." He's never been to my apartment before, if only because it's cramped and far away, and my bed can't comfortably accommodate two people.

"There's not much. I moved into my place furnished. Just my clothes and books and linens and plants, and yeah, some art. I could move in a single taxi-load, I bet. When the time comes."

When will the time come, I wonder? In the New Year? I'll have to ask my landlady if maybe I could extend my lease by six months. I'd wanted to move this fall, but if I could move in with Didier by the spring, I'd happily stick it out a bit longer. How odd that we might soon be discussing practical, grown-up things, like how to split the rent. Who would fetch the groceries. Soon enough, Didier may need more than his ancient landline telephone. I try to picture him texting, but the vision seems silly. So many hours we've spent listening to his phonograph, I want to giggle, imagining him with iPhone cords dangling from his ears.

We go through our respective bedtime grooming routines, and I dress in my pajamas, joining my naked boyfriend on top of the covers. *Boyfriend*, I think. *Boyfriend, boyfriend, boyfriend. I have a boyfriend. J'ai un petit ami.*

The storm has trickled to just the musical ping of the odd drop on the fire escape's slats.

"Are you sleepy yet?" he asks.

"Not really."

"Here." He sits up against the headboard and pats the space between his spread legs. I settle against his chest, liking the funny weight of his chin on the crown of my head. A breeze blows the curtains in, surprisingly cool in the wake of the storm and smelling clean with rain, lifting away the musky scents of beeswax and sex.

"I want to keep saying it," Didier murmurs. "But I don't want to use it up."

"I doubt I'll ever get tired of hearing those words." There was a point when I worried I might never hear them, after all. They're lyrics to a song I'll never get sick of.

"I wonder what you'll do," I say, then yawn. "For a job."

"Me too." He stiffens behind me at the mention of such a profound change to his years-old routine.

It'll never be just him and me. His disorder will likely always be with us, whispering persuasive lies in his ear. The better he gets, the easier it will be for him to ignore it, but that voice has been with him for as long as he can remember.

I realize with a buzz-killing clarity that, as wonderful as all this is, it won't be easy. He's volunteering to turn his life inside-out for me. To confront his fears in so many more ways than just a trip to the coffee shop. And I'm signing up to date a man with a disability, of sorts.

I never even waded in the shallow end of the romance pool, just fell in love with a prostitute and toppled right off the diving board the second he told me he loved me back. But I know how to navigate the outside world, enough to start a new life in a foreign country, at least. And he knows how to love, and maneuver through all those complex obstacles. Between us, we'll figure it out.

He kisses the back of my head, once, twice, three times, noisier and sillier with each smooch. I laugh and hug his arms tight around me.

"I'd like us to go on a trip," he tells me.

"Where to?"

I feel him shrug. "Within France, perhaps. Whenever I've figured out a new job. To celebrate."

A ready scene flashes across my mind. "I've always imagined being with you in Provence or somewhere. Some rustic old stone cottage with a fireplace, and crickets chirping at night."

"I would have imagined you'd want to go somewhere posh. Somewhere decadent, my little connoisseur."

True, I do love the finer things—nice clothes, rich cheeses, vintages I can't afford. "I dunno. That's been floating around in my head for a while." I turn to smile at him. "It sounds very romantic, somehow." Just him and me and the sounds of the countryside.

"Then we will go."

"On a train, maybe? Are you okay with trains?"

"It's been years. I'm not sure. I'm not very good with bridges, certainly, but neither am I good at leaving Paris. Or these walls. I don't want to shape my life around what I'm good with, though."

"Of course not."

"Each day, I think, I should do something that frightens me. I should get used to feeling the panic in my body. The way you build a tolerance to alcohol. I'll feel a little more of the fear each day, until my threshold is so high, I can function like a normal person."

"There are no normal people," I tell him. "Only people who are good at acting normal."

"Perhaps."

"But I think that's an excellent plan."

"Good. I will find a new source of income, maybe this fall, and we'll make plans for you to move in. Once you're settled, we'll take this trip. Like a honeymoon."

Such a strange tingle that word gives me. I've never once imagined being married. I've had vague thoughts of a ring and a dress, but no more significant than my fantasies about the evening gowns and jewelry I'd love to wear to a fancy party or awards ceremony. It was always about the clothes, the occasion incidental.

But the idea of a honeymoon. With Didier. Heat creeps up my chest as I realize I'll be introducing him as my boyfriend now. I'll be traveling with this handsome, charming man, arm-in-arm, and get to tell people, "This is my boyfriend, Didier."

Suddenly no dress or ring can compete. And just as suddenly, I frown.

I crane my neck to meet his gaze. "Do you ever get annoyed by how obsessed I am with…you know. How good-looking you are?"

He laughs softly. "No, I don't. You know me. I like to feel desired."

I nod. His very name means "the desired one", or so an Internet search told me. "I love so much more than how you look, though."

"I know that. You tell me all the time with words, but also with how you treat me, how you touch me."

"Okay. Just so you know you're not some fancy accessory to me or anything."

"I think that idea bothers you far more than it does me."

"Yeah, it does." I blow out a long breath, chest tight with that old anxiety. My affinity for out-of-my-league gorgeous men kept me lonely and scared for ages, and I'd started worrying I was the female equivalent of those dumpy, deluded guys who won't settle for less than a *Maxim* cover model as a girlfriend. I wanted in my heart to just fall in love with someone ordinary and kind and deserving, but some force inside me wouldn't let it happen. A hamburger would've sufficed—I'm a hamburger, myself—but I was hell bent on the filet mignon. I even went so far as to worry, would I end up falling for someone because of their looks, and stay with them despite them being a moron or an asshole or a cheater?

"You love me for my broken insides, as much as my polished surface," he says.

"I do."

"I know you do. Because I know many women who love only the latter. They give me checks and never make me go with them to a café."

I smile. "I'd still love you if you got fat," I tell him, just being silly.

"Aren't you sweet, offering to enable my physical decline?"

I turn again, shooting him a mock-horrified look. "You mean you wouldn't love me if I got fat? Because have you noticed what I eat?

Genetics can't fight off the brie and truffles and alcohol forever. And my only athletic talent is jogging to catch the subway."

"I would only want you to be happy. So perhaps if you grow fat in the fashion of Caligula, savoring ever drop of wine and bite of food like an orgy, because it gave you so much joy..." He nods. "That might be quite attractive. But if it gave you no pleasure, only numbed you as my clocks do me, I would have to return the favor and nag you into taking control of yourself."

I want to protest and say I don't nag him, but I do. "Fair enough. I guess that's what couples do."

"You've so far been a very flattering but fair-minded mirror, held up to me. And I'm the strongest, mentally, that I've been in years because of you."

"Because of you, doing the work."

"Because of you, being worth impressing." Another kiss on the back of my head, soft, warming my hair with a long breath. Then a yawn.

"Bedtime?"

"I think so. I must get my beauty sleep, lest I wake up haggard and scare you off."

I swat his hand. "Don't joke about that."

"Sorry. I don't think you're shallow. Honestly."

"Well, I do. And I don't like that about myself."

"It's not shallow or selfish to want what you want. It would be selfish to pretend you're attracted to a man you aren't, and saddle him with a dissatisfied partner who merely goes through the motions."

"I guess."

A final kiss and he urges me from between his legs. I arrange the pillows and slip under the blanket. It feels comforting—unseasonably cool air drifting in from the open window, warm dry covers—though nowhere near as lovely as Didier's arms.

He blows out the candles, all but the lowest-burning pillar. That flame will fizzle soon enough, but maybe he, like me, enjoys a bit of light as we're drifting off. I like the way it dances across the drapes hung from the bed's canopy and the pattern of the old wallpaper, how it gives the mahogany of the headboard extra layers and depth. And if I'm spooning Didier and not the other way around, I love how it makes his skin look golden against his dark hair.

But tonight he beats me to it. "Turn over."

I get comfortable on my side as he climbs into bed, and his strong, warm arm wraps around my waist, the other shoved under my pillow, his legs nested with mine. He frees his hand to draw my hair behind my ear, and kisses my neck.

This is the first time in several visits we've bothered getting under the covers. It makes me think of the coming fall, of walks that might take us strolling beneath the changing leaves in a park or along a boulevard. Of winter, and getting to choose a Christmas present for this man, then a birthday gift come January. I stroke the hand holding my wrist, imagining what Provence might be like in autumn. Cold nights with a bright fire, soft blankets stuffed with down and black velvet above, punched through with stars.

"I love you," I whisper.

"And I love you." He sounds wide awake, same as me. I wonder what thoughts are running through that peculiar mind, staving off sleep. Not anxious ones, I don't think. His body's too still and supple. Romantic ones, perhaps. Hopeful ones.

I feel his breath behind my ear, so steady and deep and easy, inside these walls. My rustic countryside fantasy tarnishes a bit. He and me in the quaint cottage of my mind's eye, but all the familiarity gone. Will he tremble all night in such a strange place, upset by the journey there and already anxious about the trip back? Will we return to Paris, his relief arriving just as my guilt is piquing? Or maybe, just maybe, will I prove familiarity and comfort enough for him?

Only time will tell. And time, somehow, miraculously, is our luxury to savor.

I hear a sound I know well, a faint, singular snore, the sound of Didier drifting off, just as the guttering candle goes dark. One fire spent and cold, but not us, not our two bodies in this bed, not our romance, wherever it might take us. I press my back tight to his chest.

This, I think, *this has only just flickered into life.* And this will burn through the night, perhaps through the autumn and winter. Let the storms come and try to upset this flame. I'll cup my hands around it against the wind and rain. Because I waited too long for this to ever let it go.

EXPOSURE

THE CURIO VIGNETTES, PART V

I 〇━━

The car bucks in a deep rut as we turn up the driveway, gravel crunching under the tires until we slow to a stop.

"Whewww." Caroly's blue eyes are wide, darting all around. Her grip on the wheel has blanched her knuckles, betraying the calm she's been faking all the way from the Avignon train station.

Those fists match my heart, tight and bloodless. But we've made it. I give her shoulder a squeeze and a pat. "Well done."

With a comically hysterical sigh, she switches off the engine and collapses over the wheel, honking the horn and startling herself. She laughs and straightens, and drops the keys in her purse. "Okay. We survived."

Yes. A cab ride from Paris' Latin Quarter to the Gare de Lyon train station, two and a half hours to Avignon. Thirty minutes in the hire-car parking lot while Caroly re-taught herself how to drive, not having done so in five years. And finally an hour's journey—with a detour to collect groceries—to our destination.

Any one of those steps on its own would be enough to mire me in churning, nauseous worry for days beforehand. All of them together, strung in a terrifying marathon? Torture.

Except...

It's bizarre, I think, opening the door and stepping into the cool air, but I've emerged nearly Zen at the end of the ordeal. As though I slipped through a wormhole into the core of my own agoraphobia and shot out the other side so coated in panic, I'm not afraid.

Stretching, I take in the countryside, the hills dyed mauve by the approaching dusk. We didn't pass any other vehicles in the final kilometers of the trip. Caroly wanted remote and rustic, and she's gotten it.

I fill my lungs with air more clean and fragrant than I've smelled in forever. Small wonder—this is the farthest I've traveled in nearly fifteen years. Heaven knows what grasses and flowers I'll prove allergic to, after breathing nothing but city air since adolescence.

Driving stress forgotten, Caroly claps, grinning at the cottage. "It's just like the photos." Photos she's been ogling obsessively on her phone for weeks.

"Nicer, even. Let's hope the inside proves just as suitable."

"Look! There's my chim-*ney*," she says in a sing-song, pointing to the roof. She's been very excited by the prospect of fireplace access.

We gather our bags and the groceries from the trunk and carry them up the flagstones. The house is ancient, pleasantly so. Stone walls, pitched tile roof sprouting flowers, the window panes thick and wavered. Caroly consults a print-out then heads to an assembly of potted plants, poking in the largest urn until she holds up a key, triumphant.

"I won't get to pick the lock then," I say, pretending disappointment.

"Ooh, neat." She returns and shows me the key, a knobby old charming thing from a more prideful time when we bothered to give flourish to everyday objects. The door lock matches, its scalloped edges boasting a decorative inlay of vines. It opens with a satisfying, loud click, and Caroly pushes the door in on whining hinges.

We head into the main room and find a lamp.

Her eyes light up, along with the bulb. "Oh. It's perfect."

"It is."

The inside's as rustic as the exterior, but with touches of modernity—old beams and stone, but the furniture is in good nick, rugs new, only the faintest whiff of mustiness. Far nicer than either of us had let ourselves expect. The ceilings are lower than in a modern home, but I don't mind. I'm fairly tall but I've lived in a slope-cornered garret flat for years, and I enjoy feeling closed in upon.

We set our bags on the couch and carry the groceries through to the rear kitchen, small but well appointed, with a garden window overlooking the valley. I slide it open to let the breeze usher some of the closeness from the room. It's early October and the rains ended a week ago. The autumn blooms have begun to make their debuts, dots of color in the distance and scrubby trees silhouetted against a darkening blue sky. We've missed the lavender, but the air is crisp, promising deep sleeps under warm blankets...should my brain allow such a thing beneath an unfamiliar roof.

I don't like new places. The only explorations I've been comfortable undertaking are those bathed in candlelight, above, beneath and inside a new woman's body. As a prostitute, my role was to navigate those landscapes with the intuition and confidence of a perennial lover, and I can say without bravado that I was excellent at my job.

But the outside world... There I'm as good as blind, lacking even the most basic internal compass, head full of static and screaming chemicals from my disorder at the mere *thought* of an unknown journey.

We're here in Provence for only four days—a short time by most vacationers' standards, yet this is monumental. I've slept in the same bed every single night for the past five years, with the exception of one evening I passed slumped in a chair at my mother's bedside in the hospital. Four days is an eternity to be away from my routines, stranded far outside my precious, hateful safe zone.

Yet somehow…

I don't feel as I'd expected. My panic faded when we left the town behind, calm growing with every kilometer we put between us and civilization.

"Ooh," Caroly calls. "This is lovely."

I follow her voice across the living room and into the master bedroom. Its double glass doors open onto an overgrown garden and in the far, far distance, you can make out a steeple and the roofs of a tiny village, and the dark stripe of a river snaking through the valley.

Caroly bounces on the bed. It's wide, made up in a thick, colorful quilt and lit by matching sconces on either side. So different than my dark bedroom, set for seduction. No pigeons roosting beyond the windowpanes, just the hum of insects getting ready for their evening shift. No twinkling city lights, but soon enough, surely more stars than I've seen in half a lifetime.

"I wonder what sort of moon it will be." I should know these things. People who leave their homes know these things; people who keep their curtains open and enjoy things as vast and crushing as the sky.

"Just past full," Caroly supplies, staring through the windows at the sinking sun. The edges of her dark-blonde curls are tinted pink by the light, skin stained rosy. I move to sit beside her, taking her hand atop the covers.

"This was a very good idea."

"How are you feeling?"

I shrug. "I'm still a bit raw from the journey. And from the...differentness. I doubt it will fade completely while we're here, but it's the being here that's important." I squeeze her hand. "Getting you your stone cottage. A trip to mark the official start of all these new changes."

And so much will change when this holiday is over. A few days of leisure in a calm place where I may stand a chance at truly relaxing, then the stress of the drive and the train and the taxi. Then home, blessed familiarity with the added excitement of Caroly. Her things have been moved in; welcome additions that make me see my flat through new eyes. A brief domestic respite before the hard adjustments begin. Necessary struggles.

I accepted a job two weeks ago, one that fell into my lap custom-made, the answer to an unarticulated prayer. The elderly proprietor of a shop in Gobelins offered me part-time work, mending antique watches and other mechanical curiosities. His eyes and back and fingers are growing too weak for the task.

I took Caroly there one afternoon and the owner had been at work, operating on the guts of a grandfather clock. He'd been struggling with the escape wheel, and Caroly volunteered me to take a look. To say I "dabble" with clockwork is to say an alcoholic "enjoys the odd tipple". I'd never have offered my help, afraid to sound too pushy or patronizing. But my help was welcomed gratefully, and we left an hour later, she with a new charm for her bracelet and I with an offer of sporadic employment, doing the thing I love best.

Well, the thing I love best aside from seducing Caroly.

The wage I'll make from the antique shop is a fraction of what I commanded as a prostitute. But I have much in savings, and I'll earn enough to feel I'm contributing. Far more worrisome than the pay cut is that the job will demand I walk ten blocks to the shop, several days a week. That's ten blocks outside my miniscule comfort zone, but a pretty enough commute, with WALK signals at most of the street crossings.

"You'll be getting paid to do exposure therapy," Caroly had suggested as we marked up a map with colored pens. You'd think we were negotiating a route into darkest, uncharted Africa, not a two-kilometer stroll through the only city I've called home. She's right though. The prospect of enjoying so many new mechanical challenges will ease the way there, and the promise of seeing Caroly when I get home will make the return trip bearable. As much as it scares me, I'm eager to look back a year from now and see just how much more manageable the journey might feel.

I've said goodbye to my clients over the past month and a half, all beloved acquaintances, welcomed visitors to my lonely realm. Yet as my world's grown bigger, I've found there's no room for them in it. The monogamy I never thought I valued has grown magnetically attractive and changed my priorities.

As much as I've cherished the years I spent with those women, their company enabled me. It fed my bank account but also my crippling anxiety, and a time has come when I finally prefer to feel frightened and alive rather than safe and numb.

I lace my fingers with Caroly's. "You did very well driving." She'd been as nervous as I've ever seen her…save perhaps for the evening she first turned up on my threshold.

"I did, didn't I? It's been so long, I wondered if I'd remember how. Thank goodness the French drive on the right. Otherwise I'd probably have drifted into the other lane out of habit and gotten us killed. But we made it."

"We did."

"I'll be our chauffeur if you'll translate. Provençal may as well be Esperanto, to my ears."

Caroly is American, and after living in Paris for two and a half years her French is strong, if inelegant. She has a keen eye for anything artistic, a thousand names for the color blue, but no ear for languages. I speak French of course, and English and Portuguese and Spanish as well, and passable Italian. These are the ways in which a shut-in does his world traveling, through language and music and books and recipes. Provençal is a blend of dialects, but I spoke well enough to make myself understood at the market.

She thumps our linked hands against my thigh. "I think it's wine time. I bet we could both use a glass."

"Agreed."

We rise and head for the kitchen. We selected several bottles at the store, and she chooses the Clairette de Die.

"Something bubbly, to celebrate surviving the journey," she declares.

I inspect the cabinets, finding no flutes but a couple of brandy snifters. "These will have to do." I set them on the scrubbed-pine table and take the bottle from Caroly, ending her spirited struggle with the cork. I wrap it in the hem of my shirt and twist it free with a mighty pop. The spray wets my shirt and the floor, but Caroly catches most of the eruption with the glasses.

"I guess that was a bumpier ride than I realized." She finds a cloth to mop the spill while I rinse my shirt, and we meet at the table and hold up our glasses.

"To Provence," she says.

"This wine is from the Rhone."

"Whatever. To France."

And we toast, the fizz teasing my tongue.

After a sip and an admiring sigh she says, "We toast a lot. Like, every single night."

"There is much to celebrate."

"And we drink a lot."

"There is much to drink."

She laughs. "And yet I don't know that I've ever seen you drunk."

"I prefer indulgence to gluttony."

She taps my glass with hers. "Well put."

I examine my wine, holding it to the light to watch the streaming bubbles. "This is lovely." White, when I so often drink red; sparkling when I nearly always drink still. It's funny to find myself enjoying the newness of everything. Perhaps my need for the predictable is just a lie I've been fed by my disorder. Perhaps it really is people I fear, more than the unknown or the open.

Still, I must walk before I can run. In Paris I crawl, it feels, but perhaps in a place like this, I could even manage to stroll. Move with ease like a normal man, mind wandering through daydreams instead of hounded by waking nightmares.

We take our glasses through the bedroom and out the doors to the side garden. The sky is deep indigo now and already the stars are emerging. So white, like holes pricked through a shade, leaking pinpoints of pure sunlight. Which is nearly what they are, I suppose. Far off suns, winking through the cold, empty vastness. I breathe deeply of the cool air, quenching as a glass of water washing away a hangover's sour glaze.

I'd worried this first evening would be lost, consumed by the task of simply waiting for my heart to recover from the journey and the change of scenery. But I feel far more at ease than I'd expected. Caroly notices.

"You look pretty relaxed," she says, rubbing my shoulder. "Or is that just relief for the transportation portion being done for a few days?"

"It is, but it's more." I sip my wine. "I thought this would bother me—this hill, this gigantic sky, all this space. But I don't mind it. Not as much as I'd feared."

"Maybe it's the chaos you're afraid of, not the environment."

I nod. "Is it what you imagined?"

"It's absolutely perfect. Like walking into a Cézanne."

We stare at the sky for ages, until all the blue has drained away, leaving pure blackness. Far-off windows glow to mark the village, a tiny provincial galaxy. The lights from the bedroom bathe the grass for a meter or so beyond where we stand, giving the hill a strange dimension, as though it ends where the light does and we could just take a handful of steps and drop off into the darkness.

"There's the moon," Caroly says, pointing. It's just breached the scrubby hills, looking big, so close to the horizon.

My father taught me a trick, one of the summers I was sent to stay with him in Portugal. I was eight, perhaps. The moon had seemed so huge above the ocean one night, and he told me, make a circle with your thumb and forefinger. If you hold the circle over the moon, you'll see how small it really is. That's why photographs of a majestic full moon never look so impressive once they're developed. Cameras know it's always the same size. It's the human eye that's fooled. The huge moon shrank, fitting easily within the ring I'd made with my finger and thumb. I had preferred believing I'd been lucky, catching the moon looking so especially grand. The trick took away a bit of nature's mystery. But my father also taught me to skip rocks and to dig deep in the sand until I found the ocean, and showed me fireflies for the first time.

I sip my wine, wondering if perhaps he thought he was letting me in on the moon's secret, not spoiling a pleasurable illusion.

And I wonder—with an odd, slow-motion panic at the very realization I'm entertaining such a thought—what would I do if it were *my* child?

Perpetuate the myths, or let science be magic enough?

I move to stand behind Caroly, stroking her arm with my free hand. Her blouse has short sleeves and her arms are prickly with goose bumps. Such simple contact, yet my body rouses, warmth collecting deep in my belly. "You're cold."

"I could stand out here for hours, it's so quiet. And dark."

"Let's go in, just until you're warmed up. We'll keep working on that bottle and eat some supper. There will be even more stars an hour from now." We can shut off all the lights and spread a blanket on the grass, and her eyes can drink in the glittering sky while I quench my greedy thirst on her body. Let the sky watch us, and the moon. Let the security of roofs and walls and familiarity go to hell, for once in my cowardly life.

I take her hand and lead her inside. One glance at the bed and I'm suddenly excited by its newness, instead of unnerved.

In the kitchen we find the cutting board and plates, and make a meal of grapes and soft cheese and good crusty bread. Caroly is in her personal idea of heaven—I see it in the way her eyes narrow each time the Banon passes her lips.

"Your face looks much the same whether you're eating cheese or approaching orgasm."

She laughs, covering her mouth with her hand to keep from wheezing crumbs across the table.

"It's only natural you moved to France."

She nods, swallowing. "I know. It's so obvious. I'd say I was switched at birth with a French baby, but I don't seem to have any inherent ear for the language."

"You speak just fine." And I like her accent, as she does mine. I like when we lapse in and out of the two languages, creating some hybrid all our own. Why shouldn't that be the case, after all? We met as a virgin and a prostitute. Everything has evolved through the perfect mix of fluidity and awkwardness, an absurd but happy coupling. It seems only natural our speech should be the same.

"Is this our future?" I ask, leaning on the table. "Lovely trips and lovely nightly cheese and wine tastings?"

"I hope so. What else could anyone want?"

"I can think of other things."

That earns me a grin. "Such as?"

"Things I'll show you once supper is finished." I take a deep drink. "So much is about to change, when we return to Paris."

She nods. "All for the better, I hope."

"I suspect so. Difficult at first, but I'll suffer for my freedom. Plus I've come to appreciate my home all the more when I've forced myself to leave it. I revel in the calm a hundred times more deeply."

Only last weekend, I finally agreed to join Caroly and two of her girlfriends for drinks. I was embarrassed to let strangers witness how I shake while in public, but her friends made it easy. They were hyper and crass and hilarious, and already aware of my former profession. Coupled with the wine, their shameless curiosity drew me out of the unfamiliar setting and into the forgotten pleasures of socializing.

"I'm proud of you," Caroly says, her tone suddenly serious.

"I know that. You tell me every day."

"And I'll keep telling you."

We eat in a natural, intimate silence, the night sounds serenading us through the open window. Once we're sufficiently stuffed with cheese and bread, we stow the food and Caroly refills my glass.

"We have to drink it all tonight. It'll be no good flat."

"What a terrible burden," I say, and take a sip.

"I could use a quick shower, to rinse away the journey."

I'd normally campaign to join her, but a few minutes alone would be well spent simply breathing deeply, adjusting to this place. "I'll go after you. "

She kisses my cheek.

"Once you've scared all the spiders away," I add.

"Oh, chivalrous." She swats my arm and leaves to collect her toiletries.

I wander the cottage, marveling at its sheer quiet. I feel very close to the earth, when I'm normally four stories up, gazing down on the ant farm of Paris from my safe little roost. Here I feel like a bird on the ground, acutely aware of what might be above, tensed and ready for flight at the slightest suggestion of danger. I can't fly though. I can't drive, and I can't sprint seven hundred kilometers back to the safety of my flat. My wings are clipped.

And yet it's not so bad. Not so bad at all.

Caroly finishes in the shower and I take my turn, fascinated by the old enamel tub propped on its lion paws, at the colored glass glinting darkly in the bathroom window's diamond panes. The water tumbles from the old fixture, a heavy stream slapping my shoulders, feeling nearly brutal after knowing only my own shower for the past half decade. It's curious, finding novelty in something so simple as water. I let it fill my mouth, thinking it tastes cleaner here. The tub is smooth and rounded, unlike the flat tiled floor of my cubicle back home. How long since I've taken a proper sit-down bath? Ages. I'll have to do that before we leave.

I shut off the taps and dry myself with a towel more thin and coarse than I'm accustomed to, another primitive distinction to add to the list. I leave my hair wet. That seems to do things to Caroly— darkens her gaze, charges it with a hungry glimmer.

I dress in fresh clothes, a thermal shirt and a pair of fine, soft pajama bottoms Caroly bought me, insisting it was strange I didn't own any "lazy pants". At first they made me feel half-dressed and unkempt, but I've come to see the appeal. When you dress for sleep on a Sunday afternoon, you often wind up in bed, I've discovered.

Caroly is in the bedroom, folding clothes and sliding them into the drawers of an old wardrobe. She smiles over her shoulder at me and her gaze catches on my wet hair—so adorable, so predictable. I'd worried this trip would have me too anxious to make much of a go at honeymoon-style sullying, but I needn't have wasted the energy. Just that look in her eyes has me half-hard, my stiffening cock teased by the fleece lining of the pants.

Once our clothes are put away, we meet beside the bed. I stroke her slender arms and smile down at that peculiar, beguiling face.

Sharp cheekbones, round eyes. The hard line of her jaw offset by the impossible softness of the damp curls tucked behind her ears. She kneads my shoulders, returning the smile.

"You look happy," she says.

"Why wouldn't I?" It's rhetorical. We both had good reason to suspect I'd be a wreck.

She rises on her toes and our kiss is chaste and fond. I rub the tips of our noses together before she drops back on her heels.

She bites her lip.

"Yes?"

"Sit on the bed with me."

I nod to tell her to precede me and she does. As her fingers twine with mine, I sense seriousness in the gesture.

"I lied to you about something," Caroly says, staring down at our hands. Her voice is quiet, warmed by an unseen smile. This is no stark confession.

"What lie is this?" I tilt her chin up so her eyes meet mine.

"I told you the lab work wouldn't be done for two weeks."

We both took blood tests shortly after I kissed my final client farewell. Caroly's was a bit of a formality, considering I'm the only man she's been with, and always with a rubber. Mine was a routine matter, as professional courtesy demanded I have them done every few months. Ignorance is not blissful, in prostitution. Trust is both a necessity and a calculated risk, and I didn't take my clients' faith in me lightly. You can't sleep with as many women as I have, careful or not, and remain as unsullied as a blushing virgin. Though neither can anyone realistically enjoy only a couple of sex partners without signing up for at least the odd, benign impurity. A steep tax for some, a pittance for others. To me, a perfectly reasonable price to pay for physical pleasure. For the deepest human connection I know of.

I've been eager for the results. If all is well, Caroly will choose a method of birth control and our days of suffering the formality of condoms will be over. No pause before penetration, no limit to how long we can wallow in a messy heap after the deed. And of course, the sinful moment of release itself. The mere thought of it makes my brain fog and my cock swell. Few sex acts remain a delicacy to a whore, but that is one. Forbidden fruit. I crave it constantly.

"So the results are already in?" I ask, rubbing her knuckles.

"Mine came the other day. And I took yours from your mailbox."

"Postal theft is a serious crime," I chide. "Nothing worrisome rewarded your snooping, I hope?"

"No, nothing."

"Good. And yours?"

"Squeaky clean."

"No surprise." I do the math in my head, calculating what this means for our countdown. Depending on what she chooses, we might be free to enjoy this new intimacy by the end of the month.

"I lied about something else though."

"Oh?"

A shy, mischievous smile, and I'm officially antsy.

"What? Tell me."

"I told you, once we had the all-clear, I'd go on something."

"Yes?" *Yes, yes, yes?*

"I did that weeks ago. Went on the Pill."

My eyebrows shoot so high I swear I hear them ricochet off the ceiling. "I see." My heart is beating hard, nothing like the way it did on the train or in the car. Blood flees my head, snaking south. I swallow, feeling pleasantly bleary. "So…"

She nods, smirking.

"It's been long enough?"

A full-blown grin now. "I timed it so it would be. For this trip."

I sit up straight, shocked by her genius and treachery. "Wicked girl."

"So whenever you want to, we can."

I rub her knuckles. "I've wanted to for months."

"Then I imagine tonight's the night."

I'm drunk on so much more than wine. On lust and surprise, and just a trace of residual anxiety.

"We have to finish the bottle, at least," Caroly had said, and now I'm tapping an invisible watch, standing beside her in the kitchen as she refreshes our snifters.

"You've waited ages for this," she teases. "What's a few more minutes?"

"It was never within my grasp before." I accept my glass and drain it in a gulp, set it down gruffly. "Okay. Now."

She laughs, still sipping.

I joke of course. This moment has been too long in the making for me to possibly rush it now. I drop the impatient act and kiss her cheek, leaving her to finish her drink while I head for the living area. I find what I'm after in a closet, a faded quilt folded on the top shelf. The perfect surface on which to make a picnic of Caroly. I grab a throw pillow from the couch and exit through the front door.

The night air is brisk, and I wish I knew how to do something as primitive and outdoorsy as build a bonfire. Caroly told me once that she's turned off by rugged men, though. Having grown up in New Hampshire, she says she's had her fill of "beer-swilling rednecks on ATVs". Luckily for me, she wants a man who can pair wine, not construct her a log cabin. Someone groomed and genteel and housebroken. A pedigreed indoor cat, that's me.

Circling around the cottage and down the hillside a few dozen paces, I scout for the right place. A view of the moon, a soft patch of ground. I locate such a spot and the overgrown grass flattens beneath the weight of the blanket, the perfect mattress.

I find Caroly still in the kitchen, rinsing the glasses. I shut off the tap for her. "Come with me."

"Where?"

"Outside."

As I lead her across the grass, she rubs her arms, smiling. "It's chilly."

"I'll have you warm in no time."

"What have you got planned?"

"Nothing so sleazy or premeditated as you plotted for me."

She laughs softly, and I take her hand as the light of the cottage fades completely, the fields frosted ghostly blue in the moonlight. I imagine coming back when it's warmer. When the dark brings relief from the heat of long summer days and the night flashes with fireflies. I imagine a life in which I can move without fear through the open air, and I realize with a physical bolt that I'm living it.

Right now.

It shocks me so much, my feet lose their rhythm for a pace.

"I see what you're up to." Caroly's words ring clear in the pure, natural darkness. No city glow slipping between the curtains, no ambient hum of sleeping electronics, no shouts or car sounds rising from the restless streets. Just the faint light of the moon, the chirp of the crickets, ours the only voices for miles.

She takes a seat on the blanket and I join her. We kick our shoes aside and lie down together, sharing the pillow. I stroke her cheek. Her eyes are drinking up the stars, and I roll onto my back as she is to stare into the sky. I clasp her chilly hand in my warmer one. In moments my body seems to rise from the ground, no periphery here on this hill, the black dome of night suspending us utterly. The starscape appears to rotate, spinning slowly, a vast, black, twirling umbrella peppered with pinholes.

"I feel very strange," I say at length. A cannabis high, lethargic and soaked in awe, a heightening of the senses, a shedding of the body.

All of this is as foreign to me as weightlessness to a normal person. Paris makes me feel small, but not like this. The insignificance I feel is thrilling, a release that dissolves every muscle, every nerve, every cell, leaving me floating. "Either that wine was spiked, or the sky is."

She squeezes my hand. "I feel it too. Like gravity's gone away."

"Like we'll peel away from this blanket and tumble into the blackness."

Another squeeze. "That's how I felt when you took me up to the roof and told me you loved me. Like I'd drift up into the clouds if you'd let my hand go."

I let her words linger before I speak, not wanting to chase them away. The stars are multiplying as my eyes adjust, too many to even conceive of.

I tighten my hand around hers. "You've brought me so many gifts. Beyond wine and clocks and clothes. This sky and this air, and all the doors you've opened."

A pause, then her voice returns, sounding fragile. "I'm glad."

"You've been so patient."

"And you've been so brave."

"Perhaps. But I needed the shove, to have stumbled out the door in the first place." So many times she's shoved, and so many times I've had to suppress my reflexive reactions to the pressure—panic and resentment—ultimately coming to recognize my disorder's voice for the liar it is.

The outside is dangerous, it whispers, selling me fear, naming it fact. *Stay indoors, where you belong.*

Indoors, safe and snug as a corpse in a sweet-smelling, satin-lined coffin, content to decay.

I turn back on to my side to trace her cheek, her jaw, the divot between her nose and lip.

"Yes?"

"I'm admiring you. I've never seen you in this light."

"Do I look different?"

"A bit. You even sound different out here, with all my walls gone. With Paris gone, and only us left. Us and the crickets."

She smiles shyly, pursing her lips.

I smile back. "Kiss me."

Cupping my jaw, she draws me close.

Her mouth is soft to start, growing bolder by the moment. The way she kisses echoes that infatuated gaze she often beams at me, a consumptive lust we act as though only men possess. But even when she came to me a virgin, I saw that look, at once a gleam and a glazing, hunger peering from behind heavy lids. I feel it in the way her lips claim mine, in the lap of her tongue, how she clutches my hair.

Seven months ago she'd never have kissed me this way. She was a passive, receptive thing, eager to learn but frightened to act. She's grown shameless since the spring, a fascinating evolution.

Curious hands stroke my chest, survey my shoulders and arms, caress my belly under my top. A deep shiver moves through me, warmth gathering in its wake. I've been wanted before, and felt it in a woman's touch. Countless times. But to know a lover cares for my mind and my future—my very happiness—as much as she desires my body...

She leaves me weak. Reduces me to a joyful ruin with the merest touch. She must sense it when my mouth has lost the rhythm of our kiss and hear it in my shallow breaths. And if she slipped a hand between my legs, there'd be no mistaking it.

But it won't do to lose control so soon. Tonight's finale is not one to be rushed.

I rise to sit cross-legged, gazing down at Caroly. She looks like art in the moonlight, alabaster against the blanket's collage, framed by the crosshatched strokes of the grass. Her blue irises seem black, her skin white as milk. Without a word, I reach for her waist to free the bow of her stretchy bottoms. She lifts her hips so I can slide them down her legs, and I watch little bumps rise along her thighs as the cold encases them.

Her voice is soft in the darkness. "So it's become that sort of picnic then?"

I lower to my hip and elbow, tracing the hem of her panties with my knuckle. "Tell me you'd prefer more cheese."

"No, no, this will do nicely." She strokes my hair, everything about the moment feeling as it has a hundred times before, in my bed, yet twisted.

We're the same, but the air is cool and so clean, the starlight so distant, not warm and close like candle flames. And it's us, only us, with more than a fortuitous Sunday lying between this moment and the arrival of my next client. There is no next client.

I stroke her thigh, run my fingertips over the lace at her hip.

This affair feels like none I've fostered before. All the ones before this were as pleasant as a beautiful song or a delicious meal. Though a twinge of sadness accompanied their conclusions, the world kept turning. With Caroly, it's rousing as a symphony, nourishing as a banquet, but vital as oxygen as well. Should all of this end, it won't go with any pang so simple as sadness. I'd grieve it like a death.

I hold her hip tighter.

No one can guarantee security. We promise it, of course. But no romantic proclamation can ensure permanence, neither can wedding vows, and even the truest love can be lost in an instant…whether that instant comes at the speed of a car, or dragging at the heels of a years-long illness. In love, there's no predicting the end, only savoring the present.

Moving down the blanket, I urge her to make room for me between her legs.

I bring my face close, detecting Caroly's scent behind the autumn air and the wild musk of the grass. No other man has smelled her, tasted her, heard her sighs and moans, felt or watched her come. No other man has caressed her sex with his hand or tongue or cock, and none but I have been invited to. It never fails to make my pulse throb, knowing that she's only ever been mine. The idea that she might someday gift that most intimate access to some other man… My blood pumps harder still, coursing with jealousy and possession and lust enough to ignite a fire.

Love hasn't banished the baser flavors from our sex. As long as there's no threat behind them, I welcome the jealousy and possession into bed with us. Security and trust are wondrous, but they don't boil the blood the way those fearful sensations do. And I do so enjoy that frantic heat. She must too, considering all the times she's asked to hear what my clients have requested of me.

I draw my thumb softly along the line of her sex through the silk, smiling at the way her thighs tense.

"No other man's made you twitch as I can."

"No man ever will."

I let my nose glance her clitoris as I breathe her in. "We can't know that."

"Maybe not," she allows, fingers combing my hair then clasping. The contact matches the tone I've set, just the slightest misgiving scraping a hot spark through my body.

"In case one ever gets the chance," I say, "I'll be sure to spoil you so rotten, he'll never compare."

"That I do know for sure."

Through her panties, I close my lips over the hardening point of her arousal, exhale to warm the spot and make her sigh.

"If I was ever with some other man," she murmurs, "I'd have to shut my eyes and imagine it was you."

Her words strike me twice—the first blow jealousy, the backhand flattery. Both sting hot with pleasure. I stiffen my tongue and draw it along her seam, wetting the silk. Her hand in my hair becomes a fist.

I want to do everything to this woman—serve her, spoil her, dominate her, submit to her. Any dish she wishes to sample, I'm hers to devour.

Hooking my thumb under the hem of her panties, I pull the strip of lace and satin aside, exposing her most delicate skin to the night air. I feel the opposite against my own sex, pure heat and confinement. Maddening.

"Cold?" I ask.

"A little."

"My mouth is warm." Before she can reply, I take her clit between my lips. Any words that might have come are swallowed in a moan, the sweetest sound I know.

With a jingling of her charm bracelet, her hand takes over for mine, holding the fabric to the side. I find her wetness with a deep, firm lap, another, dozens—until I'm panting and starved, until she can't doubt how deeply I wallow in this moment. More intimate than intercourse, more intoxicating than wine. Am I the aggressor or the servant? I can't tell, and that's what I've always loved about this act.

My cock's grown hard, aching as I imagine sliding inside her, slick from her arousal and my mouth, soon her release. And no condom, not anymore. I shiver. A whore's last unfulfilled fantasy, realized only now that he's left that vocation behind.

Against my lips and tongue, I feel every tiny mechanism of her pleasure, each pulsation, each twitch, the tensing and swelling of her flesh telling me things no words can articulate.

Is this act so different than a watchmaker's craft? Her heartbeat like clockwork, speeding with my adjustments. Then again, no beguiling piece of brass has ever loved me back, nor sighed in ecstasy as my fingertips wound it tight or snapped it snugly closed. My hobby will change soon enough—drawing me out, not keeping me in. *But this*, I think, penetrating Caroly with my tongue as my thumbs trace her lips, *this will remain my art.* Her pleasure is my masterpiece, honed nightly but never complete, never beyond perfecting.

I'm flooded with her scent, scalded by her heat on my lips. I'm dying of a sexual hunger deep in my belly to taste her, to imagine how good she'll feel around my cock and to know I must wait. I flick my tongue against the swollen nub of her clitoris and gently draw two fingers along her seam, back and forth, back and forth, then finally slip them inside.

"Didier."

As always, my name in her voice hits me like a crop. I'd scale a mountain on bleeding palms and knees to feel the sweet sting of those syllables. I'd bankrupt myself, endanger and degrade myself for the sensation, and yet she gives it freely.

"Caroly." I whisper it against her sex and the fingers grasping my hair tighten. Soon enough she'll be holding my arms or raking my back or guiding my thrusts with her smooth, soft palms on my hips. I doubt I'll register any of it. Not tonight, not with every particle of my consciousness focused on that long-forbidden prize. My cock surges as I imagine it. My mouth grows more aggressive. Her thighs tense and one heel rubs along my spine, trembling and giving her away. Her feet always tell me when she's close—restless as fidgeting hands.

"*Oh.*"

There's so much I can read into that breathy syllable. Volumes.

Don't stop, it tells me. *Keep doing that, exactly that, please. Please.*

And I obey. Normally I might back off just as I sense her wishing for me to continue, draw it out so her eventual release is a blinding, desperate necessity. I can be cruel that way. But tonight I'm as needy as I am controlling. I keep my tongue thrumming, keep my fingers delving, keep the rhythm steady and the intensity building slowly, slowly, as her pleasure winds tighter, tighter.

I'm close, her rubbing feet tell me. *Don't stop*, begs the shaking hand gripping my hair. Her hips shift, meeting the push of my fingers as they might my driving cock.

A throaty, tremulous moan rends the darkness, tingling down my back. She flutters against my lips and I slow my mouth and strokes, drawing her climax out, out, out until she jerks from the contact, pleasure turning to pain.

Smiling, I let her go, caressing her calves as she relaxes back against the blanket. I kiss her inner thigh, then its twin. "Good."

She clears her throat, sounding delirious. A sheepish giggle brightens the night. "Yes, very good. Just like always."

"I beg to differ." I sit up and she does the same, scooting close between my legs so I can shelter her in my arms from the breeze. I nip at her ear. "Nothing like always. Out here, under the stars? Away from the flat?"

"True. But you still make my legs all wobbly, just like always."

I stroke the bumps peppering her thigh. "More shivering than wobbling, it seems."

"I don't mind. I haven't seen this many stars in ages... I took this for granted, growing up in the boonies."

I kiss her neck, my wonder wrapped up not in the cosmos but in her closeness, her smell, the promise of what's to come. She reaches a hand back to stroke my hair.

"You're not thinking about stars," she says. "I can tell."

I run my nose up and down her nape. "We've got something far more rare than a clear sky to enjoy tonight."

"What if I was sadistic and made you wait?"

"I would never cook for you again."

A dramatic gasp. "That's just mean."

"Tonight then?"

She turns, kissing me. "Of course, tonight."

"Where? Here?" *In the darkness, all our senses are heightened...*

But she says, "In the bed. By the light of the fireplace."

And in an instant, I know she's right. It can be no other way. On soft, dry sheets, by the heat of the hearth. I need to see her face, and she mine. What's more, I think with a flash, I want to watch the moment when my bare flesh claims hers. And I want her to watch as well.

And what I want matters, I remind myself. With this woman, my desires count.

For years I've molded them to complement my clients' needs, or cast them aside entirely. I've stifled them for the sake of longevity, warped them to cater to borrowed appetites. It's a hard habit to break, setting aside my old roles. They became my identity, in time. I was a chameleon, adapting to the wants of whoever came to my bed. A mirror revealing their deepest, darkest needs. But Caroly's told me she doesn't want that—not every night, at least. She wants to be with *me*, not merely a reflection of her own preferences. A true lover, not a performer.

And I need, I desire, I want. I'm a man, not a machine.

A heart beats in my chest, muscle pumping blood, simple as brass and oil but warm, so warm. I fear and I hurt, and one woman in a hundred has cared to know it. Asked to see it. And though I've bared far more than simple nakedness to her before, tonight I'll bare it all.

As Caroly cinches her pants, I gather the blanket, tucking it beneath my arm. Hand in hand, we stroll through the grass and wildflowers, back toward the light.

Her thumb rubs my knuckles and I return the gesture, suddenly shy. When did I last feel so nervous before sex? As a teenager, surely. In another life. Yet here I am, stiff from a breed of anxiety I'd forgotten about—the exciting kind, full of anticipation, not dread.

It's cool inside. I hadn't noticed before, when the sun had still been dawdling on the horizon. The cottage boasts no modern heating system, only the fireplaces.

"*Alors.*" I shut the patio doors behind us. "I'm afraid I'll have to defer to you, my rugged companion."

Her brows rise.

I confess, "I don't know how to build a fire."

"Oh, it's easy. I'll teach you."

There's a rack of wood beside the bedroom's stone hearth, and Caroly disappears for a moment, returning with a bin of old newspapers.

"Always make sure the flue's open."

I kneel beside her to see what she means.

"Otherwise the room will fill with smoke. I've forgotten that step. It's the worst." She rolls up her sleeve and fusses with a squeaky lever.

Next she shows me her father's patented arrangement of crumpled balls of newspaper and stacked logs—smaller sticks on the first layer, thicker ones crisscrossed on top.

"Now we need matches."

After a search, I find some on the living room mantle.

"And all you do is light the paper," she says.

I strike a match and hold it to the newspaper. We sit back on our heels and watch as the flames spread to the smaller kindling, yellow tongues licking.

"Ta da." She balances a metal folding screen on the hearth. "You've made a fire."

"I assisted."

"Now we just have to keep an eye on it and add a fresh hunk of wood when it starts to peter out."

A branch cracks and shifts, sending orange sparks chasing up into the chimney.

How nice to be taught something by Caroly. Something practical, that is, beyond the lessons she's offered regarding my capabilities, out in the wider world.

I imagine us strolling around art galleries and museums, she teaching me terms I've never heard before, enthusing about the thing she loves most. Strange, catching myself looking forward to such outings, and with only a hint of fear tainting the idea.

When people speak of prostitutes needing to be saved from their vocation, they mean danger, exploitation, degradation. It was never that for me. In turns, I offered my clients therapy, escape, affection, decadence. They didn't take—I gave. I liked giving. Too much.

If Caroly saved me from anything, it was my own lack of momentum. She dragged me from the quicksand of my slow, passive decline into inevitable hermitdom, from a reality I hadn't stepped back from enough to even fully see. I'd enjoyed the sinking, the snug safety of my descent. Had we never met, I'd have eagerly drowned in all that reassuring immobility. But she made me choose my life instead, and I took hold of the rope. It seems I'd rather stand shaking beside her than atrophy in comfort, all alone.

Since I've rejoined the outside world, I've found there are benefits—benefits beyond keeping Caroly in my life, which can't be discounted by any means.

I've noticed that the days are longer. Not simply because time passes more slowly when you're distressed, but because the world is suddenly bigger. There are so many things to see and hear, so many new faces to study. Staying inside, it was like eating nothing but chocolate for three years. Reliably lovely and pleasing, yet my palate grew lazy. Each meal blended into the last. Outside, it is like a buffet. So much variety it shocks the senses, and though I don't love every flavor I'm fed, the choice is dizzying. So frightening, often, but also so rich.

We rinse the soot and wood flecks from our hands in the kitchen, switching off all the lights as we make our way back to the bedroom. She tosses two pillows before the crackling hearth and takes my hand. We sit cross-legged side by side, the fire nearly too hot but all the more exotic for it, with the cool air at our backs.

After a long, spacey silence, I ask, "What are you thinking of?"

"I'm thinking how lovely it would be if life was just like this."

"Like what?"

"Just this." She rubs my thigh. "Sitting in front of a fire at night, drinking wine. Someplace so quiet."

"You'd miss the city." This place suits me more than I'd ever imagined, but Caroly loves culture and shopping and events, cafés and parks with interesting people to watch. She likes the bustle, content to quietly observe, curator that she is. We're not compatible that way.

If this love stays in bloom, what shape might a compromise take? A home on the outskirts of a smaller city? Where she could leave in one direction for the activity when she wished, I in the other, seeking calm and solitude. It's not such a terrible arrangement, as long as we each play tourist in one another's outer lives now and again, and keep our time together inside stoked and glowing.

"I wouldn't be so opposed to leaving Paris." She turns to meet my gaze. "As long as I could find a satisfying job somewhere. Maybe we have a few more places to visit in the next year or two. See what it's like in Nice or Lyon."

"Your career should come first."

"My career's about being part of the art world, and making enough money to live. It's important, but I don't want it to the exclusion of you being happy." Saying the words makes her bashful, I can tell. She's not used to baring her heart to people, especially not men. Some wounded child inside her fears she'll be mocked for admitting she cares for someone. Instead I kiss her mouth, proving her earnestness will always find a welcoming ear with me.

"We'll stay in Paris for the foreseeable future," I tell her. "If I can acclimate to the outside there, get back to how I used to be, when I was functioning..."

"Then you could make it anywhere," she finishes. "Well, except maybe Bangkok or New Delhi."

I laugh. "Yes. I think Paris is as frantic as anyone can be asked to suffer."

"But in a few years, who knows?"

Who knows, indeed? Who knows where we'll be sitting, what view beyond the windows? Who knows if it'll even be just the two of us, or if...

I let the thought trail off. A curiosity for another night, another month, another year or more. Tonight there's enough fire to foster between our bodies, by the glow of the one we've laid in the hearth.

I study her smooth complexion, gilded in the flickering light, the shadow of the screen's lattice dancing across her face.

"Yes?"

"I remember the first night we met."

"So do I."

"There was a screen then too, only we sat on different sides."

She smiles, her blush all but lost in the firelight.

"Oh yes, so shy once again. Like I haven't seen a much different smile on those lips since March."

"I'm sure I have no idea what you mean," she says, feigning innocence.

"You've changed. You've opened like a flower."

"You're one to talk."

"You've hatched. I'm more like a weak bear after hibernation, stumbling half-blind out of its cave."

"No wonder we're both so shaky sometimes."

A soothing silence settles between us. As much as I'd like to freeze the moment and linger in it for ages, my body grows restless. It hasn't forgotten what's still to come, and with my nerves silenced, my libido's whispers rise to insistent murmurs.

I turn to Caroly, closing her hand in both of mine. "Let's go to bed."

She smiles, nodding. "Let's."

III 🗝

I stand first and help her to her feet.

She looks so beautiful, my chest tightens. Her eyes dart to the bed, but I stay where I am and reach for her face, cradling her jaw, my focus darting between her eyes.

"Yes?"

"You look different."

"Oh?"

"You look… I don't know. I look at you and I think, *she's mine.*"

Unable to drop her head, she averts her eyes instead.

"I've never looked at someone and felt this before. This mix of recognition and surprise. Like I understand you so well, yet there's so much I still want to know." I pause, laughing. "I'm not making sense. But I mean every word."

Her gaze returns to mine, eyes shining from more than the firelight. I wipe away a tear and lean in to kiss her forehead. Her arms close around my waist and I fold her in a tight hug, planting another kiss on the crown of her head.

The bed sits to one side of the fireplace, half the quilted comforter warm and lit by the fire, the other shadowy and cool. I coax Caroly to lie on the fire-lit side, and she lets me strip her pajama bottoms for a second time. She sheds her top, skin adorned by satin and lace, some pale color burnished bronze in the fire's glow. I peel away my shirt, muscles tensing in the coolness of the room. The soft cotton of my pants drops away, and hot as the crackling flames may be, they're nothing compared to the heat in Caroly's eyes.

I toss my clothes toward the bureau. "I'll never grow tired of the way you look at me."

"I'll never get tired of watching you undress," she says with a guilty smile.

Naked, I join her on the bed, sitting up against the headboard and urging her to do the same. She tucks herself tight to my side and I kiss her temple. "It's been a long while since you've asked for a story."

She tenses against me. Since I told her I planned to give up my clients, she's all but stopped asking about them.

Perhaps before, when she assumed I'd never consider leaving my vocation, asking me about my experiences was her way of making peace with the unseen women who shared her lover. She enjoyed those bedtime stories. I hope it's not guilt that's made her stiffen this way, guilt from worrying I'll regret sacrificing my experiences, forsaking all others for her alone.

"Let me tell you about a client I used to know."

A pause, then a wooden, "Okay."

I lean close, drawing my fingertips along her arm. "She came to me this spring. A virgin, if you can believe it."

Realization softens her expression. I palm her breast, thumb stroking slowly until her nipple stiffens and her lips part.

"She told me she wanted to experience sex with a beautiful man. The kind of man she didn't think she could ever have for keeps." I was prepared to go on, but suddenly tears shimmer in her eyes. I still my hand. "Have I upset you?"

She laughs weakly. "Of course not. I like that story best of all."

"I have another, if you'd like to hear it."

She nods.

"It's about a man, this one."

"Is he French?"

"He is. And he was a terrible coward who hid inside, because the bullies in his head told him to. His only real friends were clocks and pigeons."

"I know this one. The man was very, very handsome. And an excellent cook."

"He hid in his lonely little tower for years and years, until a leggy blonde American woman—"

Caroly snorts.

"—came to rescue him."

"Oh yes. By forcing him down the tower steps every morning and down the street to ye olde coffee shop."

"And they moved to the countryside and lived happily ever after."

She turns to plant a kiss on my shoulder. "That was a very good story. But I think maybe we ought to get busy writing a new chapter tonight."

I take her cue when she lies down, straddling her hips and dropping to my forearms, kissing her lightly.

I've been hard on and off for an hour, but now, looming above her, my cock grows stiff as stone. Her smooth, soft palms run along my sides and back and thighs, just as they have a hundred times before, but never quite like this. New space, new light, new texture under my knees and new smells mingling with her familiar vanilla-amber perfume—wood smoke and autumn crispness.

When I shift my legs, she does the same, hugging my thighs with hers, calves tugging at my backside. I know this request well, and for once I grant it without making her wait, lowering my hips and letting my erection brush her mound. She rewards me with a tiny gasp, clasping my shoulders.

Cocking my hips, I angle my shaft between her thighs and give a slow, long stroke against her clothed sex. Her moan makes me lightheaded. I drop to kiss and nip at her throat.

"This answers my question," she mumbles. "About whether you'd be relaxed enough on this trip to…you know."

I push up on my arms. "It's easy, with the way you look at me. We could be in some hotel in the heart of the city, with the din of the Champs-Élysées coming through the window, and as long as you have that look in your eyes, I'm ready." We both know it's a lie, of course. A pretty lie, one we'd both like to believe, but it's different here, undeniably. Quiet, calm, dark, easy. The peace I've worked so hard to create in my little cell in the honeycomb called Paris. An entire countryside's worth.

"Lie on your side," Caroly whispers.

I do, tucking my lower arm beneath her head and its pillow, pulling her close with the other. She strokes my chest and kisses my neck, and I feel myself turning helpless, desperate, rabid—a thousand conflicting things at once. No one's ever made me feel so wanted, so longed for, so treasured as she does. She waited for me, she's said. Avoided men for ages, then sought me out as a rejection-proof point of entry into the world of sex. Now she loves me, somehow. Wants me just as deeply as she did before those carnal initiations. Wants me as so much more.

It's as comforting as it is terrifying, because in such a short time I've come to care for her in a way I hadn't known possible. With it comes a fear I've blocked since the passing of my mother. I love Caroly so much, if I lost her, a part of me would turn brittle and crumble to dust, leaving a hollowness I'd carry with me for the rest of my life.

I've tensed, and she notices. She stops caressing to embrace me, surely thinking some tentacle of my agoraphobia has snaked between us, to turn me so rigid and unsure.

"I'm fine," I promise, and smooth her curls. "Just feeling so much. All good things." Good things chased with a fear of loss, but such is life. And I *have* a life again, a proper one. The fear is a thing to rejoice in. Proof that I can still love this deeply.

"Maybe we should get you out of your head." She strokes my hair, gazing into my eyes. I want to swim in those blue irises, dive deep and emerge under a pitch-black sky, riddled with stars.

I steal a kiss. "Maybe we should."

Another kiss, and she welcomes my tongue, making my cock throb with impatience. Her hand runs down my neck and chest, over my belly and between my legs to clasp my erection. I gasp, the sound swallowed in the kiss. I fumble to return the touch, but she grasps my wrist, halting me.

"You've already made me come, remember? Let me spoil you for a little while."

Kind words, but I hear mischief in her tone.

Let me torture you for a little while, I translate. The anxious virgin I met in March must have been a figment. The woman here on this bed with me now is too fearless, too eager to possibly be the same Caroly. My progress has been slower and more halting, but I limp steadily toward a functional life, her hand always there, guiding me.

The tender thoughts dissolve as she urges me to lie back, edging her way down my body.

I put a hand to her arm. "No. I'm too close already."

"Just for a minute." She's on her knees between my legs, palms slipping over my chest, stomach, caressing my hips, my calves, up the insides of my thighs. I moan, helpless, and gather her hair in my hands.

The barest glance of her fingers jolts my cock. A stroke and I'm shaking.

"Just imagine how good it'll feel," she murmurs, then my crown slips between her warm, soft lips.

"*Oh.*"

Needing a distraction—a chance at lasting longer than a minute—I conjure the first time she did this to me. She'd wanted to try sooner than I'd thought wise, considering her inexperience. It ended in tears. Now the fingers wrapped around the base of my shaft are strong and confident. She swallows half my length in a breath, pure slick heat. No hesitation.

"Yes."

I made you this woman, I think, and my pleasure folds in on itself, too strong and potent to ignore. I hold her curls loosely, following the bobbing motion of her head.

"Softly," I beg.

It feels so good, so absurdly good, I have to laugh. "Where on earth did you learn this, beautiful girl?"

She frees her mouth just long enough to smile at me and say, "From a very patient man."

Another minute I let her spoil me, then I know it's too far.

"Enough," I whisper. "Please."

I'm released, as relieved as I am disappointed. I can't stand to wait another second, but she escapes to tend to the fire, laying a fresh log on the pile. The flames rise and, as she returns to the bed, the fire glowing in my body spikes as well.

"Take off your underwear."

She smiles, kneeling, and reaches behind to unhook her bra. It joins my clothes on the floor and before she can get her panties off, I'm fairly tackling her for the chance to strip them. They're gone. She's beneath me, hands on my arms, gaze on my face.

"I think it's time," she whispers.

I nod. She shifts her legs outside mine, tilts her hips. It's so much like the moment she invited me to take her virginity. So like it, yet utterly new. She releases my arm to draw the side of her finger up and down my cock, and my sentimentality dissolves in a tide of lust. I lower my hips so my shaft is along her wet lips, and I start to move. She grasps my shoulders with a moan.

My attention is nailed between us, unbudging. *This is so wrong,* my conscience mutters as my flushed flesh strokes hers. With no latex veiling my cock, a flash of instinctual panic stiffens my spine. I've done just about everything a person can in bed, but this feels truly forbidden. Pornographic. It fills me with awe and shame and a hundred other exciting emotions.

Without warning, Caroly reaches between us, clasping me, drawing my head up and down along her lips. I curse, so shocked my arms nearly buckle.

"Let me feel you. Please."

I nudge her hand aside and steady my cock. I take a deep breath, then another.

And I push inside.

She's hot, soft, taut, wet. Everything I've been fantasizing about, multiplied.

For the longest time I hold us there, my cock buried as deep as it goes, impossible to distinguish my pulse from hers. Slow as the moonrise, I draw myself out, memorizing every sensation. Back again, just as deep. I shift to my elbows and drop my forehead to hers, overcome.

"You feel so good. So, so good."

"So do you."

But she can't have any idea how sweet this is. How slick and warm she feels around me, how utterly different this familiar moment has become, with nothing between us. Nothing.

My throat's so tight I can barely get the thought out. "I've never felt this close to anyone. Ever."

She cradles my head, kisses my mouth. "No?"

"Never." I edge my forearms closer to her ribs, coaxing her thighs a touch wider with mine. "Does it really feel different to you?"

"Yes." She pauses a moment. I know that look. She's struggling for words that won't make her blush too deeply. "The friction's different. More…explicit."

"Really?" I still my hips, smiling. She nods, and I ease my length back, nice and slow.

"Really." She kneads my backside, tugging. I ignore the request, maintaining my glacial pace. This moment will only come once. Let us both luxuriate in every inch of my slippery flesh driving into hers. A rare occasion indeed, for both of us to be experiencing something together in equal wonder.

I've felt this before, but it was so long ago and so taken for granted, I know it only as an intellectual fact. A more powerful fact is the one I uttered only seconds ago—I've never, ever felt so close to anyone. I want to slip inside her body, far beyond the mechanics of penetration. I want to feel what she does, see what she does. It seems I nearly can.

I slide my arms under her back and press our cheeks together, she breathing in my ear, I in hers, and I begin to thrust. Her thighs hug my waist tighter, her hips mirroring mine, deepening each thrust, lengthening every withdrawal.

Barely realizing it, I've begun moaning. Deep, needy sounds, set to the rhythm of our sex. I hear my name between her labored exhalations. Those same breaths warmed my neck the very first night we did this, steeped in this same awe. I can never give her what she's given me—exclusive custody of her sexual experiences—but I can give her this moment, this virtual first.

I speed my thrusts and let every shock of pleasure I feel escape from my mouth in grunts and sighs and groans. *Take what you want,* her hands tell me, urging my hips. And for a glorious minute, I do just that. Let the fire rage until I feel so good, so close, it frightens me that I haven't come yet. That I can burn this hot and not lose myself. Not go insane from the sheer intensity of this pleasure.

Then all at once, the hands on my sides stop begging.

"Wait," she says.

Panting, I pause, as easily as I might stop the Earth from spinning. "Yes?"

She pulls away, and my throbbing cock is closed in cold, dry air. I gasp and shiver, so primed it hurts. She twists around in my arms so we're on our sides, and I understand. I slide my leg between hers, angle my cock and slip back inside her heat from behind. Her moan is soft and tight, excitement sharpening. I wrap my arm around her, chest flush to her back, mouth just behind her ear. I shove my own pleasure into the shadows and concentrate on hers. The breast in my palm is hot from the fire.

"You like me this way," I murmur. "Behind you."

"Yes."

So often I wonder why, when her feelings for me sprouted from a purely visual attraction. Because it feels animalistic somehow, she told me once. Because she likes to hear me losing my mind behind her, all my poise gone.

We do enjoy demolishing our lovers, I muse, slipping my hand down her belly, settling it on the soft curls of her mound. We want to see our shy partners turn brazen from what we can do to them. We want to bring our domineering ones to their knees, if only for a moment, if only evidenced by a helpless look in their eyes, a shudder, a whispered plea. If Caroly wants her elegant servant torn to bits by a desire he can't control, I won't deny her.

I slip my fingertips to her lips, glancing my own sliding flesh, stealing her slickness. Her clit is already hard, a throbbing knot of nerves begging for my touch. I could circle with exquisite precision, stroke with the lightest, most excruciating pressure. But I won't. Instead, I let myself feel my own arousal. My cock, wrapped in her. I shut my eyes. My fingers twitch against her clit, unbidden. Whatever I feel, I let it spill from my mouth and into her ear. I bump her thighs with every thrust, and she reaches behind to grasp my flexing hip.

"Didier."

That alone is a sharp shove, ushering me away from reason and toward the crash. I take her harder, holding my fingers still and letting the motion of the sex dictate the strokes they give. I feel wild and reckless. Bossy. I've been crowding her body, and now she's nearly pinned to the bed but for the elbow propping her up. I drive my leg deeper between her thighs and move the other to join it.

"I've wanted this so badly," I whisper.

"Me too."

"I'm close." Saying it spurs my need, edging me closer. For ages I've had to be told when it's my turn to release. It's my job to know when a woman's taken everything she needs from me. To read the signals and seek permission. Tonight, though. Tonight I'm holding back not out of duty, but out of desperation. I don't want this to be over. But every stroke blazes with sensation, burning hotter, hotter…

She doesn't urge me. She knows some switch in my head wants her attention, needs to be flipped to inform me it's okay to be selfish, but I can sense she's denying me. I'm not a whore anymore. I'm just a man. Her equal and her lover, mortal and allowed to lose control. And how good it always feels to me, watching her come apart from our sex. She must want the same. To watch me succumb to the pleasure like most any man can.

Come, she usually says, with her voice or her gaze, with urging hands on my hips. Not now.

I feel the shapes of words forming on my tongue—*I'm so close.* I swallow them. I sink into my body, into the excitement humming in my cock, into the fire. A groan rises from my throat, erupts from my mouth, an *Ahh* harsh with need.

She whispers, "Take what you need."

Take. Not an easy order. Not when I've spent all these years only giving. Even alone, just myself and my hand, I don't come until the woman in my mind tells me to.

But tonight. *Come,* a voice inside me says. *Come, just as you've fantasized all this time. Stripped. Bare. Selfish and sinful, come like an animal in heat.*

The pleasure's sharpening, deepening. Beyond friction. Beyond taboo. It cuts like a blade; my body is begging for mercy, my cock hot and hard and screaming for relief. A gleaming knife's edge sliding along some tendon of self-control, until—

I snap.

"*Oh.*"

It rushes through me, swallows me up, pulls me under in a crush of perfect, deafening pleasure. I moan, out of control. Behind the noise and sensation is Caroly. Her soft voice chanting, "Good, good." Her arm angled back and her hand on my hip, riding my bucking spasms. The way it shakes, I know she's there. Orgasm still ringing through me, I make her join me with a flurry of practiced strokes.

"*Come.*"

I feel when she does—feel it more explicitly than I ever have, like two dimensions becoming three. Her breath, her smell, those most intimate contractions pulsing around the point of my own release, then easing. I'm shaking all over, still moaning even as the wave of my orgasm recedes.

"Didier." Her voice is cool palms cupping my face, soothing me.

My groans quiet. The world stops spinning and slowly I float back to the earth, back to the bed with the softest thump. Then…

Bliss.

No rush to withdraw and shed the condom. I can stay in her warmth as long as I like, wallowing in the beautiful, silly, mammalian mess we call sex. I wrap my arm tight around her ribs, push her hair aside with my nose so I can press my lips to the back of her neck.

I hope I never take it for granted, how close she feels at this instant. How difficult the journey was, getting to where we are now. So often I envy the careless way other people move through the world, but I don't ever want to forget how hard I've worked for this. This moment is my reward. A gift to pale all of the material ones she's given me. And for once I feel truly worthy of her offering.

Another kiss behind her ear. Another. "You're much too good to me," I whisper.

She clears her throat. "I doubt that. You're the nicest man I know."

"Am I?"

"And the most romantic, and the most sensitive."

"Sensitive, yes. I believe that. Sentimental."

She turns, just enough to make eye contact. "And the bravest."

I don't blush easily, but I feel my face warm as though I were peering into the fire. "You're too kind."

"No one could ever be too kind to you," she says, and clasps my wrist at her waist.

We lay wordlessly for a long time, the silence filled by the fire's crackling and the night noises drifting from the open window. Caroly twitches, roused from the edge of sleep. She yawns deeply and shifts against me, my cock finally slipping free between her thighs.

I peel my body from hers and toss a small log on the dwindling flames, and shut the window on my way out of the room. I find a clean washcloth and we tidy ourselves. Freeing the covers, we wriggle between the sheets.

"I don't know if I can fall asleep without the sound of pigeons cooing," she says, adjusting the pillow beneath her head. The moment she's settled, I curl my body alongside hers once more.

"Crickets will have to suffice. Or you could fall asleep with the snores of an extremely satisfied man at your ear," I suggest, and hug her tightly, settling my lips against her neck. Her skin tastes clean, only the faintest trace of sweat. I kiss her there for as long as I dare. Any more and sleep's spell will be broken, and surely she's too drowsy to wish to be pawed by some restless, lusty creature. I choose to behave, nestling my face against her shoulder.

"I love you," I tell her, barely a whisper.

"I love you." She turns in my arms, smiling broadly, sleepily. She kisses my nose, my forehead, my chin. "I can't wait to see what life will be like when we get back to the city. Us living together."

The idea tenses my arms around her. "I can wait."

Another press of her lips to my chin.

"I'm excited as well. But I hadn't imagined I'd be as relaxed here as I have been. In fact, I'm shocked."

"I wondered how you'd..." The thought catches on a yawn. "How you'd fare. Maybe you were born in the wrong province, all along. Maybe you should have been a winemaker's son. Maybe I was supposed to meet you during some vineyard tour on a trip to the Mediterranean."

"You wish I were born a cheese monger," I tease her. "Admit it."

"You're too good to be true already. Don't overstimulate me by adding cheese to the equation." Another mighty yawn.

I stroke her hair and kiss her temples in turn, and nudge her to roll back over. She softens in my arms, but my worries are never so quick to let me go.

"What are you thinking of?" she whispers.

"Are my thoughts that noisy?"

"Your breathing's all tight."

I kiss her ear. "Sorry. I'm melancholy."

"After all that?" She strokes my hand where it lays against her belly.

"About all the time I wasted, inside. Three years."

She doesn't reply right away, but after a minute or more, she says, "I wasted over a decade, not really dating or even letting myself like anyone too much. Being a stubborn, fussy coward. But you know what?"

"What?"

"I didn't waste it. Because I couldn't have met you if I'd done it differently. And I can't imagine anyone I could possibly want to be with more than you. So it wasn't wasted, it was just the way it had to happen for me to get right here. Right now." She lays her arm along mine, hugging us both.

"That's true." I wouldn't have met her if I'd stayed as functional as I was in my twenties. She wouldn't have met me. Might we have passed on some street, me going through the lonely motions of a man pretending to be at ease in his city? To hear her tell it, she'd have cast me the briefest glance then feigned utter disinterest, her old way with handsome men. Two anxious strangers passing on the sidewalk in some alternate Paris. That, compared to having her in my arms now...

"You're right," I say, and kiss her again. "This is just the way it had to happen. And I'd sacrifice another three years for one more night like this."

"How lucky that you don't need to."

Lucky. Never before a word I'd have paired with my disorder. Perhaps I'm being too rough on myself. Those years I spent in self-exile may have been pathetic, but they taught me great empathy for the women who came to my bed. I learned languages, read many books, bonded with lovers as I hadn't known a person could—briefly, yet completely. I immersed myself body and soul in recipes and wines and songs and sex, relishing their nuances as I never would have, had my life been more complex. More external.

For all its faults, it was a rich time. It made me patient, introspective, humble. It made me worthy of lying beside Caroly now. Not a waste at all. And yes, perhaps even lucky.

"You're a very smart woman."

"Isn't it supposed to be you teaching *me* deep stuff about myself?"

"We're not the same people we were in March. I'm not a prostitute or a shut-in."

"And I'm definitely *not* a virgin."

I laugh then drag my lips down her neck until she shivers. "And thank goodness for that."

Three more days we have here, days of blissful nothingness, the only stresses being drives to town for food and wine, and the thought of those journeys rouses just the faintest wriggling of worry in my belly. I want to feel everything new this place can offer. A real bath for the first time in years. Enough nights in a strange bed for it to become familiar. Days away from my routines, my cabinet and my hobbies, my kitchen, my security. Time enough that perhaps even my sanctuary of the past half decade will look new upon our return, novelty to be discovered in all the spaces and items I take for granted. That I've taken for the entirety of my universe, for so long.

I wonder what my mother would say, if she were alive to hear me announce my travel plans.

"Why in heaven's name would you want to go to *Provence?*" she might demand. She had agoraphobia as well—not as severe as mine, but it kept her happily confined to the only city she knew. "If it can't be found in Paris, it's not worth looking for."

I might tell her, "The sky is bigger, and the air smells cleaner. It's quiet and there are more stars than you can count."

She wouldn't be moved. But perhaps if I told her, "I fell in love. That's why I'm going." That, she might respect.

She'd have done anything to keep my father, of that I have no doubt. Unfortunately for her, his wife was equally attached. The mother of his three legitimate children. But to turn one's life inside out for love… Yes, I think my mother would approve. Surely choosing to have me turned hers upside-down, shook it like a *boule d'eau* until the miniature snowflakes became a blizzard, her careful landscape never to look the same once the waves settled. Settled as a woman settles for a son, when it was his father she'd truly wanted, wanted until the day she died.

I sigh noiselessly, holding Caroly tighter.

Should some child come into being as a result of our affair… Well, it will be different. Different than how I arrived. No souvenir of a love lost, no living proof of a doomed romance or a tainted marriage. Merely a new person, some odd little companion to guide through the world. A big world, at once scary and breathtakingly wondrous, to discover alongside a father who would fundamentally be seeing it for the first time himself.

If, of course.

A very big and serious *if*, and one whose answer I've been told before.

"Caroly." I whisper it, softly enough that it won't rouse her if she's fallen asleep.

A pause. "Yes?"

Do you know for sure that you don't want children? But all I manage is another, "I love you."

"I love you too."

I want to ask, as badly as I fear to.

Again, my breathing gives me away. "What are you thinking about?"

"You said once…you don't want children."

A long, heavy pause answers me. "I told you I'm not sure I'm cut out for it. And I'm scared it might end up with my mom's issues. Or mine, or—"

Or yours, she was about to say. She revises. "You told me you couldn't offer anyone that."

"Because I hadn't left my flat in over three years. You may as well have asked me if I'd like to dance on the moon."

"Have you changed your mind?"

"My mind isn't sure of anything. But my world is quite different, these seven months later."

I hear her swallow. "I don't know how I feel about it. I'm still learning how to even be somebody's girlfriend."

"Of course."

She raises my hand and presses my knuckles to her lips. So often when she doesn't know what to say, she kisses me. As though the words her mouth seeks are written on my skin.

"Next fall I'll have lived with you a year," she finally says. "I might have a new job title. You might propose to me, or break up with me. Or I could do either of those things to you."

"You're saying, ask you again, further down the road."

"I think I'm saying, never say never. Before this spring, I could only imagine lying here with a man like you..." She pauses for a breath. "I'm trying to say, *right now* is so exciting. I don't want to miss any of it, worried about predicting the future."

Yes, the present. I've never been good at basking in the moment. Anxiety's always had me squinting into the distance, scanning for threatening shadows. The only times I exult in the present are during sex, and while mired in the hypnosis of mending a clock. Even now, in this bed, wrapped around the woman I love, my mind is fixated on questions that only time can answer, lamenting wasted years that no measure of regret could ever reclaim.

At length I ask, "What are *you* thinking about?"

"How strong your arms feel."

I sigh. "You're so much better at that than I am. Just enjoying the moment."

"I was thinking about how strong your arms feel," she says again, "and how you'd look, holding a child."

My heart thumps hard, mouth going dry. "Oh."

She squeezes my hand. "So no, I'm not immune to those thoughts. I've tried to imagine it now and then. For the record, I think you'd be amazing at that—being a father."

I try to reply, but no words come.

"I'm not in any hurry though." She hugs my arms tighter around her middle. "I'd like to be selfish for a few years and have you all to myself."

"But if the idea should slide out of my brain and through my lips, from time to time…?"

"I wouldn't mind."

"Good. You're right though. For now, we should just enjoy being greedy with each other."

"Speaking of which—it's my turn." She nudges my shoulder and I obediently roll over so she can drape her arm along my ribs, bracelet tinkling.

Nearly every night we spend together, this is how she falls asleep. Since giving up my clients, I'm an owl struggling to adjust to a robin's hours, often lying awake a long time before sleep comes. But I enjoy the time and this clinging sensation, the way her arm goes limp when she nods off, how the breaths warming my neck deepen. It makes me feel wanted. That hunger that was so rarely fed as a child, the one that made me parlay my looks into modeling, then prostitution. I need to feel desired, and I've always known it.

Caroly's arm has grown heavy around my waist, and she tenses for a breath, dreaming. I wonder if she knows how like a dream my waking life feels, lying here with her, so far from my everyday world.

I shift, rousing her. "My turn."

"No it's not," she mumbles, barely awake, but rolls over all the same.

I hold her tightly, nesting her bent legs with mine. Her hair smells of the lavender already come and gone from the countryside. Closing my eyes, I breathe her in and imagine the purple fields at the height of summer.

With Caroly close, I can imagine so many places. So many possibilities. So many of the things I've excluded myself from, for so long. I forfeited years, letting them pass me by in a haze of pleasant company, pleasant atmosphere, pleasant sex, pleasant distraction. A blur of squandered days and nights. Perhaps I won't ever feel at ease, strolling down a busy city street, but at least I'll experience every second of it.

"*Beaux rêves,*" I whisper against her skin. "And thank you." For this moment and this place, and a chance to even be this way with someone.

She stirs, not waking.

"*À demain.* I'll see you when I wake." Tomorrow, and every morning after, for as long as I'm fortunate enough to call this woman mine. For as long as it's her hand, her voice, her smile, drawing me out of the shadows and back into my life. Come what may.

ABOUT THE AUTHOR

SINCE SHE BEGAN WRITING IN 2008, Cara McKenna has published over forty romances and erotic novels with a variety of publishers, sometimes under the pen names Meg Maguire and C.M. McKenna. Her stories have been acclaimed for their smart, modern voice and defiance of convention. She was a 2015 RITA Award finalist, a 2014 *RT* Reviewers' Choice Award winner, a 2012 and 2011 *RT* Reviewers' Choice Award nominee, and a 2010 Golden Heart Award finalist. She lives with her husband and son in the Pacific Northwest, though she'll always be a Boston girl at heart.

caramckenna.com
facebook.com/authorcaramckenna
twitter.com/caramckenna

ALSO BY CARA MCKENNA

After Hours

Hard Time

Her Best Laid Plans

Shivaree: The Complete Series

Skin Game

Strange Love: Remastered Tales

Thank You for Riding

Unbound

THE FLYNN AND LAUREL SERIES

Willing Victim

Brutal Game

THE SINS IN THE CITY SERIES

Crosstown Crush

Downtown Devil

Midtown Masters

THE DESERT DOGS SERIES

Lay It Down

Give It All

Drive It Deep

Burn It Up

Ride It Out

AS C.M. MCKENNA

Badger

AS MEG MAGUIRE

Caught on Camera

Headstrong

The Reluctant Nude

Trespass

The Wedding Fling

Wild Holiday Nights

THE WILINSKI'S SERIES

All or Nothing

Going the Distance

Takedown

www.ingramcontent.com/pod-product-compliance
Lightning Source LLC
Chambersburg PA
CBHW072108250626
47159CB00007B/2352